"I do not think I have seen you before. What is your name?" Lord Satterwaite asked.

Fredericka was amazed. She had never been accosted with such familiarity. She still had not found her tongue when the gentleman pulled out his handkerchief and seized her chin between his long fingers. "Hold still. You have a smudge of dust on your cheek."

Fredericka stared up at him wide-eyed as he cleaned her face for her. He flicked her nose with a gentle forefinger and then released her.

Lord Satterwaite threw himself into a chair nearby and crossed his feet at the ankles. "Have you been with her ladyship long, my shy beauty?"

Fredericka merely looked at him. A gentleman never sat down in the presence of a lady. It was simply not done. The truth had slowly been dawning on her, and the full realization burst upon her stunned mind. He had taken her for a housemaid.

Her eyes began to dance. Lord Satterwaite thought her to be a maid. Very well, then. She would try to see whether it was a role that she could carry off for a few amusing moments.

Fredericka's Folly

Gayle Buck

A SIGNET BOOK

SIGNET
Published by the Penguin Group
Penguin Books USA Inc., 375 Hudson Street,
New York, New York 10014, U.S.A.
Penguin Books Ltd, 27 Wrights Lane,
London W8 5TZ, England
Penguin Books Australia Ltd, Ringwood,
Victoria, Australia
Penguin Books Canada Ltd, 10 Alcorn Avenue,
Toronto, Ontario, Canada M4V 3B2
Penguin Books (N.Z.) Ltd, 182–190 Wairau Road,
Auckland 10, New Zealand

Penguin Books Ltd, Registered Offices:
Harmondsworth, Middlesex, England

First published by Signet, an imprint of Dutton Signet,
a division of Penguin Books USA Inc.

First Printing, August, 1996

10 9 8 7 6 5 4 3 2 1

Chapter One

Lord Sebastion Satterwaite was returning from a fortnight of duck shooting with friends in the shires. He had planned to go straight back to London, but in a moment's reflection decided to deviate a short way out of his course to his ancestral home, Chalmers. His parents, the Earl and Countess of Chalmers, would be in residence and since he had not spent above a day or two with them over the Christmas season, he thought that it was as good a time as any to pay them a visit.

The viscount was traveling with his valet and his groom. When he spoke aloud his intentions, his groom merely looked wooden-faced, but the valet was moved to diffident protest. "M'lord, is that wise?"

Lord Satterwaite threw his man an amused glance. "You are thinking of the earl's expression wishing that he need not see my face again for a twelvemonth when last I was there, are you not? But you know as well as I do that his lordship's tempers do not last, Turby."

"Yes, m'lord, quite true. But his lordship was in rarer trim than ever before," said the valet earnestly, with all the privileges of a valued retainer.

"Be that as it may, I have a wish to visit her ladyship. I doubt that I shall have the opportunity to do so for some months to come," said Lord Satterwaite. He did not feel it in the least incumbent upon him to explain his reasonings to his servants, but he knew their concerns and their genuine loyalty to himself. In any event, surely just a day or two at Chalmers would not end as badly as had the last visit.

"Yes, m'lord. It is to be hoped that his lordship is feeling in better pin," said Turby, resigning himself.

A light snow was falling and the narrow road was edged by the drifts of earlier falls. It was bone-chilling cold and the breaths of horse and man alike were puffs of white on the frigid air.

The conditions of the road and the likelihood of increasingly bad weather might have daunted other travelers, but Lord Satterwaite was not among their fainthearted number. An acknowledged whip who knew to a hair the ability of his spirited highbred horses, he had seen nothing in either the weather or the deterioration of the roads in this unfamiliar part of the country to give him cause for anxiety. Though he did not know precisely where he was, his sense of direction was good and he knew that within a very few hours he would likely reach a main post road and the availability of a posting house in which to put up for the night. Then, he judged, it would be but a gentle push to make Chalmers on the next day.

Suddenly the phaeton bounded into the air and the valet clutched instinctively at the seat rail. When the phaeton came down again, there was an ominous shivering of its smooth gait. "M'lord! What is amiss?"

Lord Satterwaite was drawing in his team. "You may well ask, Turby," he said shortly. "The back wheel has struck a rock that was hidden beneath the snow."

When the phaeton was stopped and the groom had gone to the horses' heads, Lord Satterwaite snubbed the reins and jumped down to the icy ground. He took a considerable amount of time, or so it seemed to the anxious valet, to inspect the underpinnings of the carriage.

"Turby, go hold them. Nimms, pray come look at this," said Lord Satterwaite.

"Aye, m'lord." The groom's voice was matter-of-fact.

The valet clambered down. It was beneath him to do so, but he obeyed his master's command without a word, going at once to relieve the groom of the task of holding the bridles. "Testy brutes," he muttered, when one threw up its head.

Lord Satterwaite had pulled off his gloves and now he pointed at what he discovered. "I've cleared the ice off of it, Nimms. What do you think?"

The groom took a long, thoughtful look and straightened again. "It appears to be cracked, right enough."

"Just as I thought. We shall have to unhitch the team and ride to the nearest village to find a wheelwright," said Lord Satterwaite, pulling on his glove again.

"That we won't, m'lord. The leader was kicked and is fair to being lame," said the groom laconically.

Lord Satterwaite gave a slight smile. "Then we shall walk. Back them out of the traces, Nimms."

The groom took Turby's place and the valet trotted back around the side of the phaeton. "You will not wish to leave the baggage, m'lord, where any passerby may make off with it."

"No," agreed the viscount. "We will strap it to one of the horses."

While the valet was engaged in this task, Lord Satterwaite glanced up at the lowering sky. His expression was thoughtful. Though he had set out without thinking much of the weather, matters were a bit different now. It looked as though a heavier snow was in the offing and, too, it was growing late. What sun there had been was swiftly fading away. It would not be long before nightfall was upon them and then they would be in the basket, he thought dispassionately.

"We shall be fortunate to reach the next village before nightfall," he remarked.

"Yes, m'lord. That thought had occurred to me," said Turby with a shudder.

"Nimms, you must ride in ahead and send back help for us. Turby and I shall follow as quickly as we can," said Lord Satterwaite.

"Aye, m'lord." The groom pulled himself up on the uninjured horse and urged it into a canter.

The valet morosely watched the mounted groom disappear around a bend in the hedgerow-bordered road.

"Well, Turby, let us make the best of it," said Lord Satterwaite, taking hold of the lead for the lame horse and starting off.

The valet sighed and fell into step with his lordship. It was naturally his duty to remain by his lordship's side, but just this once he found himself wishing that he had entered the quite lower service of the stable.

Lord Satterwaite was completely unaware of the trend of his valet's miserable thoughts, and if he had been privy to them, he would have laughed and given a bit of a shrug. Such self-pitying reflections were alien to him. It was not to be supposed that a gentleman of nerve and spirit would regard such a thing as a cracked wheel as of any great moment. True, it was fair to being freezing and his boots were not made for walking. However, he would far rather be moving toward succor than he would to remain beside the phaeton and hope that the threatening skies did not let go their load before the groom had returned.

A horse flew over the hedge into the road ahead of the plodders. The rider must have caught a glimpse of them as he came over the hedge, for as soon as the mare's hooves had touched the ground, it was turned around. "Hallo! Have you met with an accident?" asked the rider in a light voice.

Lord Satterwaite realized that his impression of the rider's gender had been in error and he blamed the bulky overcoat and close-drawn hat, as well as the wide muffler that was wound around the rider's face, for his mistake. "Alas, yes, ma'am. A rock concealed under the snow has made short work of one of the back wheels of my phaeton. It is cracked, as a matter of fact. How far is it to the next village?"

"That will be Littleton and it is still some five or six miles distant," said the rider. Despite the low-drawn hat and muffler, it could be discerned that she was frowning. She glanced up at the sky. "The sun will be down soon and it will begin to snow again. You will be frozen before ever you reach the inn."

"I have sent my groom ahead on the other horse. This one was lamed, as you see, and I dare not take him at more than a walk," said Lord Satterwaite. "I trust that Nimms will return with a gig before we have quite expired."

"Yes, I would ordinarily agree with you. However, this lane does not give directly upon the post road. I would not be surprised if your groom did not take a wrong turn before he is quite aware of it. That is, if he is unfamiliar with the road."

"Unfortunately, he is," said Lord Satterwaite dryly.

It was not the best news that he could have been given, and perhaps the rider recognized it, for she went into a peal of throaty laughter. "I do apologize. It was not my intent to breathe gloomsday tidings to you!" Amusement laced her voice.

The rider had walked her horse closer and the viscount could see now that she had a pair of striking hazel eyes. "Oh, not a bit of it, ma'am. However, I doubt if my valet has greeted this intelligence with any but the gravest of forebodings," said Lord Satterwaite.

The rider chuckled. "And no wonder. I doubt that it is anyone's ambition to freeze." She gathered her reins. "I shall ride to the nearest farmstead. I expect that there will be room to stable your brute until the morrow and someone will be able to drive you into the village to the inn, if you wish."

"I thank you, ma'am," said Lord Satterwaite. He was on the point of inquiring the lady's name when she gave a nod and touched a spur lightly to her mount's side. The mare lifted gracefully over the hedge, leaving the viscount with a vision of as pretty a piece of horsemanship as he had ever witnessed.

"We shall be all right now, Turby. No doubt the farmer and his whole household shall turn out to rescue us at our fair lady's word," he said.

"I hope so, indeed, m'lord," said the unhappy valet. He spared a thought for the groom, who would undoubtedly hurry back as soon as he was able, only to find his lordship and his manservant vanished. However, it was no concern of his and as he very well knew, Nimms was quite capable of taking care of himself.

It was not many minutes before an unwieldy farm cart came rumbling down the road toward Lord Satterwaite and his valet. The driver stopped, pulled his forelock, and said that he had been sent to fetch the gentlemen.

Lord Satterwaite thanked the man and tied his lamed horse to the cart. "Up you go, Turby!" he said cheerfully, himself climbing into the back of the cart and letting himself down on a bed of crackling straw.

The valet clumsily followed suit, muttering disapproval. "Surely you would be more comfortable on the seat, m'lord."

"Come, Turby, surely you realize that this straw will keep us as warm as toast," said Lord Satterwaite, stretching at his ease.

"Be that as it may, m'lord," said Turby stiffly, plucking the straw from the sleeve of his coat. He foresaw that his duties that night would include brushing his lordship's coat and breeches free of bits of straw, and he sniffed with distaste. This adventure was quite beneath him.

The farmstead was reached, the lamed horse was placed into the competent care of the farmer's son (who had run an experienced eye over it and expressed his opinion that it was a rare 'un), and his lordship, along with his uppity servant man and baggage, had been bumped over the lanes to the village. The slow ride had rattled the passengers a good bit and Lord Satterwaite was glad to be able to get out of the cart at last. He thanked the farmer graciously and tried to press a coin on him. The farmer spurned the gesture, saying laconically that he would not turn his back on the roughest customer alive on such a cold evening.

"Which shows you, Turby, that I am not a very bad fellow at all," said Lord Satterwaite.

"Aye, m'lord." The valet's tone was repressive.

Lord Satterwaite entered the inn. His valet came behind him, directing the ostlers to bring in m'lord's baggage and to be sharp about it. Lord Satterwaite began to explain the particulars of his odd arrival, but the landlord was already in possession of the circumstances.

"Aye, m'lord. Your man is 'ere and fit to be tied, him not being able to hire a gig seeing as how it is on loan to Mr. Potts until Wednesday night, and swearing that he must 'ave it at all odds," said the landlord. He bade the tapster to convey the tidings to the regular jawbone in the public room that his lordship was astanding in the front hall. Then he turned back to the viscount. "Ye'll be wanting a room and a private parlor, of course, my lord. I will see to it instantly, and no doubt dinner and our best wine would be agreeable to you, as well."

"Stay a moment," said Lord Satterwaite, as the landlord seemed about to take flight. "Is there a wheelwright available in this village?"

"Aye, in a manner of speaking, m'lord. But he shan't be able to do anything this night, begging your pardon," said the landlord apologetically.

"I had guessed as much," said Lord Satterwaite. "Pray send a message requesting him to wait upon me in the morning. In the meantime, I should like that room and private parlor, as well as accommodations for my valet and groom. Ah, there you are, Nimms!"

The groom was relieved to see his lordship. "M'lord! I scarce hoped to see you."

"I am perfectly well, as you see. Remind me to have Turby describe to you our ride in a farm cart," said Lord Satterwaite.

The groom's seamed face eased a fraction.

While Lord Satterwaite had consulted with his groom, the landlord had nabbed a waiter and spoken a flurry of orders into that individual's ear. The waiter replied, and the landlord stared. He was not unnaturally ruffled to learn that his lordship's manservant had taken it upon himself to commandeer the best rooms in the inn for the viscount and had already bespoken dinner. Instead, he took it in stride. He was not the man to take an affront over something so paltry as that, he hoped. Not when it could be plainly seen that this guest was the most well-heeled that his house had seen in some little time.

The landlord respectfully reclaimed the viscount's attention by suggesting that his lordship might like to step upstairs now to his rooms, where his lordship's man was even then directing the waiters to lay out a dinner that, it was hoped, would meet with his lordship's approval. His lordship acceded to this proposal and the landlord himself led him upstairs and ushered him into a snug little parlor.

Within an hour of his arrival, Lord Satterwaite pushed back from the table upon which were the remains of a very fair repast. Though the dinner had consisted of plain fare, it had suited the viscount admirably. At his lordship's hand was a glass of wine of surprisingly good year.

A fire was crackling in the grate and the room was small enough that it had warmed to a comfortable degree. Outside, a howling wind had risen and the threatened snow flew in flurries.

Lord Satterwaite lifted his glass in tribute to the unknown lady who had so providentially come to his aid. Without her unexpected appearance, he and his valet might well have spent the most miserable hours of their lives in the freezing weather.

It was a pity that he had neglected to inquire her name before she had ridden off, he thought in lazy regret. He recalled the lady's peculiarly attractive laugh and the way that her eyes had gleamed with amusement. It would have been pleasant to have pursued his acquaintance with her.

Lord Satterwaite shrugged, a lingering smile still curling his lips. Draining off the last of his wine, he set down the glass. The lady was probably wed fast to a genial country squire, to whom she had presented a full nursery. It was better to recall her as a passing angel of mercy, with the lightest hands and seat that he had ever seen on horseback.

Turby softly entered the parlor just then and inquired if his lordship required anything further.

"Nothing that a night's sleep won't produce," said Lord Satterwaite. He stood up and stretched. "I am going to bed, Turby. You may wake me at eight o'clock. We shall no doubt be able to leave by luncheon."

"Very good, m'lord."

Despite Lord Satterwaite's optimism that he would certainly be back on the road before noon, it was actually three o'clock before he was able to continue on his interrupted journey. The wheelwright had indeed been able to accommodate him, but the job of repairing the phaeton's wheel took a bit longer than his lordship had anticipated. In addition, the lamed horse was still favoring its leg, as became obvious when it was brought to the inn by the farmer's son, and the viscount was forced to make arrangements for the horse's upkeep at the inn until it was fully recovered. His groom had volunteered to remain at the inn until that time, in order to be certain that all was properly done for it, and had pledged himself to bring the horse back up to London in easy stages.

Therefore it was only the devoted Turby who accompanied Lord Satterwaite when he left that afternoon. The pace of the remainder of the trip was necessarily slower than previously, due to the necessity of hiring a job horse to replace the viscount's own leader, but they were still able to reach Chalmers before dinner.

The viscount's unexpected arrival was greeted with a mixture of mingled surprise and dismay, quickly veiled but not so quickly that Lord Satterwaite did not catch it. As he gave his hat, gloves, and whip into the footman's hands, he looked at the butler and bluntly inquired, "How is his lordship, Moffet?"

The butler hesitated, torn between discretion and honesty. "In rather poor trim, I'm afraid, my lord."

Lord Satterwaite grimaced. With the help of the footman, he shrugged out of his greatcoat. "Then I shall not remain more than a night before I get on to London. Let Turby know, Moffet. I shall go up to see her ladyship. Is she in her sitting room?"

"Aye, my lord, and very glad her ladyship will be to see you."

Lord Satterwaite ran up the stairs. His reception at his mother's hands was all that he could have wished for. However, after they had exchanged greetings, he said quizzingly, "I am told that my father is in queer stirrups."

"Yes; so unfortunate when you have come to see us. We are not entertaining just now," said Lady Chalmers.

"As bad as that, is it? Well, I am not intending to remain above a night, so you may rest fairly easy," said Lord Satterwaite, his expression rueful.

"That would probably be wisest, my dear. Your father does seem to be reminded of his grievances against you whenever he sees you," said Lady Chalmers, smiling a little.

"Never fear, Mama. I shall be on my best behavior this evening and I shall leave tomorrow directly after breakfast so that we do not have a chance to come to cuffs," said Lord Satterwaite.

"Thank you for understanding, Sebastion," said Lady Chalmers. "Now, you must sit down for a long cose with me and tell me all the news. I have had only a very few letters from my friends this past month."

Lord Satterwaite did as he was bid, and regaled the countess with such *on dits* and descriptions of his own recent movements that might be thought to be of interest, only expunging those details of his own dealings that he thought it unnecessary to divulge. It would serve no good purpose to inform her, for instance, that besides the excellent shooting he had seen there had been some very deep play, from which he had risen an indifferent winner.

At length the viscount left his mother and repaired to the bedroom that had been prepared for him. His valet was waiting for him with a change of raiment. Lord Satterwaite sat down to have his boots pulled off. "We shall not be staying beyond breakfast tomorrow, Turby."

"I did not think so, m'lord," said Turby, gently setting aside the top boots.

"So you have heard already, have you?" said Lord Satterwaite with the shadow of a grin. "Perhaps you would care to remind me that you advised against this visit?"

"I would not so demean myself, m'lord," said Turby primly.

Lord Satterwaite did not reply, but instead submitted himself into the expert hands of his henchman. Shortly thereafter, he returned downstairs and entered the drawing room, where he found his mother sitting alone. "What, is my father not joining us?" he asked, as he took his mother's hand.

Lady Chalmers shook her head and smiled. "I know that I should not be glad of it, but your father stated that he preferred to keep to his rooms this evening rather than share a table with you."

"Hardhearted and uncivil, to boot," said Lord Satterwaite, a quick frown coming into his eyes.

Lady Chalmers gave a small laugh. "Yes, I suppose it is. But you must believe me when I say that all of us will be more comfortable this way. It is the gout that makes him so testy, Sebastion. He knows it and he does not like to be cross, but the pain is hard to bear at times."

"I absolve my father of ill will, Mama," said Lord Satterwaite. "However, I do wish that he could curb his atrocious temper, for your sake."

Lady Chalmers laughed and disclaimed and requested that her son escort her into dinner. They dined alone, enjoying themselves, and when the countess rose to leave Lord Satterwaite alone with his after-dinner wine, he said, "This has been comfortable, has it not?"

"Yes, my dear. Now I shall bid you good night, for I must go up and look in on your father," said Lady Chalmers, dropping her hand upon his shoulder. "You will come to see me before you leave tomorrow?"

"Of course," said Lord Satterwaite. He watched his mother exit, and his expression was somber. Whatever his thoughts, he did not linger long over the wine before he, too, left the dining room.

Chapter Two

The earl's voice in the library was raised in anger. The footmen exchanged uneasy glances, shifting at their stations in the grand hall. His lordship was at it again. It seemed to have become a regular occurrence whenever the viscount came to visit. The entire household at Chalmers was aware of the ongoing disagreement between the earl and his heir. It was a pity that the viscount's short visit should end in this way.

The footmen suddenly stiffened to attention. The Countess of Chalmers was coming down the broad front stairs. Her ladyship was occupied in adjusting her Norwich paisley shawl over her shoulders, but as she neared the bottom of the staircase, the earl's furious voice came to her ears. She looked up, her expression at once registering dismay.

Lady Chalmers paused on the bottom stair to listen. At what she heard, her slim fingers tightened on the banister. Her natural air of repose fled. "Those idiotic obstinate fools," she murmured under her breath.

Suddenly the earl's voice exploded. "Damn your impertinence! You'll do as I say, or I swear that I will do it!"

A harsh laugh rang out. "Then you shall do so, indeed!"

Suddenly the library door was flung open and Lord Satterwaite strode out. His powerful shoulders were set off by a dark blue superfine coat of excellent cut. His obstinate jaw was held tight above an impeccably arranged snow-white cravat. The breadth of his chest was admirably displayed by an embroidered waistcoat and frilled shirt. Well-cut breeches molded tightly to muscular thighs and he was shod in glossy top boots.

At any other time, Viscount Satterwaite was a vision that would gladden any fond mother's heart. But at the present moment his lordship's face was tight and his green eyes held an exceedingly annoyed expression.

A voice from within the library roared, "And have the kindness to close the door behind you!"

The viscount shut the door behind him. He rounded on one of the footmen and snapped, "Order out my carriage! And notify my man!"

"Immediately, m'lord!" The footman raced off.

The other two menservants leaped forward to help his lordship with the greatcoat and beaver that had been laid on a chair in the hall. The viscount had not noticed his mother who stood watching him from the stairs. He pulled on his leather gloves and took his whip as it was offered to him.

The Countess of Chalmers stepped down and swept across the grand hall to her son. She laid a detaining hand on his arm. "Sebastion."

Lord Satterwaite turned his head swiftly. He stared down into his mother's face and the furrow between his brows deepened. There was no lightening of the expression in his eyes. His voice was clipped. "My lady. I am taking my leave, as you see."

Lady Chalmers said, "Pray spare me a moment, Sebastion. Come up to my boudoir with me."

Lord Satterwaite hesitated. He was not in the mood to curb his annoyance, nor to listen to his mother's conciliating words. But he had no ready excuse to deny her the audience that she desired of him. His carriage was not yet at the door. Reluctantly he nodded his acquiescence. "Very well, my lady."

Lord Satterwaite followed his mother upstairs into her private boudoir. She moved unhurriedly across the Oriental carpet toward a striped satin-covered settee. Lord Satterwaite closed the door. With his hand still on the doorknob, he looked across at his mother rather sardonically. "Well, my dear?"

"What has transpired, Sebastion? I did not overhear all," said Lady Chalmers, seating herself. The settee was angled in front of the grate. A fire burned brightly to ward off the winter chill of December, but it scarcely warmed the apprehension in her heart.

Lord Satterwaite uttered a sharp laugh. "My father has ordered me to wed. I am to settle down and set up my nursery. Otherwise he threatens to cut me off and disown me."

The countess's gray eyes were troubled. "I had not anticipated that things should come to such a pass as this. I had hoped for moderation between the two of you during this short visit."

The viscount shrugged. "I made the mistake of thinking that I could take civil leave of my father this morning. Unfortunately, his lordship chose to speak his mind, ma'am. The old argument was raised as always."

"But this time it ended altogether different, I think," said Lady Chalmers gently.

Lord Satterwaite slapped his whip impatiently into his palm. "Father disapproves of my untrammeled life. He sees marriage as the means of steadying my character and, of course, of securing the line." His well-formed mouth twisted. "How I have grown weary of the argument. But we are told to glory in tribulation, knowing that it works patience, are we not?"

"That is a misguided use of scripture, Sebastion, as well you know, for you use it to excuse your disrespect toward your father," said Lady Chalmers, her eyes flashing.

Lord Satterwaite's lips tightened. "My pardon, ma'am. You are correct. I should not excuse myself in such a way. However, it is insupportable that my father should desire to force me into a conformity that I have no desire to occupy. I am well satisfied with my life at present. I see no reason to change."

"The strained relationship between you and your father in recent visits has naturally been a source of grief to me. But I shall not reproach you on that point at this time, Sebastion. It is scarcely the moment," and Lady Chalmers.

Lord Satterwaite bowed with a careless grace. "I thank you, madame, for your gracious forbearance."

"Pray do not mock me, Sebastion," said the countess calmly.

The viscount flushed slightly. He drew his whip through his fingers. "My apologies, Mama. I am awash with such annoyance that I scarce can keep a civil tongue in my head, even with you."

"What will you do?" asked Lady Chalmers, voicing her major concern.

Lord Satterwaite laughed again and his green eyes glittered. "It is to London and the devil this night!"

"That will scarcely solve matters," said Lady Chalmers.

"Let be, Mama!"

There was a moment of tense silence as mother and son locked glances. The struggle of wills was almost palpable. A log fell in the fireplace, scattering sparks up the chimney.

Lady Chalmers acknowledged defeat. "Very well, my son. I shall not tax you further." She rose from her place and walked over to stand on tiptoe to kiss her son's lean cheek. Quietly, she said, "Do not do yourself a true mischief out of anger or spite, Sebastion. I love you too well to be able to bear the heartbreak."

Lord Satterwaite shook his head. A tight smile stretched his mouth. "No, Mama. I shall not come to permanent harm, I promise you."

Lady Chalmers nodded. It was all that he would vouchsafe to her and she knew it. "Very well, then. Go with my blessing. I shall speak to your father after he has calmed. It is the gout that makes him fly into such a flaming passion, you know."

Lord Satterwaite laughed, rather bitterly. "Oh, yes! That is a fine excuse, is it not? But pray do not put yourself to the effort on my account, Mama. It is already far too late. Matters are such that—" He caught himself. "But I shall not burden you with my opinion. I must go."

The countess gave her hand to him. The viscount saluted it briefly. Then he abruptly turned and strode to the door. Lady Chalmers did not follow him out of the room. Instead she stood listening to her son's rapid hard steps fading away.

Lady Chalmers went to the window. The glass was glazed at the corners with ice and outside a light snow was falling. Lady Chalmers looked down onto the drive. The viscount's phaeton was waiting. The horses were stamping in their traces, their breaths blowing white on the cold air.

Below, Lord Satterwaite emerged from the house and ran swiftly down the steps. He climbed into his phaeton and placed a rug over his knees. His valet was already aboard. The viscount nodded to the groom holding the horses' heads and the man released the bridles. There was a shout, the crack of a whip. Then Lady Chalmers faintly heard the creaking of the wheels. She watched as the phaeton was tooled away, until it was lost to sight in a bend in the snowy drive.

The Countess of Chalmers stood immobile at the frosted window for a moment longer. Her fine brows were drawn together. Her first impulse was to go downstairs at once and confront her husband. But she knew too well the earl's temper when his gout had flared up and he had been put out, besides. His lordship was normally the most logical of beings, but at such times as these there was no dealing with him in a rational manner. The earl would not even give her a proper hearing while he was in such a state, she thought. No, it would be far more prudent to exercise patience and wait until the earl's initial wrath had had time to cool.

A smile just touched her ladyship's lips. It was an irony that her son should quote a scripture on patience, for she felt that she had seen patience become one of her virtues.

Ever since the viscount had graduated out from under his tutors there had been a seemingly endless round of disagreements between father and son. Lady Chalmers had mediated, sometimes more successfully than others. It had been a grievous wound to her soul to watch as the two most beloved individuals in her life rubbed so ill against one another. The roots of the problem laid in the earl's certainty that he knew what was best, and the viscount's equally strong will to be his own man.

When Lord Satterwaite had inherited his own snug property from an uncle and had the full use of the income deriving from it, he had set some distance between himself and his parents. It had eased the relationship to a degree, though there had still been one or two points that sire and heir could never seem to come to agreement on.

By far the most serious point of contention was this determination of the viscount's not to wed. He was not entirely set against the necessity, of course. It was simply that he did not wish to enter the state of marital bliss just at that point in his life.

Lady Chalmers thought that she understood a little about why her son stood so resolute against the idea. She had thought it a great mistake to refuse to grant the viscount his desire to go into the army without offering some alternative.

Lord Satterwaite was an energetic young man with deep-held beliefs and loyalties. He was restless when he was not employed in some venture that interested him. Society offered nothing more than self-indulgence. It was scarcely to be wondered at that Lord Satterwaite should channel his energies into reckless escapades and fast living.

The countess sighed. It did little good for her to refine on those things that were long past and could not be changed. She had to deal with that day's ill-conceived confrontation. Her first task was to see that the earl was put into a more benevolent frame of mind. Matters would be helped along immensely if the earl was to discover all of his favorite dishes served at dinner, Lady Chalmers thought dispassionately. Accordingly, when she exited her boudoir, she went away to talk with her cook.

That evening Lady Chalmers was gratified to see that her wise strategy was bearing fruit. The viscount had left several hours before and the Earl of Chalmers had had time in which to come down from his towering rage. It had helped that his lordship's valet had suggested that he be allowed to apply a treatment for the gout that had been prescribed by the earl's physician, and that had seemed to give a small measure of relief.

The earl was further mellowed by a simple repast that was just to his taste. There was a barley soup, removed by fish, a cutlet, a roast fowl, and some game. Lord Chalmers made a hearty meal and restricted himself to a light wine during the course of dinner.

A roaring fire heated the dining room and bunches of brightly-lit candles added to the cheerful aspect. Lord Chalmers touched his mouth with his napkin and sighed in contentment. He was very nearly in charity with the world again.

At a solicitous inquiry by Lady Chalmers, the earl allowed that the pain in his gouty foot had waned.

"Not that I regard it, my dear lady. I am not one to complain," said Lord Chalmers.

"No, indeed. I know it well," said Lady Chalmers. "Shall I leave you to your port?"

The earl grimaced. "The port is like to inflame the gout to an insupportable degree all over again. I shall not take a glass tonight."

"Then perhaps you will join me in the drawing room for coffee and dessert," suggested Lady Chalmers. She signaled to the butler. The man bowed his understanding and at once left the dining room. Two footmen began to discreetly clear away the clutter and remove the covers.

"Aye, that will be pleasant enough," agreed Lord Chalmers, smiling

The couple rose from the table. The earl retrieved his ebony cane before he offered escort to his lady. The countess laid her fingers upon his elbow. Together they exited the dining room and made their way upstairs to the drawing room. Their pace was necessarily slow since the earl limped painfully as he leaned on his cane.

The grand hall and the staircase were drafty and Lady Chalmers inevitably became chilled as she matched her steps to the earl's. Her Norwich shawl and merino gown were not proof against the eddies of cold air. Consequently, Lady Chalmers was glad to enter the drawing room, where another fire blazed on the hearth.

The coffee and a tray of small tarts and a bowl of walnuts was already being set out. The butler inquired whether there would be anything else. At his mistress's soft negative, he bowed and exited, closing the doors behind him.

Lady Chalmers left the earl's side and went to sit down behind the coffee. She lifted the silver pot. "Will you want dessert, too, my lord?"

"No, nothing. I shall leave it to you to satisfy the cook's anxious conceit, my dear."

"I fear that Cook will be disappointed in us both, then, for I want no more than one of these tarts," said Lady Chalmers, smiling.

Lord Chalmers grunted. He sat down heavily in his favorite chair. A comfortable footstool had been strategically placed and he propped his afflicted foot on it. He placed his gold-headed ebony cane within easy reach.

When he was settled, he looked about him at the cozy domestic scene. It was uncommonly agreeable not to have to do the civil to dinner guests that evening, he thought contentedly. He knew that with the ending of winter most of the entertaining had already gotten through. He was not an unsociable man, of course, but he did hope that they could scrape by without too many more parties.

It suited him just now to have only the company of his wife for an evening.

The fire gamboled on the hearth and the flickering light shone friendly upon his countess's face. Lord Chalmers thought that his lady had endured the years well. She was just as much a beauty that evening as she had been on the day that he had wed her. "You are still a dasher, Sarah," he said aloud.

Lady Chalmers looked around in surprise. She smiled as she met her husband's admiring, fond glance. "You were always a dear flatterer, Edward. But I thank you all the same."

"I am in all seriousness, Sarah. I am glad that I married you these thirty-odd years past," said Lord Chalmers. He took the cup that his wife proffered to him and lifted it to his lips. He tasted the brew and sighed in contentment. "You always knew just how to sweeten it, my dear."

"If I had not learned, you would not have been so impressed with me and asked my father for my hand," said Lady Chalmers teasingly. She poured her own cup and set down the silver pot. She chose one of the tarts and nibbled on it.

The Earl of Chalmers laughed. It was a hearty, relaxed laugh. "True enough," he admitted. "I was looking for a wife and you were not the only eligible beauty."

"How lowering it is to reflect that it was my housewifely attainments that won for me your affection," said Lady Chalmers, still smiling.

"Aye, but it was a happy choice, was it not?" asked the earl.

The Countess of Chalmers chuckled a little. She cast him a roguish glance. "Oh, indeed. I have never regretted it. Though you have tried me often and often, I love you still."

The earl's ruddy face turned a deeper shade of red. He said gruffly, "You put me to the blush, my dear."

The countess judged that her moment had come. It was a pity, really, to bring unpleasantness into such a moment, but it could not be avoided. She was a firm believer in confronting troubles so that there could be no festering of bitterness or misunderstanding.

"I should like to see Sebastion settled as happily," said Lady Chalmers, setting aside her cup and saucer.

The earl's expression tightened. His former affability totally disappeared. "I'll not have that name aired, if you please!"

Lady Chalmers looked straight into her husband's hardened eyes. Quite coolly, she inquired, "Why ever not? He is still our son. For the moment, at least. I think that there has never been a better time to air the trouble that exists between you and Sebastion."

"Aye, trouble, indeed! So he told you, did he?" The earl's voice was harsh. "I might have known that he would run to your skirts."

Lord Chalmers's grating assumption did not set well with the wife of his heart.

"My dear sir, I overheard the discussion between you and our son from the grand hall, as did every servant within earshot. I scarcely needed Sebastion to give me the particulars. I could have easily inquired them of my maid, for no doubt the entire household became aware of what occurred within moments of its happening," said Lady Chalmers, a small edge to her voice.

Lord Chalmers was momentarily silenced. It was never his intention to air the disagreement between himself and his heir to all and sundry. He shifted uncomfortably in his chair. At his indiscreet movement, a spasm crossed his face. The pain in his gouty foot reignited his temper. His lordship's jaw tightened and he snapped, "You won't turn me up sweet, Sarah. I shall stand firm this time. The boy must be made to toe the line."

"I quite agree, Edward. It is high time that Sebastion find himself a suitable mate and set up his nursery," said Lady Chalmers.

Chapter Three

There was an arrested moment, which Lady Chalmers took in stride. She gestured at the earl's cup. "Would you care for more coffee, my lord?"

"Eh?" The earl was staring at his wife with a mixture of astonishment and suspicion. He looked down at his empty cup, and handed it to her. "Aye, aye! Now what is this turnabout, madame? Is it some new ploy to work on Sebastion's behalf?"

Lady Chalmers took note that the earl had actually said his heir's name and a smile of quiet satisfaction crossed her face. She calmly poured fresh coffee. "No ploy, I assure you, my lord. I am completely sincere. I have given much thought to the matter since Sebastion left. I, too, would like to see an end to our son's wild gaming and his foolhardy escapades. Situated as we are in the country, I nevertheless hear much of what goes on in London. We still have many friends there, as you know, and I maintain a wide correspondence. I doubt that there is much that I have not been made aware of through my friends."

"Gossips! How dare they bandy my son's name about!" growled Lord Chalmers, his color deepening to an alarming shade. Of all things that he found most reprehensible were tattling rumors and rampant speculations. It was especially abhorrent to him when a member of his own family became the subject.

"Precisely so," said the countess. She handed the refilled cup of coffee to her husband and then picked up her own again. Sipping meditatively, she said, "It would be very nice not to have Sebastion's name figure so prominently in the latest *on dits*."

"The boy has no sense, none at all! Is it any wonder that the tattlemongers find food for their grist in him?" The Earl of Chalmers banged his fist on the arm of his chair. His violence made his coffee slop onto the saucer. He thrust the cup and saucer down on the occasional table beside him with unwonted force. "I never imbibe two cups at night, Sarah! You should know that."

"I had forgotten, my lord," said the countess meekly. "It was the pleasure of your quiet company that addled my memory, no doubt."

The earl stared at his lady with lowered brows. Then his lips twitched. "Aye, you've always had the knack of turning me up sweet. Very well, I shall not shout anymore. Now, what do you think of my ultimatum to Sebastion?"

"I think it was borne out of fury and desperation and perhaps a lack of proper forethought," said Lady Chalmers.

The earl grunted. His expression had tightened again and his eyes were narrowed. In a voice of ice, he asked, "Is that the whole of your observations, madame?"

"Not at all. When have you ever known me to be at a lack, my lord?" replied Lady Chalmers with a fleeting smile. There was no answering gleam in her husband's eyes and she abandoned her small attempt at humor. "Very well, Edward. I shall tell you precisely what I think. You and Sebastion have created an impossible situation. You are both too proud and obstinate to back away from your positions. That leaves you, sir, without an heir. Except, of course, for your brother's son, Lucius. And Sebastion is left without a family or means of support. The options left open to him are the pasteboards or the army. I shall allow you to contemplate the future that you have wrought between you."

The earl was scowling. His jaw worked. "I have never cared for Lucius. A smooth toad-eating libertine! At least Sebastion, for all of his wild progress, can never be accused of being bad ton."

"Sebastion's willful nature will propel him into the army," said Lady Chalmers quietly.

"Aye! Aye, that is just what the ingrate would do to spite me," exclaimed Lord Chalmers, at once perceiving the truth of her observation. "I denied him permission these three years past to join Wellington's staff. Now the war is at last turning in our favor and every young hotheaded fool left in England is panting to take part in the glorious conclusion! Phah! What do these sprigs know of war? No, madame! I shall continue to deny my permission. I will not have my heir blasted into eternity upon a Spanish battlefield."

"But he will no longer be your heir and therefore you will no longer have the right to restrain him," said Lady Chalmers reasonably.

The Earl of Chalmers thumped his chair arm again. "Do you think that I do not know that?" he roared.

The countess raised her brows in reproof.

Recalling his promise not to shout, Lord Chalmers moderated his volume. "It is a devilish coil, Sarah! But I cannot go back upon my word. The boy must be made to understand that I meant what I have said!"

"Of course he must. But do you not think that giving Sebastion only a week was a bit unreasonable, my lord? I could scarcely believe my ears. After all, what sort of match can he possibly contract in just a few days' time?" asked Lady Chalmers.

The earl subsided sullenly in his chair. He carefully shifted his foot on the footstool. "One that will be more than suitable, I suppose. There were any number of girls brought out last Season and not all have yet accepted offers, I dare swear."

Lady Chalmers gave an unladylike snort. "Yes, indeed! Shall I describe the remnants of last year's crop to you, my lord?" She proceeded to number them off. By the time she had described a hoyden, one lady with a squint, and another with a squealing laugh, the earl was openly dismayed.

"Did you say that she sounds just like a stuck pig?" he asked.

"Just like one," said the countess firmly.

"I could not abide such a noise in my drawing room," said the earl forcefully.

"No, nor I," agreed Lady Chalmers. "Even if Sebastion should happen to favor the girl."

"He would not be so lost to sense. No man would," declared Lord Chalmers.

"Edward, do you not think that you could at least give Sebastion the length of the Season to contract a betrothal? It is only proper that he should be given time to make his choice. Then he could select the lady most suitable to himself and who would most befit our family," said Lady Chalmers.

Lord Chalmers had been reflecting with foreboding on the young lady who was possessed of such an unattractive laugh. Though he had handed his son an ultimatum, it would not suit him to welcome a daughter-in-law whose very presence would grate upon him. He was struck at once by the practicality of her ladyship's reasoning. "Aye! You have hit upon it precisely, my dear. We do not wish to be entirely precipitous in this matter. Very well, then! I shall write Sebastion on the morrow and let him know of my leniency."

"Perhaps it would be best if I wrote to him," suggested Lady Chalmers.

The earl looked at her. Then he began to chuckle. "Do you fear that he would consign my letter to the flames unread, Sarah?"

"The thought did cross my mind," admitted Lady Chalmers.

"You are undoubtedly right. I shall let you write to him as you will. But mind, do not allow him to think that I have softened, for I have not. I shall see the boy respectably wed or cut him out of the succession," said Lord Chalmers.

"I perfectly understand, Edward," Lady Chalmers smiled at her husband. "The hour grows late, my lord. Shall I call for more tapers or shall we retire?"

The Earl of Chalmers carefully maneuvered his foot to the carpet. Retrieving his cane, he levered himself up out of his chair. He held out his hand. "Allow me to escort you to your chambers, my dear lady. It has been an uncommonly restive day and I discover myself ready to retire."

Lady Chalmers rose gracefully and accepted his proffered escort. "You have always been the perfect gentleman, Edward. I do not think that I should have liked anyone half as well as you."

"Of course you would not. The rest of your swains were all prosy bores," said the earl, sweeping the memory of his competitors away in one grand stroke.

Lady Chalmers laughed and agreed.

The following morning after she had breakfasted, the Countess of Chalmers returned to her boudoir and sat down at her cherrywood desk. She penned a short letter to her son. Then she sanded it, folded it, and pressed her ring into the hot wax seal.

After she was finished, she stared unseeingly out of the window for several minutes. Then with resolution Lady Chalmers pulled a fresh sheet of stationery toward her. She inked her pen and began to set in motion her own little plot for the future of her son, Lord Satterwaite, Viscount.

Several days later the countess's second letter found its way to a quiet village. It was addressed to a Lady Hedgeworth and its delivery set in motion an extraordinary sequence of events.

Lady Hedgeworth was a widow. She was set in comfortable circumstances, being in the enviable position of enjoying all the privileges of her former position due to the fact that her underage son had inherited his father's relatively unencumbered estate. Luting Manor was a snug property and provided a decent living from its revenues for the widow and all of her youthful offspring.

Many years earlier, Lady Hedgeworth had been the closest bosom-bow to the girl who had become the Countess of Chalmers. The two young misses had whispered secrets and dreams to one another and in those days there had never seemed to be a lack of either.

Lady Hedgeworth sighed reminiscently as she perused the letter from her old and dear friend. "Fancy hearing from Sarah Allyn after all of these years," she murmured to herself.

For a moment she let the several sheets drop to her lap, and a small smile played about her mouth as she let the past unfurl in her mind. Oh, those had been good days. They had had such hopes. Sarah had attained hers, of course. She had made a spectacular match and it had proven to be a happy marriage, as well. As for herself, thought Lady Hedgeworth, she had not done so ill, either.

Lord Hedgeworth had not been of a stature to compare to an earl, of course; but he had been a good man, a kind husband, a fond father. Lady Hedgeworth's only regret was that her late spouse had not had a bit more sense.

The Hedgeworths had retired from society many years before due to his lordship's rather careless grasp upon his fortune. The pasteboards had been Lord Hedgeworth's downfall. Too late, he had realized the pit into which he had slid. But being an honorable man with a sense of responsibility toward his young family, Lord Hedgeworth had made the determined sacrifice of leaving London and all of its temptations behind.

The baron had never returned to the metropolis and had instead made himself a gentleman squire. All that he had had left of a comfortable inheritance had been his estate, and he had fortunately come to his senses before either mortgaging it or setting it up as the collateral for a wager.

Lady Hedgeworth had never been more grateful for anything in her life than to realize that the roof over her head was not going to go the same way as had her jewels and the family heirlooms. And so she had relinquished the fashionable life without bitterness and had settled contentedly into her new life as mistress of a country manor. The advent of several more children occupied her time and the years passed.

The Countess of Chalmers and Lady Hedgeworth had remained fast friends for a time after their marriages. They had shared the pleasures of London and the trials of new motherhood. After Lady Hedgeworth's retirement from society, however, the friendship had gradually and by degrees lost its former closeness. They had corresponded avidly for a time, but even that had eventually fallen away to the occasional note.

Now had come this marvelously thick letter from the Countess of Chalmers. Lady Hedgeworth again picked up the sheets. The letter was chatty and contained all of the news that her ladyship had gleaned from her London friends. Lady Hedgeworth read with unabated enjoyment until the third sheet. Then her eyes widened in shock and her hands began to tremble. Her mouth opened and closed. She reread the unbelievable lines.

"My dear Victoria, you must by now be wondering why I have written such a lengthy correspondence after all of this time. The truth is, my dear, that I am a coward. Dare I to broach that subject which is so prominent in my thoughts? But I must. Therefore, dear Victoria, I have determined to put it down at last.

"As you may recall, we made a pledge between us many years ago. Lord, how ancient it seems now! Victoria, do you not remember that we pledged to ally our families one day? Was it a silly girl's pledge or did we indeed mean it for a sacred vow?

"This Season my son Sebastion, Viscount Satterwaite, looks about him for a bride. He has not before shown any in-

*dication that he means to settle into wedded bliss and pro-
duce a sturdy brace of children, but he has at last been
brought to realize that the lineage must be secured.*

*"As I seem to recall, your eldest girl is of an age to com-
pare with Sebastion. Is it too much to hope that we might not
promote an alliance between these two? That is, of course, if
Fredericka is not already wed. But you have never sent me
word of any betrothal, so I rest fairly easily that it is not so.*

*"Pray do not fear that I shall be offended if you consider
this to be an outrageous suggestion. It was a pledge made
very long ago and between two naive young girls, after all.
However, if this suggestion does find favor in your eyes, I am
offering to sponsor Miss Hedgeworth for the Season. I cannot think of anyone whom I would rather call my in-law than
your dear self, Victoria, just as I am certain that the sweet
child I remember could not be other than a meek, beautiful
young lady today. I am fully persuaded that you have
brought her up just as she ought to have been.*

*"Oh, do say yes! I should so like to do this for the daugh-
ter of my dearest of friends. In fact, even if you do not wish
the match, I shall still bring out Miss Hedgeworth and I
pledge myself keen to launch her successfully.*

*"For the sake of an old, old vow, I remain ever your
friend,*

"Sarah"

Lady Hedgeworth stared around her at her comfortable sitting
room, dazed. She had difficulty believing that nothing had
changed. There was the fire crackling on the hearth, the wingback
chair opposite hers, the settee pushed against the lemon papered
wall, the faded velvet draperies at the tall windows.

The full implications of the countess's communication finally
penetrated. Lady Hedgeworth shrieked and jumped up from her
chair. Unable to contain her exuberant feelings, she danced a little
jig and her muslin cap slipped over one brightened eye.

The door of the sitting room was thrust open. At once Lady
Hedgeworth abandoned her gyrations. She drew herself up and
looked around, her breathing a bit agitated. "Yes?"

A housemaid had put her head inside the room and now she

stared at her ladyship. Anxiously, the maid inquired, "Do ye require anything, m'lady?"

"No—yes! Require Miss Fredericka to come downstairs immediately!" exclaimed Lady Hedgeworth, clasping the sheets of the countess's letter to her ample bosom.

As the door closed once more, Lady Hedgeworth could not resist indulging in a few more capering steps. "How wonderful! How perfectly marvelous!" she chortled.

Lady Hedgeworth waited in all impatience for her eldest daughter to make an appearance. She had sufficient time in which to readjust her cap, rearrange the flowers in the vase on the occasional table, and see to a few other minor details. She brushed the top of the mantel with her fingers and frowned. "I shall have to make certain that the maid dusts in here," she murmured, and promptly forgot her resolution an instant later.

While Lady Hedgeworth fidgeted about the sitting room, she managed to reread the pertinent paragraphs of the countess's letter twice. Each time she nodded and she was unable to restrain a wide smile from blooming across her face.

"Oh, was there ever anything more marvelous! Fredericka shall be positively stunned with amazement!" she exclaimed.

The precious words contained in that one paragraph had opened up a new world to Lady Hedgeworth's imagination, one that she had long yearned to give to her eldest daughter, and had regretfully realized was beyond her scope. She had never had any real hope of ever launching her eldest into the elite circles of polite society, but now the unattainable was going to come to pass.

Her daughter was going to have a proper London Season. And perhaps, just perhaps, Fredericka might wed a viscount.

Chapter Four

When the door of the sitting room opened, Lady Hedgeworth hastily folded the sheets of the letter. It would not do to let her daughter actually read the countess's communication, for Lady Hedgeworth thought she knew how Lady Chalmers's extraordinary proposal to ally their families might be received by Fredericka. It would be best to keep her own counsel on that little detail.

Lady Hedgeworth turned to greet her daughter with barely suppressed excitement. "My dear! Pray come in. I have something of importance to convey to you. It is very good news."

A tall, stately young woman entered the sitting room. She shut the door and stood for just a moment with her hand remaining on the knob. A humorous light glinted in her hazel eyes. "Mama, you look just like the cat after it has had a bowl of cream. What has occurred that has put you into such spirits?"

Lady Hedgeworth held out her hand. "Come, dear Fredericka, and sit down beside me. If I look like that idiotish overfed cat it is certainly not to be wondered at, for I feel as though I am standing in the midst of a delightful dream!"

Fredericka advanced and took her place on the settee beside her mother. She was wearing a simple day gown of brown merino with a high-standing collar ending in a small neck ruff, and trimmed in champagne ribbons. Her auburn hair was dressed modestly and her throat and hands were bare of jewelry. She did not have the appearance of one born and bred to a position, yet her easy manner and innate grace proclaimed the lady.

"My dear ma'am, surely not! You are too sensible to be knocked into jackstraws by a simple dream," she said, smiling.

"You are perfectly right, Fredericka. It is not at all a dream, but a very pleasant reality." Lady Hedgeworth drew in her breath and then said, "My dear, I have had a correspondence from the Countess of Chalmers. She reminds me of the old, old friendship between us, and indeed, she would have been your godmother except that your father thought it would be best to humor your great-great-aunt Agatha. He was quite wrong, of course."

"It is quite true that my great-great-aunt Agatha never showed me the least partiality," said Fredericka with a hint of laughter in her expressive eyes.

"How could she have done so, when she died two years after you were born?" asked Lady Hedgeworth with asperity. When her daughter began laughing, she said sternly, "Now none of your funning, Fredericka. What I have to say is most important to your future."

At that, Fredericka immediately sobered. "This becomes ominous, ma'am."

"No such thing! It is quite the best surprise that I have ever had. What do you think, Fredericka? The Countess of Chalmers has very kindly offered to sponsor you for the Season!"

Lady Hedgeworth waited for the same excess of transports that had come over herself, but she was disappointed. Her daughter sat quite still, a frown forming between her rather marked brows. Rather impatiently, her ladyship said, "Come, Fredericka! Do you not realize what I have said? Why, it is an opportunity that I never dreamed of for you. A Season in London! You have the chance of a lifetime handed to you and you sit there and say nothing!"

"I am honored, of course, that the Countess of Chalmers has been so magnanimous. But why has she done so, Mama? For I can mean nothing to her. I have no claim upon her ladyship," said Fredericka.

"My dear child, *I* mean something to the countess. We were the dearest of friends in seminary and even after our marriages. We attended the christenings of one another's first child. Poor Sarah's other two children succumbed at a young age to virulent fever and then she lost her last baby. I have been singularly blessed in having seen all but one of my own offspring survive out of infancy," said Lady Hedgeworth, with justifiable pride.

"It is a fortunate thing, indeed, for Jack and Betsy and Thomas and Sarah," said Fredericka dryly. "But I fail to understand what they have to do with the Countess of Chalmers."

"Of course you do not, for you cannot see past the nose on your face, Fredericka. Really, one would think you were a slowtop not to recognize how singularly fortunate this is," said Lady Hedgeworth. "Why, my dear child, once you contract an eminent marriage you will be able to open doors and provide things for your brothers and sisters that I cannot!"

Fredericka stared at her mother, dismayed. "But I don't wish to wed. At least, not just yet!"

"You will have the whole Season to decide upon someone who strikes your fancy," said Lady Hedgeworth soothingly. "It is not like the quiet society here, where there are just a handful of eligible young gentlemen from which to choose. And indeed, I cannot quite fault you for refusing Mr. Hollingsworth. He is a worthy young man, of course, but there is that queer trick he has of staring one out of countenance. Reverend Reading, while a good kind man, is rather too old for you, and Sir Julian too young, and—"

"Yes, yes!" Fredericka threw up her hand, laughing again. "Pray stop parading my failures, Mama. I am well aware that I am the despair of a fond mother's heart, for I am quite uninterested in any of the gentlemen who have come to court me."

"Well, you are not precisely a despair, my dear, but I could wish for a little more feminine feeling," said Lady Hedgeworth frankly.

Fredericka rose from the settee and walked toward the window. The clear winter sun shone on her lovely face as she looked out on the snow, but her expression could not be read. "Am I such an oddity, Mama?"

"No, no! Of course you are not!" said Lady Hedgeworth hastily. "You are quite a lovely girl and you have such a generous nature and you are always so cheerful. It is just that—well, Fredericka, you are very nearly twenty and you have yet to fall in love!"

Fredericka turned at that. A rueful expression flitted over her face. "I have never cared for romantic novels, you see."

"Yes, and that is just what I mean. Why, when Sarah Allyn and I were girls together, we sighed over all the novels of our day. We had a taste for romance and we confided our closest confidences to one another."

Lady Hedgeworth sighed. She shook her head. "I cannot comprehend how you can care more for striding about the estate than you do about a frivolous dress or a party or new ribbons! Your conversation is far more likely to consist of observations about the cost of grain and the conduct of the war than it does of recipes and beaux!"

"I am unnatural indeed, ma'am. Perhaps it is due to my being the firstborn," said Fredericka lightly.

"Nonsense! You are a female and a female is obligated to be a female," said Lady Hedgeworth.

As Fredericka regarded her mother, the bright light of laughter leaped again into her eyes. "But of course. How could it be otherwise?"

"Fredericka! You are being deliberately provoking!" exclaimed Lady Hedgeworth.

Fredericka went quickly to her parent, her hands held out. She caught up her mother's hands and bent down to place a quick placating kiss on her cheek. "Indeed I am, ma'am! I am sorry! But you must see how idiotish it all is. I have no wish to wed anyone. There is not a man in the country who is up to my weight, and as for London—why, Mama, I daresay that I should be bored in a week with the fops and the dandy set."

When Fredericka would have released her hands, Lady Hedgeworth retained hold of her daughter's fingers. She looked up into Fredericka's smiling face and said urgently, "But you will go to the Countess of Chalmers, my dear. You will have a London Season, just as I have always wished for you."

Fredericka looked down into her mother's eyes. She sighed, and slowly straightened to her full height. "Do you truly wish it, Mama?"

"Yes, I do, Fredericka," said Lady Hedgeworth firmly.

"Then I shall go, of course," said Fredericka quietly.

Lady Hedgeworth squeezed her daughter's slim fingers and then let her go. "Thank you, my dear. I know that you think me unfeeling of your desires and wishes. Believe me, I do not wish to force you into anything that you would dislike, but this is an opportunity that must not be let go. Can you not understand that, Fredericka?"

"Of course, Mama. I am perfectly sensible to the honor that is done me by the Countess of Chalmers. I shall endeavor to be a credit to you, dear ma'am," said Fredericka.

"Oh, Fredericka!" Lady Hedgeworth regarded Fredericka with dismay. This restrained calm of her daughter's was certainly not the reaction that she had hoped for. "Indeed, indeed, I mean it for the best. You cannot remain buried here forever, especially not when you have such an opportunity. Why, I have wracked my brains for longer than I like to recall about how I was ever to provide such a thing for you."

"Well, you need not wrack your brains any longer, Mama," said Fredericka, smiling again. "The Countess of Chalmers has stepped handsomely into the breach."

"Quite! I was never more surprised nor pleased. Why, Sarah Allyn is as sharp as she can put together. You will not go far wrong in being guided by her, Fredericka!" Lady Hedgeworth's thoughts raced on into even pleasanter straits. "Even though you will have only a modest portion, I know that will not prove a great impediment to your obtaining a very credible marriage once you are gotten to London. The countess's invitation is really most providential."

"Providential indeed, ma'am," said Fredericka with a marked lack of enthusiasm. She was already seeing what was her mother's prime object in sending her to London for the Season. Obviously Lady Hedgeworth's thoughts were firmly fixed upon a wedding.

Fredericka felt a sinking sensation. A marriage of convenience seemed to be staring her in the face. Naturally she had always assumed that she would wed, but just the same it came as a distinct shock to be told that she was expected to do so in a matter of months. She hadn't realized that her mother had hidden away such deep ambition for them all. She asked the question paramount in her mind. "What if I do not contract this eligible marriage, Mama? What then? Would my sisters and brothers truly suffer for it?"

"No, of course they shall not. Our means are modest, but I hope that I have been wise enough to remain in contact with a few people of influence who might be persuaded to take an interest in the boys," said Lady Hedgeworth. "As for your sisters, naturally I should like to see them credibly established. You will be able to aid me in that, once you are yourself well-situated."

Fredericka was silent a moment, while her mother watched her. Aware of her mother's puzzled regard, she gave a quick smile and said, "I had no notion that the future of my sisters could come to rest on my shoulders."

"Pray put it out of your head, Fredericka. It is your future that is most pressing at the moment," said Lady Hedgeworth, practically turning her attention to the matter at hand. "I have no doubt at all that you shall go off very well. You shall undoubtedly make a splendid match, and naturally your credit shall be an advantage to your sisters when they are grown a bit older."

"But if I do not take, Mama? What then?" Fredericka asked, frowning.

"My dear!" Lady Hedgeworth regarded her daughter with astonishment. "Surely you are not afraid! Why, you have never balked at a fence in your life. Your father would never hear of it."

"This is not a fence, Mama, and Papa is not here to give me that hearty support that he used to do. In any event, I assure you that I am not frightened. It is simply that I should like to know what will happen in the event that I do not bring some town buck up to scratch," said Fredericka.

"What a vulgar term, Fredericka. I shall not inquire whom you have had it from," said Lady Hedgeworth, knowing very well that her elder son's influence was at fault. "But in answer to your question, of course you would return here to me. Luting Manor shall always be your home. At least, until Jack comes of age and decides to wed. Then his wife may see things a bit differently. She will naturally take up those responsibilities that you have been used to carrying."

"Oh, dear," said Fredericka. A chasm was steadily widening under her feet. All that she had depended upon and taken for granted was being cut out from under her with every word her mother had spoken.

Lady Hedgeworth smiled at her daughter's dismayed expression. She shook her head. "You are such a funny, Fredericka. At

one and the same time you have a shockingly logical mind and a
streak of impracticality. My dear, did you not think what changes
the future might bring? Our little family will grow up and away.
Why, Jack will enter his majority the year after next. Betsy is already at a select seminary and Sarah will soon follow. As for
Thomas, he is mad for the sea. I shall not be able to keep him
home much longer—a few years at the most. So you see, my dear,
it is really in your best interest to make the most of this Season
that the Countess of Chalmers has so handsomely offered to you."

"Yes, Mama, I do see it." Fredericka was troubled. She had
never been one to see the worst of any situation, instead dealing
with problems with the buoyancy of a naturally optimistic dispo-
sition and well-developed sense of humor. However, her mother's
explanations had served to cloud a future that she had not a quarter hour past looked upon with serene contentment and as yet she
could not discern anything at all redeeming in it.

Fredericka sounded subdued and Lady Hedgeworth pitied her
daughter, even when she did not perfectly understand her. But it
was all for the best, Lady Hedgeworth assured herself. Her dearest and oldest friend had pledged to see that Fredericka would be
successfully launched, and if her mother's heart cherished the ambition to see the girl become a viscountess, could she be faulted
for that? Lady Hedgeworth did not believe so.

"Come, Fredericka, give me a kiss. You may go now, for I
know that I have given you much that you will want to consider
in private," she said, holding out her arms.

Fredericka obediently saluted her mother. Then she quietly
withdrew from the sitting room. She did indeed have much to
think on. The announcement that her mother had relayed to her
about going up to London had astonished and dismayed her, but
no more than what Lady Hedgeworth had outlined about what the
future held for her family.

Fredericka had never thought about it, but of course her brother
Jack would one day take over the management of Luting Manor
and the estate. He was already nominally its owner since the
death of their father two years before. Until he attained his majority, though, the estate would remain in the hands of trustees. It
was universally agreed that young Lord Hedgeworth needed to be
seasoned before he could embark with confidence upon his re-

sponsibilities. He had thus been carefully trained by a group of dedicated individuals who were devoted to the family interests.

However, it was not Lord Hedgeworth, but Fredericka, who had always taken the keener interest in management. It was she to whom the bailiff and agent and trustees went to whenever there arose a question about the estate. Lord Hedgeworth might be the heir, but Fredericka was the quiet authority upon whom the everyday management of the estate had gradually devolved.

Lord Hedgeworth had expressed himself content to leave it that way. "For I don't mind telling you, Freddie," he had confided frankly, "I find it a dashed bore to be tied to Luting when I could be jaunting up to London of a Season."

"You are a bit young to be thinking about jaunting anywhere," Fredericka had observed.

Lord Hedgeworth had hunched his shoulders. His handsome face had expressed his discontent. "You don't understand. You're just a female, and one who likes such things as grubbing in the dirt, besides. I want to be more than a country gentleman. I want to see something of the world."

"Do you so dislike Luting, then?" Fredericka had asked, surprised. For herself, she could not imagine that there could possibly be anywhere better to be.

"Not dislike, precisely," Jack had said, frowning. He had given a restless shrug. "I cannot explain it. Never mind! How you do worry at a fellow, Freddie!"

Now recalling that conversation, Fredericka decided to search out her brother. Surely Jack would not want her to abandon him just yet. Surely she was not required to wed this Season. Surely she was not constrained to enter into a marriage of convenience. Fredericka's dismayed thoughts tumbled faster than her hurried steps.

Fredericka had already started downstairs when she heard Lord Hedgeworth's cheerful voice drifting up from the entry hall. She glanced over the banister and saw that her brother was just coming in from riding. His breeches and top boots were liberally sprinkled with mud. He had given his riding crop and gloves to the footman and he was engaged in ridding himself of his dampened overcoat.

"Jack!"

Lord Hedgeworth turned, looking up in surprise. He unwound the wide muffler from around his neck as he greeted his sister. He grinned. "Hullo, Freddie! You shouldn't be hanging over the banister in such a hoydenish fashion. Whatever would your old governess have had to say about that?" His brown eyes were sparkling and his cheeks were ruddy from the cold outdoors. Riding always put him into a good mood.

"Stay right there, Jack," said Fredericka, completely disregarding her brother's joking reference to the strict preceptress who had once ruled over her. She swiftly crossed the landing and ran down the remainder of the stairs.

Reaching the bottom stairs, Fredericka said at once, "I wanted to catch you before you disappeared again. I know that this is the afternoon that you planned to go over to Ned's, but I need to talk to you before you leave."

Lord Hedgeworth eyed his sister. There was an unusual agitation in her manner that alerted him that she had something of a serious nature on her mind. "What's afoot, Freddie? Have you gotten into some coil or other? If it has to do with the estate you had best apply to Bartram. He's the best of agents."

"No, it has nothing to do with estate business. Come into the library and I shall tell you," said Fredericka. She was mindful of the footman standing attentively nearby. However easy were the manners of the family toward their servants, she was aware that there was still a line to be observed.

"Oh, very well. Let me change out of my dirt and—"

"Please, Jack! I really must speak to you directly," said Fredericka.

Lord Hedgeworth was surprised and alarmed by her insistence. "Very well, Freddie. Of course I shall come." He allowed himself to be led across the hall into the library.

A small fire was banked on the hearth, putting out only enough heat to take the worst chill off of the air. Fredericka wrapped her arms about herself and ran her palms once or twice up and down her arms in their long sleeves. She was not usually bothered by drafts. It must be the agitation of her spirits that had made her so susceptible to the cold, she thought.

When he had shut the door, Jack demanded, "Now what is it

that has disquieted you, Freddie? If you are in a scrape, you may rely on me, you know."

"Yes, I do know it. That is why I had to talk to you," said Fredericka. She took a breath. "Jack, the most awful thing has happened. An old school friend of Mama's, the Countess of Chalmers, has written and offered to sponsor me for the Season."

Chapter Five

"A London Season?" Envy warred with understanding on Lord Hedgeworth's face. "You don't care for it, of course! But if it was me—What I wouldn't give to be in your shoes right now, Freddie!"

Fredericka gave a small laugh. "You would look rather ridiculous in petticoats, my dear. You've not the build for it."

Lord Hedgeworth grinned at her, for he was rather proud of his wide-shouldered physique. He knew that he looked somewhat older than his eighteen years and he cultivated a confident air in both manners and fashion. Not for him the dandified padded shoulders or the nipped-in waists of the man on the strut. Jack looked his best in riding coat and breeches, just as he was wearing that morning. Privately, Lord Hedgeworth thought that he would look even better in a Hussar's uniform. But that was simply a mild private observation, never voiced, for he really had no ambition to go into the army. His ambitions ran on far different lines. Certainly Fredericka's startling news had newly aroused those in his breast, but he was a kind brother and he concentrated on his sister's feelings rather than his own.

"Thank you for that, sister. But what has really got you so overset, Freddie? All you have to do is tell our mother that you don't care for it. She knows what you are, that you don't care a rush for the beaux," said Lord Hedgeworth. He shrugged. "Though I don't see how you can be so indifferent when there are any number of clotheads trailing you around anytime we attend one of the assemblies! In any event, Mama won't force you to go to this countess of hers."

"But she wishes it more than anything, Jack. I have already asked her and she has made it very plain to me, so naturally I must abide by her wishes. Jack, Mama wants me to make a credible match," said Fredericka despairingly.

"And so you should," said Lord Hedgeworth sternly from his brotherly perspective as head of his household. "It ain't natural that a young miss as fair as you should declare that she wishes to be a spinster!"

"Oh, Jack!" Fredericka gave a gurgle of laughter. "I did not say that I *wished* to be a spinster! I merely said that I preferred my own company to that of any of the gentlemen who have come calling on me."

"It's the same thing, isn't it? You haven't got a partiality for anyone, and what's more, I don't believe you ever have had," said Lord Hedgeworth shrewdly.

"No," said Fredericka on a sigh. "I haven't. Oh, Jack! I should just like to go on as I always have here at Luting! And that is what truly has me in a pucker, Jack. Mama has pointed out to me that you shall wed and your wife won't want me here, and Betsy and Sarah and Thomas will all be gone away. She says that there will be no place for me here then."

"What?" Lord Hedgeworth stared at his sister. His brown eyes were opened wide in complete astonishment. "What maggot has Mama got into her brain? Why should everyone leave? What wife?"

An unwelcome thought occurred to him and he asked uneasily, "Freddie, has Mama got her eyes on someone for me? Is that it?"

Fredericka shook her head. "No, of course not! At least—no, I do not think so. She said something about your attaining your majority and then settling down. But I do not believe that she has anyone in mind just yet."

"Thank God! I was afraid for a moment that she had," said Lord Hedgeworth, immensely relieved. "I don't mind telling you, Fredericka, a fellow don't want to feel himself to be legshackled before he has had a chance to look around him."

"What about Dorcus Delacorte? Surely you do not find her totally unacceptable?" asked Fredericka teasingly, a smiling expression in her eyes.

Lord Hedgeworth flushed. "Well, that is a different matter altogether. Miss Delacorte and I have been friends since we were in our cradles. Of course we like one another. But that doesn't change matters. There are a few things that I'd like to see and do before I settle down." He drew himself up and said with dignity, "And I might find someone who suits me better than Miss Delacorte."

"That's true. And she might find someone whom she prefers, also," said Fredericka. She saw the quick frown that came to her brother's face. Apparently it was a new and unpalatable idea. Fredericka reached out to pat his arm reassuringly. "Never mind, Jack. You needn't be anxious about it. It is unlikely that you will be replaced in Dorcus's affections so easily."

"Kind of you to say so," he said gruffly. He returned to the major point. "But what about you? Surely you are not against this Season in London because you have made up your mind not to wed at all. That would be foolish, Freddie, and so I tell you to your head."

"Oh, no, Jack, of course I have not decided any such thing. It is just that"—Fredericka gestured rather helplessly—"I so much prefer my life here at Luting that I cannot conceive of anything better happening to me. But if I don't take, and I haven't got a place here at Luting, I do not know what I will do."

"Here, now, what's this?" Lord Hedgeworth was alarmed. He could count on one hand the number of times that he had seen his elder sister weep, and here she stood with tears suddenly trembling on her lashes. Uneasily, he said, "There is nothing in this to make you cry, you know."

Fredericka dashed her hand across her eyes. "I'm sorry, Jack! I never meant to act like a watering pot. It is just so lowering. What must I do?"

Lord Hedgeworth handed his linen handkerchief to her. "Well, first you must get hold of yourself and look at this thing in a logical manner."

Fredericka gave a watery laugh. She blew her nose. "Mama said that I have a shockingly logical mind, but that I have a streak of impracticality, too. That is why she said that I must look at what the future might bring."

"And so you should," said Lord Hedgeworth. He leaned against the edge of the massive mahogany desk that dominated the room. "Now what is there in that to put you into such a quandary? I daresay that Thomas *will* go to sea and the other two girls will naturally wed one day."

"And you will wed, too, and Mama says that I cannot stay at Luting after that," said Fredericka. Her brow was knit as she folded the handkerchief and tucked it inside her cuff.

Lord Hedgeworth frowned at his sister. "What a nonsensical thing to say. What has my marrying have to do with any of the rest of you? I shall not thrust you or Thomas or the girls or Mama out of the house. What a rascally fellow you must think me, Freddie. Yes, and Mama, too!"

Fredericka shook her head. When she lifted her eyes, her gaze was somber but steady. "No, Jack, you don't understand. Mama didn't mean that. She meant that your wife would be mistress of Luting Manor, and that then there would be no place for me."

"Oh, I see," said Lord Hedgeworth slowly, comprehension at last coming to him.

It was tacitly recognized that though Lady Hedgeworth was nominally in charge of the household, it was actually Miss Hedgeworth who was applied to for concrete direction. Fredericka had always been careful to defer to her mother and show a proper respect for her mother's authority, but more often than not Lady Hedgeworth was perfectly willing to allow her daughter to run the day-to-day affairs while she concentrated on evolving various entertainments.

"Yes." Fredericka sighed. "I suppose it is different for Mama. She will relinquish the reins quite graciously and end her days happily traveling about from one of her offspring's houses to the next."

"You have hit on it exactly," said Lord Hedgeworth. "Mama would like nothing better. I have always suspected that she missed London and all of her friends and the fine parties. She never complained, though. But we always did more entertaining than anyone else in the county, even after Papa died. No, indeed, Mama shall not be unhappy to allow any wife of mine to become lady of the manor."

"You do see, then! But it is different for me, Jack, you know it is. I have managed Luting Manor and the estate since Papa died and I have loved it. I have never felt more useful. It never occurred to me that that should end," said Fredericka. She raised her hand in tacit acknowledgment. "Oh, certainly, I knew that when you came of age you would want to take on more. And I suppose I expected in a vague way that you would one day wed. But I thought that we would continue on in the same comfortable way. I never realized that there was the possibility that I would lose Luting as my home!"

Lord Hedgeworth's sympathy was thoroughly roused. "Freddie! I would never allow you to be driven away. I shall always stand by you. You know that."

Fredericka shook her head. There was a despairing expression on her face. "Oh, Jack, Mama was right. Now that she has pointed it out to me, and as I have told you about it, of course I can see that I might someday become a thorn in your side. And I could not bear to be the cause of a breach between you and whomever you made your wife."

"Nonsense! We have both got better sense that that," said Lord Hedgeworth staunchly.

Fredericka straightened her shoulders. She summoned up a determined smile that nevertheless wavered at the corners. "No, Mama was right. I must go to London for the Season and accept the first suitable offer made to me."

"No, dash it, you don't!" Lord Hedgeworth said explosively. "You have had fellows dangling after you ever since you emerged from the schoolroom and you haven't once succumbed to even a tendre for any of them. I'll tell you what it is, Fredericka! You aren't one of these females who gives her heart away again and again. When you love, it will be for always. So you mustn't accept any offer unless you are absolutely certain that it is the right one!"

Fredericka stared at her brother, impressed and more than a bit discomfited. She gave a small laugh. "Really, Jack! One would think to hear you that I am too particular for my own good."

"You are loyal to the bone. I know it, and so will the fellow you finally choose," said Lord Hedgeworth.

He placed his hands on her shoulders. He topped her by a few inches already and so he was able to stare sternly into her face. "Now you listen to me, my girl. I am the head of the household and I say that you are to go up to London and have your Season. If you should find a fellow who is worthy of you, then make a match of it. But if you don't, then come back to Luting Manor. There will always be a place for you here, I promise you."

Fredericka felt tears coming to her eyes again. "But what about when you do wed, Jack? I shall be in the way, you know that I shall. I am too self-willed to take second place to anyone."

"I won't reach my majority for two years. I don't see why I should wed before then, do you? Not when I want to see something of the world first. A fellow doesn't drag a bride about with him when he wants to kick up a few larks, you know!" he said.

When Fredericka laughed, Lord Hedgeworth gave her a fond little shake. "And as for what might happen, let's leave that worry for the future. Doesn't Reverend Reading say that we are not to take thought for the morrow, for the morrow shall take care of itself?"

"Yes, but—"

"Besides, if you do not find a gentleman acceptable to you this Season, we'll see whether I am not able one day to introduce you to a set of fine fellows myself," said Lord Hedgeworth. "I shall make new acquaintances. It stands to reason. There must be someone who is worthy of you. We shall simply set ourselves to rooting him out. And as for Betsy and Sarah, I shall see to it myself that they make splendid matches."

Fredericka smiled and shook her head. She was unreasonably comforted by her brother's confident declaration. "Thank you, Jack," she said simply. "You make a wonderful head of the house, you know."

"Go on, then," he said roughly, giving her a little push. He was embarrassed but pleased. "I must rush if I am to meet Ned in the village. If I am late, I shall tell him that it is your fault!"

Fredericka laughed and went away in a much happier state of mind. Her brother had given her just the assurance she needed. Of course, she would like to please her mother by contracting an acceptable match. But now she did not feel compelled into doing so.

She could still afford to wait and perhaps find someone whom she could love.

Fredericka naturally wanted to find someone with whom she could willingly share her life. But her heart had yet to be stirred and she knew that she did not want to go where her heart did not lead her. A marriage of convenience was of all things the most appalling that she could imagine.

Her brother would stand by her, whatever her decisions during this London Season. Fredericka felt that she could breathe freer. If she required it, she still had two precious years in which to make up her mind.

Fredericka was thus able to regard the Countess of Chalmers's invitation with a degree of tranquillity. She would regret leaving Luting, but the London Season might prove to be rather interesting, and just perhaps she would meet the one gentleman she had been vaguely waiting to claim her.

Fredericka laughed at herself for that flight of fancy and went away to talk with the housekeeper about an inventory of the linens closet.

At dinner, Fredericka was able to answer quite truthfully to her mother's tentative query. "Yes, Mama, I am perfectly amenable to going up to London and placing myself under the Countess of Chalmers's aegis."

"Oh, my dear! You have made me very happy," said Lady Hedgeworth.

The news that Fredericka was going to London set off surprised and envious exclamations from her younger siblings. The sister next in age demanded, "What is Freddie talking about, Mama?"

Lady Hedgeworth explained the treat that was in store for Fredericka. "Lady Chalmers has written to me and invited Fredericka to stay with her during the Season. Her ladyship has very kindly offered to bring out your sister and I expect Fredericka to enjoy immediate social success."

"London!" The youngest of Fredericka's sisters stared at her in wide-eyed wonderment. "Oh, Fredericka! How grand! What will you do first?"

Fredericka gave her throaty chuckle. "Why, I don't know, Sarah. I suppose that I shall go to a great many parties."

"You'll go shopping first," said Thomas shrewdly, out of his vast observations of his world. "That is what every female wants to do when she goes to London. Mrs. Spalding could talk of nothing else when she came back from visiting with her sister."

"It isn't fair! Mama, it isn't! Why, I am all of seventeen and I am pining for a Season, while Freddie doesn't care one whit for such things," exclaimed Betsy, a buxom miss of fair complexion and golden curls. Her pretty bow mouth trembled. "Why could not the Countess of Chalmers have chosen me instead?"

"Perhaps Mama might write to the countess and ask her to have you, too, Betsy," said Sarah with all the practicality of her fourteen years.

Betsy's face brightened. She turned at once to her dismayed parent. "Oh, Mama! Do you think—"

"I do not," said Lady Hedgeworth firmly, recovering swiftly from her consternation. "Fredericka is the eldest and her ladyship has specifically asked for her company."

"But why should she pick Freddie? It isn't fair," said Betsy, throwing a darkling glance at her sister.

"Betsy, it is not my fault, you know," said Fredericka. She was in perfect sympathy with her younger sister. "I would gladly let you go in my stead, you know I would."

"It is all just so odd!" exclaimed Betsy, unheeding of Fredericka's magnanimous statement. "The countess doesn't know Fredericka from any of the rest of us, for I know that we have never set eyes on her in our lives!"

"The countess of Chalmers was present at Fredericka's christening. I do not consider it at all odd that she should ask for Fredericka, Betsy," said Lady Hedgeworth repressively.

Not for worlds did Lady Hedgeworth want the uncomfortable notion that there was something unequal about the invitation to take root in her eldest daughter's mind. She had been anxious over the girl's chances for two years. This Season, with the Countess of Chalmers acting as her daughter's sponsor, was a golden opportunity not to be scorned.

Lady Hedgeworth was determined that Fredericka would be able to make the most of the Season. However, she much preferred that her eldest daughter obey her wishes gladly rather than

out of rebellious obligation. She did not want foolish statements
flying about that might bias Fredericka against the opportunity
that had been granted to her.

"I should think that you would be happy for your sister, Betsy,"
said Lady Hedgeworth reprovingly, hoping to stem any further
expressions of envy.

"But, Mama!"

"That will be enough from you, Betsy, my girl," said Lord
Hedgeworth sternly, taking a hand in matters. His sister's mouth
opened to deliver a stinging setdown, and he warned, "If you do
not pipe down, I shall see to it that you regret it. You will not be
allowed to return after the holidays to that nice seminary that you
like so well. I shall keep you here and put you back under Sarah's
governess."

"Mama would not let you!" exclaimed Betsy.

"Oh, wouldn't she just!" retorted Lord Hedgeworth. "Mama
knows as well as I that you need a firm hand. If this tart tongue
and selfish air is what you are being taught at that seminary, then
you shall do much better here where we can keep an eye on you!"

"Mama!" Betsy turned her pretty face and trembling lips toward her parent.

"There is much in what your brother says, Betsy," said Lady
Hedgeworth. She was grateful for her son's assumption of authority. Though she would never have thought of threatening her
daughter in such an ignoble manner, she was willing to impart her
authority to it. "I'll not have you upsetting us all, and especially
Fredericka, with your tempestuous starts."

Betsy subsided, eyeing her older brother with sullen respect.

Sarah tried to smooth oil on the troubled waters. "Shall Fredericka have to have a great many pretty new dresses, Mama?"

Lady Hedgeworth smiled, glad for the change in topic. "We
must see to that, indeed. Thank you for reminding me, Sarah.
Fredericka, I shall take you into the village tomorrow to be mea-
sured. Though your wardrobe is well enough, it is rather meager.
We shall need to refurbish it a bit, for most of your things were
made over from your mourning clothes. You will need outfits
with a bit more color and dash."

"Oh, no, Mama! I could not let you go to the expense," said
Fredericka, appalled. She was already made uncomfortable at

being the cause of poor Betsy's distress and now this unexpected decision upon her mother's part merely added to her discomfiture.

More than anyone else, with the exception of the trustees, Fredericka knew precisely what was the family's financial state. Life at Luting was not crimped in style. None of the Hedgeworths were extravagant, discounting Betsy's occasional lapses, but still that did not mean that the estate could bear an exorbitant expense. The complete outfitting of a young lady for a London Season could conceivably qualify as just that.

"Nonsense, dear. I shall enjoy it. After dinner we shall have out the fashion plates and decide what we shall order from the seamstress," said Lady Hedgeworth. This was a topic into which her other daughters could not resist interjecting their own opinions and preferences even before the covers were removed. By the time that the family had repaired to the drawing room, the conversation was full-blown.

The sullen air had dropped away from Betsy as she became absorbed in what was of true interest to her. If she repined because none of the gowns or dresses were to be her own, she did not show it. Instead, she willingly advised her eldest sister on what styles would best compliment Fredericka's height and warm coloring. "You must on no account wear anything too pale, Fredericka, for it would make you look too brown. A lady's complexion must appear fashionably pale," she said with worldly wisdom.

"Gracious! Then I am undone," said Fredericka with a hint of laughter in her voice. "I suppose that you shall have to lend me some of your creams, Betsy, if I am not to disgrace myself entirely."

Betsy graciously consented to make this sacrifice upon her sister's behalf. "For naturally we must all do what we can to insure your success." She shook her head. "It is a pity that you will go outdoors so much, Freddie."

"Perhaps she can wear a veil attached to the front of her bonnet," suggested Sarah.

"Nothing would persuade me to do so," said Fredericka firmly.

Thomas had listened to the unfolding discussion with growing disgust. Finally he burst out, "What I want to know is, are you going to see Astley's Circus and the zoo, Freddie? And the harbor! I'd give anything to see those, by Jove."

"Of course she isn't! That sort of thing is for children. Fredericka will be far too busy with balls and routs and driving in the park and—and that sort of thing," said Betsy, her nose going up in the air.

"Such dull stuff!" said Thomas scornfully. He lost interest in his sister's projected trip and ambled over to the sideboard. There was a browned apple tart made from the winter stores that he had been eyeing for some minutes and he had determined to have it.

Fredericka and Lord Hedgeworth both laughed at their younger brother's neat judgment.

"Yes, well, scrub, I tend to agree with you," said Lord Hedgeworth. "What do you say to a game of billiards while these females prose on about ribbons and bonnets and fripperies?"

Thomas's eyes brightened. He made hurried work of the tart. "You are on, Jack!"

As Lord Hedgeworth and Thomas left the drawing room, the latter tossed a triumphant glance at Betsy, who chose to ignore him. Time spent with their eldest brother was a treat for any of the three younger siblings.

After the fashion plates had been diligently discussed and finally set aside, Fredericka wandered away from the cozy circle in front of the hearth. She drew back a drape so that she could look outside. The moon was full and cast crystalline shadows over the snow. She felt that the storm last night was the last of the winter. Soon she would be off to London.

Fredericka thought that she had not felt such a lowering of her spirits since her father had died. By rights, she knew, she should be excited at the prospect of traveling for the first time and of entering into a society that she had only heard and read about. She was the daughter of a peer. It was her natural heritage to make her bows and establish herself credibly in the ton. But the fact of the matter was that she had never been farther from home than the next county and her life was wrapped around the gentle changes wrought by the seasons at Luting. She really had little desire to expand her present horizons.

The affinity Fredericka had for her home was not unusual

among those of her social circle, for love of the family lands was bred into the daughters of her class. It was always a painful wrench for a daughter to leave the land behind when she wed. It was a surrender of pride and identity. She was no longer associated with all that had formed the course of her life up to that point. Instead, she became submerged in her husband's identity and substituted his pride of place for her own.

For Fredericka, however, the depth of feeling ran even deeper. She was not only the daughter of the house, but she had virtually acted in the capacity of steward for Luting for two years. Her emotional ties to Luting were stronger than her contemporaries to their own homes because she had learned to manage and husband the lands. Fredericka could not conceive of giving up all that she had learned and come to love simply because it had suddenly become her duty to wed.

It would be different, of course, if she was to wed a gentleman whom she loved.

Fredericka felt a flare of rebellion. Alarm had initially attended what she had heard from her mother. But it was subtle anger that now flickered through her veins and fueled her thoughts.

Already she was beginning to recognize that, her brother's assurances not withstanding, it still behooved her to accept an eligible offer if one were made to her before the Season ended. She could not rely upon Lord Hedgeworth's airy promise to introduce her to some respectable parties, and it did not bear thinking of to find herself in the end in exactly the situation that she most wished to avoid. Her best course to prevent herself from becoming a future burden upon her brother was to make the most of her opportunities in London.

Fredericka determined that she would do everything that was expected of her by the Countess of Chalmers and by her mother, but there was a line to be drawn. She would not accept any offer that came from a gentleman who had not proved himself worthy of her.

Fredericka resolved that the gentleman who sought her favor would be willing to sacrifice something of his own pride in order to claim her. After all, she would be sacrificing herself. Should she not be assured that the gentleman she chose to wed would be so firmly attached to her that he would put her even before himself? If she was to enter a marriage of convenience, then she at least wanted to be able to respect and esteem the gentleman she accepted.

Fredericka dropped the drapery and turned back to her family. A smile quivered upon her lips. There was something of a martial light in her eyes, but since her manner was much as it always was, none of her family felt the least trepidation for what the future might hold.

Chapter Six

Lady Hedgeworth lost no time in sending off an affirmative reply to the Countess of Chalmers. She sat down at her desk that very night. Her daughter's serene acquiescence was an unexpected balm to her anxious conscience and she wanted to finalize the matter before anything might occur to shake Fredericka's confidence in the decision. Only let some emergency occur with a family member or a knotty problem arise with the smooth working of the estate and Lady Hedgeworth knew that Fredericka would balk. The girl had a high sense of duty that was disconcerting, thought her ladyship with mingled pride and frustration.

Now Lady Hedgeworth pondered how she should word her acceptance. After all, Fredericka had not been precisely overjoyed at the prospect of a Season. Though Fredericka had entered readily enough into the discussion on various fashions and expressed her opinion with her usual frankness, Lady Hedgeworth had still been able to detect a certain reluctance in her daughter that was of concern to her.

It was leaving Luting Manor and everything that Fredericka was attached to, of course, thought Lady Hedgeworth regretfully. It was a pity that the running of the estate had fallen so firmly upon Fredericka's shoulders. If that had not been the case, then perhaps this first foray away from Luting would have been easier for her daughter to accept.

Lady Hedgeworth made up her mind to talk to her eldest son. He must begin to take his rightful place and so free his sister of her unusual burdens. It made matters so much more complicated for Fredericka when she saw herself as necessary to Luting. How was the child ever to be weaned away unless Jack proved himself capable and willing to shoulder his responsibilities?

Perhaps Fredericka would have long since begun to look more favorably upon at least one of her suitors if she had not felt herself to be so attached to Luting Manor and all that the estate entailed, thought Lady Hedgeworth. Her own neglect of those responsibilities that should have been hers was something that she guiltily glossed over. Fredericka needed to know how to properly order a household, after all. And certainly her daughter had grown to be completely competent in such matters. She never had a moment's anxiety for anything when she knew that Fredericka had things well in hand. Really, she should congratulate herself on her wisdom in allowing Fredericka such freedom of decision.

Having neatly dispensed of her own twinges of conscience, Lady Hedgeworth came full circle back to the dilemma at hand. She sat idle for a few more minutes, at a loss as how to describe her daughter to the Countess of Chalmers. She felt it would be doing a disservice to Fredericka to reveal how thoroughly her daughter disliked the notion of angling for a husband. The girl was intelligent, but she had no common sense at all, thought her fond mother in regretful exasperation.

Lady Hedgeworth was positive that Fredericka would not put herself forward in any way. Undoubtedly, the Countess of Chalmers would need to give her a little push.

Lady Hedgeworth finally had to be satisfied with the inclusion of a cautioning note into her acceptance letter.

"*I must tell you, Sarah, that I have not breathed a word of our schoolgirl vow to my daughter. Fredericka has the greatest dislike for being made to stand in the limelight. Indeed, she would far rather be out of doors riding her mare over the fields than she would to make a few passes over a ballroom floor. She is not unsociable, precisely. On the contrary, she is quite assured in company. But I fear that she is unlike other misses. Her head is not filled with romantic fancies. I quite despair of her at times.*

"*However, I do repose the fullest confidence in you, my dearest Sarah. It is naturally my fondest wish that your dear Sebastion and my Fredericka shall make a match of it. I shall not repine, however, if either of the two should prefer*

*another, for I would never wish to force our dear children
into a connection which either would dislike.*

"*I remain, cordially,*

"*Victoria*"

Lady Hedgeworth reread what she had written. Again she hesitated, thinking of another phrase that could be added here or there, or seeing how she could have said this or the other thing a little better. In the end, however, she did not change her letter. With a shrug, she sanded the sheet and sealed it, believing that perhaps the least said was for the best. The countess would take Fredericka's measure soon enough.

Lady Hedgeworth was confident that her friend, whom she recalled as a strong-willed lady, was fully equal to the task of shepherding and puffing off a miss who was reluctant to leave behind all that she had ever known.

The only thing remaining to be settled was when Fredericka should travel up to London. That, of course, depended upon the Countess of Chalmers's wishes. Lady Hedgeworth anxiously hoped that there would be time for the seamstress to finish a few items for Fredericka's new wardrobe. She did not want her daughter to look unfashionably countrified when she arrived on the countess's doorstep.

Lady Hedgeworth posted her letter and a few days later the Countess of Chalmers was making herself mistress of its contents.

Lady Chalmers smiled as she finished reading the carefully worded letter. It was obvious to her that Lady Hedgeworth had taken pains to excuse her daughter's dull conventionality and was anxious that it not be seen as a liability. But there was little chance of that, thought Lady Chalmers. Her son needed stability in his life, something to steady him, and becoming responsible for a rather lackluster wife was indeed one way to attain that goal.

Lady Chalmers had set out to put into effect her little scheme on the basis of a close friendship and an old vow, trusting that the Hedgeworths' exile in the country would mean that their daughter had been brought up quietly and in an unspoiled fashion. This, plus the fact that she had known the parents intimately, guaranteed her that the girl would be of good ton. Lady Hedgeworth's description of her daughter was all that Lady Chalmers had hoped for and more.

"It is better than even I thought. The girl sounds perfect," she murmured to herself. Now the trick would be to get her son interested in Miss Hedgeworth. Really, for an arranged marriage it would work out very well.

"I am sorry, my lady. Did you speak?" asked the dresser as she put the final touches to her ladyship's coiffure.

"I was merely thinking aloud, Dorsey," said the countess, folding the letter and tucking it away into her jewel box.

"Yes, my lady."

"We shall be going to London quite soon, Dorsey. You will make arrangements for the packing of my things," said Lady Chalmers.

"Of course, my lady," said the dresser calmly. The announcement had come as a complete surprise, but she obviously knew her place too well to allow even a flicker of expression to cross her face.

The Countess of Chalmers swept out of the bedroom and went downstairs for dinner. Once again, she and the earl were dining tête-à-tête. It was always so when the earl's gout was a particular plague to him. His lordship found the task of playing host onerous at such times.

It was tacitly understood in the county around about that whenever Lord and Lady Chalmers withdrew themselves from social commitments, it meant that the earl was sadly out of curl. No one took affront, therefore, whenever polite regrets were received from Chalmers.

The Earl of Chalmers was informed by his lady over the turtle soup that she was sponsoring Miss Hedgeworth for the Season. He frowned, his spoon pausing in midair as he considered the news. "Hedgeworth?"

"Surely you must remember Lord and Lady Hedgeworth, Edward. Why, Victoria and I were the closest of bosom-bows even after we married," said Lady Chalmers. "They were at Sebastion's christening and we attended when their daughter was christened."

"Of course I remember them," said the earl testily. "I remember, too, that Hedgeworth exiled himself from town to preserve himself from his fatal gaming instinct."

"It was the only thing that he could do under the circumstances," said Lady Chalmers.

"Undoubtedly true. Hedgeworth was completely rolled up," agreed Lord Chalmers. "But I do not understand why you must sponsor this girl. She has no claim on you. You were not made her godmother, as I recall."

"No, she is not my goddaughter, however much dear Victoria would have liked her to have been. However, I do recognize a claim, my lord, even if it is only one of friendship," began Lady Chalmers. "You must know that Lady Hedgeworth lives quietly in modest circumstances."

The earl snorted. "That I well believe. As I said, Hedgeworth ran himself off of his legs before they removed themselves from London," said Lord Chalmers. "I doubt that he had two groats left to rub together. It was astonishing that he managed to keep possession of his estate."

"Very well, then. You must see Lady Hedgeworth's predicament. How is she to credibly launch her daughters unless one steps in and offers a hand?" asked Lady Chalmers.

"And, of course, it is only natural that Lady Hedgeworth should choose to call upon you," said Lord Chalmers irritably.

"Really, Edward!" Lady Chalmers did not think it important to correct his mistaken impression that it had been Lady Hedgeworth who had initiated the contact. "I, for one, cannot turn my back upon an old friend. Certainly not on Lady Hedgeworth, who was closer to me than even my own sisters."

"Aye, and I suspect that you are thinking of throwing the girl at Sebastion's head, too," said Lord Chalmers.

The countess smiled a little. "My dear, why should I not take a hand in things? The Hedgeworths are known to us. Sebastion could do worse than ally himself with that family. In any event, I have already pledged myself to launch the girl even if she does not take Sebastion's fancy."

The Earl of Chalmers waved his hand. "Oh, very well. I perceive that you are quite set on it, so you must do as you think best. I suppose that this will require us to open up the house in London?"

"Of course," said Lady Chalmers in surprise. "I shall wish to launch the girl from our own ballroom, naturally." Then she realized all that her husband had implied. She stared across the table at him. "Edward, do you mean to go up to London with me?"

"I cannot leave you without a proper escort, can I?" he said grumpily, moving his gouty foot gingerly.

Lady Chalmers noted the twinge of pain that the slight movement caused him. "You need not travel up if you do not wish it," she said gently.

"I do wish it. That is the end of the matter," snapped the earl.

"Very well, Edward. I should be glad of your company," said Lady Chalmers quietly.

Lord Chalmers reached over to lay his hand over hers. "But you wish that I was in better trim, do you not? Well, perhaps a change of place shall do me good. I am heartily bored with my own company, and it has been abominably slow this winter here at Chalmers. At least in London I shall not have time to brood so much about this foot of mine. I expect, too, that old acquaintances shall keep me occupied to good effect. What do you think? Could you put up with me, my dear?"

Lady Chalmers's hand turned under his and she grasped his fingers. She smiled at him. "I should like it of all things. You know that I have always had a preference for your company."

"How unfashionable of you, my dear," said the earl, smiling now. It had always been a source of immense gratification to him that his lady wife was not indifferent to him, nor pretended to be, even though fashionable society derided such faithfulness.

"Shall you object if I put in immediate orders for all the packing and closing of the house? For I should like to leave for London in two days," said Lady Chalmers, her thoughts already running ahead.

"Why should I object? The sooner we go to town the sooner I may be comfortable again," said Lord Chalmers, shrugging. He returned to his soup.

The countess rose and dropped a kiss upon his bewigged head. "Then I shall leave you now to talk with the housekeeper. I must also write to Lady Hedgeworth and tell her when we shall expect Miss Hedgeworth to come to us."

"But what of the rest of your dinner?" asked Lord Chalmers, surprised.

"You know how I am when I am excited over something, dear Edward. My appetite quite deserts me. I shall be very much better company once I have taken care of these small matters," said Lady Chalmers. She smoothed his lordship's wide collar and smiled coaxingly. "I shall join you later in the drawing room."

The Earl of Chalmers growled his assent. However, as she made to go, he caught her hand. "One moment, Sarah! I have bethought myself of something."

Lady Chalmers turned in surprise. "Why, Edward, whatever is the matter?"

Lord Chalmers stared at her with frowning eyes. "This Miss Hedgeworth—I trust that she will not be a burden to you, Sarah."

Lady Chalmers raised her brows. "But why ever should she be, Edward? You know how much I adore playing hostess. It shall be a wonderful treat for me to bring the girl out. I have never sponsored anyone before and I suspect that it will be vastly entertaining."

"I am thinking of Hedgeworth's gaming tendencies. You know little about Miss Hedgeworth. Who is to say that she has not inherited her father's taste for the tables, along with his lamentable lack of skill? Sarah, I shall not hide from you my foreboding that the girl may turn out to have the gaming fever in her blood," said Lord Chalmers. He grimaced. "It would be just like that whelp of ours to be drawn to someone as rackity as himself. That is not what I wish to accomplish through my ultimatum to Sebastion."

Lady Chalmers stared down at the earl for a long considering moment. She said slowly, "As you say, I know very little about Miss Hedgeworth. It never occurred to me that she might take after her father in such a fashion. However, Lady Hedgeworth has never hinted at any such thing to me."

"There is nothing in that," said Lord Chalmers, brushing it aside. "Naturally her ladyship would not trumpet such a thing about, if it does exist. But Miss Hedgeworth's possible propensities are not what exercise me so profoundly, as you must realize.

She may be the toast of the Season and contract a spectacular marriage, or sink beneath the waters. She may gamble every day and night of the week, if she pleases. *That* is all one to me! It is Sebastion who I am thinking of now."

"Yes, I perfectly understand you." Lady Chalmers frowned, apparently turning something over in her mind. She looked down again at the earl. "Do you wish me to hint Sebastion away from Miss Hedgeworth?"

Lord Chalmers shrugged. "You must do as you feel best, my dear. I shall tell you frankly, however, I would vastly prefer a daughter-in-law who laughs like a pig to one that will aid Sebastion in running himself into the ground!"

"Your point is well taken, my lord. I shall see to the matter," said Lady Chalmers with decision. "I shall soon discover whether Miss Hedgeworth is a gamester. And if she is, I shall let Sebastion know that she is unsuitable in our eyes."

"It is all that I ask," said the earl, satisfied. "Have you already written to Sebastion?"

Lady Chalmers nodded. "Oh, yes. These several days past. He will naturally be relieved."

"That I do not doubt. I am positive that he will be hoping to betroth himself to a lady who reminds him most of his lovely mother," said Lord Chalmers. He raised his lady's hand to his lips.

Lady Chalmers colored. She tugged at her hand. "Edward, really! What if the servants should come in?"

"What if they do? I shall not be embarrassed to be discovered making charming love to my wife," said Lord Chalmers, smiling with a wicked light in his eyes.

"Oh, Edward, I do love you so," murmured Lady Chalmers, brushing her free hand against his jaw.

"That is just the sort of thing that gives a man life and breath," declared Lord Chalmers. He lifted his wife's hand to his lips again and brushed a fond kiss over her knuckles. Then he released her. "I shall join you in a short while in the drawing room. That is, if you think that you will be finished with your instructions to the housekeeper?"

"Oh, yes. I shall not be kept long at that. As for my letter to Lady Hedgeworth, that may wait for the morning. I should not wish to deny myself the pleasure of your conversation, my lord," said Lady Chalmers.

The earl chuckled, satisfied and content. There was a small glass of port at his elbow. "I shall not keep you waiting, my dear lady. As you see, I do not overly indulge myself this evening."

Lady Chalmers left her lord seated at the table and went away to summon her housekeeper. Even when she became busy in giving instructions to her housekeeper, her mind mulled over what the earl had said. At last the housekeeper expressed herself to be quite clear on her ladyship's wishes and took leave of the countess.

Lady Chalmers lay back in her chair and contemplated the drawing room fire, a frown between her brows. The possibility raised by Lord Chalmers was indeed a valid one. It was well known that the propensity for gaming ran in families. It would be unfortunate indeed if Miss Hedgeworth had inherited her father's obsession, for it would mean that Lady Chalmers would be unable to promote the match that she had proposed to Lady Hedgeworth. Lady Chalmers fully concurred in the earl's observation that Sebastion scarcely needed that sort of helpmate.

"How lowering," Lady Chalmers murmured to herself, annoyed. She saw now that she had been rather shortsighted when she had contacted Lady Hedgeworth. All was not lost, however. When she wrote to Lady Hedgeworth on the morrow, she would bluntly inquire about Miss Hedgeworth's attitude toward gaming.

Lady Chalmers hoped for a good report from Lady Hedgeworth which would assure her that the girl was entirely free of her father's love of the pasteboards. However, if Lady Hedgeworth admitted that her daughter had been stricken with the same curse, then certainly Lady Chalmers could not in good conscience promote a match between their respective progeny.

She would still honor her pledge to sponsor Miss Hedgeworth, of course. She would do all in her power to see that the girl was suitably established and as quickly as possible. It would never do if the girl remained unattached long enough for Lord Satterwaite to take an interest in her. If Miss Hedgeworth was indeed a gamester, that would indeed be fatal.

Lady Chalmers comforted herself with the thought that it was not wise to borrow trouble. Perhaps all of this alarm was completely unnecessary. Miss Hedgeworth could still turn out to be the sweet, stable creature that Lady Chalmers had envisioned her to be. Certainly Lady Hedgeworth's letter had influenced that same vision.

In the morning, she would write to Lady Hedgeworth and send the letter by personal messenger. It was imperative that she should have Lady Hedgeworth's reply in her hand before Miss Hedgeworth came up to London, for then she would know how to proceed with her son, the wayward viscount.

How complicated it had become of a sudden, she thought, annoyed. Depending upon Lady Hedgeworth's answer, she would either endeavor to place Miss Hedgeworth in Lord Satterwaite's way or she would do her utmost to keep them apart.

Chapter Seven

Lord Sebastion Satterwaite had received his mother's brief communication with mixed feelings. Uppermost was relief that he had been given a reprieve. After all, seven days was little enough time to enjoy himself before he must contemplate the utter devastation of his future.

He had not intended to bow to his father's decree and get himself a wife, and he had viewed the probable loss of his favored position as the heir to Chalmers with defiant resignation. It had been a hard thing to contemplate. But his ground was as it had always been—he was not one to be driven into a marriage when it did not suit him to enter that blissful state. He had always thought of entering that contract at some hazy future date. He would not be ramrodded into a marriage of convenience simply because his sire was beginning to feel twinges of his own mortality.

Lord Satterwaite was also annoyed by his mother's note. Her ladyship should not have interfered this time between himself and his sire. The matter had become a point of honor. His will was set against that of his father. The decision had been made, his stand had been declared. The outcome would be known in less than a week and the unnerving wait would be done with.

As a result of Lady Chalmers's interference, when the Season was over in several months, he would have to endure once more this unsettling, tense time that was the result of calling the Earl of Chalmers's bluff.

He had had time enough to regret the hasty indiscretion of his tongue that had led him into exchanging words with the earl. It had been a bitter lesson in the truth of the maxim that a wise man is slow to anger and guarded his tongue, thought Lord Satterwaite with a twisted self-derisive smile.

The unbidden thought whispered to his mind, and not for the first time, that he could very well retain his inheritance simply by complying with his father's wishes. But Lord Satterwaite thrust it aside brusquely, not happy that he had entertained the reflection for even a moment.

He would never wed at someone else's order. If he had already been betrothed, if he had already had even a passing interest in some lady, then perhaps the earl's ultimatum could have been better swallowed. But as it was, there were no such ties already existent. Bowing now would mean the entire humbling of his pride and his will, and that was insupportable to him.

Already the earl had forbidden him to go into the army and get himself a position on Wellington's staff. It would have been something indeed to have been part of the war. Lord Satterwaite knew with every fiber of his being that Wellington was the one man alive who could possibly defeat the brilliant Napoleon Bonaparte. He knew also that he would have made a fine staff officer and it would have satisfied him to contribute something worthwhile to his country.

But he was, on the whole, a dutiful son. He had acceded to his father's wishes not to enter the army. He had understood the earl's fears that he might be killed and thus leave the earldom to fall into his cousin's rapacious hands.

Whatever their differences through the years, Lord Satterwaite and the Earl of Chalmers had always been one in their aversion to the Honorable Lucius Everard. Born to a younger son and possessed of a competent independence in his own right, blessed with a handsome if somewhat cold face and good figure, Lucius Everard should have been a prime favorite of his uncle, the Earl of Chalmers. But his cozening ways, his malicious tongue, and his extremely disreputable way of life had set him beyond what was pleasing to his noble relations. If the mantle of the earldom were ever to fall on that gentleman's shoulders, there was no question that the estate would be glutted by the man's greed, the tenants exploited, and the very name of Chalmers would be disgraced in the eyes of the world.

If he had married before this and had gotten himself a nursery full of hopeful babes, then perhaps he could have set his face toward the army in all good conscience. But he had not done so.

There had never been an attachment strong enough with any damsel to validate tying himself in tandem for life. He had never desired the lukewarm sort of relationship that he had observed among many of his social set.

Lord Satterwaite's thoughts idled on. He could still do it. He could wed and set up a nursery in a matter of a year or two, before joining the army. It wouldn't matter that he and his lady cared tepidly for one another. He would be out of the country, likely for some years if the war dragged on.

Lord Satterwaite realized the temptations of those thoughts and he grimaced. His strength of mind or will must be lacking that he would even entertain such reflections. No, he would continue to hold to his purpose. His honor and his pride would remain intact, even though it cost him everything that he held dear and the position for which he had been bred up to step into.

Lucius Everard would have the earldom and he would have nothing.

The stark thought was not palatable. Lord Satterwaite stared into the middle distance for a moment, his mouth grim. He wondered whether his father had realized that possibility yet.

Lord Satterwaite thrust his mother's letter into the drawer of his desk and got up. Striding over to the door of the study, he set up a shout for his hat and gloves and overcoat. Within moments, his valet was carefully helping him into the overcoat.

Lord Satterwaite pulled on his gloves. "I am going out. If any of my particular cronies should call, you may tell them that I may be found at Jackson's Saloon." He placed his hat on his head and departed from the house.

Lord Satterwaite came upon one of his closest friends on the way. The Honorable Fitzgerald Howard-Browne was sauntering casually down the flagway toward the viscount. When he saw Lord Satterwaite, he hailed him. "I say, Sebastion! Where have you been keeping yourself? I have not seen you in days."

"I spent a few weeks in the shires for the shooting and then turned aside to visit at Chalmers," said Lord Satterwaite, grasping his friend's wiry hand.

"Where are you off to now?" asked Mr. Howard-Browne.

"I am for Jackson's to enjoy a round or two," said Lord Satterwaite.

Mr. Howard-Browne gazed at him with experienced eyes. "Up in the boughs, are you?" he stated shrewdly. "I think that I'll go along with you and see whether anyone has the courage and the bottom to stand up to your rattling style. You are always good for a pound or two when you are in a fury."

Lord Satterwaite laughed reluctantly. He did not deny his friend's observation. "You are a bloodthirsty fellow, Fitz. But you are likely to be disappointed if you are looking for a raree-show."

Mr. Howard-Browne had turned and now matched the steps with the viscount's lengthy stride. "Oh, I have no doubt that I shall be fully entertained. I have seen that look in your eyes before. Blood, my boy, blood."

"Nonsense!" said Lord Satterwaite impatiently.

Mr. Howard-Browne did not protest the validity of his observation, merely saying, "What has put you into such a pucker that you must needs pound some poor fellow's brains out of his head?"

Lord Satterwaite threw his companion a smoldering glance, which Mr. Howard-Browne met with such bland sapience that he was forced to grin acknowledgment. He grimaced. "I have been to Chalmers. Is it needful for me to say more?"

Mr. Howard-Browne threw a sideways glance at the viscount. "Indeed, it is scarcely necessary. I have no intention of prying, of course."

Lord Satterwaite shook his head. All the evils of his situation came up in his roiling thoughts. "It was worse than you suppose, Fitz. My father and I had words again, yes. However, we parted in more rancor than ever before."

Mr. Howard-Browne shook his head. "Very bad, of course. My sympathies. I am fortunate to be placed as I am with two brothers. Was it the same disagreement?"

"Yes, and no," said Lord Satterwaite, the grim smile again touching his lips. "An ultimatum was made me this time, Fitz. I am to be disinherited, cut out of the succession, in fact, if I do not seek to tie the knot. I told my sire what he could do with his ultimatum. It was an ugly scene, believe me."

Mr. Howard-Browne gave a low comprehending whistle. "I

have no difficulty in believing it, my boy, none at all! What will you do?"

Lord Satterwaite shrugged, and laughed. "Damned if I know, Fitz. I suppose that I shall end up in the army, which, as you know, would not altogether displease me."

"But not if it means that you must enlist as a common foot soldier," murmured Mr. Howard-Browne.

Lord Satterwaite's brows drew together. He did not vouchsafe an answer, for that possibility had also crossed his mind. Stripped of his title and his position, it was extremely unlikely that any influence would be exerted upon his behalf. In essence, he would be barred from becoming a staff officer. He would have no more preference than any other untitled individual. The best he would be able to do would be to buy a commission and then work toward promotions. It would be a slow way to curry favor and position.

A carriage passed the two gentlemen. The feminine occupants of the coach acknowledged the viscount and Mr. Howard-Browne. Mr. Howard-Browne touched the brim of his hat and gave a slight bow. Lord Satterwaite nodded his own acknowledgment of the ladies' bow.

When the carriage was well past, Mr. Howard-Browne voiced his thoughts. "You cannot simply drop the plum into Lucius Everard's hands, dear fellow. It is not to be thought of. Such a turn would make me feel positively unwell."

"Believe me, the thought nauseates me far more than it does you," said Lord Satterwaite brusquely. "But I cannot see my way clear. My cousin shall step into my vacated shoes unless I comply with my father's ultimatum. And that I cannot and will not do! It is a point of honor."

"Of course. That is well understood," agreed Mr. Howard-Browne. He unhappily regarded their way. After a moment, he offered a tentative suggestion. "I don't suppose that you could let go of your pride for a higher purpose? Such as that of taking a wife to keep Everard from what he most desires?"

"Fitz!" exploded Lord Satterwaite.

"No, I suppose not," said Mr. Howard-Browne, sighing. "A pity. I have the most cordial dislike of Everard. It quite blinded me for a moment, so much so that I forget myself. Forgive me, Sebastion. Of course you cannot do it. It is a point of honor and all that."

"It would be different if I were already contracted to some lady," said Lord Satterwaite.

"Oh, there could be no question of it," said Mr. Howard-Browne. He cast a hopeful glance at the viscount. "I don't suppose that there is any lady whom you have favored lately?"

Lord Satterwaite's lips curled in a fleeting grin. "Unfortunately, no."

Mr. Howard-Browne sighed, and nodded. There was nothing more to be said. Jackson's Saloon having been reached, the two gentlemen passed through the portals and ascended the stairs to that elite club of boxing.

Lord Satterwaite enjoyed a couple of brisk rounds with another gentleman of like mind. There were several gentlemen already in attendance and as usual, Jackson stood out from among his more soberly dressed noble clients in his scarlet coat, lace cuffs, breeches, and silk stockings.

Mr. Howard-Browne watched as an interested spectator. He had no interest in putting on the gloves himself, preferring other more sophisticated sports over this rough recreation. When the viscount was finished, he was so fortunate as to be given the nod of approval by the great pugilist himself. Mr. Howard-Browne remarked, "It makes no odds to me, of course, but you were a bit brutal with poor Connolly."

"He would scarcely have given me any quarter if our positions had been reversed, Fitz," said Lord Satterwaite.

Mr. Howard-Browne nodded. "Quite true. Connolly is a bit of a bullying sort." He looked at his immaculately manicured nails and flexed his fingers. "Give me the small sword any day. That is a weapon far superior to one's fists, and the weapon of a gentleman, besides."

Lord Satterwaite laughed. "You are a snob, Fitz. Come, you will bear me company to Tatt's. If I am to be cut off penniless in a few months, I must make the most of my present opportunities. I hear that that team of Wyndham's are on the block."

Mr. Howard-Browne at once pricked up his ears. "Indeed! Of a certainty I shall accompany you. I have an interest in that direc-

tion myself." He sauntered down the walkway with Lord Satterwaite.

"You don't mean to bid against me, I hope," said Lord Satterwaite.

Mr. Howard-Browne waved a languid hand. "It sorrows me to
contemplate the possibility of a rift between us, naturally. We
have always been the closest of friends heretofore."

Lord Satterwaite laughed. "Come along, then. We shall see
who shall have them!"

The viscount and Mr. Howard-Browne repaired to Tattersall's,
the horse auctioning house. They met several friends and acquaintances there, for the subscription rooms were a fashionable con-
gregating place for sporting gentlemen to discuss horseflesh, to
trade the latest *on dits*, and to buy or sell some of the best horses
in England.

A mutual acquaintance came up to Lord Satterwaite and Mr.
Howard-Browne. After exchanging pleasantries, Sir Gregory
dropped the comment that he had just seen Lord Satterwaite's
cousin, the Honorable Lucius Everard, a few moments before.

"Everard means to bid on the very team that you say that you
have your eye on, Satterwaite. He's been boasting in that sicken-
ingly soft way of his that he is the only whip who can properly
handle them," said Sir Gregory. He was a large, bluff gentleman
and had the red face and square jaw of the country squire. His
manner was broad and unsubtle. He nudged the viscount and guf-
fawed. "That man-milliner! I wish I may see it!"

Lord Satterwaite smiled. "My cousin may choose to bid however he pleases, of course."

Sir Gregory made a few more derogatory remarks about Mr.
Everard before he spotted another acquaintance and took himself
off. Mr. Howard-Browne looked after the gentleman reflectively
before turning to the viscount and saying, "He is always very forward with his opinions. One is never forced to conjecture at his
meaning. Your cousin's waspish tongue has been stinging that
gentleman's hide, unless I miss my guess."

"Yes, I think you have hit the mark squarely, Fitz. Our good-
natured friend seemed unusually ruffled this morning," said Lord

Satterwaite. He looked beyond his friend's shoulder. "The bidding begins, my friend. Do you bid against me?"

Mr. Howard-Browne shook his head. "I shall give you free rein. If Everard is to bid for that team, I prefer not to muddy the waters. However, if you should chance to be run off your legs before you have acquired that team, only inform me. I shall be glad to lend you a monkey or two to beat him out."

Lord Satterwaite laughed. "Kind of you, Fitz. I shall keep it in mind."

The bidding began and the gentlemen ringing about made their preferences known to the auctioneer. Lord Satterwaite waited until the team that he wanted was led out into the ring. The bidding was begun at a rather substantial amount, but he lifted his hand.

Across the way, an unusually tall gentleman turned to see who had forestalled his own opening bid. The gentleman's eyes narrowed when his gaze fell on the viscount. He turned and nodded to the auctioneer.

Within moments, all other bidders had withdrawn to leave the arena to Lord Satterwaite and his opponent. It was recognized that the bidding between the viscount and Mr. Lucius Everard was becoming a contest of clashing wills, and the onlookers freely expressed their opinions over which of the gentlemen would emerge the winner.

In the end, Lord Satterwaite carried the day. The team was led out of the arena and his lordship started to go submit a draft on his bank for the horses. But before Lord Satterwaite and Mr. Howard-Browne had gone any great distance, they were approached by the gentleman who had lost in the bidding.

Mr. Everard smiled. His teeth were very white and gleaming. His dress was impeccable, inclining toward the dandy with exaggeratedly high starched shirtpoints and a richly hued waistcoat. Several fobs dangled at his waist and jewels flashed on his fingers. He hailed the viscount, saying, "So, cousin! You have outbid me. I must congratulate you."

Lord Satterwaite nodded coolly. "Lucius. I trust that you do not hold it against me."

"Oh, decidedly not! The team is such a pretty acquisition. I understand how one of your noted stature as a whipster could not resist," said Mr. Everard. His words were friendly enough, but there was a cold look in his hard blue eyes.

"As you say," said Lord Satterwaite noncommittally.

"I must wish you joy of them, cousin, of course."

Mr. Everard smoothed an imaginary wrinkle out of his coat sleeve. He said meditatively, "One does so wish that convention did not place such constraints for insipid civilities upon us." He glanced up, still smiling. "You will understand my meaning, I know."

Lord Satterwaite smiled. "I do not pretend to misunderstand you, no."

"I did not think that you would," said Lucius Everard softly. He glanced at the viscount's silent companion. "Good day to you, Howard-Browne. Shall I see you at the races later, I wonder? Ah, but I have forgotten. It is rumored that you have had several reverses of late."

"Nothing of any concern," said Mr. Howard-Browne briefly.

"Of course not," said Mr. Everard soothingly.

Mr. Howard-Browne flushed with anger. Lucius Everard gave a low satisfied laugh. He made a short negligent bow that was almost mocking in its execution. Then he sauntered off, twirling his cane.

"I do not care for your cousin one whit," said Mr. Howard-Browne emphatically.

"Nor I," said Lord Satterwaite. "He is as subtle and as dangerous as an adder. When we were boys, I often bruised his head. I would that I had broken it. Perhaps it would have done him some good. Alas, I was too compassionate."

"Sebastion, you cannot allow that fellow to step into your shoes!" said Mr. Howard-Browne forcibly.

"I own, the prospect pleases me less and less," said Lord Satterwaite, glancing after his cousin.

"Give it some thought, I beg," said Mr. Howard-Browne earnestly. "Surely one should take into account the greater of the evils in this situation."

"Very well, Fitz. I shall consider what you have said," said Lord Satterwaite quietly. His expression was distant, as was his voice.

Glancing swiftly at the viscount, Mr. Howard-Browne realized that he had overstepped the bounds. He flushed. "My pardon, Sebastion! I forget myself. My own antagonism toward that—but pray disregard everything I've said. It is not my business, after all."

Lord Satterwaite nodded. "Fitz, have you had reverses? You have only to say so and—"

"Would I have offered to spot you a monkey just now if I was in dun territory?" demanded Mr. Howard-Browne, his face reddening.

"My apologies, Fitz," said Lord Satterwaite.

Mr. Howard-Browne shook his head, his angry color fading. "I shouldn't have allowed that fellow to prick at me. He has a trick of implying the worst of everyone, and the sad thing is that he is so often believed."

"Let us agree that my cousin is a malicious wasp and leave it at that," suggested Lord Satterwaite.

Mr. Howard-Browne laughed and agreed. He accompanied the viscount over to make payment for the new team and arrange for its delivery to his lordship's stables.

After the visit to Tattersall's, Lord Satterwaite and Mr. Howard-Browne separated with promises of meeting one another at their club for dinner.

Chapter Eight

The ton trickled back into London for the beginning of the Season and Lord Satterwaite began the customary round of social calls and amusements that an unmarried gentleman of expensive habits and impeccable lineage could be expected to enjoy. It was several days before he learned that his worthy parents had come up to London for the Season. He was surprised. He knew that his father was still enduring a period of particularly painful gout, because his mother's last letter had mentioned it.

Since the blazing interview between himself and the earl, Lord Satterwaite had suffered pangs of conscience for adding to his sire's discomfort. The old gentleman most certainly would not be in the mood for jollity and socializing, so why had his lordship quit Chalmers for London? The Earl of Chalmers was notorious for shutting himself away from company of any sort when he was in such torment.

The only possible explanation that came to Lord Satterwaite's mind was that the earl wanted to oversee his son's progress with the ladies.

That supposition not unnaturally incensed Lord Satterwaite to no little degree. His mouth tightening, he murmured aloud, "I'll not give him the satisfaction. He may thunder and threaten till he is blue, but I will not dangle after some simpering miss at his order!"

"M'lord?"

Lord Satterwaite discovered that he was staring at his valet. "It is nothing of your concern, Turby."

The valet said nothing more, but he shot a keen glance at the viscount's frowning profile.

In the normal course of events, Lord Satterwaite would have gone at once to pay his respects to his parents. But after he had

drawn the only possible conclusions for their sudden appearance
in London, Lord Satterwaite deliberately chose to allow a few
days to lapse before he adhered to this civility. Certainly he
needed the time for his annoyance to abate enough that he could
meet them with any degree of equanimity.

In any event, he knew that it would be an uncomfortable interview, for he had already determined that he would not submit
himself to the possibility of his father's cross-examination, nor to
his mother's attempts to persuade him to fall docilely into line
with the earl's injunction. That was all that he could expect to
come out of the visit.

Lord Satterwaite's determination lasted until he received a
short note from his mother, the contents of which aroused his curiosity and drew him to her drawing room at Chalmers House.

As Lord Satterwaite was announced and stepped into the drawing room, he glanced around to see whether there were already
other callers. There were not and he wondered if his mother had
given orders to deny her to her several acquaintances that morning. The suspicion made a smile flicker to his lips. He had indeed
stepped into the lair. Now it remained to be seen how he would
fare.

Lady Chalmers received her son with outstretched hands. "My
dear Sebastion! Thank you for coming to see me. I had hoped that
you would."

The viscount kissed her fingers before releasing her hands. He
smiled down at her. "How could it be otherwise when you sent
me such a titillating note, Mama?"

Lady Chalmers looked around as though anxious that they not
be overheard. Satisfied that the door to the drawing room was se-
curely closed, she drew her son over to the settee, saying, "Truly,
I did not wish to put myself forward in this matter, Sebastion. But
I felt that I had little choice. You are my son, after all. I wished
there to be no question of my position."

Sebastion sat down and regarded his mother with the faintest of
frowns. "What is this, Mama? Surely my father has not gone back
on his word?"

Lady Chalmers looked blank for a moment. Then understanding came over her face. She shook her head, her expression re-
proving. "Of course not! Why would you think such a thing?

Your father is the most honorable of men, Sebastion. His word has always been his bond."

Lord Satterwaite's lips twisted. "Then I might suppose that I shall be disinherited at the end of the Season. I knew as soon as I heard that you were in town that my father must have felt compelled to come up so that he could keep his eye upon me. I do not intend to satisfy his lamentable curiosity!"

Lady Chalmers looked calmly at him. "Pray do not do anything that you might regret, Sebastion. Perhaps your father did indeed have something of that sort on his mind. I really do not know, for we have not discussed it. However, even if it is so, pray do not use our presence in town as an excuse for deliberate ruination. You have been granted ample time to look about you and find someone suited to your taste. It is not as though you had to offer for the first female that you clapped eyes on when you returned to London!"

"No, fortunately not, since that female was one of dubious reputation," retorted the viscount.

"I have never understood why men are such pigheaded, proud fools," said Lady Chalmers meditatively.

"I did not come here to argue with you, Mama," said Lord Satterwaite.

"No, indeed! You came in anticipation that I was going to throw myself upon your manly chest and beg you to reconsider your hasty declaration to your father. But I shall do no such thing," said Lady Chalmers tartly.

"Will you not, ma'am?" asked Lord Satterwaite, a smile of skepticism on his face.

Lady Chalmers shook her head. "No, I shall not! I have quite made up my mind that you must wed. A good wife will be the making of you, Sebastion."

"Thank you, ma'am! It is naturally a mildly disagreeable surprise to me that you so heartily endorse my father's opinion," said Lord Satterwaite, his upper lip curling.

"Pray do not take that high tone with me, Sebastion. I recall quite well that I once wiped jam from your face and hands. Well, you have gotten yourself in quite a sticky mess once more, but I am unable to make it all right. Only you can do that, and you have been made aware how it can be done," snapped Lady Chalmers.

Lord Satterwaite gave a low laugh. "Oh, indeed! That has been made abundantly clear to me."

"I only trust that you see the sense behind your father's ultimatum before the Season's end, Sebastion, for I have made up my mind to it that I shall not interfere, and that is my warning to you," said Lady Chalmers. "I shall make no appeal to your father. What you have wrought between you is devilish, and I shall suffer because of it. But I, too, have my pride. I shall not lift my finger to help either of you. I am retiring from the lists. It is high time that you two learned to deal with one another without having to resort to a mediator."

Lord Satterwaite stared at his mother. The expression in his green eyes was unreadable. "Have you informed my father of this determination of yours to sit back and watch us go to the devil?"

Lady Chalmers smiled. "Informed him, my dear? I have no need to do so, for he has already seen it. I told him just what I have told you. This standoff was borne out of imprudent anger and stupid pride. So be it! You have both done your best to make your own beds. Now you may lie in them, if you will. Meanwhile, I intend to enjoy the Season. I am sponsoring the daughter of an old friend. You may perhaps remember Lady Hedgeworth, Sebastion. You were, I think, three years old when their daughter was christened."

"No, I am sorry. I do not recall," said Sebastion, frowning heavily and replying with spurious interest.

Lady Chalmers's neat wrapping up of the matter that had most exercised his mind and emotions every moment of every day was disconcerting, to say the least. And then, once her startling declaration had been made, she had quite coolly turned the conversation into mundane waters. Lord Satterwaite felt as though everything of importance to him in his life had suddenly been relegated to the background. It was insupportable.

It dawned slowly and with unwelcome clarity upon Lord Satterwaite that he had subconsciously leaned on the confidence that his mother would make intercession on his behalf with the earl.

Lady Chalmers had always served to smooth the path between the two males in her household. But it seemed that this time her good nature and natural compassion had been imposed upon once too often. The countess appeared quite adamant about allowing the dice to fall where they might. It was a radical changeabout, and the viscount wondered grimly what his father thought about it.

His attention was brought abruptly back to what his mother was saying when he heard an admonishment. Lord Satterwaite narrowed his eyes on his mother. "What was that you said, Mama? I am not to pay my addresses to Miss Hedgeworth? Is that not a strange thing to say, considering my own unenviable position and the fact that you are sponsoring her?"

"Not at all," said Lady Chalmers calmly. "Miss Hedgeworth has but a modest portion. She has lived in the country most of her life and as I recall she was quite timid as a very small child."

She did not bother mentioning the earl's concern about Miss Hedgeworth, for she had already gotten back Lady Hedgeworth's astonished and indignant denial that her daughter had an affinity for gaming whatsoever. It had relieved Lady Chalmers of a pressing worry so that she felt quite able to promote her original scheme without reservation. With that in mind, she concluded, "In short, Sebastion, Miss Hedgeworth has not the prerequisites that you require in your viscountess, and so I prefer that you cast your eyes elsewhere."

"What do you know of my requirement in a wife, Mama? I have never aired them to you," said Lord Satterwaite. "Actually, Miss Hedgeworth sounds to be eminently suitable."

"Oh, I beg to differ with you, Sebastion. I doubt very much that she would suit," said Lady Chalmers coolly. "At this juncture, I do not believe that you have the inclination to change your habits. Though I do believe that a good alliance must present a steadying influence upon you, certainly you will not be transformed. Your future wife must be able to turn a blind eye to your wild progress. And too, she must be able to look elsewhere for her own companionship. I doubt that Miss Hedgeworth will have been brought up to understand these things."

Lord Satterwaite flushed and his mouth tightened. "I thank you for your opinion of me, Mama! It is flattering indeed! What a hopeless fellow you must take me to be that you assume that this is the way that I shall conduct myself after I wed. Or that I should tolerate that sort of free behavior in one I called my wife! That carelessness may be discreetly accepted by much of society, but it will not do for me."

"Am I mistaken, then? Would you truly want a wife who looked to you for her emotional support? I would not have thought it, for you do not in the least wish to wed. Do you, Sebastion?" said Lady Chalmers, raising her brows.

"No, I do not!" grated Lord Satterwaite. "As well you must know, ma'am!"

Lady Chalmers smiled, shaking her head. "If you do wed, it will be solely for the sake of securing your inheritance. For you do not love, Sebastion. You are far too selfish to fall into that trap, are you not, my son?"

Lord Satterwaite was stung. He rose hastily and took a quick turn about the room. His emotions could no longer support inactivity.

Lady Chalmers watched him with an interested gaze. She had said such deliberately insulting things to her son. Never in her life had she treated him with such callous disregard for either his sensibilities or his pride. It would be interesting to see how the viscount would react.

A measure of shame touched her for what she was doing, but she assured herself quickly that the circumstances called for desperate measures. She simply had to break through the wall of the viscount's obstinate pride and thus force him to reflect on his future.

Lord Satterwaite stopped before the fireplace. One hand braced on the mantel, he stared down at the crackling fire. He tossed over his shoulder, "You are wrong, ma'am. Where I loved, I would do all in my power to please my lady. She would have no need to turn a blind eye, nor to look elsewhere to ease her loneliness."

"You interest me profoundly," said the countess. "In fact, you have greatly relieved my mind."

Lord Satterwaite turned swiftly, his brows snapping together in a deeper frown.

Lady Chalmers smiled at her son and held out her hand. "You are undoubtedly too angered to talk with me any more today. I apologize, Sebastion. I have deliberately brought forth things in a provoking way so that I might see what were your true feelings. I am glad to see that you do have some proper notion of how a marriage should go."

The viscount went forward and took her hand. Forcefully, he said, "I have the example from my childhood, ma'am. You and my father have always been before my eyes. How could I contemplate a bloodless connection such as you have painted when I know that there is more that can be had?"

"Oh, my dear," said Lady Chalmers, at once overcome.

Lord Satterwaite bowed. He brushed her fingers with his lips. As he straightened, he forced himself to smile. "I shall indeed take my leave of you, ma'am. You have given me much to think about. Perhaps I shall see my way clear before the Season ends."

"Then you shall wed?" asked Lady Chalmers, at once curious and hopeful.

The viscount grinned. His green eyes glinted with a mocking light. "Perhaps. Then again, perhaps not. We shall see."

With that, he was gone.

Lady Chalmers sat for a long time thinking over the short visit with her son. She was not dissatisfied with the way the interview had gone. She had seen at once that her assurance that she would not intercede between the earl and his heir had struck the viscount forcibly. Then her wounding words had done something in breaking down the stubborn blind resolution that Lord Satterwaite had against marrying. However, she was still overwhelmed to discover that the relationship between herself and the earl was held in such high esteem by their son. It was something to give humble thanks for in her evening prayers.

As for the scheme that she had begun to weave around Miss Hedgeworth, her ladyship was not ill-pleased there, either. She thought that she had placed just the right amount of opposition in the viscount's path to arouse his competitive nature and his curiosity about Miss Hedgeworth.

Lord Satterwaite had nibbled at the bait. He would at least give more than a passing glance at Miss Hedgeworth, which was one of the objectives that Lady Chalmers had hoped to accomplish.

The other and greater objective, of course, had been to draw the viscount out of his self-absorption. Lady Chalmers hoped that she had planted the right seed that would do just that.

Lady Chalmers sighed. She was using Miss Hedgeworth in an unscrupulous manner. It pained her sense of fairness. But she had determined on her own course and she would not turn back now.

It was possible that with the best will in the world for it to be otherwise, Sebastion might not be drawn to Miss Hedgeworth. The viscount might not wish to offer for the young woman at all. He might turn his sights in quite another direction once he had become used to the notion of marrying. That would certainly leave the question of Miss Hedgeworth's future dangling in midair.

The only consolation that Lady Chalmers could offer her uneasy conscience was that she had pledged herself to successfully launch the girl. By hook or by crook, she would collar a suitable husband for Miss Hedgeworth. She might not fulfill the girlhood vow between herself and Lady Hedgeworth, thought Lady Chalmers, but at least she could make certain that her dear Victoria would be relieved of the anxiety of an unwed daughter.

Lady Chalmers tugged the bellpull. When her butler entered, she requested that her writing materials be brought to her. She would post a letter to Lady Hedgeworth, requesting that Miss Hedgeworth be sent to her at once. There would be dresses and gowns to be commissioned and all sorts of fripperies to buy, thought Lady Chalmers, and naturally she would bear the expense. It would be to her advantage that Miss Hedgeworth should be tricked out in as fashionable a manner as possible, for she knew her son well.

Lord Satterwaite might have nibbled at the bait, but he would not look twice at a complete dowd.

Chapter Nine

When Lord Satterwaite left his mother's drawing room, he stepped around to Albemarle Street, where resided the countess's uncle, Mr. Alfred Allyn.

Mr. Allyn was pleased to see his nephew and he greeted the viscount warmly. "Nevy! Glad to have you. Sit down, sit down."

Lord Satterwaite availed himself of this genial invitation by sweeping a chair free of racing forms, calendars, a muffler, and other assorted items. "How have you been, Allyn?" he asked.

"Tolerable, tolerable," said Mr. Allyn comfortably. "I make no complaints." He was an obese gentleman and seldom put himself to the trouble of physical exertion of any kind, so he had not risen upon the entrance of his guest and he adjured his servant to set a tankard of ale at his lordship's elbow (which his lordship declined) before taking himself off. When the man had exited, he waved a hand at the remains of a ham and some cutlets on the sideboard. "I am just finishing a light breakfast. Join me, Satterwaite."

"I breakfasted earlier," said Lord Satterwaite, smiling.

Mr. Allyn shook his head. "I can't understand you young fellows. All up and go at the crack of dawn, as like as not. In my day, we played deep all night into the small hours and rose at a decent hour, when the sun was at its zenith, to partake of a good hearty repast. Those were good times and I could tell you tales that would make you sit up and take notice, my boy."

He broke off his fond reminiscences to look shrewdly at his visitor. "But you haven't come here to listen to me run on. Nor is it entirely for the pleasure of my company. What is it, nevy? You may open your budget to me, as you know." He patted his pocket suggestively. "Perhaps you are a trifle behind the wind?"

Lord Satterwaite laughed. "I am fond of you, Allyn, but I'll tell you to your head that you are an insulting old bird. I have not come for a loan, so you may wipe that knowing expression off your face."

"I am glad of it, my boy, for truth to tell I am myself badly dipped at present. It all comes from ignoring my instincts and allowing myself to be persuaded by my friend, Topper, to sport my blunt on a slug." Mr. Allyn shook his head in self-disgust. "A slug, my boy! Me! I was never more annoyed."

"You will come about," said Lord Satterwaite, knowing that this was the reassurance his uncle wanted to hear. It did no good to caution the old gamester, for his habits were too ingrained and too compulsory. Still, it could not be denied that his uncle was one of the shrewdest gamesters alive.

"There is no doubt of that," said Mr. Allyn comfortably, if not quite accurately. "Now, what is it I may do for you? If it is not a loan or a tip?"

Lord Satterwaite turned in his chair and stretched out his legs, crossing them at the ankle. He frowned as he contemplated one toe of his highly polished boots. "It is my father, sir. I sustained a most unpleasant interview with him during a flying visit to Chalmers."

"Drove away under a cloud, eh?" asked Mr. Allyn sympathetically.

"More like from out of the midst of a tempest," said Lord Satterwaite dryly. "The earl has laid down an ultimatum to me that I must shortly wed. If I disoblige him, his lordship threatens to disinherit me. What think you, Allyn?"

"He won't do it," said Mr. Allyn instantly. "My brother-in-law may be a testy fellow at times—in the gout, was he? I thought as much. You take my advice and stay away when his lordship is hipped. He don't mean half the things he says, and those things he does say he regrets later. You lay low a few months and see if this trifle isn't good as forgotten."

Lord Satterwaite's lips curved, though not exactly in amusement. "That's just it, Allyn. I don't think he will forget this time. His lordship gave me a week to get myself betrothed. Then Mama wrote me that he has agreed to give me until the end of the Season."

Mr. Allyn frowned. "That's bad. I would have expected your mother to have sent you word that it was all blown over than otherwise."

"Quite. Perhaps you have not heard. The Earl and Countess of Chalmers have set up residence for the Season," said Lord Satterwaite.

"No!" Mr. Allyn stared. "I wouldn't have thought it, not with his lordship in such queer stirrups as you have been relating. What has brought them up to town?" His mouth dropped open. "Never tell me that his lordship means to drive you himself?"

"That was my initial thought, I must admit," said Lord Satterwaite. "You may conceive the measure of my dislike for the notion."

Mr. Allyn uttered a rumbling laugh. "Aye! I can well imagine your chagrin. It is infamous, indeed! What does the earl hope to accomplish by these roughshod tactics, pray?"

"I suspect that he intends to force me to contract a marriage," said Lord Satterwaite. He rose from the chair and crossed the sideboard. Unstopping a decanter he poured out a small measure of wine. Lifting the glass, he tossed back the wine. Looking across at his uncle, he said, "I have not told you the whole. Mama has chosen to add her weight to my father's. I have just come from an interview with her. She told me that she hopes that I come to see the sense of falling in with my father's dictum before the end of the Season, for she declares that she has washed her hands of the matter."

Mr. Allyn swore.

"My sentiments exactly," said Lord Satterwaite shortly.

"But what is my sister thinking of?" exclaimed Mr. Allyn, roused to unusual agitation. His round rubicund countenance deepened almost to brick. "I shall speak to her, my boy. I promise you."

"I shall not ask it of you, Allyn," said Lord Satterwaite.

"Aye, but I see that it is my duty to do so. It is plain that she has completely lost her senses," said Mr. Allyn forcibly.

"No, I do not think that," said Lord Satterwaite, frowning. "Rather, I believe that Mama has simply had enough of the strife between my sire and myself. She said something of the sort, and so she has determined not to intervene."

"But what then, pray, *does* she intend to do? Surely my sister means to do more than wave her fan while disaster engulfs her house!" exclaimed Mr. Allyn with awful sarcasm.

A flicker of a smile lit Lord Satterwaite's face. "Mama informs me that she is sponsoring the daughter of an old friend, Lady Hedgeworth, for the Season. She intends to be gay to dissipation, in fact."

Mr. Allyn frowned. "Hedgeworth?"

"Why, do you know the name?" asked Lord Satterwaite curiously.

"Aye, of course! I remember now. Sarah's closest bosom-bow was married to Lord Hedgeworth. As I recall, Hedgeworth made a pretty scandal with his gaming reverses and was forced to retire to the country." Mr. Allyn's expression had turned thoughtful. He shot a glance at his nephew. "So Sarah is bringing out the gal this Season, is she? Now that is interesting, indeed."

Lord Satterwaite easily interpreted his uncle's expression. "You must not think that Mama intends to throw Miss Hedgeworth in my way," he said sardonically. "She has already warned me off, implying that I am too unsteady to make an eligible partner for a country-bred miss."

Mr. Allyn regarded the viscount with a fixed stare. "That was an unhandsome thing to say. I should not wonder at it that you were not put into a proper flame."

Lord Satterwaite laughed in genuine amusement for the first time in days. "Well, yes, it did for a moment or two. However, it served to make me reflect upon my future with a clearer eye than before. And, too, I recently had the doubtful pleasure of running into my cousin Lucius."

Mr. Allyn puffed out his cheeks. He contemplated the matter for a moment, then thrust aside his plate with an expression of loathing. "Lucius is the next in succession, barring you."

"Precisely, sir. I saw my esteemable cousin a week or more ago at Tatt's, and I was struck more forcibly than ever by the undesirability of his stepping into my shoes," said Lord Satterwaite.

"So I should imagine," snorted Mr. Allyn. He eyed the viscount with a good deal of sympathy and understanding. "You are over a barrel, my boy."

"So I have perceived, sir," said Lord Satterwaite, grimacing.

Mr. Allyn's manner underwent a subtle change. In a brusque voice, he said, "You want to know the odds of his lordship holding his leaders, don't you?"

"You have anticipated my thoughts perfectly," said Lord Satterwaite.

Mr. Allyn nodded. He frowned heavily, steepling his fingers. He threw a sharp glance at his nephew. "Does anyone else know of this rat's coil? For I shall tell you plainly that the more people who do know, the more determined the earl will become."

"I have told only Fitz Howard-Browne. He may be trusted to keep a confidence," said Lord Satterwaite. He hesitated, then said, "It is Fitz's reluctant opinion that I must swallow my pride and find me a bride, if for no other reason than to put Lucius's nose out of joint."

Mr. Allyn nodded. "Howard-Browne is not a fool. It has often crossed my mind."

"I shall be certain to relay your kind observation, sir," said Lord Satterwaite, bowing.

Mr. Allyn nodded in acknowledgment, but his countenance did not lighten. "I shall tell you, since you have inquired, that I consider your situation to be in very bad case. For one, your mother has not come down on your behalf. My esteemed sister is as shrewd and as strong-willed a female as I have ever known. She will not have retired from the lists without good reason. This, coupled with your own obvious concern and Howard-Browne's reaction, has given me very low hopes that the earl will not hold to his purpose. As I see it, the only card that you hold at this moment is that my brother-in-law's dislike for Lucius Everard exceeds yours. His lordship will not easily stomach him as his heir."

Lord Satterwaite shrugged. There was not a shred of amusement in the smile that curved his mouth. "That is a facer, indeed. Well, Allyn, what do you suggest to be my better course? Shall I get myself a wife immediately, and save myself the bother of my sire's recriminations, or shall I relinquish what is mine to my cousin?"

"Neither," said Mr. Allyn promptly. "Play out your hand as long as you can remain at the table. There is inevitably, even in the worst of moments, something that turns the game in one's favor."

Lord Satterwaite was not impressed with this piece of gamester's advice. He thought it hid the depth of his uncle's true feelings. "You believe my situation to be next to hopeless, then, do you not?"

"Let us merely say that I should not like to lay heavy odds against the earl's changing his mind," said Mr. Allyn. "However, we must trust that something might occur that will put an entirely new deck on the table."

Lord Satterwaite looked over at his uncle with a suddenly hardened expression. "I do not look for my father's demise, sir!"

"My boy!" Mr. Allyn was shocked. "The thought never once occurred, I promise you! Why, I have the utmost respect and regard for his lordship. I am wounded, nay, insulted, that you could suspect me of something so vile!"

Mr. Allyn's appalled indignation was such that Lord Satterwaite's expression relaxed into a rueful grin. "My apologies, sir. This business has turned my wits to a degree. I should not have cut up ugly with you, for well I know that you and my father hold one another in genuine, if baffled, affection."

Mr. Allyn chuckled. "Aye, his lordship does not understand that I prefer my mode of life, while I shudder at the thought of such respectability as he exemplifies. We are oil and water, oil and water! But for all that, we like one another tolerably well."

Lord Satterwaite rose to take his leave. "I do not ask you to see me downstairs, for I know you are far too indolent to flatter me with such a show of civility."

"Quite right. You may very well show yourself out, nevy. I shall undoubtedly see you about town sometime this Season. You'll go to the races, of course?"

"Of course," said Lord Satterwaite, smiling as he exited.

Mr. Allyn sat for a moment, thinking. He came to a decision. "I must make an effort to do the pretty this Season," he said aloud. "I must let my sister know that she may rely upon me to make up her numbers." His rumbling laugh shook him. It would surprise the countess to be informed by her brother of his willingness to attend just those sort of gatherings that he had often expressed pungent dislike for; but the opportunity to watch the unfurling play was too tempting to set aside. Mr. Allyn had the liveliest curiosity to see exactly what would come out of this particular Season.

Chapter Ten

Lady Hedgeworth was thrown into alt when she received the Countess of Chalmers's latest letter. She could scarcely believe her good fortune, nor regard with too much gratitude the countess's gracious generosity.

As she told her eldest son and Reverend Reading, who had come to call on her ladyship, "I could not ask anything more for Fredericka. The countess has thought of everything and assures me that I need not be anxious over any point. She will provide all that Fredericka could possibly require, even to bearing the cost of her court dress. I shall be able to cancel most of the orders that I have made with the seamstress for Fredericka, and instead concentrate on outfitting Betsy and Sarah to a much greater extent than I thought possible."

"It is a fortunate circumstance, certainly," agreed Reverend Reading. "You must feel it, indeed."

"I am eternally grateful to her ladyship," declared Lady Hedgeworth. Her most dwelt-on thought was spoken aloud. "Oh, I do so hope that this Season results in Fredericka accepting a suitable offer and becoming credibly established!"

Reverend Reading looked thoughtful. He appeared about to say something, then seemed to think better of it.

Lord Hedgeworth frowned, his square young face appearing unnaturally somber. "I am aware of your feelings, Mama, and certainly the Countess of Chalmers has far exceeded any definition of generosity. But has it occurred to you that this might not be right for Fredericka herself? My sister is a sensible girl and one used to having her own head. She will not wish to ally herself with just anyone."

Reverend Reading looked at her ladyship, interested in that lady's response. It was perhaps unfortunate that he had remained silent because Lady Hedgeworth was in a fair way to having completely forgotten his presence in pursuit of her delightful reflections.

"That is precisely why I have been so eager to accept the countess's invitation on her behalf," said Lady Hedgeworth. "Fredericka deserves better opportunities than what she has been granted in our small society."

Her ladyship did not notice the good reverend's wince, but Lord Hedgeworth did. He said hastily, "That is as may be; but we still have not considered Freddie's feelings of the matter." He turned to the reverend. "What do you think, sir?"

Reverend Reading smiled. He said gently, "I think that it is time that I take my leave. Such a discussion is far better engaged in when there are only family members present. My lady, your devoted. Jack. You will naturally tell me how this matter is resolved later."

Lady Hedgeworth graciously allowed her visitor to make his excuses, and when he was gone turned to regard her son's frown with surprise. "Why, Jack, what can you be thinking of? Surely you would not wish me to turn down the countess's magnanimous offer! That would be foolish indeed!"

"No, not turn it down precisely," said Lord Hedgeworth slowly. He wanted to explain his feelings on a subject with which he had little experience and it was proving difficult to form the proper line of reasoning. "I just do not wish Fredericka to feel obligated to accept some offer that don't suit her."

"Of course she must not! How strange of you to say such a thing, Jack. Fredericka knows very well what is due her name. I trust that she will bring the same sensible head that she has for managing Luting to the managing of her own affairs," said Lady Hedgeworth. "And that reminds me, Jack. I wish to have a serious talk with you. Pray sit down there."

At that, Lord Hedgeworth looked faintly alarmed. However, he obediently took the chair his mother had indicated. He looked over at his parent with an anxious expression. "What is it, Mama? Have you had bad news of some sort?"

"Nothing of that nature, Jack. I wish to talk to you about taking on the responsibility of your position," said Lady Hedgeworth.

Lord Hedgeworth looked relieved. "Is that all? I had thought from your expression that it was something important that you wished to convey to me."

Lady Hedgeworth shook her head impatiently. "It has become of the upmost importance, Jack, as you would see if you would but try. Fredericka has agreed to accept the countess's largess, but I know my daughter well. Her heart is not truly in it."

"No, I should say not," agreed Lord Hedgeworth, recalling his sister's almost despairing way of relaying the news to him.

Lady Hedgeworth was satisfied that he was following her. "My dear, has it not occurred to you that Fredericka's reluctance to go up to London is grounded to a large extent upon her sense of duty toward Luting? I do not wish to see her waste an opportunity to establish herself well because she feels pressed to remain in halter to Luting!"

Lord Hedgeworth stared at his mother. The thought had not once crossed his mind that his own inaction could possibly be detrimental to his sister's life. Slowly, he asked, "I had never considered that, Mama. Do you truly think that is true?"

Lady Hedgeworth sighed. "My dear son, I know Fredericka's heart as well as anybody. She loves Luting, which is natural since it is her girlhood home. But she has never given herself a chance to look beyond Luting. Jack, your sister is very nearly on the shelf without discovering whether she would prefer another sort of life. I am speaking of a life given over to her own household and her own pursuits. It would pain me very much to watch Fredericka waste her youth and dwindle into a maiden aunt by default. She deserves more than that."

"Yes, by Jove," said Lord Hedgeworth, much struck.

"Then you must help her to leave Luting. Yes, my dear, you!"

"But how? I do not see how I can—"

Lady Hedgeworth interrupted him with a wave of her hand. "Listen to me, pray! There is only one way to accomplish it. Jack, you must take over your rightful place and duties. Free your sister of the burden of guilt and obligation that she assuredly bears and allow her to enjoy this Season with a clear conscience."

Lord Hedgeworth got up out of the chair. He made a quick turn about the sitting room, his hands thrust into his pockets. Over his shoulder, he said, "I understand what you are saying, Mama, of course. I never realized—"

He suddenly turned toward his parent and squared his shoulders. "Very well, Mama. I shall do just as you ask. It is not as though I am not capable of it. I shall relieve Fredericka at once of all responsibility of Luting."

"Thank you, Jack. You have relieved my mind considerably. I know that Fredericka will feel more comfortable leaving us with the reins held firmly in your hands," said Lady Hedgeworth, settling back against her lounge. She was well pleased that her son had so readily accepted the necessity of changing the way of things. "And I know that I also shall be able to place my full confidence in you."

"Yes, Mama," said Lord Hedgeworth.

He left his mother's sitting room with mingled feelings. He was at once proud that she reposed such trust in him, and dismayed that his untrammeled carefree days were about to come to an end. His steps were slow as he walked down the hallway, his thoughts running faster than his feet.

It was true that he had relied on Fredericka in a selfish manner. He was fair enough and honest enough with himself to admit that. But he had done so because of his own dreams. He had hoped to leave Luting someday, and had assumed that the estate would remain in Fredericka's capable charge until such time as he tired of his foray into the world and returned.

Now Lord Hedgeworth saw that had been a complacent pipe dream. He could not hold his sister hostage to his own selfish desires. He had to let her go so that she could discover whether her own dreams would come to encompass something other than Luting.

He stopped abruptly in the middle of the hall. "What a coil it all is!" he exclaimed, running his hand through his thick hair.

Lord Hedgeworth wanted to jump on his horse and travel as far as the animal could carry him, for he felt the walls to be closing in on him inexorably. He might never leave Luting now. He might never taste of things that he had only dreamed of or heard about. He would remain at Luting, a gentleman squire tied to the land all of his days.

An inarticulate denial rasped in his throat. "No! I shall not do it!" he exclaimed forcefully. "I will not do it!"

"What won't you do?" asked a curious voice.

Lord Hedgeworth turned quickly. His brother stood looking at him. Thomas was nearly of a height with him now, Lord Hedgeworth realized. Soon, Thomas would be granted his wish and be allowed to go to an old family friend who had promised to sponsor him onto a ship. Thomas would sail the far seas and see wondrous sights. He would experience hardships and at times fight for his very survival. He would live the life he had always yearned for because he was not tied to the land in the same way that Lord Hedgeworth was.

Lord Hedgeworth was the heir. He had succeeded to his father's title. He was the baron, though few actually thought of him in that guise. When he came of age, he would have all of the benefits and monies accruing to a landed gentleman.

His was the position of privilege, but it was also one of servitude. He could not sell or entail away the estate even if he so desired. He would be responsible for maintaining and improving the estate. His obligations would include looking out for the welfare of his tenants, to provide for their housing, doctoring, and possibly even the schooling of their children. His influence would be felt throughout the county, for Luting was the largest estate around. His opinions would be sought, his whims catered to, his favor curried by those less fortunate or less socially exalted.

How had his father, who by all accounts had been a regular out-and-outer and general man-about-town, ever borne it?

Lord Hedgeworth did not know. He did not know how he was to bear it. He shrank from the very thought of taking on such awesome, massive responsibility. He was all of eighteen, a man in his own eyes and yet possessed of a boy's faltering heart. At that moment the fear was very nearly choking him as he thought of his place in life.

The dim perception of that fear, and jealousy for his brother, lent sharpness to his voice as he replied to his brother's question. "Never you mind! I haven't time to dally. I have important matters on my mind, such things as you would never understand."

"Oh! Then you will want to talk Fredericka," said Thomas, quite unabashed. He was solid in his perception of his own worth and he would have been astonished if he had had even an inkling of what conflicting emotions were battering his brother.

"Fredericka! Where is she?" asked Lord Hedgeworth quickly.

"She'll be out in the south field, I expect. I overheard her tell Bartram yesterday evening that she would go out with him this afternoon to inspect the new irrigation project," said Thomas. He wrinkled his nose in disparagement. "I am glad that I do not have to worry my head over such stuff."

His slighting statement stung Lord Hedgeworth on the raw. "Yes, and so am I! You would undoubtedly make a rare mull of it!" he snapped, and strode off.

Thomas looked after his eldest brother, somewhat surprised and even a little hurt. But he shrugged it off. Ever since Lady Hedgeworth had received that letter from the Countess of Chalmers, nearly everyone had been acting a bit peculiar. Fredericka was moping about and pretending not to. Betsy was so jealous that she could scarcely speak a civil word to anyone. Lady Hedgeworth could talk of nothing else but the fine times that were in store for Fredericka and the grand opportunities she would have to find a husband. Now Jack was feeling thin-skinned. Only Sarah and himself seemed to be unaffected.

Thomas shook his head. "A rare taking over something so paltry," he said musingly. "Now if it was an invitation to see the sights, that would be different!" And off he went to his room to discover the roll of string that he wanted.

Lord Hedgeworth had his horse saddled and cantered out to the south field. There he found his sister and Mr. Bartram, the estate agent, conversing at length and in detail over some new irrigation methods. Fredericka acknowledged his appearance with a flickering smile and uplifted hand, but she did not break off her conversation.

Lord Hedgeworth listened impatiently for a few minutes before interrupting and appropriating his sister's attention. "Fredericka, I should like to speak with you."

Mr. Bartram glanced up at Lord Hedgeworth's expression. He nodded. "I shall see to it, then, Miss Hedgeworth." He left the brother and sister then, smiling at the young master's impatient manner. It was just like Master Jack to think so little of such a discussion that he must needs put an end to it.

Fredericka's thoughts ran along the same lines. Half-laughing and half-scolding, she said, "Really, Jack! Whatever must Bartram think of you for cutting him short in such a fashion."

"I don't know and I care even less," said Lord Hedgeworth brusquely. "Fredericka, I must talk with you."

Fredericka looked at him in surprise. Her brother was not normally a rude person, having a healthy awareness of others' opinions of him. They had begun to walk back across the field, leading their horses. "What has so exercised you, Jack?"

Suddenly Lord Hedgeworth found that he could scarcely find the words to tell her. Whatever he said would make him sound the height of selfishness. Therefore, rather sullenly, he said, "I have been talking to Mama."

"Oh, dear! What has she said to upset you?" asked Fredericka.

Lord Hedgeworth made an impatient gesture. "It is not so much what she said as what it has made me realize, Freddie." He stopped abruptly and turned to face her. "Freddie, will you be anxious about Luting and things here while you are away?"

Fredericka was taken aback. "Why, of course I shall. I shall wonder about you and Thomas and the girls and Mama, too, of course."

"What about all of this?" Lord Hedgeworth waved his hand at the field. Since the melting of the last snow, the earth had remained muddy. It was not a pretty vista at that time of year.

"Well, I shall probably give it a thought or two," admitted Fredericka, smiling, but with a puzzled expression in her fine eyes. "Jack, what is it that you are trying to get at?"

Lord Hedgeworth took a deep breath. "Freddie, I have decided to take on more of the responsibility for Luting. It is high time that I did so. I have let you carry the burden alone too long and I need to learn how to manage things on my own. I think this Season of yours in London will give me the perfect opportunity to begin."

Fredericka looked at her brother for a long moment. "Mama put you up to this, did she not?" she asked shrewdly.

Lord Hedgeworth shook his head. "Something she said struck me, that is all. Freddie, Luting is my inheritance. I don't know much about the estate or its workings. I've been content to let things slide into your lap, for one reason and another, but I realize now that that was wrong of me. Forgive me, Freddie, for I never meant to be so selfish."

"What unutterable rot! Jack, pray do not be such a fool. I would have told you long ago if I felt that I carried an unfair burden. Why, I never enjoy myself more than when I am busy about business," said Fredericka, laughing.

"But don't you see, Freddie? It's selfish, too, of you to want to hold on," said Lord Hedgeworth, just discovering it for himself. He laid his arm over his sister's shoulders. "Dear, dearest Freddie! You are the best of sisters. I do not know what I will do without you, but I must learn. One day you might wed and leave me just at a crucial point and with my not knowing how to go on. Luting and the family and our tenants would all suffer from my ignorance. I *must* learn how to manage things on my own!"

Fredericka stared into his face. Lord Hedgeworth's expression was earnest, even sad, but there was determination in the slant of his jaw and the firmness of his mouth. "I see," she said slowly. A part of her was beginning to unravel. It was a strange feeling. "I did not realize that I was standing so squarely in your way. I am sorry, Jack. I never meant to hinder you."

"You haven't, you silly clunch. It is entirely my fault. I was such a baby when Papa died. I could not have taken up those decisions that were needed, nor accomplished what you have. And as for Mama! My trustees naturally looked to the one lone voice of authority that was heard. Yours, Freddie. You have acted as my regent, you know," said Lord Hedgeworth, with a heavy attempt at humor.

She shook her head, not daring to reply just at that moment. Her throat seemed to have closed up a little and she had the silliest urge to utter a protest.

Lord Hedgeworth seemed to sense her struggle. He sighed and gave her an affectionate squeeze. "The time has come to wean us both, Freddie. You must let loose of the reins and I must take them up. I think that will go easier at a time when you are not here and able to look over my shoulder, do you not? I know that I think so, for otherwise I shall constantly ask your advice or look over at your face to see how things strike you."

"I—I do see what you mean, Jack." Fredericka took a determined breath. She felt something much like grief welling up insider her, but that was nonsense, of course. There was nothing to be sad about. Her brother was simply saying that he was at last willing to take up what were, after all, his lawful responsibilities. She should be rejoicing that it was so.

Jack was the heir and he did need to know how to go on. She should have realized that months ago and herself begun to give him a gentle shove in that direction. Instead, it had taken some oblique reference made by their mother, who had not the least sense of what went on in the estate business, to have made the matter plain.

"Of course you are right. It is just the right time," said Fredericka determinedly. "I shall be able to turn all of my energies to making the most of this Season, as Mama has bid me. It—it will be quite an adventure since my mind will be relieved of its most pressing anxieties."

"Good. I am glad that is settled," said Lord Hedgeworth. He gave her another squeeze, then released her. "I think that I shall begin at once. Bartram will be surprised at my sudden interest, but he will soon become reconciled, I think."

"Oh, indeed," Fredericka managed a more natural smile. Her eyes even lighted a little with a teasing expression. "But I hope that he will not be so shocked at first that he swallows his pipe."

Lord Hedgeworth cracked a laugh. "I hope not, indeed!" He laced his fingers together and offered her a foot up into the saddle. Fredericka placed her boot on his palms and he tossed her up. When she was settled in the saddle and had shortened her reins, Lord Hedgeworth detained her for a moment with a hand on her bridle. "Freddie. We shall both be happy."

"Of course we shall," said Fredericka. "I am never despondent, as you know."

"Yes, you are the most resilient girl," agreed Lord Hedgeworth. He grinned up at her. "I would give much to see you all decked out in new finery, Fredericka. By the by, Mama said that the countess means to bear the brunt of the expense for your come-out. She is in high gig, as you may imagine."

"Yes, indeed," said Fredericka dryly. She shook her head. "I suppose that I should return at once so that she may tell me the news. It is an odd time for me, Jack."

"For us all, Fredericka, for us all." Lord Hedgeworth stepped back, his reins still in his hand. He lifted a hand to her. "I shall see you at supper, Freddie."

Fredericka nodded. She set spur to her mare and rode away from him. Once, she glanced back. Her brother was striding across the field toward the estate agent. His shoulders were squared and his head was held high.

Fredericka turned away again and spurred the mare to a greater pace. How odd it was to realize that a part of her life had just ended, she thought.

Chapter Eleven

A fortnight later, Fredericka was in London. She had traveled up from Luting in the Chalmers's own coach, which the countess had been gracious enough to send for her. One of the respectable ladies from the village, who had been intending to travel up to London to visit relations, was persuaded by Lady Hedgeworth, as a favor, to accompany Fredericka.

"For I do not conceal from you, Mrs. Inching, that I would feel more comfortable knowing that someone whom I knew that I could rely upon went with Fredericka, even though she will be traveling in her ladyship's own carriage," Lady Hedgeworth had said.

Mrs. Inching had entered wholly into her ladyship's sentiments, quite overcome that she had been granted the high treat of traveling in such comfort and style when she had meant to take the Mail coach.

The journey had indeed been comfortable, but from Fredericka's point of view it had also been tedious. The countess's driver apparently did not believe in allowing his team to get above a mild trot. Fredericka had more than once toyed with the temptation to urge a faster pace, but since the driver appeared to be an old and trusted retainer, she thought he would more than likely turn a deaf ear to such a shocking proposal. Fortunately, London was not so distant as to require more than one night on the road, which gave Fredericka the opportunity to judge the advantages of a posting house.

Fredericka's companion was in due course delivered to her destination, and very important Mrs. Inching thought herself when she descended from the crested carriage in full view of all her relations. Fredericka declined an invitation to alight for a few moments and waved farewell as the coach tooled on its way.

At Chalmers House, Fredericka was received by Lord and Lady Chalmers with every cordiality and courtesy. Her ladyship suggested that Fredericka might wish to lie down and refresh herself after the fatigues of the journey, but Fredericka had at once demurred. "I am never fatigued, my lady," she said, smiling. "I am quite ready to place myself at your disposal."

Lady Chalmers had looked at her guest. Except for the signs of travel on her attire, Miss Hedgeworth appeared as fresh as though she had just stepped out of her bedroom. Undoubtedly it was the effect of all that fresh air and the early hours that were kept in the country, her ladyship thought.

"Then we shall not tarry here, my dear," she said. "When you have changed and come back downstairs, I shall take you at once on a tour of the shops."

Lady Chalmers mentioned that she had provided a maidservant for Fredericka, who was already waiting to help Fredericka change out of her travel-creased pelisse.

Fredericka had agreed and followed a footman upstairs to the chamber that had been prepared for her. Her bedroom, with its view of the garden behind the house, was delightful and the maid most solicitous.

A half hour later, Fredericka returned downstairs attired in a well-cut dark blue walking dress. A velvet bonnet, adorned with a small plume of feathers, was on her head and she carried a small muff along with her reticule.

Lady Chalmers swept her guest with a critical gaze and she was obliged to own that though Miss Hedgeworth was not dressed in the height of fashion, she was quite presentable.

The countess's carriage was ordered to be brought around to the front door. Lady Chalmers and Fredericka descended the front steps to the flagway, followed at a discreet distance by Lady Chalmers's maid. The coachman opened the door and handed the ladies up into the carriage. The maid climbed in and took the seat with her back to the horses. The coachman climbed up onto his box seat, unsnubbed the reins, and picked up his whip. He flicked the leaders with a touch of the whip. The carriage lurched forward and rolled away from the curb into the thronged street.

After several stops, during which Lady Chalmers gathered a fairly accurate notion of her guest's tastes and inclinations, the ladies returned to the countess's carriage to be driven to their last destination of the day. They carried nothing but their reticules, having allowed all their purchases to be carried by the maid back to the carriage.

Lady Chalmers was delighted with Miss Hedgeworth. The young woman had proven herself to be practical and surprisingly knowledgeable about fashion. Also, she had carried herself well whenever they had chanced upon one of Lady Chalmers's many acquaintances. Fredericka's manners were easy but she did not put herself forward in an unbecoming way. Lady Hedgeworth had done a marvelous job in teaching the girl how to go on, thought Lady Chalmers. The countess was already enjoying her novel role of benefactress.

Of course, there had been some initial demurement on Fredericka's part over what she should allow the Countess of Chalmers to do for her; but that was quickly smoothed away. Lady Chalmers had carried the day, declaring that she had already set herself to be responsible for Fredericka's wardrobe and her court dress for her formal presentation at St. James's Palace.

"You are to be responsible only for those small purchases you might require that can be made from your own pin money, my dear," she said. "Your mother and I have already agreed between us how everything else is to be accounted for."

"Very well, my lady," said Fredericka, laughing. "I bow to my mother's higher wisdom."

"So you should, indeed," said Lady Chalmers. She had not been displeased at Fredericka's natural hesitancy. Such finer feeling spoke of a well-bred character, rather than one of grasping, spoiled greed.

It would indeed be a pleasure to bring this girl out, thought Lady Chalmers complacently. Miss Hedgeworth was well-favored of face and figure; she was well-mannered and well-bred; and she was practical and possessed good taste in fashion. Even if her son disappointed her by ignoring Miss Hedgeworth's manifold qualities and did not offer for her, Lady Chalmers decided that it would be well worth the effort to see that the girl was otherwise credibly established.

"I am so glad that you have come to me, Fredericka. You have no notion," said Lady Chalmers, smiling. Her eyes twinkled. "I do so like to entertain and sponsoring you gives me the perfect excuse."

"I am grateful to you for your generosity and kindness toward me, my lady. I never thought of such fortune becoming mine," said Fredericka, quite truthfully.

Lady Chalmers waved aside her guest's expression of gratitude. "It is nothing, my dear. It is only what I should have done two years ago. Why, your mother and I were once closer than sisters. How long ago that seems! However, that is quite beside the point. I had a high regard for your mother and I should have kept in closer touch with her. If I had, I would probably have extended this belated invitation to you much sooner! You would now in all probability have been wed these past two years and had at least one beautiful child to show for it already!"

Fredericka blinked at the vision that had been conjured up. Her mouth curved in a slight smile. "You have painted a pretty picture indeed, ma'am. Somehow it is not one that I have ever envisioned for myself."

Lady Chalmers threw her a curious glance. "Have you not? But every young woman thinks of these things sooner or later."

"Then perhaps I am one of the latter, my lady," said Fredericka with a hint of humor. "My mother quite despairs of me, you know. I am not of a romantic turn of mind. I fear that it is not a handsome face that turns my head, but rather, a kind heart and a ready hand on the bridle. I am told that I have a shockingly practical intellect."

Lady Chalmers smiled. Miss Hedgeworth's almost self-deprecating confession pleased her. She said warmly, "I am not at all dismayed, Fredericka. Why, I do not doubt that you will go off very well. Your manners are frank and engaging. You are perfectly lovely and you are not a ninnyhammer. You will find any number of gentlemen who desire just such qualities."

"Do you think so, ma'am? Well, perhaps you are right," said Fredericka, smiling. Her hazel eyes held a gleam of laughter. "It ought to prove interesting, in any event. I have little or no ambition to make a spectacular match, I warn you. My requirements are exceedingly high and I doubt that there are many gentlemen who shall measure up to my weight."

"My dear!" Lady Chalmers was both taken aback and amused. She eyed her charge with considerable speculation. "With that lofty attitude, I predict that we shall have half of London positively tripping over themselves to win your smiles."

Fredericka laughed. "I am more sanguine, my lady. I doubt that there will be many who will actually put themselves to the exertion as to bother with me," she said. "And I shall not mind it in the least, I assure you. I have my family and a place at Luting, if I so desire. I care little for the amusements that so many females seem to find essential to their lives."

"Then we must endeavor to change your mind, Fredericka. I shall make it my personal mission to see to it that you positively loll in amusements and become the toast of the town," declared Lady Chalmers.

Fredericka laughed again and shook her head. "Oh, you shan't convert me into a town beauty so easily, my lady."

Lady Chalmers smiled at her, but she wagged her finger at the younger woman. "Mark my words, Miss Hedgeworth, you will quickly come to enjoy yourself as frivolously as any other young lady and feel yourself to be pining away of boredom if you spend even one quiet evening at home."

"Not I!" declared Fredericka.

But the Countess of Chalmers merely laughed. The carriage had by this time reached their final destination and the ladies had alighted to enter yet another modiste shop. Lady Chalmers adjured Fredericka to gaze upon a particularly pleasing watered silk. "It will make a delightful domino, my dear. I shall have it made up for you. And that wonderful blue merino will highlight your auburn hair. We shall have a day dress done out of it, I think."

"You have already showered me with gowns and bonnets and stockings and every other sort of possibly frippery," said Fredericka, gently objecting. She had already seen a fortune spent on herself and something as frivolous and expensive as a domino seemed to her simply too much. "Surely I do not require a domino as well."

"You may never have occasion to wear it, it is true. However, one must have a domino in her wardrobe just the same. It would be a sad day, indeed, if you were to be invited to a private masquerade and were unable to procure a domino in time," said Lady Chalmers. "One should always be prepared for any eventuality, Fredericka. You must learn this lesson well. I am certain that your mother has told you the same thing any number of times. A lady is always prepared for whatever social situation that may arise. Why, one could be invited to Carlton House and not have a new gown to wear that has never been seen. What then?"

"I do not know, ma'am. Pray tell me," said Fredericka, regarding her ladyship with a fascinated expression.

"One ends by attending in a gown that has already been remarked by friends and acquaintances. It is quite fatal to wear the same gown so many times that it becomes recognized, my dear, and especially to Carlton House. It is almost an insult to His Royal Highness," said Lady Chalmers.

"I shall allow myself to be entirely guided by you, my lady," said Fredericka solemnly. "It is quite obvious that I should commit just those faux pas that are least calculated to please if I do not give heed to your voice of experience."

"Just so," said Lady Chalmers. She was not certain, but she thought that she detected a glimmer of laughter in the younger woman's eyes. She chose to ignore it. "I shall do my best to steer you safely past all of the dangerous shoals. I promised your mother to launch you successfully and so I shall."

Fredericka turned full-face toward the countess. Her expression was unreadable. Her voice held just a hint of mild interest in its even tones. "Did you do so, my lady? I am more indebted to you than I had known, then. I hope that I do not disappoint you."

"You shall not. I am certain of that," said Lady Chalmers serenely. "You are just the sort of young miss that I am most happy to have charge of and I know that we shall get along famously."

They left the modiste's shop and stepped back up into the carriage. It was the last of the several stops that Lady Chalmers had wanted to make that afternoon, and she gave the signal to the coachman to return to the town house. It was an uncomfortable ride with all of the packages stacked on the seats and on the floor of the carriage. The maid sat across from the countess and her ladyship's guest, her arms also full of wrapped packages.

Upon the carriage's arrival at the town house, the front door was flung open and the porter and two footmen descended to the front steps. The ladies were helped to alight and then the footmen turned their attention to removing the mountain of packages from the carriages, under the expert supervision of Lady Chalmers's maid.

As Lady Chalmers and Fredericka walked up the steps, her ladyship noticed the slanting shadows and she realized that the hour was already rather advanced. Lady Chalmers's thoughts naturally turned to her spouse. She wondered with a twinge of guilty anxiety how his lordship had spent the day.

If the gout had flared up, he would not be in the mood for genteel conversation that evening. In his uncertain tempers he had been known to indiscriminately bite off the heads of friends and strangers alike. Their guest should be warned that it was possible that she might be the recipient of rather turkish treatment at the earl's hands under such conditions.

Lady Chalmers turned to Miss Hedgeworth as they entered the house and stepped into the entry hall. She said earnestly, "You will do well to go quietly around the earl for a few days, child. His lordship is not in the best of curl just now due to the gout in his foot. Pray do not be surprised if—if he has a tendency to growl a bit at you."

"I am sorry, my lady. I did not know," said Fredericka, at once sympathetic. She accompanied the countess up the stairs toward the first floor. "I trust that his lordship is not in terrible distress?"

"His foot pains him considerably some days, while at other times it scarcely seems to affect him. We had hoped when we left Chalmers that a change in locale might be beneficial to him, but up to now it does not seem to have answered very well," said Lady Chalmers, rounding the corner and proceeding up toward the second floor, where the bedrooms were located. She threw her guest a slightly anxious glance. "You will naturally understand if his lordship appears somewhat severe or impatient, my dear. He prefers his own company on such days."

"Of course, my lady. I understand perfectly," said Fredericka. "Is there anything that I might do to further the earl's comfort?"

Lady Chalmers regarded her with surprise. "Why, that is very good of you, Fredericka. However, I do not believe there is anything that can be done that will answer the purpose. It is just a matter of time waiting for the gout to dissipate and his lordship begins to feel more the thing. I do hope that it happens before your come-out ball, for I should like Lord Chalmers to stand in the receiving line with us."

"Oh, pray do not insist upon it, my lady. I would feel terribly guilty for adding to Lord Chalmers's distress," said Fredericka, rather appalled that her host should be put out to such a degree for her.

"No, of course I shall not insist upon it. I shall have my son, Lord Satterwaite, to stand up with us if Lord Chalmers is still indisposed," said Lady Chalmers calmly.

"Lord Satterwaite?" Fredericka combed through her memory of the several personages who had stopped to chat with Lady Chalmers and to whom she had been introduced. "I do not believe that I had the pleasure of meeting the viscount today, my lady."

"No, we did not see him. Sebastion was present at your christening, but of course you will not recall that," said Lady Chalmers. She glanced at her companion. "It is a pity that your parents left London when you were still so very young. Otherwise, you and Sebastion might have grown up in one another's pockets and then you would already have an acquaintance in the city."

"Yes," agreed Fredericka. "It would have been very much like being able to call upon one of my brothers, for you have made me feel very much at home, ma'am."

"What a sweet thing to say," managed Lady Chalmers. She had thrown a quick, startled glance at her guest. She did not at all care for the correlation that Miss Hedgeworth had made.

"It is true, you might have indeed looked upon Sebastion as another brother," she said slowly. The unhappy thought that the young woman might see Lord Satterwaite as other than a potential mate had never occurred to her. "Well, once you are made known to one another, I trust that there will be an easy discourse between you. Your mother and I were such good friends that I hope that our children will feel an equal cordiality, even an attachment, toward one another."

"I hope so, too, dear ma'am," said Fredericka, quite willing to please the countess in this minor fashion. "I look forward to making the viscount's acquaintance. Does he wait on you soon, my lady?"

Lady Chalmers hesitated before she replied. "Sebastion is very much his own man. He will not pay us a morning call until after your come-out, I expect," she said. "However, in the event that Lord Chalmers finds himself incapable of providing us with an escort, I trust that he shall put himself at my disposal. Certainly Sebastion would be the most logical gentleman to call upon in a pinch."

"Is Lord Satterwaite a fond son, then?" asked Fredericka curiously.

Lady Chalmers shot her a sharp glance. "Fond? I suppose that he does have a fondness for his father and me. However, Sebastion runs only in his own traces. He can be a difficult, if not undutiful, son." She noted Miss Hedgeworth's mildly surprised expression and realized that she was probably revealing more than she should. "But I shall say no more. Otherwise I shall give you quite a false impression of him. You must judge his character for yourself, dear Fredericka."

Fredericka asked no more about the viscount, but her curiosity was aroused. She parted ways with the countess at the head of the stairs, each of the ladies turning aside to go to their own bedrooms.

As Fredericka entered her own apartment, her expression was thoughtful. Lady Chalmers seemed proud of her son, but also a little disappointed in him. Perhaps the viscount was a worthless fop, thought Fredericka. That would explain the countess's attitude. It would also explain the Earl of Chalmers's oblique reference to his heir which Fredericka had chanced to overhear as she had left Lord and Lady Chalmers and gone upstairs to prepare for the shopping trip.

Lord Chalmers appeared to be holding a grudge against his son. Although Fredericka did not know what had caused the rift between them, she was fairly certain that it would be an accurate guess to lay much of the blame at the viscount's door. Nothing could have exceeded the Earl and Countess of Chalmers's kind-

ness toward herself and she could not imagine them treating their
own son with any less. It was a puzzle, indeed.

No doubt she would learn much more about Lord Satterwaite
once she entered into society. Since they would be moving in the
same exalted circles, she would naturally come into the viscount's
way, especially since the countess was sponsoring her.

Fredericka only hoped that she would be able to treat Lord Satterwaite with true civility, no matter what the viscount's character
proved to be. She owed that much and more to her benefactress.

Chapter Twelve

As it was, Fredericka met Lord Satterwaite sooner than anticipated, and certainly under circumstances that in Lady
Chalmers's subsequent opinion were calculated to blight Cupid's
course.

That evening over dinner, Lord Chalmers had complained that
he had been unable to find a particular reference because over the
years the shelves had been put into such chaos by zealous, unedu-
cated maids who had had no better notion how to group the books
than that of arranging the volumes according to height.

"I have never been more annoyed, my dear. I cannot find a
thing until the shelves are put into some sort of proper order, and
here is Cunningham writing to me and begging for a particular
reference to an obscure law of the north. It seems that he is writing a treatise and he is insisting that there is a precedent existent
in the work that I have mentioned to you," said Lord Chalmers
disgruntledly. "I do not know what I am to do, since Peadmire had
to take off so suddenly. One does not wish to speak ill of any individual, of course, but I cannot help wishing that his father had
chosen to take ill after my shelves had been put into a semblance
of order."

"It is difficult for you, of course," said Lady Chalmers sympathetically. "But perhaps Mr. Peadmire shall return sooner than expected."

"It won't be in time. Cunningham must have his answer by
next month at the latest. I shall have to inform him that I can be of
no help to him in this matter," said Lord Chalmers, brooding.

"My lord, if you should not dislike it, I would be most happy to
organize your library for you," said Fredericka. "I helped my
brother's agent catalog my father's collection after Papa's death,
so I do know something about it. And I am certain that Lady

Chalmers will not begrudge me to you, for we have already done as much shopping as we possibly can."

"We will never do enough shopping," said Lady Chalmers firmly, which made the earl laugh. She smiled at him. "There! I do like it when you are able to appreciate one of my small jokes. It does you so much good, for a merry heart is like a medicine."

"Undoubtedly true, my dear," said Lord Chalmers. He turned to look at their guest with approval and speculation. "Do you truly wish to do it, Miss Hedgeworth? I warn you, it is a formidable dusty task."

"I shan't mind that in the least. I would be happy to do this for you," said Fredericka. She turned to the countess. "Unless you should dislike it, ma'am?"

"No, of course I do not dislike it. You must do just as you please. I am certain that Lord Chalmers will be grateful for any help that you may give to him, for without his secretary, Mr. Peadmire, his lordship is completely helpless in these sorts of things," said Lady Chalmers.

The earl grunted reluctant endorsement of Lady Chalmers's statement. Fredericka had repeated her willingness to oblige his lordship in this fashion, and thus it was that she came to be ensconced in the library with his lordship the following afternoon.

Lord Chalmers had already begun a lengthy letter to his correspondent, making reference to several books that Fredericka was so fortunate to unearth for him almost at the beginning. He had been well-pleased and had remarked that she was an unusually sensible young woman.

There was a thick coat of dust on the backs of the books, which Fredericka had anticipated, and so she had put an apron on over her plainest gown to protect it and had borrowed a mobcap from one of the undermaids to cover her hair. She looked very like a servingwoman, which scandalized the butler when he came into the library to inquire of the earl whether his lordship needed anything.

Lord Chalmers tried to send the man away with an irritable wave. "No, nothing! Can you not see that I am busy, Moffet? Perhaps Miss Hedgeworth has a commission for you."

The butler turned to Miss Hedgeworth. Attempting to ignore

her ignoble outfit, he kept his expression wooden. "Do you wish anything, miss?"

"Yes, a duster, if you please. The dust is so thick that his lordship and I are likely to choke on it," said Fredericka cheerfully.

A quiver passed over the butler's face. He bowed. "I shall have a girl sent up immediately to assist you, miss."

Fredericka was amused by the butler's stiff attitude. It was naturally very bad ton for her to do her own dusting and she had been as good as told so. Obviously she had damaged her credit in Moffet's eyes. However, she did not mind in the least that a maid would be sent to do the dusting, for that would free her to concentrate on the actual organization of the books.

"Blister it!" exclaimed the earl.

Fredericka turned, startled. Lord Chalmers was attempting to lever himself out of his chair with patently small success. His expression was grim, forbidding any expression of sympathy.

"My lord, is there anything that I can get for you? I can probably find it much quicker than you shall, at this point," she said quietly, hoping not to offend his sense of pride.

Lord Chalmers glared at her. "I need my newspaper," he snapped. "I have just recalled reading an article yesterday evening about the very thing that Cunningham is interested in and I know that he does not subscribe to this journal."

"That is easily dealt with, my lord. I shall get your newspaper for you, and then you will not be obliged to completely lose your train of thought," said Fredericka.

The earl's brows were lowered in irritation. "Nonsense! I can fetch it myself! I am not yet in my dotage, miss! I can very well manage for myself. For that matter, I can ring for a servant."

"All that you say is perfectly true, my lord. However, I do not mind in the least performing this small favor, for I can see that you have been in deep reflection over your correspondence and I know you would prefer not to leave it even for a few moments. And while a servant could indeed bring you the newspaper, you would have to waste a few moments in instruction over precisely where the newspaper is located, for as I recall it was left in one of the chairs. Depend upon it, I shall locate it much faster than one of the footmen," said Fredericka, smiling.

Lord Chalmers regarded her for a moment. He was reluctantly pleased by her insistence to cater to him. "Very well, Miss Hedgeworth. It is true, this letter much exercises my thoughts and I do not wish to lose hold of what I am trying to convey."

"Then I shall go at once for the newspaper," said Fredericka, walking to the door.

"Thank you, Miss Hedgeworth," said Lord Chalmers gruffly. "And I apologize for my immoderate language just now." He turned back to his correspondence and before Fredericka had finished closing the door, his pen was already moving steadily across the page.

Fredericka went quietly down the hall and entered the drawing room. It was deserted and she crossed over to the chair that Lady Chalmers had sat in the previous evening. She hoped that the servants had not been too zealous in tidying the room earlier in the day and found the newspaper and carried it off to be tossed away. That would annoy Lord Chalmers very much, she thought, smiling.

However, her fears were groundless. After a short search, she found the newspaper stuffed down between the several cushions, where it had remained unnoticed.

Fredericka was engaged in rearranging the cushions and pillows, plumping them up, when the door opened silently behind her and a gentleman entered the drawing room. He closed the door and stood watching her for a moment, before drawling, "What have we here?"

Startled, Fredericka whirled, a cushion clasped to her breast.

The gentleman was tall, dressed in a fashionable coat and breeches, and a pair of gleaming Hessians. His lean face was handsome and his green eyes were alight with appreciation. Strangely there was something familiar about him. It was almost as though she had met him someplace, but of course that was nonsense.

Fredericka was still attempting to puzzle out what had given her such an impression as he sauntered toward her. "I do not think I have seen you before. You are a beauty. What is your name?"

Fredericka was amazed. She had never been accosted with such familiarity before. The suspicion that the gentleman was drunk flashed across her mind. But there was nothing to indicate it in his lively smiling gaze or in his lithe approach.

She still had not found her tongue when the gentleman pulled out his handkerchief and seized her chin between his long fingers. "Hold still. You have a smudge of dust on your cheek."

Fredericka stared up at him, wide-eyed, as he cleaned her face for her. He flicked her nose with a gentle forefinger and then released her.

The gentleman threw himself into a chair nearby and crossed his feet at the ankles. "Have you been with her ladyship long, my shy beauty?"

Fredericka merely looked at him. A gentleman never sat down in the presence of a lady. It was simply not done. The truth had slowly been dawning on her and the full realization burst upon her stunned mind.

The gentleman had taken her for a housemaid.

Fredericka's sense of the ridiculous rose. Her eyes began to dance. The gentleman thought her to be a maid. Very well, then. She would try to see whether it was a role that she could carry off for a few amusing moments.

Putting on the broad accent of her own county, Fredericka said, "Ow, sir! You did startle me that bad, to be sure! I was just fetching 'is lordship's paper to him and thought to plump the cushions, besides."

The gentleman smiled. "You have made a very good job of it, too. Now, what is your name, girl? I should really like to know."

It occurred to Fredericka all at once that her imposture was not at all the thing. The truth of the matter was that she had responded to the laughing gleam in the gentleman's eyes with a bit of fun and had not even given a thought that it was an unkind thing to do.

She was about to confess her little joke, when the drawing room door opened and Lady Chalmers entered. "Sebastion!"

The gentleman immediately arose and stepped around the chair, his movement unintentionally shielding Fredericka from the countess's view. "Good afternoon, ma'am. You are in high good looks."

Fredericka was ready to sink. In that instant, she realized that she had been duping none other than the viscount himself, Lord

Satterwaite. And there was no possibility of apologizing and keeping the matter between themselves now.

The opportunity presented to her had been irresistible. The trick had been played and it couldn't be undone now. She would simply have to carry things off with a high manner and hope that the viscount would not consider himself to be humiliated in front of his mother.

Lady Chalmers held out her hands to her son. "I was but informed just this moment that you had called and—"

Lord Satterwaite turned to draw the countess toward the settee and as he did so he no longer blocked Fredericka from her ladyship's view.

Lady Chalmers's mouth dropped open. She stopped in her tracks, an utter expression of dismay upon her face. "Fredericka!"

"Is that the wench's name? She would not tell me," said Lord Satterwaite, smiling. "I interrupted her pillow plumping and I fear that I offended her."

Lady Chalmers appeared thunderstruck.

Fredericka recognized that her hostess was utterly speechless and took the lead. Having already retrieved the earl's newspaper, she stepped forward with an air of composure that she was far from feeling. "Forgive me, ma'am. His lordship took me for a maid, attired as I am, and I fear that I could not resist teasing him just a little."

Fredericka held out her hand to the viscount. His expression had altered ludicrously upon hearing her genteel tones. "You must be Lord Satterwaite. I am sorry! I do hope that I have not embarrassed you, but you must see that it was quite an irresistible opportunity. I am Miss Fredericka Hedgeworth."

Lord Satterwaite recovered himself quickly. His face smoothed into a civil smile. He took her hand and made a slight bow. "The honor is mine, Miss Hedgeworth. Alas, I admit that I was quite taken in."

"I trust that you are not annoyed?" asked Fredericka, searching his eyes. There was a disquieting gleam in their green depths.

"Not at all, Miss Hedgeworth. It was a novel experience, merely," said Lord Satterwaite, still smiling. "My mother had naturally mentioned to me that she would be sponsoring you for the

Season. I had looked forward to our meeting, but I had not envisioned it to take place in quite this way."

Lady Chalmers uttered an inarticulate moan.

"No," agreed Fredericka. She suspected that the viscount was more annoyed than he had let on and she regretted more deeply still succumbing to her sometimes unfortunate penchant for fun. "I apologize yet again, my lord. I hope that you will excuse me, my lady, but I had promised to return Lord Chalmers's newspaper to him as quickly as possible."

"Of course, my dear," said Lady Chalmers, managing to summon up a wan smile.

Fredericka exited the drawing room, glad to escape what was becoming a rather tricky situation. Her little joke had managed to discompose herself, the countess, and Lord Satterwaite. It was too bad of her, she readily admitted to herself as she traversed the hall. But when she recalled the look on the viscount's face when he had realized that he had unwittingly duped himself, she could not help laughing.

When the drawing room door had closed behind his mother's guest, Lord Satterwaite demanded, "What is Miss Hedgeworth doing dressed as a common maid? I completely mistook her, but how was I supposed to see her quality in such a guise?"

Lady Chalmers had sunk into a convenient chair and covered her eyes with one hand. She looked up with a sigh. "Miss Hedgeworth has volunteered to organize your father's library here. Apparently she discovered what a disagreeably dusty task it is and decided to put on the apron and cap to save her gown. How mortifying that she was seen dressed thus!"

"Exactly so, ma'am," said Lord Satterwaite rather dryly. "But I do not understand. How is it that a houseguest is doing such work? Surely that task is better suited to my father's secretary than a miss who will shortly be introduced to society."

"I saw no harm in acquiescing to the scheme when it was proposed. Miss Hedgeworth very prettily volunteered her services at a moment when your father was rather disgruntled because he could not find a particular obscure reference. I was actually rather grateful to Miss Hedgeworth for diverting your father's attention,

for he was fast falling into the mopes. You know how he does,"
said Lady Chalmers.

Lord Satterwaite uttered a short laugh. "None better."

"Yes, well, that is how it came about," said Lady Chalmers
hastily. "Miss Hedgeworth's offer pleased your father and gave
his thoughts quite a turn for the better."

"Still hipped, is he?" asked Lord Satterwaite. "Well, I shall not
wait on him, then. He will likely demand an explanation of me
why there is not yet a notice in the *Gazette*."

"You do not mean to visit him, then?" asked Lady Chalmers,
disappointed.

"You may convey my respects to my esteemed sire after I have
taken my leave. I think that will be the more politic strategy at
this juncture, for I know all too well that you do not wish your
peace cut up yet again with a vulgar quarrel, and especially with a
guest in the house," said Lord Satterwaite. "Though I doubt that
much can rattle a young lady who brazens out such a trick as she
has played."

"Oh no, no! You quite mistake, Sebastion. Miss Hedgeworth is
all that I could possibly wish for," assured Lady Chalmers
earnestly. "I have been enormously pleased in her since she has
come to me. She is well-mannered, quiet in her speech, and acts
just as she ought."

Lord Satterwaite uttered a crack of laughter. His green eyes
narrowed with amusement. "Act is precisely the word to apply to
Miss Hedgeworth. I have never been so fortunate as to be the butt
of such a consummate performance."

"I am certain that charades is still a favorite pastime in the
country," said Lady Chalmers, valiantly upholding her guest's
credit but feeling herself to be inexorably sinking. Oh, was there
anything more provoking than that Fredericka should have been
caught looking such a fright? she thought, dismayed. Or to discover that the wretched girl had such a perverse sense of humor?

Lord Satterwaite merely smiled. He turned his mind to the purpose behind his visit. "I did not call on you to bandy words about
Miss Hedgeworth's talents, or lack thereof, Mama! I came to tell
you that I am leaving London for a few days. I have received
word from my agent that there is an urgent spot of business that
must be attended to at once. So you must not count on me to

make up one of your dinner guests or depend upon my escort until my return. I know that you will understand."

Lady Chalmers thought her plate had been full. She now understood that she had not even seen the first course. "Sebastion, naturally I do understand that you must attend to your own affairs. However, are you certain that this has nothing to do with your father's ultimatum to you? You are not being deliberately mulish, I hope."

Lord Satterwaite grimaced. "I thought that you might see my temporary defection in this light. Surely you must realize that I know my duty better than anyone. Not withstanding the quarrel between myself and my father, I intend to hold myself ready to render whatever service you might require of me in your efforts to launch Miss Hedgeworth. I am better aware than most what fortitude it requires of you to give up your pleasures and amusements whenever my father is out of curl."

"You must not think that. It is but a small sacrifice when I know that he is so sadly pulled. I do not mind in the least when it is but the two of us at table," said Lady Chalmers quietly.

"But you cannot stay at home when you have Miss Hedgeworth to puff off. And my father will not bestir himself upon your behalf if he remains cross as patches," said Lord Satterwaite.

Lady Chalmers gave a tiny sigh. "It is quite true that I have thought I might require you to stand in for your father on occasion this Season. I had hoped that his gout would have subsided by now, but it has not to any degree."

"Then you will need me at some point to escort you and Miss Hedgeworth to some of the functions. I will do so, I promise you." A smile flickered over Lord Satterwaite's face. "I only trust that my father does not come to think that I am dangling after Miss Hedgeworth, for nothing could ever be further from the truth."

"My dear, of course nothing will be said," said Lady Chalmers. "And if your father should chance to utter such a thing in my hearing, I shall naturally disclaim any such design on your part."

"Thank you, Mama. I knew that I could depend upon you," said Lord Satterwaite. He lifted his mother's hand to his lips and

briefly saluted it. "I am off in an hour. I hope to return before the
week is quite out."

"Will you, my dear? Well, I wish you a very good journey. No
doubt you shall call upon me after your return when it proves
convenient for you to do so," said Lady Chalmers, almost indifferently.

Not for worlds would she make the mistake of appearing too
anxious about her son's movements. He was a man grown, after
all, and would naturally resent too close a watch set over him. She
was wise enough not to overplay her cards in that way, at least,
thought her ladyship.

Lord Satterwaite agreed to it, and a few minutes later took affectionate leave of the countess.

Chapter Thirteen

Meanwhile, Fredericka had returned to the library with the earl's newspaper.

Lord Chalmers took it, thanking her, but also quizzing her a little. "I was beginning to wonder whether you were able to find it, after all, Miss Hedgeworth."

"I own, I did fear for a while that it had been thrown out, my lord. However, I found it tucked neatly inside the cushions of your chair," said Fredericka.

She wondered whether she should confide in the earl about her unusual meeting with the viscount. Then she decided that his lordship would hear something about it from Lady Chalmers and it was better to make a clean confession at once. "Actually, I was delayed longer than I would have been because Lord Satterwaite called. He came in while I was looking for your newspaper. Apparently Moffet did not realize that I had gone into the drawing room, or otherwise I know that the viscount would not have been allowed to enter. However, it was a very few minutes before Lady Chalmers came into the room. Her ladyship is with Lord Satterwaite now."

Lord Chalmers regarded her with a keen gaze. "So you have met my heir! What did you think of him, Miss Hedgeworth?" His eye was caught by the maid who was busily dusting the stacks of volumes beside the shelves. Testily, he dismissed her. Then he turned once more to Fredericka and repeated his question. "Come, now! You must not hesitate for fear of offending me or appearing too forward. This confidence is between friends."

Fredericka gave a small laugh. "I fear, rather, that it was Lord Satterwaite who was offended, my lord."

The earl's curiosity was at once thoroughly aroused. "Now what do you mean by that, miss? I'll have the round tale, if you please!"

Fredericka began to relate her story, at first somewhat hesitantly and then with greater confidence as she realized that the earl was becoming entertained. "So naturally his lordship took me for a housemaid due to my unorthodox appearance today. I could not resist the temptation to tease him a little and I put on a country burr. But I was completely unmasked when Lady Chalmers came in."

Lord Chalmers roared with laughter. "That was a good joke, indeed! I wish I might have seen it."

"Unfortunately, Lord Satterwaite was not as amused as you are, my lord. I thought that he was rather annoyed to discover the trick that I had played on him," said Fredericka ruefully.

The earl's eyes glinted. "I warrant that he was, indeed. I would have given much to see Sebastion's face when he realized that he had been so neatly duped." He regarded her thoughtful countenance. "Never mind Lord Satterwaite's reaction, my dear. It will not have hurt him in the least to have been thrown off his dignity by a hair. Indeed, it would do him a great deal of good to come down off his high ropes occasionally and laugh at himself. Thank you again for fetching my newspaper, Miss Hedgeworth. The incident that you have just related has put me in a very good humor."

Fredericka smiled at that. The earl turned back to his correspondence, able now to refer to an article that he had wished to quote, and Fredericka went back to her self-appointed task. Most of the volumes had already been dusted by the maid who had been sent in for the task, but it fell to Fredericka to reshelve and straighten the books. That task the earl would never have trusted to the maids, for they would not have known how to group the different subjects and treatises.

Several minutes were whiled away in their separate peaceful pursuits. Then the door opened and Lady Chalmers entered. Her gaze went at once to Fredericka and her eyes raked her guest's unkempt appearance. She gave a slight shudder, reliving again that moment when she had realized that her son had met Miss Hedgeworth in this awful guise. But she was able to greet her husband and Fredericka with admirable aplomb.

After a moment or two of conversation, Lady Chalmers referred to the matter that was most exercising her thoughts. "Fredericka, I am most sorry that you have met Lord Satterwaite in such an appalling fashion. It was unfortunate in the extreme. However, I do not refine too much upon it. After all, it could have been worse. One of the patronesses of Almack's might have been shown in and *that*, you will allow, would never have done!"

"The fault was entirely mine, my dear. I sent Miss Hedgeworth to fetch my newspaper for me," Lord Chalmers interposed. "She very obligingly did so, for which I am most grateful." He glanced at Fredericka as he ended, and gave a broad wink.

"Indeed! Well, in the future pray call for one of the servants to run his lordship's errands, Fredericka. You are our guest and we should not expect you to place yourself into potentially embarrassing circumstances," said Lady Chalmers.

"Nonsense! Miss Hedgeworth is very able to manage for herself whatever the circumstances might be," said Lord Chalmers, beginning to frown.

"You are not quite aware of what has happened, my lord." Lady Chalmers took a sustaining breath. "Fredericka was taken to be one of our housemaids by Sebastion. I could not have been more mortified on her behalf than if it had happened to myself."

"I fear that I am something of an insensate creature, my lady. I was not the least put out of countenance, I assure you. I suspect that Lord Satterwaite was disconcerted, however, and for that I most sincerely apologize. I should have made myself known to him at once," said Fredericka.

Lord Chalmers snorted derisively. "More fool he!"

"I doubt that Sebastion would have had the least difficulty in perceiving Fredericka's quality if she had been properly gowned. Instead of which, she is creased and covered over with dust and is wearing an apron and a mobcap, too!" said Lady Chalmers, her careful control fraying. It was patently obvious that her ladyship was operating under powerful emotions, the root of which became clear when she said, "And I had so wanted you to meet under auspicious circumstances!"

Lord Chalmers shot his lady a sharp glance. He gave a slight cough. "Unfortunate, indeed."

Fredericka realized that Lady Chalmers must be referring to her hopes that the close friendship that had existed between herself and Lady Hedgeworth would be reciprocated in their progeny. Lady Chalmers was naturally disappointed that she and the viscount had gotten off to such an odd start. "Pray do not distress yourself, my lady. I am certain that before our acquaintance is much older, Lord Satterwaite and I shall become the greatest of friends."

Lady Chalmers stared at her, a rather blank expression on her face. "Friends?" With an effort she pulled herself together. She displayed a determinedly cheerful smile. "So I should hope, Fredericka. Indeed, I trust that there will grow to be such a warmth of feeling between you and my son that it shall quite astonish me."

"I shall endeavor to please you, my lady," promised Fredericka.

Lady Chalmers's expression relaxed. "Thank you, my dear. I am sorry if I sounded fretful. It was just such a disquieting thing to have happened. You will own, I know, that it will not do for you to be seen abroad again in such a costume."

"Yes, ma'am. I do know it," agreed Fredericka meekly.

Lord Chalmers had listened with a gathering gleam of amusement in his eyes. "For my part, I think Miss Hedgeworth handled the situation with admirable aplomb. I give her high marks for that, my dear."

"Yes, indeed." Lady Chalmers's agreement sounded rather half-hearted, even in her own ears, and she said hastily, "But how do you come to know that, my lord?"

"Miss Hedgeworth had already confided to me the peculiar circumstances of her meeting with Sebastion," said Lord Chalmers. "I thought it a very good joke, my dear. I have not laughed so heartily since we came to London."

Lady Chalmers smiled, but privately she wondered at the aberration in her lord's sense of humor. For herself, she had seen nothing at all amusing in the fact that the viscount's initial impression of Miss Hedgeworth must always be the picture of a housemaid. It was disastrous, from her ladyship's point of view. But she had not confided the whole of her hopeful scheme for linking Miss Hedgeworth's future with her son to the earl, so perhaps that accounted for his lordship's queer amusement.

Lord Satterwaite must not see Miss Hedgeworth again until the dresses and gowns that had been ordered for her had been received.

Lady Chalmers was suddenly glad that the viscount was going out of town for a few days. It would allow that awful memory to fade in his mind, and hopefully, when he returned he would be knocked off of his feet by Miss Hedgeworth's improved appearance. She was even glad that her son had declined to dine with them that evening *en famille*. Of course his refusal had been couched in almost disrespectful terms, but she did not mind that now. It was unquestionably for the best.

"Yes, very well. I came to tell you, my lord, that I am leaving in a few minutes. I promised Letitia Savage that I would call upon her this week and I have decided to do so this afternoon. You must not expect me back too quickly," said Lady Chalmers.

"Shall I change and accompany you, ma'am?" asked Fredericka. She had seen that Lady Chalmers had been overset by what had happened earlier and she was anxious to make amends. Surely offering to go with Lady Chalmers on a social call would help to mollify her ladyship's exacerbated feelings.

Lord Chalmers uttered a crack of laughter. Fredericka glanced at the earl in surprise. She was even more surprised when her ladyship said hastily, "I think not, my dear. It would not be at all the thing."

"I do not understand," said Fredericka slowly.

"Letitia Savage is a reformer," said Lord Chalmers, still chuckling. "It is not her sort of society that my lady wishes to launch you into, Miss Hedgeworth."

Lady Chalmers gave him a look of reproach. "Mrs. Savage runs a foundling home in one of the poorer districts of London, Fredericka. I am one of her patronesses and I go to see her whenever I feel that she may have need of my largesse."

"But I should of all things like to accompany you, my lady! Indeed, it sounds to me to be a fascinating project. Pray say that I may go with you," said Fredericka. She was keenly interested and curious. In her own county, she had observed the orphaned parish children and wondered what would eventually become of them. She had wanted to do more than offer food and clothing for their sustenance, but she had had no notion how it could be accomplished. She had never heard of a foundling home. It was a novel concept to her. She had had no idea that such places existed or that a lady of the Countess of Chalmers's stature would lend herself to such a worthy cause.

Lady Chalmers looked rather helplessly toward the earl. His lordship shrugged. "Take Miss Hedgeworth with you, my dear. I daresay that the visit will be instructive, at the least."

Lady Chalmers made up her mind. "Very well, Fredericka. You shall go. I have already requested that the carriage be brought around in a quarter hour, but I shall leave it wait in order for you to change."

"Thank you, my lady. I shall go up at once." Fredericka turned to the earl. "I am sorry, my lord, to leave you before my task is quite finished."

Lord Chalmers waved his hands in dismissal. "Nonsense. The books can easily wait for another day when they have already been disarrayed these several years. In any event, I believe that you have made enough of an inroad that I shall be able to discover a few treasured volumes on my own now."

Fredericka gracefully dismissed herself and left the library. She went upstairs to her bedroom and tugged the bell rope to call for her maid. She did not wait for the tiring-woman, but began unbuttoning her cuffs and disposed herself of the apron and cap.

When the maid came in and was told what was needed, she set at once to work to help Fredericka finish changing. Within minutes, Fredericka was outfitted in a walking dress, with a warm pelisse buttoned over it, and her feet were shod in walking boots. Though her attire was obviously of the first quality, there were no frivolous knots of ribbon adorning her outfit nor an inordinate number of feathers curling over the brim of her bonnet.

"For you don't wish to appear too flashy, miss, not down in those parts," had commented the maid.

Fredericka had agreed to the common sense of the maid's observation. She had visited the poor often enough in the capacity of her responsibilities at Luting to know that it was not kind to tout off one's consequences, either in manner or dress, before those who were less fortunate. As she finished tying the ribbons of her velvet bonnet, she said as much.

"Yes, miss. Howsoever, I was thinking about pickpockets and the like," said the maid, holding ready a pair of pale kid gloves.

Fredericka glanced at the maid as she took the gloves. "Is it very bad, then?" she asked.

The maid folded her lips. "You shall see for yourself, miss."

Fredericka went downstairs. A footman indicated that she would find Lady Chalmers in the drawing room. When Fredericka entered the room, she saw that the countess was attired in a similar fashion as herself. Her ladyship's pelisse was cut on rather severe lines and besides her reticule, she carried a large ermine muff.

Upon setting eyes on Fredericka, Lady Chalmers said, with an approving smile, "Very well, indeed, Fredericka. I perceive that you do have some notion of what is appropriate."

"The maid advised me, my lady. Of course, I have for many years dealt with our own tenants and visited the poor and the sick in the village, but I expect that this will be a bit different," said Fredericka.

A footman came into the drawing room to announce that her ladyship's carriage was at the front door. As the ladies left the drawing room in the footman's wake, Lady Chalmers glanced at Fredericka. "Yes, I believe that you will find this expedition quite a bit different than what you are used to, my dear."

Fredericka was wondering exactly what the countess meant when they emerged from the town house onto the front steps. The wind was sharp and she was glad for the warmth of her pelisse and bonnet.

Just before she was handed up into the carriage after Lady Chalmers, Fredericka chanced to glance up at the driver's box. She was surprised and a little disturbed when she saw that a stalwart footman was seated up beside the driver, and that he was checking the priming of a large horse pistol.

A warm rug was placed over the ladies' knees and a hot brick was put under their feet. The door was latched and the signal given to the driver. The house servant stepped back up onto the curb and watched while the driver flicked the reins.

As the carriage lurched forward, Fredericka said, "My dear ma'am, the footman accompanying us is armed. Surely you do not expect trouble here in the heart of London?"

"Certainly not in this neighborhood," said Lady Chalmers calmly. "But we will shortly be entering quite a different part of town. It is wise to be prepared for any contingency."

Fredericka said no more, but her curiosity was heightened even further. She was learning something about the Countess of Chalmers which she had never suspected of that fashionable lady. It would be interesting, indeed, to see what other revelations would come out of this particular call.

Fredericka gazed out the window. The streets teemed with other elegant carriages, hackneys, dray wagons, and coaches. Soon the fashionable quarters of town gave way to less respectable neighborhoods, and the traffic also changed. There were fewer carriages and more of the heavy wagons and disreputable hackneys. Tradesmen seemed to predominate in the area, and Fredericka wondered whether this was the dangerous territory that the countess had alluded to.

However, their carriage did not stop. It continued to wend its way and the streets became narrower and more crooked. There were hardly any equipages of any kind to be seen. The buildings were tumbledown, some still bearing blackened signs screwed to the front plates that bore witness that at one time this had been a respectable part of the metropolis.

Now squalor abounded on every side. Sewage ran in shallow ditches on either side of the street. Unkempt folk loitered or poked through heaps of trash. Ragged children, shouting shrilly, flashed past the slow-moving carriage.

Hard flat stares were leveled on the carriage as it passed and Fredericka was suddenly glad for the armed footman on the roof. She had never seen such impersonal hostility as she saw in those unknown faces. What shook her most was that it was not just the men, but the women, too, who had such stark expressions.

"I never dreamed of anything like this," she murmured.

"Quite," said Lady Chalmers dryly. "It is a different world altogether, one that I am eternally thankful that I was not born into. Most of our class do not think of such places as this, nor of the people who inhabit these rabbit warrens; or if they do, they prefer o put it out of their minds. It is unpleasant and horrifying when one learns that people actually live in this way."

"But surely there is something that can be done," said Fredericka, her natural compassion stirred. "These children! It is so cold and yet they run about in threadbare garments and with rags tied about their feet."

"I see that you feel just as you ought, my dear. However, I must warn you. Do not give a single coin out to any of these urchins, or otherwise we shall be swamped with beggars," said Lady Chalmers.

Fredericka stared at the countess. "Surely you are not serious. Why, I would willingly turn out my purse."

"Yes, and advertise that we have considerable means, at least in the eyes of these poor souls. Not even Stephen and his pistol would be able to hold them all off then," said Lady Chalmers. She rested her hand lightly for a moment upon her companion's arm. "You must be guided by me, Fredericka. I know whereof I speak. It is not an unusual story for a nobleman, who has overimbibed through the night, to be set upon and waken in one of these gutters completely stripped of all on his person, including his fine coat and breeches! No, my dear! I shall shortly introduce you to a lady who is far better able than we to provide help to those who so desperately need it."

Fredericka nodded her understanding. "I shall follow your lead, of course," she said quietly.

"Thank you, my dear. Now we have arrived and you shall meet one of the greatest ladies of my acquaintance," said Lady Chalmers.

The carriage had passed through the gates of what appeared to be an old coaching inn. The horses were drawn up at the front door. The driver snubbed his reins and climbed off his box. He let down the iron step and opened the carriage door. The footman remained seated on the box, his attitude one of vigilance.

The ladies descended into the muddy yard. Lady Chalmers spoke a few low words to the driver and he nodded. Then the countess lifted the hem of her skirts and approached the door of the old inn, Fredericka following her.

The door had been opened by a short dour individual wearing a leather waistcoat. As Lady Chalmers stepped through, the man nodded brusquely to her ladyship. He cast a suspicious glance at Fredericka and closed the front door.

The light was dim inside the wide hall. Without a word, the man showed the two visitors into a parlor and went away to tell the mistress of the establishment of their arrival.

Chapter Fourteen

Lady Chalmers went over to the grate and spread her gloved hands to the blaze. She saw that Fredericka was glancing around with a frankly curious gaze. "It is a gloomy, overlarge room, but serviceable."

Fredericka also approached the fireplace. "Indeed, one can still see the blackening of soot in the beams. Was this once part of a common taproom, ma'am?"

Lady Chalmers smiled. "I believe that it was. There was much that was torn down and redone inside these walls. You will find this place to be vastly different from your tenant cottages, my dear."

Before her ladyship could say more, the door opened. A woman entered. She was tall and spare of frame. Her features were patrician, almost severe in line. Her hooded eyes were keen and sharp. She glanced toward Fredericka, but addressed her greeting to the countess. "Lady Chalmers. This is a welcome surprise. I did not expect you until later in the week, as is your usual custom."

"I hope that I do not take you away from something of importance," said Lady Chalmers.

Mrs. Savage gestured gracefully. "Not at all, my lady. I was merely instructing a few of the girls in what makes for a properly stocked linen closet. I have left Nan in charge of the lesson. Pray be seated. I have sent Thomas for refreshment."

Lady Chalmers sat down on a settle, indicating the place beside her to Fredericka. Obediently Fredericka took her place. Their hostess sat down opposite in a wingback chair. "I hope that you do not mind that I have brought Miss Hedgeworth with me. When she learned that I meant to call on you, she requested that she be allowed to come. Miss Hedgeworth is just up from the country. I am sponsoring her this Season."

"I see. A new turnout for you, is it not, Sarah?" asked Mrs. Savage, with the glimmer of a smile.

Lady Chalmers laughed. "Indeed it is. Fredericka, this is Mrs. Letitia Savage. She is the proprietress of this establishment and my good dear friend."

"How do you do, Mrs. Savage? I am happy to make your acquaintance," said Fredericka formally. She did not know what to think of the lady. Mrs. Savage was obviously well-bred and she stood on apparently intimate terms with Lady Chalmers. Yet she lived in this squalid part of London and ran a foundling home. It was awkward, indeed, not to instantly be able to place the lady in the social structure, for then one did not know quite what to say or relate that would be of interest.

Mrs. Savage graciously inclined her head. She appeared about to say something, but just then the door opened and the dour manservant entered, bearing a tea tray. Mrs. Savage instructed him where to put it and when he had done so, and been dismissed, she turned again to her visitors to offer them hot tea. "For well I know how chill it is outside. You will not wish your horses to stand about for long in this air, my lady."

"No," agreed Lady Chalmers. She accepted a cup and saucer. "And I know, too, how very busy you keep yourself, so I do not wish to keep you too long."

Fredericka had also been given a cup of sweetened tea and she quietly sipped the steaming brew. She was content merely to listen, feeling herself to be somewhat out of her milieu.

Mrs. Savage looked over at Fredericka. There was a rather aloof expression in her eyes. "What brings you with her ladyship, miss? Curiosity, perhaps?" There was a steely disdain in the lady's voice.

"Perhaps," agreed Fredericka quietly. "But also a sincere interest. Lady Chalmers had mentioned to me how you have made a home for foundlings. I have long wondered about the abandoned and orphaned children in my own county, and so I wished to see what was being done here."

Mrs. Savage nodded. There was a glint of approval in her eyes. "Yes, I provide a home for young girls and their babes. Later, when the girls are able, I provide proper training so that they may enter a respectable service. As for the babes, we try to place them with loving families."

"But is that not a formidable task?" asked Fredericka.

Mrs. Savage actually laughed. Her stern countenance lightened to an amazing degree. "Yes, it certainly is, Miss Hedgeworth. Come, I shall give you a tour. That is, if you think that it will not harm your team, my lady?"

Lady Chalmers shook her head. "I have left instructions with my driver to walk them about the yard if we tarried."

Mrs. Savage nodded, and rose from her chair. She waited while her guests set aside their cups and then she led them out of the parlor. By the end of the short tour, she had warmed considerably to Fredericka, remarking that it was refreshing to meet such a sensible young miss. "In general, the young misses these days all seem to have more hair than wit," she said disparagingly.

Mrs. Savage saw the ladies out to their carriage. Lady Chalmers had asked Fredericka to precede her, as she wished to say a few private words to Mrs. Savage. Fredericka had nodded and gone ahead. She had glanced back in time to see Lady Chalmers and Mrs. Savage exchange a close embrace.

Fredericka was curious as to how Lady Chalmers had ever become associated with such an unusual charity. She had witnessed the discreet exchange of a bank draft from Lady Chalmers to Mrs. Savage and had understood from the few words spoken that the countess had been a faithful benefactress.

When Lady Chalmers was settled into the carriage and they were well off again, Fredericka ventured to inquire of the history of the connection between her ladyship and Mrs. Savage.

Lady Chalmers smiled at the question. "Do you think it strange that I should be on such intimate terms with Mrs. Savage? Actually, there is nothing at all odd about it. There is a family connection, you see. Letitia is my cousin twice removed."

Fredericka was astonished. "But how is it, then, that Mrs. Savage came to be here, and doing this sort of thing? Surely her family objected to it!"

Lady Chalmers laughed. "Indeed they did! But Letitia was always a formidable, self-willed female. None of them could ever control her once she got the bit in her teeth. Most of the relations washed their hands of her when the foundling home came into existence. It was an embarrassment that one of their own should make a byword of herself by indulging so closely in a charitable work."

"But you did not feel the same," said Fredericka.

"No, I did not. As a girl, I had always admired Letitia. My admiration for her has never abated," said Lady Chalmers. She was silent a moment, then said, "She came out a few years before I did, and contracted with what most of her family thought was a rather lusterless marriage. However, Mr. Savage is a very worthy man. Indeed, he is one of those whom I would not scruple to trust with my life."

"But is Mr. Savage alive, then? I assumed that Mrs. Savage was a widow," said Fredericka.

Lady Chalmers shook her head, smiling. "Oh, no. The Savages have been happily wed for nearly forty years. At present Tom is traveling. He visits different parishes to determine the existence of families who are willing to adopt the babes, or where there might be decent places to indenture the girls. It is an exacting work that Tom and Letitia have embarked upon, but they are really quite dedicated. Their commitment to their Christian faith is nothing short of amazing."

"Of course I have heard many times in our own worship services at home the admonishment that we are to care for the widow and the orphan. Is that what the Savages are trying to accomplish?"

"Something very like," agreed Lady Chalmers. She shook her head. "Sometimes I wonder at my own selfishness, but I am too used to my comfortable existence to do anything remotely like what the Savages do. And so I assuage my conscience by giving out of my largesse."

"We are told, too, that the giver is blessed of God," said Fredericka quietly.

Lady Chalmers reached out and squeezed her hand. "Thank you, my dear. That was good of you to say." She settled back against the seat squab. "Now, we must turn our attention to your come-out ball. I have decided that it shall be three weeks from Tuesday. That shall give us ample time to send out the invitations and to make all the necessary arrangements. You must tell me if there is anything that you particularly wish in the arrangements, my dear."

Fredericka shook her head, smiling. "I am quite at a loss, ma'am. I do not know what is considered de rigueur and I submit myself to be entirely guided by you."

Lady Chalmers was pleased. "You are an amiable creature, to be sure! I anticipate scarcely a wrinkle to mar the Season. Very well, then. I shall tell you what I have been thinking of."

Fredericka was quite willing to encourage the countess in this admirable vein. She sat listening with amusement and some awe as her ladyship outlined a function that was destined to excite admiration and envy among all the haughtiest hostesses.

In the following few days, Fredericka was introduced to any number of people. Lady Chalmers made a point of taking Fredericka with her on all of her morning calls and afternoon visits. The ladies drove in the park in Lady Chalmers's crested landau each afternoon during the fashionable hour between five and six o'clock, which assured introductions and chance meetings with an amazing number of society's elite. Lady Chalmers and Fredericka also promenaded in Bond Street, a maid trailing discreetly behind to carry whatever purchases might be made.

As a result, a shower of invitations descended upon Chalmers House, all begging for the honor of the Earl and Countess of Chalmers, with their guest, Miss Hedgeworth, to attend every imaginable sort of function.

"My goodness, ma'am! We shall not be able to attend the half of them," said Fredericka, amazed, picking up one gilt-edged card from the stack.

"Wait until you are properly launched, my dear. Then you will see something, indeed!" promised Lady Chalmers.

Fredericka could scarcely imagine that there could possibly be a greater number of invitations sent to them, but she knew that she was very green in such things. "I trust that we shall not be run off our legs," she murmured with a touch of humor.

Lord Chalmers laughed. "Aye, you may well wonder, Miss Hedgeworth. But you are young. You will survive."

"I do hope so, my lord," said Fredericka.

Lady Chalmers was still going through the cards when she was astonished to come across one from her son. Lord Satterwaite begged that Lord and Lady Chalmers and Miss Hedgeworth accompany him to the theater that same evening. He included in a postscript that he was certain that Miss Hedgeworth would enjoy the playacting.

Lady Chalmers chuckled when she read it, and felt a measure of relief. Perhaps that unfortunate meeting was not so very bad, after all, since it had tickled the viscount's interest in such a way as to result in this exceedingly gratifying invitation.

Lady Chalmers relayed the proposed outing to Miss Hedgeworth, saying with a smiling glance, "Depend upon it, Lord Satterwaite found some humor in the situation. It is to be hoped that your relationship shall continue to progress on amiable lines, Fredericka. I shall send Sebastion our acceptances at once, for there is only a small card party for this evening and I am persuaded that you will enjoy this much more."

"Yes, my lady. I shall look forward to it, indeed," said Fredericka. "I have never been to the theater before."

She had liked the viscount's good looks and the liveliness in his eyes. That as much as any anticipation of going to the theater prompted her tranquil acquiescence. She felt no constraint about meeting Lord Satterwaite again, for upon their first meeting she had sensed that he would appreciate her joke, and now her instinct was apparently proving to have been correct. The only embarrassment attached to the situation had been being caught out by Lady Chalmers, but in light of the viscount's invitation her ladyship was obviously ready to view the episode with an amused tolerance.

The earl begged off from the theater outing, preferring to remain home ensconced in his library. But he urged his wife and their guest to enjoy themselves. "It is not every day that my son chooses to show his dutiful side," he said dryly.

Lady Chalmers hurriedly turned the subject. "I have been thinking of that lovely jonquil muslin, my dear. I have a shawl that should go very well with it." She bore Fredericka off to her room in order to see if a certain silk shawl wouldn't be just the thing for that evening.

Lord Satterwaite was not surprised that the earl did not make up one of the party. He had known that his father did not care for Shakespearean comedy, but he had chosen that particular play with thoughts for the entertainment of his mother and her protégée. It was quickly apparent that he had chosen well, for both ladies enjoyed themselves very much. Indeed, Miss Hedgeworth was actually betrayed into a throaty chuckle.

Lord Satterwaite quickly turned his head, his brows snapping together. Surely he had heard that attractive laughter before. He stared intently at Miss Hedgeworth. She seemed to sense his scrutiny and briefly glanced over at him. When her gaze met his, he saw that her hazel eyes danced with amusement. She turned away to look again toward the stage.

Lord Satterwaite was certain then that he was not hallucinating. Miss Hedgeworth was indeed the lady of the magnificent horsemanship who had sent aid back for him on that cold snowy evening.

Lord Satterwaite leaned close to Miss Hedgeworth's chair to catch her ear. "Forgive me, Miss Hedgeworth, but have we not met before on a cold narrow road?"

Fredericka turned toward the viscount quickly. She stared at him, then her eyes widened. "Of course!" She smiled warmly. "I had had the oddest feeling that I knew you from somewhere, but I could not place you. I am glad to have the mystery explained. I trust that all worked out well that day?"

"Indeed it did. My valet and I were rescued and transported to the inn in a farmer's cart. It was a mode of transportation quite unlike any I have ever experienced," said Lord Satterwaite. As he had meant for her to, Miss Hedgeworth laughed.

Fredericka's eyes were brimming with amusement. "I am very sure of it, my lord!"

"I did not get an opportunity to do so then, but I wish to convey my admiration to you for your horsemanship. I do not think that I have ever seen a mare take a hedge from a standing jump so beautifully," said Lord Satterwaite.

"Yes, she is a beauty," said Fredericka with instant enthusiasm. "I trained her myself. It was very hard to leave Cricket behind when I came up to London for the Season."

"Did you ride often?" asked Lord Satterwaite sympathetically, watching her face.

"Oh, yes. Not a day went by that I did not throw on my habit and go for a good gallop," said Fredericka. She shook her head, smiling a little. "You can have no notion how much I miss it, my lord."

"Then you must have a mount given over to your use from my father's stables," said Lord Satterwaite.

"I could not possibly impose further on Lord and Lady Chalmers's hospitality," said Fredericka. "They are already going to such lengths upon my behalf."

"Nonsense. I am surprised that my father has not already thought of it, for he used to ride a great deal. His lordship was known as a neck-or-nothing rider," said Lord Satterwaite with a flickering smile.

"That I can well believe, my lord. The earl's strength of personality would allow for nothing else," said Fredericka dryly.

Lord Satterwaite laughed, quickly appreciating her wit. "I perceive that you have cataloged his lordship very well." He leaned over to catch his mother's attention. "Ma'am, I have learned that Miss Hedgeworth is pining for equestrian exercise. Would it be possible to provide a mount for her from my father's stables?"

"Why, of course. I should have thought of it weeks ago. Fredericka, you should have said something! Naturally you are used to riding. I would not deprive you of one of your pleasures," said Lady Chalmers. "I shall leave orders tonight with Moffet to have one of the hacks ordered out for you tomorrow and you may be assured that it will remain at your disposal for whenever you wish."

Fredericka expressed her thanks with a brief but eloquent squeeze of the countess's fingers. "Thank you, dear ma'am. It is what I should enjoy above all things."

Lady Chalmers nodded. "We have a groom who can attend you, of course, but it occurs to me that riding can be quite boring without a companion. I shall discover whom among my acquaintances have sons or daughters of like mind so that you may be assured of company."

"I shall be glad to offer my escort, ma'am," said Lord Satterwaite, with the glint of a smile. "In fact, I appoint myself as Miss

Hedgeworth's companion for tomorrow morning, if she has no objection."

"Of course I do not, but I do not wish to impose upon you, my lord," said Fredericka, not at all certain that she wished to be in the viscount's sole company. She felt an odd constraint at the thought. It was surprising, for in general she felt herself at ease with almost anyone.

Lady Chalmers ignored her guest's interjection. "Wonderful! Now I shall be quite relieved of care when you go out in the morning, Fredericka, for I can trust my son to bring you safely home. He is himself an accomplished rider." Lady Chalmers bestowed a calm smile upon them and returned her attention to the play.

"Do you dislike the notion of riding in my company, Miss Hedgeworth?" asked Lord Satterwaite quietly.

She looked at him quickly and shook her head. "It is not that, no! It is only that I am unused to town ways. You must understand, my lord, that I am in general a very independent lady. At home I ride whenever I please, and most times I do not bother to take a groom with me. Does that shock you, perhaps?"

"Not at all. You forget, I witnessed a very pretty piece of horsemanship by you. I do not think that you are a lady who will be content with a placid hack, nor will you be satisfied with a sedate circuit of the park. With that in mind, I unhesitatingly offer myself as a competitor," said Lord Satterwaite, smiling.

Fredericka's eyes sparkled. "A race, in fact! How I wish I had Cricket with me! Then I should not hesitate. But there is no knowing what sort of mount that Lady Chalmers will think will best suit me, so I must reluctantly put off your challenge until tomorrow when I see what is brought to me."

Lord Satterwaite's eyes narrowed in appreciation. "You are too cautious by half, Miss Hedgeworth! Any gamester would fling his hat over, trusting in fortune to smile upon him."

"Well, that is a rather idiotic thing to do. For myself, I prefer to know precisely what I am getting myself embroiled in," said Fredericka, smiling.

"My uncle would deplore such prudence. He would advise you to take your fences at all speed and not give a thought to consequences until they stare you in the face," said Lord Satterwaite.

"Oh, is your uncle a bruising rider, then?" asked Fredericka.

Lord Satterwaite cracked such a laugh that his mother looked around inquiringly. "Forgive me! I am not laughing at you, Miss Hedgeworth, but at the vision of my uncle Allyn seated on a horse. He is quite fat, you see, and dislikes any form of exertion most excessively. I only referred to him because his fondest entertainment is gaming of all sorts. If he had been privileged to see you on horseback as I have, he would not hesitate to back you whatever mount you were seated upon."

Fredericka felt her cheeks warm. She had received compliments before. She did not understand why Lord Satterwaite's should so affect her, unless it was because he was complimenting something other than her face. It was quite true that she was an accomplished rider. She had always had an affinity for horses. How strange it was that this man, after having seen her only once on horseback and for just a few moments, had intuited that much about her.

Fredericka managed to recover her equilibrium. "I am certain that you exaggerate, my lord. Oh, do look! Isn't that the drollest costume?" With that broad attempt, she was able to turn the viscount's attention from her back to the stage. Glancing toward Lord Satterwaite, Fredericka took note of the grin that edged his mouth and she had the suspicion that he had allowed her to do so.

Lady Chalmers had listened with half an ear to the conversation beside her and she could not have been more pleased. The acquaintance between the viscount and Miss Hedgeworth seemed to be coming along nicely. It was a surprise to discover that the two had previously met in such a fashion, but it certainly had done no harm. Her son's interest was obviously stirred, at least for the moment.

Lady Chalmers hoped that he would continue to find Miss Hedgeworth worthy of interest. It would tie up the Season so neatly if an engagement could be announced between them. Her pledge to Lady Hedgeworth would be fulfilled and her son's inheritance would be secured.

After the play, Lord Satterwaite escorted his mother and Miss Hedgeworth back to Chalmers House. He declined an invitation to come in and bade them good night, lingering only long enough to express his enjoyment of the evening and to assure Miss

Hedgeworth that he would be faithful to their tryst in the morning.

As the ladies ascended the stairs, Lady Chalmers said, "I shall not see you in the morning before you have gone out, so I will tell you now to have a splendid time. Lord Satterwaite is an accomplished rider and I have no doubts that he will take excellent care of you."

"Thank you, my lady. I know that I shall enjoy myself very much," said Fredericka. "Is there a time that you prefer that I return, ma'am?"

"Oh, no. I had planned only to make a few calls and that can be put off. After so unthinkingly excluding you from your usual habit, I have no wish to cut your first ride short, my dear," said Lady Chalmers.

"You are too generous, my lady," said Fredericka, appreciating the countess's thoughtfulness.

Lady Chalmers smiled and, as they reached the head of the stairs, parted from her houseguest with unabated good humor for the night.

Chapter Fifteen

Fredericka wakened early with a sense of anticipation. She wondered at it until she recalled suddenly that she was going to go riding with Lord Satterwaite that morning. She immediately got out of bed, calling for her maid.

A half hour later, Fredericka descended the stairs and crossed the hall to the breakfast room. She was dressed in her riding habit, the long hem of which was caught up over her arm. She did not expect to meet Lady Chalmers so early, for the lady seldom left her bedchamber before noon, preferring to take her breakfast in bed. However, when she entered the breakfast room, she saw that Lord Chalmers was at table.

The earl started to rise upon her entrance, but Fredericka at once begged him not to do so, saying, "Pray do not allow me to interrupt you, my lord. I shall join you directly." She was seated by a footman and indicated her preferences to him from the sideboard.

Lord Chalmers waited until she had finished with the footman and then said, "I see that you are going out riding this morning. It is a fine day for it. I would join you if it were not for this cursed foot of mine. Have you a party or will you be accompanied only by a groom?"

The poached egg and toast that Fredericka had asked for was set down in front of her. She picked up her fork. "Lord Satterwaite has been kind enough to offer his services this morning, my lord."

"Has he, indeed. Well, well." Lord Chalmers looked thoughtful. "I hope that a decent mount was brought round for you, Miss Hedgeworth. If not, you have only to send it back and request another that is more suitable."

"Thank you, my lord. I appreciate your generosity," said Fredericka, touched.

"Nonsense! It is only right that I should provide a guest of mine with a decent mount, especially one who went to the trouble of organizing my library. I do not believe that I should have done half as well with it," said Lord Chalmers. He glanced toward the door. "Unless I much miss my guess, I hear Lord Satterwaite now. He will be shown into the drawing room to await you. You will want to dash upstairs, I suppose."

"Yes, my lord," said Fredericka, smiling, as she rose from the table. "I need to collect my hat and gloves and whip."

"Well, go along then. I shall let his lordship know that you will be down in a few minutes," said Lord Chalmers. "Though you should take my advice and keep him kicking his heels for a while. It will not hurt him in the least to wait upon a young woman's whimsy."

"How shocking of you to make such a suggestion, my lord," said Fredericka, just before she went out of the room. The earl's hearty chuckle followed her and she smiled again. She did like the Earl of Chalmers, despite his lordship's frequent lapses into irascibility.

In the end, she did not remain upstairs for longer than it took to make herself ready. When she entered the drawing room, she found Lord Satterwaite standing at the window. He turned when he heard the door open and smiled at her. Fredericka found that an answering smile was on her lips. "Good morning, my lord. I hope that I have not kept you waiting."

"Not at all." He walked over to meet her and took her hand. "You are in looks this morning, Miss Hedgeworth. Are you quite ready?"

"Yes, of course."

Lord Satterwaite and Fredericka left the drawing room and shortly thereafter emerged from the town house. At the bottom of the front steps was a groom, holding the reins of three horses.

Fredericka knew instantly which horse belonged to the viscount. It was a magnificent black gelding of powerful sloping shoulders and excellent proportions. "A beauty, my lord! It is easily seen that he is made for speed."

"Yes, my Topper has been known to win his share of races,' said Lord Satterwaite, matching steps with her down to the flagway. "And I believe that the chestnut is meant for you, Miss Hedgeworth."

Fredericka ran a critical gaze over the chestnut. She nodded her approval. "He will do, though he in no way compares with your black. I do not believe that I shall take up your challenge today, my lord!"

"I am devastated, ma'am, but scarcely surprised. You had already struck me as knowing something about horseflesh. And you made it quite clear that you do not gamble," said Lord Satterwaite, offering his own linked hands for her to step up into.

Fredericka let him throw her up into the saddle. As she settled herself and gathered the reins, she said, "It is true that I do not gamble against certainties, my lord. However, if I had a mount such as my Cricket under me, I would endeavor to give your Topper a run that he would remember."

"Is that what you call your mare? It is a fitting name, for as I told you I have never seen a horse jump quite like her," said Lord Satterwaite, smiling. He had mounted also and now touched a spur to the gelding's glossy side. "It will not take many minutes to reach the park."

With the mounted groom bringing up the rear, Fredericka and Lord Satterwaite negotiated the early morning traffic. As they turned into the park, Fredericka looked about her with frank curiosity. There were a few carriages already rolling sedately under the large trees and several pedestrians were taking their gentle exercise. A few others had had the same happy notion as she and the viscount and were cantering along the green verge.

"It is a delightful place," said Fredericka. "I should like a good gallop. Will you join me, my lord?"

Lord Satterwaite shook his head. "I am afraid that you cannot indulge your whim, Miss Hedgeworth. A neck-or-nothing gallop in full view of society is simply not done. You would run the risk of being thought rather hoydenish."

Fredericka regarded him with slightly contracted brows. "You are serious, I believe."

"Never more so, Miss Hedgeworth. Believe me, your credit would suffer and it would inevitably reflect upon Lady Chalmers, as well. You would jeopardize your opportunity this Season of setting yourself up as a toast of the town," said Lord Satterwaite.

"How unfortunate, particularly since I have never had a desire to puff myself off as a person of consequence," said Fredericka. She regarded him with a thoughtful expression. "My lord, it occurs to me that, if this is so, then your suggestion to me of a race between us was most ungentlemanly."

Lord Satterwaite laughed. "Yes, if I had meant to subject you to the scrutiny of society. However, I had in mind a private race held so early in the day that there would be none out to see it. Though unusual, such a contest could scarcely cause comment when there would be a lack of witnesses."

"I perceive that you are a gentleman of enterprise," said Fredericka.

The viscount was hailed by name and Lord Satterwaite looked around. He smiled and, as the horseman reached him, stretched over his horse's withers to shake his friend's hand. "Fitz! What are you doing out so early in the day? I thought you meant to make a night of it at Waiter's."

"And so I did," said Mr. Howard-Browne gloomily. Ever polite, he acknowledged the viscount's companion with a slight bow. "You must ask my sister why I am up betweentimes, for I don't know!"

His companion, a young lady in a smart habit of pale blue and a saucy hat, laughed. Miss Howard-Browne turned her vivacious countenance to the viscount. "You must not regard Fitz, my lord. He is wearing that Friday face because he is determined to show how unhappy is his lot! The truth of the matter is that when he stood up with me last night, I badgered and cajoled him into accompanying me this morning and he could not withstand my entreaties. So he hopes to give me such a disgust of his melancholy company that I shall not importune him in the future."

"Here now, that isn't so," objected Mr. Howard-Browne. "I am always happy to be of service. Ask anyone."

Miss Howard-Browne rolled her eyes. "Oh, yes! That is why Mama and I must bullock you into giving us escort to Almack's or to stand up with the plainest girl in the room at our own affairs!"

"Well, that is dashed dull work," declared Mr. Howard-Browne. "You cannot expect a fellow to actually like it."

"You see, my lord! And riding with me this morning falls under the same ignoble heading, according to my brother," said Miss Howard-Browne.

Lord Satterwaite replied with suitable gravity. "Indeed I do, Miss Howard-Browne. Fitz is too irresponsible by half. You must continue in your endeavors to bring him to a full consciousness of what is owed to his duty."

"Just whose friend are you, Sebastion?" demanded Mr. Howard-Browne. "I am of half a mind to call you to account for such out-and-out betrayal."

Lord Satterwaite laughed. "No, no, you shall not pick a quarrel with me, Fitz. Allow me to make known to you Miss Fredericka Hedgeworth. Miss Hedgeworth, these two squabblers are my good friends, the Honorable Mr. Fitzgerald Howard-Browne, and his delightful sister, the Honorable Miss Amelia Howard-Browne. Miss Hedgeworth is lately come to London and will be sponsored by my mother, Lady Chalmers."

Fredericka had listened to the lively exchange with a great deal of amusement and she was quite willing to become acquainted with the engaging Howard-Brownes. She nodded and expressed her pleasure at the introduction.

"Oh! I am so happy to make your acquaintance," said Miss Howard-Browne with a friendly smile. "Do, pray, draw a little ahead with me so that we may talk comfortably. It is so difficult to try to converse across others, is it not?"

"Yes, it is," said Fredericka, touching spur to her mount.

When the ladies had drawn a few lengths ahead of their escorts, Miss Howard-Browne glanced at Fredericka. There was a shade of curiosity in her eyes. "Is Lady Chalmers your godmother, then?"

"Unfortunately, no, since I am certain that no one could have been kinder to me," said Fredericka. "However, the countess was a bosom-bow of my mother's and that is how it came about that her ladyship extended her invitation for the Season. I never had any expectation of coming to London, so you may imagine my astonishment."

"I am certain of it! Why, it must have taken your breath away.

You must wonder whether you are daydreaming such good fortune," said Miss Howard-Browne.

Fredericka laughed, a trifle ruefully. "Quite true."

Miss Howard-Browne was quick to hear the reserve in her tone. "You are not completely delighted with the opportunity?"

Fredericka was slightly embarrassed to have been so transparent. She shook her head and smiled at her friendly companion. "It was so difficult to leave my home, you see. I was used to seeing to the household and the details of the estate and oh, all sorts of things. Now of a sudden I am embarking upon a London Season and expected to make the most of my opportunities. It all seems very strange to me yet, but no doubt I shall become accustomed."

Miss Howard-Browne eyed her with a degree of compassion. "Yes, I think I do understand. No doubt you have sisters?"

"Yes, two younger than myself. Also two brothers," said Fredericka. "I am quite attached to all of them, but Jack, who is the one closest in age to me, is my dearest friend."

Miss Howard-Browne nodded. "Of course. I suppose the estate is hideously mortgaged and you are to repair the family fortunes by making a spectacular marriage."

Fredericka burst out laughing. "Oh, no! Is that what my situation sounds like? Truly it is not so. Luting is not mortgaged at all and Jack is beginning to take an interest in managing his affairs at last. And while it is true that Mama would like to see me credibly established, it is as much for my own sake as for my sisters. I shall be de trop at Luting once Jack marries, you see, for I am a managing sort of female and it would not suit me at all to live under the authority of a sister-in-law."

"Ah! I do feel for you, indeed. It is very uncomfortable to think of being ousted from one's former position." Miss Howard-Browne bestowed a particularly warm smile upon her. "But you shall no doubt do wonderfully well this Season. Lady Chalmers will see to that! I shall have Mama send you an invitation to the musical soiree that we are holding next week. You will come, won't you?"

Fredericka, torn between amusement and exasperation that she had been unable to disabuse Miss Howard-Browne's mind of its mistaken notion that she was some sort of sacrifice on the altar o— family expediency, said that she was delighted by the invitation.

"I am beginning to recognize any number of personages since Lady Chalmers has been so obliging as to take me about with her. However, it will be particularly nice to mingle with new-made friends," she said.

"Well said, Fredericka! I may call you that, mayn't I?" asked Miss Howard-Browne. "And you must address me as Amelia."

"Yes, I should like that," said Fredericka.

Miss Howard-Browne introduced a new topic and the remainder of the ride passed pleasantly in exploring one another's tastes in everything from gloves to the best hunting country in England.

It had not gone unnoticed by Lord Satterwaite and Mr. Howard-Browne that the ladies appeared to be getting along famously. Lord Satterwaite remarked that he was glad that Miss Hedgeworth was forming a friendship with Miss Howard-Browne. "She will no doubt be relieved to know at least one younger lady at the first functions she attends," he said.

"Miss Hedgeworth seems to be a friendly sort," agreed Mr. Howard-Browne. "I was surprised to hear, though, that Lady Chalmers was shepherding her for the Season. I thought the earl was too—er—low-spirited to mingle in company."

"My sire is not low-spirited in the least. I had the felicity of greeting the earl this morning when I called at Chalmers House for Miss Hedgeworth. He had the audacity to ask me when he could expect to see a notice in the *Gazette* of my approaching nuptials," said Lord Satterwaite.

Mr. Howard-Browne shook his head in disapproval. "Very bad of his lordship to tax you with it like that. I am surprised that you are not in a rare pelter over it."

Lord Satterwaite shrugged. "No, why should I be? It is only what I expected, after all. I do not mean to allow his lordship's barbs to get under my skin again. On the contrary, I shall treat the earl's pronouncements upon my character with utmost respect. I shall also endeavor to stay out of his vicinity as much as I am able, despite my mother's hope that I shall take a hand in bringing Miss Hedgeworth into fashion."

Mr. Howard-Browne looked at him with faint alarm. "My dear fellow, don't do it. Doing one's duty is all well and good, but not when it involves an unattached female who has your mother's nod."

"Nonsense! What could possibly befall me in squiring Miss Hedgeworth now and then?"

"You may find yourself riveted to Miss Hedgeworth," said Mr. Howard-Browne solemnly.

At the viscount's shout of laughter he shook his head. "You don't know how these things work, Sebastion. I've watched my mother launch two of my sisters into brilliant marriages in the slyest way imaginable. She'll do the same with Amelia, give you my word. Lady Chalmers means to do the same with you, except that she had to go about it in a roundabout way. Stands to reason that her ladyship don't want to see you come to grief with the earl. She'll make a push to put Miss Hedgeworth in your way."

"Now there you are out, Fitz. My mother expressly bade me to look elsewhere for a bride, for Miss Hedgeworth is not used to our sophisticated ways and she could take a pet at my extravagances," said Lord Satterwaite.

Mr. Howard-Browne was aghast. "Never say so! Well, if that don't beat all. It's a wonder that you are able to bear up under such insult."

Lord Satterwaite smiled and shrugged. "I find it a dead bore to talk about. Instead, tell me what you think of the chances of that gelding of Connolly's beating out Sir Gregory's Choice Lady."

Mr. Howard-Browne unhesitatingly stigmatized Mr. Connolly's offering as a short-backed nag, and by quick degrees the conversation plunged into sporting waters. When the ladies dropped back to rejoin them, Miss Howard-Browne at once cried, "What, are you talking horrid sports? Here Fredericka and I have had a delightful cose on all manner of things and you have no doubt talked all this time about your silly bets and horses and gaming!"

"Naturally you would not understand the importance of such things," said Mr. Howard-Browne in a condescending manner.

"Well, I shall not argue the truth of that," retorted Miss Howard-Browne, not at all abashed by her brother's loftiness.

Fredericka gave a throaty chuckle. "Indeed! But allow me to divert the conversation for a bit, I pray you! As I have just been telling Amelia, Mr. Howard-Browne, I have truly enjoyed meeting you both. However, and I know that Lord Satterwaite will agree, it is coming close to time for me to wait on Lady Chalmers and so I must take my leave of you."

Mr. Howard-Browne bowed gracefully from the saddle. "I trust that we shall meet again, Miss Hedgeworth."

"Oh, there is to be no doubt about that, for Fredericka is to come to our musical soiree next week. You must come, too, my lord," said Miss Howard-Browne.

Lord Satterwaite and Mr. Howard-Browne exchanged a glance of mutual repugnance. Very politely, Lord Satterwaite said, "I shall naturally look forward to it, Miss Howard-Browne. I only trust that I do not have a conflicting engagement."

The party divided and, after exchanging mutual assurances of forming other outings on horseback, went their separate ways. Lord Satterwaite returned Miss Hedgeworth, with the groom, to Chalmers House and left her after charging her with civil messages to his parents.

Chapter Sixteen

Lady Chalmers could not think or talk of anything else but Fredericka's come-out ball and supper. She ordered massive preparations to be made and Chalmers House took on the air of a frenzied beehive.

Champagne was laid in; the dinner menu was carefully chosen; a promise was extracted from the confectioner to provide tempting treats; an orchestra, consisting of a pianoforte, a trumpet, a cello, and a violin, was engaged. The silver was polished; the ballroom and adjoining parlor were made bare of unnecessary furniture and card tables were purchased to be put into the parlor. The carpet was rolled up out of the ballroom and the floor was scrubbed and buffed until it gleamed.

The servants were worn out with rushing here and there, fetching and carrying, cleaning and polishing; but they had caught the excitement. It had been many years since Chalmers House had seen such a bustle, and it quite reminded the older servants of better days, before the earl had been struck down with the gout, when scarcely a fortnight had passed without some gala event taking place under the roof of the town house.

Fredericka was not unaffected. Between fittings for her ball gown, shopping for various articles that Lady Chalmers stipulated as necessary for a young lady entering into her first Season, paying morning calls with Lady Chalmers, attending a sprinkling of evening engagements such as the Howard-Browne musical soiree, and frequent riding assignations with Miss Howard-Browne (and several other young ladies and gentlemen of that damsel's wide acquaintance), Fredericka scarcely had a private moment for reflection. She was therefore astonished when the date of the gala event suddenly burst upon them.

An awning was stretched out from the front door down to the curb. The authorities had been notified days before that there would need to be some monitoring of traffic that evening and were already in evidence. Huge sprays of flowers were delivered and carefully placed in the ballroom and elsewhere. Lady Chalmers's ball gown had been delivered that morning and Lord Chalmers, though he had frowned at the necessity of ordering a new coat made, was pleased with his purchase when his valet eased him into it. Lady Chalmers's subsequent admiring compliment was all it took to set him in a benevolent mood.

The town house was redolent of the scents of fresh beeswax and flowers. The staff of Chalmers House stood ready. Lady Chalmers anxiously ticked off on her fingers every item that she could think of and it appeared that all was in readiness at last. All that was now lacking were their guests.

Lady Chalmers had wondered right up to the last minute whether Lord Chalmers was going to be able to officiate as host. But after she had seen him in his new coat, looking quite as handsome as she had known he would when she had gently suggested that he consult his tailor, she was able to relax. At a quarter to eight, she and the earl, with Fredericka alongside, took their places in a receiving line at the top of the stairs.

Fredericka's come-out was a resounding success. Nothing could have been more wonderful than to greet the number of personages that trod up the stairs. Indeed, there were so many guests in attendance that presently Lady Chalmers had the gratification of hearing the function described as a horrible squeeze. There was no higher accolade a hostess could ever receive.

An hour after opening the doors, Lady Chalmers released Fredericka from her side so that she could mingle with the guests. Lord Chalmers had also drifted away with friends some minutes before, and so it was only Lady Chalmers who still stood at the head of the stairs when Lord Satterwaite arrived.

Lady Chalmers greeted her son warmly and gave her gloved hand to him. "I appreciate your putting in an appearance, my dear."

Lord Satterwaite bent to kiss the countess's cheek. When he straightened, he glanced at the assembly with a comprehensive lifting of his brows. "You have outdone yourself, Mama."

Lady Chalmers smiled, her expression one of immense satisfaction. "It is rather a triumph. I have already been told by Sally Jersey that she will sponsor Miss Hedgeworth to Almack's, and Mrs. Drummond has unbent enough to compliment me on Miss Hedgeworth's pretty manners. And, Sebastion, I was never more astonished in my life. Your uncle has come tonight. Of course I sent a card to him, but in general he does not attend these sort of functions and so I was perfectly speechless when he wheezed up to me and professed himself glad to have been invited. As though I would ever slight him!"

"A triumph indeed," said Lord Satterwaite. He looked at his mother in a quizzing way. "Though I must admit that I am more impressed by your ability to draw my uncle here than by all the rest."

Lady Chalmers laughed. "You are being horrid. Go away now, for I shall not be teased."

Lord Satterwaite was perfectly willing to obey this injunction and he sauntered into the ballroom. He was immediately hailed by various acquaintances. He paused to make easy conversation, before continuing his leisurely progress through the crowd. Coming upon the Earl of Chalmers, he exchanged polite civilities that, if not particularly warm, were not acrimonious. He soon excused himself to his father and continued in quest of his quarry.

The viscount found Miss Hedgeworth surrounded by admirers. She had already made a number of friends among ladies and gentlemen alike, so it was perhaps not entirely surprising that she was acquiring a court. Nevertheless, Lord Satterwaite felt a vague astonishment that a lady who had never been up to London before was enjoying the attentions of several gentlemen.

Perhaps the reason for this extraordinary sight lay in the fact that Miss Hedgeworth was in exemplary looks. Her auburn hair, cropped short in the fashionable style, glinted fiery sparks in the blaze of candles and her neat figure was set off by a gown of pale gold silk overlaid by a spider gauze. There was a good deal of vibrancy in her expression as she fielded another outrageous compliment. "No, no, my dear sir! You must be speaking of someone else, for I know too well that I am not such a paragon," she said, giving her throaty chuckle.

Lord Satterwaite stood to one side for a moment, watching her. It was odd. He did not consider Miss Hedgeworth to be a beauty in the classic sense, for her height and her strong coloring were not in the admired mode. However, that Miss Hedgeworth had appeal there could be little doubt. He thought it due as much to a trick of expression as it was to the lovely cast of her features. The amusement that was never far from her expressive hazel eyes or her mobile mouth was what was captivating.

The orchestra was beginning to strike up for a country dance. Lord Satterwaite made his way through the loosely circled gentlemen until he reached Miss Hedgeworth's side. He smiled, saying, "Your most obedient, Miss Hedgeworth."

Fredericka greeted the viscount like an old welcome friend, at once extending her elegantly gloved hand to him. "Lord Satterwaite! I am glad that you have come."

He smiled down at her. "As am I, Miss Hedgeworth." When she would have withdrawn her hand, he retained it lightly clasped in his. "I have come to rescue you from this pack of exquisites. May I have the honor of this dance from you, ma'am?"

"No, Satterwaite, it is too much, so it is! Here we have all been vying for the opportunity to lead out Miss Hedgeworth and you walk up as cool as you please and expect her to go off with you," said Sir Thomas. There were other good-natured outcries at the viscount's attempt at piracy and several other claims were put forward.

Fredericka's face was alight with laughter. "I am sorry, gentlemen, but I shall not be wrangled over like an old bone. My lord Satterwaite, I shall be pleased to dance with you."

Lord Satterwaite bore her off toward the dance floor, leaving behind his chagrined challengers. "That was very prettily done, Miss Hedgeworth. They shall now all wish to carve me up into little pieces for calling down your rebuke upon their heads."

Fredericka chuckled. She glanced up at him, her eyes brimful of amusement. "No, is that what I have done? If so, I do apologize, my lord. I never meant to put your very life into jeopardy!"

"I shall attempt to survive, ma'am," said Lord Satterwaite.

Fredericka laughed again. She thought that she had never enjoyed a gathering more. She was used to the small assemblies in her own county, and naturally as an acknowledged beauty she had

had her share of admirers, but it had come as something of a shock to discover that she could command such admiration in London. She had assumed that because she was an unknown and had little portion that she would not cause much stir. However, she had not taken into account that the Countess of Chalmers's august sponsorship counted for something and so had Lady Chalmers's untiring efforts on her behalf. Those factors, added to her own claim to beauty and her unaffected manners, were in a fair way to catapulting her into popularity.

As Lord Satterwaite led her to her place in the set that was forming, Fredericka touched on her thoughts. "I am astonished and amazed at my reception, my lord. I had never considered that so many might attend my come-out, nor that I could lay claim to so many preposterous compliments in the first hour!"

Lord Satterwaite glanced down at her, his brows rising. "Are you not accustomed to being mobbed, Miss Hedgeworth? I own, I shall think that your county is inhabited by a bunch of slowtops if they have not yet recognized your worth."

Fredericka colored slightly even as she smiled up to him. Deep amusement lit her eyes. "You flatter me, my lord! Indeed, I have not ever been the recipient of such extravagant phrases as I have already heard tonight."

"You shall grow accustomed before the Season is out, Miss Hedgeworth."

"Shall I? But how horrid if I should become so puffed up in my own esteem that I expect to receive those sorts of compliments," said Fredericka. She shook her head. "No, my lord. I prefer to believe that I shall simply enjoy the flattery for what it is."

"And what is that, Miss Hedgeworth?" asked Lord Satterwaite, mildly curious.

"Oh, flummery and nonsense," said Fredericka with a quick smile.

The movement of the vigorous country dance separated them and it was no longer possible to carry on a conversation except in disjointed sentences. Lord Satterwaite was not so improvident as to even make the attempt. When the set was over, however, he did not immediately escort Miss Hedgeworth back to her chair. She had captured his interest enough that he did not mind spending a moment or two longer in her company.

Noticing that she was becomingly flushed from the exercise, he said, "Allow me to take you over for a lemon ice."

"Thank you, my lord. It is already rather warm, is it not?" said Fredericka, laying her fingers lightly on his lordship's elbow. As the viscount led her toward the far end of the room, where the refreshments had been set up, Fredericka looked about her. She had never seen such a crowd of fashionables. Nor so many smarts, she thought on a smothered laugh, eyeing a passing gentleman whose ridiculously high shirtpoints and extravagant waistcoat proclaimed him to be one of the dandy set.

Something of her amusement must have escaped, for Lord Satterwaite instantly asked, "What do you find so diverting, Miss Hedgeworth?"

Fredericka bit her lip, glancing up into the viscount's face. She wondered if she dared to bare all of her thoughts, but there was a genuine interest in his gaze that encouraged her. "I was thinking just now how very fashionable some of these gentlemen are. I have never seen such magnificence of dress or observed such exquisite manners."

"You are obviously referring to our dandies." Lord Satterwaite glanced around and a smile touched his lips. "Fribbles and fops is what you mean."

"I never said anything so uncivil," said Fredericka.

"Nevertheless, it is what you meant," said Lord Satterwaite, his narrowed eyes gleaming with laughter. "For shame, Miss Hedgeworth. You should be standing in all admiration and awe."

"I beg pardon," said Fredericka meekly. She accepted the lemon ice that he offered to her.

"Here comes one of those fribbles now," said Lord Satterwaite. "How are you this evening, Fitz?"

"I would be in far better form if I knew that you were not going about maligning me," retorted Mr. Howard-Browne. "Your servant, Miss Hedgeworth. I have come to solicit a dance from you later this evening."

"Certainly, Mr. Howard-Browne. I would be happy to be partnered by you," said Fredericka.

"You are making a mistake, Miss Hedgeworth. Though I admit

that he has a pretty toe, Howard-Browne has not the least sense of timing. He will have you skipping and plodding by turns across the floor," said Lord Satterwaite.

"You must not believe a word that his lordship has uttered, Miss Hedgeworth. I assure you that I am a far better dancer than he has given you to suppose," said Mr. Howard-Browne.

"I already know it, Mr. Howard-Browne. One cannot possess such charming manners and so elegant an air without having acquired an equal brilliance upon the dance floor," said Fredericka, twinkling at the gentleman.

"You are a lady of discernment and taste," declared Mr. Howard-Browne.

"It seems that I have been completely cut out," said Lord Satterwaite. He noticed that he was being waved at and he suddenly grinned. "It appears that my uncle wishes our attention. May I take you over to him, Miss Hedgeworth?"

"Of course. I believe that I met Mr. Allyn during the receiving line, but I did not have an opportunity to exchange more than a word or two with him," said Fredericka, setting down her ice. She gave her hand into the viscount's care and allowed him to lead her over to a couch set against the wall, where Mr. Allyn had ensconced himself. Mr. Howard-Browne sauntered alongside them.

"Well, nevy! I thought I might see you here tonight. And Howard-Browne! Good to see you, my boy. I have a tip for you both if you care to have it, but I shall not bruit it about in this atmosphere. You may come by my lodgings on the morrow whenever it should suit you." Having handily disposed of the gentlemen, Mr. Allyn turned his smiling countenance to the lady who was on the viscount's arm. "Miss Hedgeworth, my compliments. You are truly one of the most elegant young misses that has yet to grace the Season."

"Thank you, Mr. Allyn. I know that is the height of compliment, coming as it does from you," said Fredericka, not failing to misread Mr. Howard-Browne's boggled expression.

Mr. Allyn gave vent to a rolling rumble of amusement. "Aye, you have your wits well about you! I am not one to dish out pretty phrases. I leave that to Satterwaite and the other youngsters. You shall do, Miss Hedgeworth, you shall do." His gaze moved past the trio and he flapped his hand in easy dismissal. "Here comes my friend Topper. He'll want to tell me all the racing news. Dashed if I know how he finds it out so quick. By the by, nevy, I don't think that I ever told you. Topper was flattered that you named that gelding of yours after him."

"What else could I do, sir, when it was he who put me on to him?" said Lord Satterwaite.

Mr. Allyn laughed again. He made a lazy introduction of his friend to Miss Hedgeworth and then recommended that his nephew take her off to the dance floor. "For like every young lady, Miss Hedgeworth will want to dance the night away. I never could understand what anyone saw in capering about, but there is no accounting for tastes."

Lord Satterwaite gracefully extracted himself and Miss Hedgeworth from his uncle's vicinity, but Mr. Howard-Browne did not go with them. Having heard mention of a new colt, he lingered behind with the two older gentlemen to hear more of what promised to be a most interesting conversation.

"That was very much in the grand manner," remarked Fredericka.

"Yes, do you mind it?" asked Lord Satterwaite, glancing down at her. "I am extremely fond of the old gentleman but I am not unaware of his eccentricity."

Fredericka shook her head. "No, I found Mr. Allyn to be very droll and good-natured, too. I liked him very much."

Lord Satterwaite appreciated Miss Hedgeworth's kind statements. Not many ladies of his acquaintance would have been so forebearing. He started to speak, but was prevented by a gentleman coming up and accosting them. Sir Thomas reminded Miss Hedgeworth that it was his dance and proudly bore her off to the dance floor.

Fredericka was thereafter occupied in the lively diversion that Mr. Allyn had spoken of so slightingly and she enjoyed herself very much.

Watching as Miss Hedgeworth went down the floor with yet another gentleman, Lady Chalmers was quite pleased. She had hoped that her protégée would take and apparently Miss Hedgeworth had. The young lady had not lacked for a partner all evening.

Lord Chalmers had also observed his young guest's progress

and it pleased him, making him feel that the sacrifice he had made that evening had been well worth the effort. He had borne up admirably in his capacity of host. Though his gouty foot bothered him, and it was observed by many that he leaned heavily on a cane, it was generally agreed that the earl had acquitted himself well over the course of the evening. The scope of his scathing tongue was well-known and it was a marvel to his intimates that his lordship still remained civil and polite.

Lady Chalmers had kept a close eye upon her lord, casting an occasional thoughtful glance in his direction. Satisfied that Miss Hedgeworth was well-occupied, she leisurely made her way to the earl's side and put forth a solicitous inquiry. Lord Chalmers replied testily, "I am well able to stand the business."

"Quite. I merely wondered whether you wished to discreetly retire to the cardroom or to your library, perhaps with Sir Arthur and Lord Toydon," said Lady Chalmers. "For I know well that you do not care for this sort of thing near as much as I and would infinitely prefer instead to be with your particular cronies."

The earl was tempted. It would be pleasant to retreat to his own quiet bastion with two old friends. After the merest moment of hesitation, however, he shook his head. "I am not yet teetering at the grave's edge, my lady. I know where my duty lies and what is due to our guest, Miss Hedgeworth. I shall not short my responsibility to either."

Lady Chalmers nodded. "Of course, dear Edward. I should have known better than to press you so unhandsomely. You shall do just as you think best."

Lord Chalmers glanced around in critical approval. "As you have, my dear. It shall be a memorable evening for you, I suspect."

"Oh, Edward! It is going well, isn't it?" asked Lady Chalmers, pleased.

"I have found the ball to be quite enjoyable," said Lord Chalmers. His gaze fell on a particular guest, and he frowned. "With the exception of your inclusion of Lucius Everard."

Lady Chalmers grimaced. "Indeed, I did not wish to include him. But he is, after all, one of the family. I could not very well ignore his claims upon our hospitality."

"More's the pity," said the earl shortly. "Man-milliner. Watch him around Miss Hedgeworth. I do not care to see her caught up in his oily charms."

"No, indeed, my dear!" Lady Chalmers had also seen Mr. Everard's approach toward Miss Hedgeworth and she hastily left the earl.

Chapter Seventeen

B ut before the Countess of Chalmers could reach her, Fredericka had already accepted a dance with Mr. Everard. She
speedily came to regret her acceptance. It was not a lack of skill
on Mr. Everard's part that caused her to wish that the set would
be quickly over. In fact, there was nothing that she could actually
point to, other than that the gentleman made her vaguely uncomfortable. Mr. Everard's smile was very white, but it did not quite
reach his eyes. Instead, his glance was a bit bold. And perhaps his
handclasp was a little too firm.

Altogether, Fredericka was not unhappy when the set ended
and Mr. Everard returned her to her chair. Lady Chalmers was
standing beside the chair, a smile fixed firmly upon her face. "Lucius. I trust that you are enjoying yourself this evening?"

Mr. Everard said gently, "Indeed, Aunt. I have nothing of
which to complain in either the entertainment or your lovely
charge. Miss Hedgeworth, I hope to further my acquaintance with
you." He bowed to the ladies and sauntered off.

Lady Chalmers turned to Miss Hedgeworth. "Fredericka, I
most earnestly beg of you not to admit Mr. Everard into your circle of intimates. While it is true that he is my nephew, I do not in
general introduce him to young ladies of my acquaintance. You
see, his reputation is such that—"

"You need say no more, my lady. I have already taken Mr.
Everard's measure, I assure you. He is what is commonly known
as a wolf and he no doubt delights in preying on the young and
inexperienced. But I cut my eyeteeth long ago and I shan't be
taken in by his charming manners," said Fredericka.

Lady Chalmers looked at her in surprise and relief. "You relieve my mind considerably, my dear! I can see that I need have
no anxiety for you at all."

Fredericka laughed. "I wish it was so, my lady! I have just a quarter hour past refused an impassioned offer from a youth who was no older than my own brother!"

"That will be young Alterwrop," said Lady Chalmers. "The silly boy tumbles into love and out again constantly with the most inappropriate females. He is the absolute despair of his poor mother. Last month it was his sister's governess. Before that it was Sally Jersey. She was put into absolute whoops, of course, to be presented with a billet of poems."

"I am to have a sonnet written to my eyes," said Fredericka demurely.

Lady Chalmers sighed. "We shall have him hanging about the drawing room then, I daresay. But hopefully his violence of passion shall not last more than a fortnight or two."

"You dismay me, ma'am. Surely all of my suitors shall not be so fickle," said Fredericka humorously.

Lady Chalmers chuckled. "Not all of them, my dear. I entertain no doubts whatsoever that you shall garner quite a respectable number of offers. You shall be the best judge of what suits you, of course." Since Mr. Howard-Browne came up at that moment to solicit Miss Hedgeworth's hand, she said no more. Instead, she nodded her approval and moved away, never realizing that her assured words had given Fredericka considerable food for reflection.

Fredericka made a determined effort to set aside her somber thoughts for a more appropriate time and she succeeded so well that she was able to enjoy the next hour. She had a comfortable cose with Miss Howard-Browne, that young lady declaring that she was quite green with envy at the overwhelming success of Fredericka's come-out, and she renewed her acquaintance with one of Lady Chalmers's closest confidantes, Madame Potterly.

Madame Potterley did not often attend fashionable squeezes, having the frail health of the semi-invalid. However, she had made the effort to attend Miss Hedgeworth's come-out for her dear friend's sake and Lady Chalmers had relayed to Fredericka how touched she had been. "For in general, you know, Margaret prefers to entertain through her own select parties," said Lady Chalmers. "It is quite a caveat for me to have her in attendance tonight."

So Fredericka had spent quite twenty minutes chatting with Madame Potterley. She had done so in such a friendly way that later, as Madame Potterley took leave of her hostess, she pronounced Miss Hedgeworth to be very obliging and quite the most engaging miss of her acquaintance.

"I shall be glad to offer whatever assistance is in my power to make her Season a success, dear Sarah," she said, just before a footman gently assisted her from the ballroom.

Lady Chalmers thought that the evening could not be crowned with anything better than this tribute, but she found that she was wrong. She had the felicity of seeing her son escort Miss Hedgeworth into supper. Really, things were coming along quite nicely, she thought.

However, if her ladyship had been able to overhear the conversation between Lord Satterwaite and Miss Hedgeworth, she might not have been so complacent.

Lord Satterwaite had virtually snatched Miss Hedgeworth from under the nose of his cousin, Mr. Everard. That gentleman had not been particularly pleased. It galled him to be outjockeyed by anyone, but especially by his cousin. Lord Satterwaite had already taken out of his hands a prime team of cattle. Now, it seemed, the viscount was establishing an interest in Miss Hedgeworth.

Mr. Everard was not interested in Miss Hedgeworth as anything other than a new flirt. Her beauty was not what moved him to try his luck with her, but the fact that she was launched from under the wings of his aunt, the Countess of Chalmers. It amused Mr. Everard to cause agitation to his august relations, for he bitterly resented their respected position in the world and their disdain toward him.

He had already experienced the jealous watch that Lady Chalmers placed over Miss Hedgeworth. It had both annoyed and amused him that her ladyship should be so obviously disapproving when he had led Miss Hedgeworth onto the dance floor. And so he had conceived the happy notion of importuning Miss Hedgeworth to go in to supper with him.

Miss Hedgeworth had hesitated, but she had been on the point of agreeing when Lord Satterwaite had seemingly materialized out of nowhere. "Pray excuse me for interrupting, Lucius. Miss

Hedgeworth, are you ready to go in to supper?" he had asked, with the glint of a smile.

Fredericka had been glad to see the viscount. She had conceived a faint dislike for Mr. Everard's too ready address and bold glances. She naturally preferred to have Lord Satterwaite as her partner and at once followed his lordship's lead. "Of course, my lord. I am sorry, Mr. Everard, but his lordship's claim does take precedence."

Mr. Everard showed his gleaming teeth. He threw an unreadable glance at his noble cousin. "Of course, Miss Hedgeworth. It is understood," he said smoothly, and stepped aside.

Lord Satterwaite walked off with Miss Hedgeworth gracing his arm. When they were out of earshot of his cousin, he said, "Allow me to drop a word of advice in your ear, Miss Hedgeworth. My cousin is a rather unsavory character. You would do well to keep him at a distance."

"Yes, I am aware of it, my lord. Thank you for your timely intervention," said Fredericka, bestowing a smile and a nod on another couple.

Lord Satterwaite mistook her cool reply as lack of discernment. Knowing well that Miss Hedgeworth's behavior must inevitably rebound to his mother's credit or discredit, he attempted to bring his companion to a proper comprehension. "I do not think that you perfectly understand, Miss Hedgeworth. I am warning you against my cousin. You need only grant him common courtesy when you meet in company. There will be no comment made over that."

Fredericka looked up at him, rather surprised. "My lord, I assure you that I am perfectly able to judge men of Mr. Everard's stamp. I appreciate your concern, but truly there is no need for it. Indeed, Lady Chalmers and I have already discussed this very matter."

"And still you were about to go in to supper with the fellow? That was not wise, Miss Hedgeworth, nor respectful of my mother's wishes," said Lord Satterwaite.

Fredericka stared at him, her brows slightly drawn. "Lord Satterwaite, I have no intention of going against her ladyship's wishes in this or in anything else. I found myself in an unanticipated circumstance, from which you very handsomely rescued me. However, I do not believe that has given you the right to censor my conduct."

Lord Satterwaite glanced down swiftly. There was quiet anger in her gaze. Stiffly, he said, "I beg your pardon. You are quite right. I have no right nor duty toward you whatsoever."

Fredericka nodded, and they passed into the supper room. Lord Satterwaite seated her with friends and made certain that she was served a plate of choice offerings. His duty performed to a nicety, he did not linger but excused himself and sauntered away to speak to a convivial group of friends. From there he left the supper room, and Fredericka did not see him the remainder of the evening.

Fredericka regretted that she and Lord Satterwaite had come to a slight disagreement, but it was not, after all, of any great moment. Though she naturally noticed that his lordship had left the ballroom, she scarcely felt the loss of the viscount's presence. There were several other gentlemen who were willing to command her attention and she spared hardly a thought more on Lord Satterwaite.

The come-out ball at last came to a close. When all of the guests had been seen out, Lady Chalmers and Fredericka were free to retire.

Lord Chalmers had already preceded them upstairs, leaning heavily upon his cane and supported at his other side by his solicitous valet. He had been heard to complain loudly that all of this dissipation was ridiculous in the extreme. "I am glad that I haven't a daughter. It is all nonsense. Not that it wasn't a pleasant evening and the attendance most gratifying. However, I would have been surprised if the company had been thin, very surprised indeed! But pray do not expect me to officiate at another such gathering, for I tell you that I shan't do it!"

Lady Chalmers had replied in a soothing way and sent him on his way, slightly mollified but still grumbling. When she turned back to Fredericka, she smiled and said, "His foot is paining him, poor man. I was afraid that it might prove so if he stood up all the night. But his lordship is very stubborn and he would not sit down with his particular cronies when I suggested it to him."

"I hope that the earl will feel better in the morning, ma'am,' said Fredericka.

Lady Chalmers spoke a few quiet words to the butler, instructing him to finish locking up and to snuff out the candles. "The rest may be left until the morrow, Moffet." Then she turned back to Fredericka and chuckled. "My dear, it is already morning. It is all of three o'clock! I daresay that you may not rise quite so early as you are in the habit of doing."

"No, indeed!" Fredericka smothered a yawn and apologized.

"Never mind, my dear. Let us go up to bed. I am sure that it has been a most entertaining evening, but I for one am heartily glad that it is at last over!"

Fredericka's maid was waiting up for her and helped her to undress. Scarcely had her nightshift been thrown over her head before Fredericka tumbled into bed. She was asleep almost at once.

Chapter Eighteen

The days after Fredericka's come-out were a whirlwind of activity in the company of the Countess of Chalmers. Her ladyship appeared determined to make Fredericka known to everyone of her acquaintance. Her strategy proved effective, for Lady Chalmers had the satisfaction of being able to announce to her husband and Fredericka that their visits had resulted in such a number of invitations that she had had to put her secretary to work in scheduling the various amusements into her social calendar. Already nearly every evening was claimed, and some by more than one function.

"It is really quite a nice start to the Season," said Lady Chalmers contentedly. She snipped off her embroidery thread and chose a new color. "We will be obliged to go out every evening. There will be balls and routs and musical soirees. And of course the theater and opera, too."

The earl agreed, somewhat morosely. His gout still troubled him and he could not view any such round of diversions with anything but a jaundiced eye. "I suppose that we shall be having dinners and parties and such here as well?"

"But of course, my dear," said Lady Chalmers serenely. "We are obliged to return the hospitality of our friends."

"I thought as much," muttered Lord Chalmers, frowning heavily.

Fredericka looked up from her embroidery, sensitive to the earl's fretfulness. Several weeks earlier she had offered to read aloud when Lord Chalmers had seemed particularly out of sorts and it had answered very well. Since then she had done the same many times. "My lord, would you like me to read to you for an hour?"

Lord Chalmers nodded, his expression at once lightening a little. "Pray do so, Miss Hedgeworth. You will find the newspaper folded there on the occasional table." His lordship settled more comfortably in his chair in anticipation. He had found that it was enjoyable to listen to Fredericka's soothing voice, whether she was reading the day's newspapers or a few chapters from the Bible of an evening. It was a pity that the young lady's days would become so taken up with frivolous pursuits, he thought, for he would sorely miss these quiet times.

Fredericka at once set aside her embroidery and rose to cross the drawing room in order to retrieve the newspaper. Lady Chalmers shook her head and leaned over to whisper, "You have become quite spoiled, Edward! Never did I imagine that you would put our young guest to such dull work."

"She enjoys it as much as I," said Lord Chalmers defensively. "Miss Hedgeworth understands such solemn things as the forming up of Liverpool's Ministry and 'Change."

"Never tell me that she is a bluestocking," said Lady Chalmers, rather taken aback.

"No such thing!" said Lord Chalmers testily. "Miss Hedgeworth is simply shrewd and knowing. She has managed her brother's estate for two years, you know, ever since Hedgeworth's death."

"Why, she never mentioned a thing about it to me. That is interesting, indeed," said Lady Chalmers. It was a pleasant surprise to learn that Miss Hedgeworth had had such experience. It augered well for the young woman's ability to be able to handle a larger house, such as Sebastion's, thought her ladyship.

Fredericka returned and no more was said. She took up her customary place beside the earl's chair and began reading the day's news in a well-modulated voice.

Though Fredericka seemed completely engrossed in the task, her thoughts ranged on far different planes than what the newspaper contained. She was reflecting on all that Lady Chalmers had said about what they might expect out of the Season. Certainly such heady heights must delight any young lady making her first foray into polite society and Fredericka found that she was not altogether immune.

Fredericka had come up to London as her own mistress, having made up her mind to do her duty toward her family. Thus far, it had not been an onerous task, for she was enjoying herself very much. She derived as much amusement out of observing the foibles and posturings of the fashionable as she did out of the various elaborate functions.

However, always present at the back of her mind was the understanding she had gotten from her mother that her stay in London must end in a credible match. Lady Hedgeworth had pinned all of her hopes on this single Season.

Fredericka did not wish to enter into a marriage of convenience, but she was beginning to wonder whether she was too nice in her requirement. She had any number of admirers and not a single day went by without some new billet or posy of flowers being delivered to the front door for her.

Young Lord Alterwrop seemed always to be on hand and had made of himself nearly a nuisance. Indeed, Lord Chalmers had once growled, "Does that puppy reside in the drawing room?" Once, his lordship had walked in while Lord Alterwrop was reverently expressing his sentiments to Fredericka, while Lady Chalmers looked on benignly, with several lines of very bad poetry. The earl had stared, uttered something completely unintelligible, and hastily backed out of the drawing room.

Fredericka could smile over that, for young Lord Alterwrop was no longer one of her faithful suitors. Upon the occasion of his pressing an impassioned proposal into her palm for the third time, she had told him in stringent accents that she had decided to renounce London and all of its frivolities. "I have never truly liked the metropolis," she said.

Lord Alterwrop had been utterly shocked. For him, nothing existed outside London. "Not like London?" he faltered, still on his knees before her.

"Oh, no. I have a fancy to live in a quiet watering place such as Bath, for you must know that I should like very much to take the waters. I am persuaded that my constitution would derive much good from it," said Fredericka calmly. She smiled on his lordship. "I daresay the slower pace of Bath would admirably suit us both, dear Lord Alterwrop. I understand that the assemblies are much smaller than what we have been subjected to here in town."

Lord Alterwrop was horrified by the vision that she had conjured up. He stammered a polite agreement and shortly thereafter took his leave. He did not call the following day, as was his habit and when next Fredericka saw him she was favored with a slightly embarrassed bow. She greeted his lordship cordially without any hint of what had passed between them. Within a week Fredericka heard that Lord Alterwrop had found himself a new inamorata and herself had the felicity of seeing him dangling after a pretty maiden.

Lady Chalmers had expressed herself glad that young Lord Alterwrop's passion had burned itself out. "For I do not know how I was to sustain one more poem," she said.

"Nor I, ma'am. That is why I gave Lord Alterwrop the impression that I should like to live in Bath and take the waters," said Fredericka.

Lady Chalmers stared at her and then she started laughing. "Oh, my dear! How very handy of you! I perceive that I should have no fear of any ineligible importuning you, for you are clever enough to send them to the roundabout on your own."

Fredericka had hoped that her ladyship was correct, for even as she smiled and accepted compliments and gave every appearance of enjoyment, she was conscious of a constraint within herself. She found herself privately and critically analyzing each gentleman presented to her.

For the most part she could not imagine allying herself with many of her present admirers. Of course, the gazetted fortune hunters did not come her way since it was well known that she would have only a small portion. Lady Chalmers had no need to warn off this sort of ineligible; but there were others who were just as ineligible in Fredericka's estimation, if not in the eyes of the world.

Mr. Thatcher, for instance, who had lately made himself one of Fredericka's court. He was Lord Comberley's heir and was expected to have a handsome fortune when he stepped into his father's shoes. His manners were excellent, he was generally considered to be handsome, and his ease of deportment was admired. He favored a dandified mode of dress and affected a lisp, but that was not so unusual. Several other young sprigs aspiring to be leaders of fashion did the same. Certainly that could not be held against him except by the fastidious. Unfortunately, Fredericka found herself among that number.

Then there was Sir Lawrence. The gentleman was generally acknowledged to be quite a matrimonial catch, but Fredericka could not like him. She thought his nicety of manner imperfectly concealed a selfishness of heart that she could not abide. He had once made a slighting comment about Lady Chalmers and others whose compassion had led them to support various charitable works.

Fredericka had stared at the dandy with undisguised astonishment. "Forgive me, Sir Lawrence, but I cannot agree. I believe administering charity to those less fortunate than ourselves is required of us if we are to be able to look into our mirrors with any sort of sense of self-worth."

Sir Lawrence had smiled deprecatingly. "You are naturally entitled to your opinion, Miss Hedgeworth. For my part, I see no reason to encourage these rascals to think that they may simply hold out a dirty paw and expect it to be filled."

"Quite right," agreed Lady Towrand, a dowager of formidable personality. She gave a regal nod. "The poor must be made to understand that they must not be lazy."

When Fredericka recalled the ragged children running in the streets and all that she had seen at Mrs. Savage's foundling home, she felt anger rising up inside her. She knew that she should quickly and with as much grace as possible extricate herself from the conversation. It was intolerable to her to listen to such complacent ignorance without saying something that she was certain to regret later.

"Pray excuse me," she said quietly. "I believe that I have just seen Lady Jersey arrive."

She had not forgotten that incident and decided that Sir Lawrence had revealed his true character in those brief moments. Cold selfishness was not a quality that Fredericka wished for in a husband, and she was therefore dismayed when Sir Lawrence began to pay her marked attention.

Mr. Howard-Browne was another who had quickly become one of her inner court. Fredericka liked him very much. He was an amiable gentleman, always ready to do anyone the least favor. He seemed to have a large friendship and he was a general favorite.

Lady Chalmers, apparently noticing that she showed a partiality for Mr. Howard-Browne, had delicately inquired what she thought of the gentleman.

Fredericka smiled, but she shook her head. "He is a dear, of course, my lady. But I do not think him in the least steady."

Lady Chalmers had to agree. Mr. Howard-Browne had birth and fortune and an amiable character. But he was as likely to tool off to watch a cockfight as he was to fulfill a social obligation. Every hostess knew that Mr. Howard-Browne, though very correct in manner and protocol, had the lamentable flaw of being undependable.

Lady Chalmers had not actually believed that Mr. Howard-Browne would make an offer for Miss Hedgeworth. That was a profound commitment that she felt quite certain that the gentleman was patently unready to make. Rather, Mr. Howard-Browne paid Fredericka court because it was fashionable and because he liked her. Lady Chalmers put much more construction on Sir Lawrence's pursuit and Sir Thomas's punctilious attentions.

Fredericka had indicated a preference for Sir Thomas's company over some others of her admirers and there was beginning to be speculation over the possibility of a match. Sir Thomas was eminently suitable in every way and he was a gentleman of honor and integrity, besides. Fredericka fully recognized the gentleman's worth, and she thought of all of her suitors, she might be able to form a connection with him. He was stolid and respectable. However, it was regrettable but true that Sir Thomas had no dash. Also, he did not always catch the nuances of her humor. Fredericka thought it might prove rather trying to always have to explain one's own little jokes. It was so much more amusing when there was someone who instantly understood what she meant. Someone, for instance, like Lord Satterwaite.

Fredericka's mouth curved in a faint smile as her thoughts turned to the viscount. They rode together or drove in his phaeton often and they met one another constantly at different functions. Usually she enjoyed talking with his lordship. His sense of the ridiculous was akin to her own. She could not begin to count the number of times that something idiotic was said by someone and her eyes would meet his gaze and discover her own amusement mirrored there.

Fredericka thought for a moment of Lord Satterwaite as a potential suitor. Lord Satterwaite was not backward in his attentions, but neither was he pressing. He had not made her the sole object of his devotion, but paid indifferent court to other young ladies as well.

Fredericka did not know what his thoughts might be toward her. But certainly she understood her own feelings on the matter. Lord Satterwaite was eligible, true, and they were much alike in wit. But she doubted if they would suit, for he was as likely to reprove her as he was to compliment her. More than once, he had proffered unsolicited advice about how she should go on. The first time had been over Mr. Everard. Since then there had been a half dozen small instances. Apparently Lord Satterwaite had assumed that since Lady Chalmers was sponsoring her, he had the obligation to make certain that she did not place a foot wrong. It was really rather annoying at times.

Fredericka realized that she had exhausted the contents of the newspaper. Yet she could not recall a single item. That's what came of woolgathering, she thought. "I have finished, my lord. Shall I read something else for you?"

"No, thank you, Miss Hedgeworth. That was delightful," said Lord Chalmers.

Fredericka folded the newspaper and set it aside. She knew that the earl liked to spend private time with his countess and so she made a graceful excuse to leave them. "If you do not have any objection, my lady, I believe that I shall go finish a letter that I had started earlier today."

"Of course not, my dear," said Lady Chalmers with a warm smile.

When Fredericka had exited, Lord Chalmers said, "What think you, Sarah? What are the chances that Sebastion will choose our Miss Hedgeworth?"

Lady Chalmers shook her head. "I do not know, Edward. I should like him to show more interest in Fredericka, of course, for she is a delightful girl. However, Sebastion seems to have drawn back slightly from her. I attribute that to the gossip that was beginning to arise in those first few weeks of her come-out when he was good enough to squire Fredericka and me to several functions."

Lord Chalmers grunted, a scowl descending on his face. "Aye, his perverseness is well known to me. Sebastion will go precisely contrary to what you will him to do."

"It is provoking, of course. However, I am encouraged that he is bestowing notice on a few other young misses. We must be satisfied with that, my lord," said Lady Chalmers.

"Aye, it is more than he has done before," said Lord Chalmers on a sigh. He levered himself up out of his chair and took hold of his cane. "I am off to my club, my dear."

"Very well." Lady Chalmers lifted her cheek for the earl's kiss and there was a gleam of amusement in her eyes. "Pray do not be late this evening, my lord. We are holding a small ball."

Lord Chalmers grimaced. "Aye, I remember it. Deuced nuisance, but I shall do the pretty, never fear."

"No, my lord," said Lady Chalmers demurely, as his lordship turned and left the drawing room.

Chapter Nineteen

Fredericka had faithfully written home from the first week that she was in London, and so the excuse she had given to the countess was a legitimate one. Seated at the desk in the library, she finished crossing several sheets with descriptions of the shopping and the sights, as well as touching on the kindnesses that had been shown to her by the Earl and Countess of Chalmers and others. She dwelt most particularly upon her court presentation, which had occurred the week before.

The entire monumental event had taken only a few moments, but Fredericka had been glad when it was over. She related to her mother that her heart had still been pounding when she had backed out of the audience room, feeling utter relief that she had not committed some awkward faux pas, such as tripping over her heavy hem.

The presentation to Her Majesty the Queen had marked Fredericka's formal entrance into fashionable society and made her eligible to attend a court ball or concert. Lady Hedgeworth would naturally be aware that this was a vital consideration since everyone who was anyone attended such a function at least once a year.

When Fredericka at last put down her pen, she had managed to create a thick chatty packet. She scarcely mentioned Lord Satterwaite, however, even though the viscount seemed to be on her mind more than she could have wished.

Fredericka had ended her letter on an unconsciously nostalgic note. "I am happy here, and well. However, I do miss all of you and Luting, but most of all I miss my mare. You are not to be thinking that I do not appreciate you, dear ones, for I do! But I am so confined here as I was never restricted at Luting. Oh, I long for a gallop with Cricket across the fields. I have not had a bit of proper exercise since coming to town. A few walks and sedate rides and dancing to all hours, but I do not count that! Betsy shall disagree, but I do not count shopping as a form of exercise that I should choose above all others!"

A week later when Fredericka was whiling away an hour in the library, she was told that a gentleman had called to see her. "He has sent up his card, miss," said the butler, and proffered it to her.

Fredericka did not take the card with any great interest, but her attitude swiftly underwent transformation. She stared at the card. "Jack? Here?" She flew out of her chair and made her way quickly to the drawing room.

The butler proceeded her and opened the door. When Fredericka entered, Lord Hedgeworth turned toward her. There was an amused expression on his face. "Hallo, Freddie."

"Jack! Oh, how glad I am to see you!" Fredericka rushed over and threw her arms around him.

"Here, Freddie!" exclaimed Lord Hedgeworth, exasperated. He tried to fend her off. "You're crushing my neckcloth!"

"Oh, never mind that, Jack. Just tell me all about Mama and the girls and Thomas and—" Fredericka realized there was an even more important question. She stepped back and looked up at him. "Jack, what are you doing here?"

Moffet, having benevolently observed these transports, was satisfied that there was a proper attachment between Miss Hedgeworth and her brother. "Shall you be wanting any refreshment, miss?"

Recalled to her surroundings, Fredericka colored and laughed at herself. "I am sorry! I have quite forgot my company manners. Yes, please, Moffet. Some sandwiches and biscuits and whatever else you might think of that will appeal to a ravenous young gentleman!"

Lord Hedgeworth flushed. "Freddie!" he muttered, embarrassed.

The butler permitted himself a small smile and closed the door behind him.

Fredericka at once turned back to her brother. "Now, Jack, you shall tell me how you come to be in London." A slightly anxious expression touched her face. "There is no emergency at Luting, is there? Or illness?"

"No, not a bit of it. I came up to London for the express purpose of seeing you. And I have brought you a handsome present, so you must be kind to me," said Lord Hedgeworth, grinning.

Fredericka was frowning at him. "You have not quarreled with Mama, have you, Jack?"

He was insulted. "Now I like that! I've come up to town to see you and you suspect it was because I flew out at Mama! Fine opinion of me you hold, Freddie, I must say!"

"Then why, Jack?" Fredericka threw up her hand to forestall him. "And no more of your evasions, if you please. If it is nothing to do with Luting or one of the children or Mama—well, I know very well that *something* must have occurred."

Lord Hedgeworth hunched a shoulder. "Oh, very well! If you must know, I was restless after you left. I could not stop thinking how unfair it all was. I mean, you never wanting to leave Luting, while I have always wanted to cut a dash in London. Finally, I could scarcely bear it any longer. Then your letter came, and I told Mama that I would bring Cricket up to you, and here I am!"

"Oh, truly, Jack?" Fredericka directed such a look of astonishment and dawning hopefulness at her brother that he laughed.

"Am I in a fair way to being forgiven?"

"Oh, Jack, you are so nonsensical! Where is she?"

"She is out front. I have a boy looking after her for me. You may see her from the window, I daresay."

Fredericka swiftly crossed to the window and lifted back the curtain so that she could look down into the street. There was her beloved mare. "Oh, Jack." She looked across her shoulder at him. "You are such a good brother."

Lord Hedgeworth flushed, embarrassed. "There's nothing in that," he said gruffly. "I just hope that the earl will be amenable to putting her up."

"His lordship has been very kind. I am certain that he shall not begrudge me a place in his stables for Cricket," said Fredericka.

"Good. That's all right, then. Oh, I almost forgot. I am charged with notes from Mama for you and for Lady Chalmers," said Lord Hedgeworth.

Fredericka took the sealed correspondence from his hand. "Do you mind if I read this now, Jack?"

The door opened and the butler entered with a footman in tow. The two bore trays piled high with plates of sandwiches, cold cuts, cheeses, and a host of just those things that might be expected to tempt a vigorous young gentleman's appetite. The trays were set out on the occasional table along with a decanter of wine.

Lord Hedgeworth eyed these preparations for his refreshment with approval. "Of course not. I shall entertain myself very well. By Jove, this is something like!"

Fredericka returned to her chair and broke the seal on her mother's letter to her. She spread out the sheet and with a smile curving her lips read all the news. Toward the end, a small frown knit her brows and she glanced over at her brother. Lord Hedgeworth was oblivious to her scrutiny, being happily engaged in making inroads into the sandwiches and jellies and fruit and cheese.

Fredericka did not say anything to her brother, but instead she folded the sheet and tucked it away into her pocket. She picked up the sealed correspondence for Lady Chalmers. "I shall put this aside for her ladyship. I should like you to meet her, Jack, for she is the kindest creature alive. I believe that his lordship has gone out to his club or otherwise you would meet him as well."

When Lord Hedgeworth expressed himself perfectly amenable to making the countess's acquaintance, Fredericka went to the bellpull. In answer to her summons, the butler entered. Fredericka quietly asked that a message be relayed to the Countess of Chalmers that Lord Hedgeworth had dropped in, and Miss Hedgeworth wished to know if her ladyship was available to callers.

A few minutes later Lady Chalmers entered the drawing room. "Why, what is this that I am told? Lord Hedgeworth himself is here?" The countess advanced on the young gentleman, who had hastily risen upon her entrance, and held out her hand to him. "I am happy to make your acquaintance, my lord."

"It is entirely my pleasure, my lady." Lord Hedgeworth made an elegant bow, carrying her ladyship's hand to his lips. His grace and savoir faire was such that his sister stared, half in amusement and half in astonishment. Surely her brother had attained a polish and assurance that he had not had even a few short months before.

Lady Chalmers sat down and invited Lord Hedgeworth to join her. She approved of the young gentleman's manners. He blended just the right touch of deference with confidence in his own worth. "But what brings you up to London, my lord? Fredericka mentioned not a word of it to me."

"My sister was unaware that I meant to come to visit, my lady. She had written a quite pitiful expression of wanting her mare with her, and so I designated myself as the one best to be spared to bring it up to her," said Lord Hedgeworth.

"How charming for you, Fredericka! This is a kindness, indeed," said Lady Chalmers, turning to her houseguest.

"Yes, indeed. I hope that you do not mind my having Cricket here, ma'am," said Fredericka.

"Of course not. I was thinking only the other day that it would be wonderful indeed if you were mounted on a horse that did you justice," said Lady Chalmers.

"But, ma'am, the gelding you have put at my disposal is quite adequate," exclaimed Fredericka.

"Nonsense. I am persuaded that you privately think him a bit of a slug, for you are a splendid rider. Your mother had mentioned to me in one of her letters that you liked nothing better than coursing over the fields, and certainly you do not get that here," said Lady Chalmers, smiling.

Fredericka blushed slightly even as she laughed. "I fear that is true, my lady. I was practically born in the saddle and I have missed careering over the countryside very much."

"Freddie is a bruising rider to hounds," said Lord Hedgeworth. "She never balks at a fence or hedge. I've not yet seen her like on horseback, my lady."

"This is high praise, indeed! Lord Hedgeworth, I perceive that you are the perfect brother. Considerate and supportive! I am glad that you brought the mare up to town yourself. Do you make a long visit? For I must tell you that you are very welcome to stay here at Chalmers House for however long you wish," said Lady Chalmers.

"That is very kind of you, my lady. However, I have already

bespoken some rooms at an hotel." He ignored Fredericka's thoughtful expression and smiled with engaging boyishness at the countess. "I've never been to London before, you see, and I wished to indulge my curiosity a little before I return to Luting. Although I shall naturally make myself available to whatever schemes that your ladyship may have in train while I am in town."

"Certainly I shall hold you to that, Lord Hedgeworth. You must come this evening to dinner. It will be only a small dinner party, very intimate, with not above thirty couples. I shall introduce you to a few individuals who might be expected to share many of your same interests and who may be persuaded to point you to those entertainments and sights most guaranteed to appeal to a young man on the town for the first time," said Lady Chalmers.

Lord Hedgeworth was nearly overcome and thereby showed his youth. "Thank you, ma'am. I accept your kind invitation with all anticipation," he said sincerely.

Lady Chalmers nodded. "Very good. I shall invite one or two others to round out the numbers." She rose and extended her hand to Lord Hedgeworth. "I look forward to our next meeting, my lord."

"And I, my lady," said Lord Hedgeworth, also rising and bowing over her hand.

"I shall leave you with your sister now, for I know that you both must have much to relate," said Lady Chalmers, moving toward the door.

As soon as Lady Chalmers had exited, Fredericka turned to her brother. He seemed to be anticipating her attention, and he smiled, somewhat sheepishly. "Well, Freddie?"

"Jack, Mama writes to me that you mean to spend a few weeks in London. Is that true?" she asked quietly.

Lord Hedgeworth made haste to offer his explanation. "Mama has given her permission, Freddie. And I made all right with Bartram. He will handle Luting while I am gone. So you need not look at me like that, dear sister!"

Fredericka shook her head, a small smile curving her lips. "No, I shan't scold you, as you seem to fear that I might do. You are of an age to make your own decisions. It is not difficult for me to understand why you decided to come to London just now. I only hope that as you plunge into your amusements that you will keep a level head about you. It is a very different world, my dear."

Lord Hedgeworth laughed. His eyes sparkled and he retorted, "Just so! I mean to have a capital go while I am here. And now that I am thinking about it, how have things gone for you, Freddie? Her ladyship seems to be all that amiable, just as you wrote. But you have said next to nothing of beaux in your letter to Mama. Believe me, she took note of that omission."

"Oh dear, did she?" Fredericka gave a wry smile. "I was taking such care to say nothing that would disappoint her, too! The truth of the matter, Jack, is that there are very few gentlemen whom I have yet met that I would trust for their good sense or even their taste in fashion!"

"As bad as that?" asked Lord Hedgeworth sympathetically. His natural optimism was not dampened, however. "Well, you shall discover someone worthy of you, I don't doubt. What about this Lord Satterwaite that you mentioned?"

Fredericka raised her brows. "The viscount?" She seemed to reflect. "It is true that his lordship is not a fribble, nor a fool. I suppose that I could like him well enough."

Lord Hedgeworth lost interest in the viscount at this lukewarm accolade. "Oh, well. Someone shall turn up that will suit you, dear sister. If not during this Season, then later on. I've already promised to help you, haven't I?"

"Indeed, you have, Jack." Fredericka smiled warmly at him. "You are the best of brothers, Jack."

"Don't I know it," he retorted. "Now are you going downstairs to greet Cricket or not?"

"Of course I am! Let us go down immediately," said Fredericka. She at once led the way from the drawing room. A few minutes later brother and sister emerged out of the front door of the town house and Fredericka ran down the steps to the curb.

"Dear Cricket!" The mare snuffled in recognition and pushed against her mistress. Fredericka laughed and stroked her. "I am sorry, girl! I did not think to bring you any sugar."

While Fredericka was making up to her mare, a curricle and four drove up to the curb. Lord Satterwaite got out and sauntered toward them.

Fredericka greeted him as though he was an old friend. Her eyes sparkling, and quite unconscious of loose horsehairs that had attached themselves to her day dress, she said, "Hallo, my lord. Pray let me make known to you my girl, Cricket."

Lord Satterwaite smoothed the mare's neck, looking over her points with cool appraisal. "She is a fine specimen. How did she come to you?"

"Oh! I am sorry! My lord, this is my brother, Lord Hedgeworth. He was so obliging as to bring Cricket up to town for me, for he suspected how much I have missed her. Jack, this is Viscount Satterwaite."

The two gentlemen exchanged greetings while they shook hands. Both approved of what they saw in the other. Lord Satterwaite inquired what Lord Hedgeworth's plans were while he was in London.

The younger man flashed an engagingly frank smile and said, "I am not certain, my lord, except that I hope to amuse myself. Lady Chalmers has been kind enough to invite me to her dinner this evening and I daresay that will be a splendid start."

Lord Satterwaite agreed to it gravely and then turned to Miss Hedgeworth. "I had come to beg you to drive out with me, but I can see that you would much rather catch up on old times with your mare."

"Yes, that is true, my lord," agreed Fredericka with laughter in her eyes. "It is abominably rude of me, of course."

"I am an adaptable fellow, however. Indeed, I shall engage myself to ride out with you," said Lord Satterwaite. He turned his smile on Lord Hedgeworth. "And naturally you must make up one of the party, Lord Hedgeworth."

"That's handsome of you, my lord. However, I haven't gotten a hack yet and—"

Lord Satterwaite held up his hand. "I shall loan you one of my own, of course."

"Thank you, my lord. I should like it of all things," said Lord Hedgeworth.

Lord Satterwaite nodded and looked again at Miss Hedgeworth. "Shall we say a half hour, Miss Hedgeworth?"

"Of course, my lord. I must have Cricket taken round to the

stables until I am ready for her," said Fredericka, looking toward the front door in order to catch the eye of the porter.

The mare's immediate future dispensed with, Fredericka took leave of her brother and the viscount. Lord Satterwaite had offered to give Lord Hedgeworth a lift to his lodgings and Lord Hedgeworth accepted with alacrity. He had already taken shrewd measure of the viscount's matched team and he fairly leaped at the opportunity to actually ride behind such a sweet-looking pair. He assured his sister that he would shortly rejoin her at Chalmers House ready for their expedition.

Fredericka went inside and upstairs to her bedroom to change into her riding habit.

Chapter Twenty

The ride in the park was a great success. Lord Satterwaite had hastily invited a few other personages of his acquaintance, most of whom were a few years younger, in an effort to introduce Lord Hedgeworth into exactly that set of kindred spirits that would best suit a youth's first foray into London. Included in this party were Miss Howard-Browne and her brother, one of Miss Howard-Browne's admirers, Lord Markam, and his lordship's sister, Miss Stoker.

Mr. Howard-Browne gravitated toward Lord Satterwaite and Miss Hedgeworth, while Lord Hedgeworth became acquainted with the others. "Quite a friendly fellow, your brother, Miss Hedgeworth," observed Mr. Howard-Browne. "And he sits that hack of Satterwaite's like one born to the saddle. I'd like to see his lordship on the hunts. I'd wager that he is a neck-or-nothing rider."

"Indeed, Jack enjoys nothing better, Mr. Howard-Browne," said Fredericka. She glanced up at Lord Satterwaite's profile. "I appreciate your kindness toward my brother, my lord."

"I merely provided a mount and a few boon companions, Miss Hedgeworth. It was the least I could do when I discovered that Lord Hedgeworth was engaged to my mother's dinner party this evening," said Lord Satterwaite, smiling.

Fredericka tucked away a smile, murmuring, "It is to be a very respectable dinner, my lord."

Mr. Howard-Browne gave a crack of laughter, hastily covering it with a cough. "Precisely so, Miss Hedgeworth."

"Quite," said Lord Satterwaite dryly. "Oh, I have no doubt that your brother will enjoy it to a certain extent since it will be novel to him. However, I doubt that such entertainment will not soon become rather tame in his eyes. If I am not mistaken, Lord

Markam will soon introduce Lord Hedgeworth to entertainments that will be much more to his taste."

"I wish Jack to have an amusing time, of course," said Fredericka, completely comfortable with the idea of the shy, rather inarticulate, Lord Markam becoming her brother's guide. She thought she could rest easy when her brother was off with such a harmless companion, and it did seem that Lord Hedgeworth and Lord Markam were hitting it off marvelously well. They made plans to meet again on the morrow, when Lord Markam promised to show his new friend the sights.

Miss Howard-Browne was a bit chagrined that two such handsome cavaliers should ignore her and chided them on their callousness. Miss Stoker put in her own laughing objection. "Indeed, Miss Howard-Browne, one would suspect that we were merely so much baggage," she said, directing a melting glance in Lord Hedgeworth's direction.

Instantly, Lord Hedgeworth declared himself ready to climb any mountain or accomplish any feat that either lady wished. Lord Markam was not to be outdone and promised to do the same, at least for Miss Howard-Browne. "You may do the pretty for m'sister, Hedgeworth," he explained.

Miss Howard-Browne was delighted. She turned around in her saddle and said, "Fredericka, I am in awkward straits. Here I have two knights willing to do my least bidding and I am unable to envision a single quest to send them on!"

"Nor I," said Miss Stoker, shaking her head.

"It is melancholy, indeed, that there are no dragons left to slay," said Fredericka. "I suppose that we must all be satisfied with their squiring us about the dance floor or gallantly giving us a hand up into our carriages!"

The gentlemen protested that this was tame stuff and put forward several outrageous and improbable scenarios, to the vast amusement of the entire party. The hour passed pleasantly, at the end of which the riders took leave of one another with reluctance.

Lord Hedgeworth did indeed dine at Chalmers House that evening, and if he was awed by the company and his surroundings alike, he yet recognized that it was not precisely the sort of thing that he was hoping to attend while in London. He confided to his sister's ear alone that he had not known that such important people could be such a dull set.

Fredericka laughed, but admonished him. "These are the earl's particular friends, Jack. They are all connected to government and his lordship wished to expose me to the political circle in case I come to wed a great public man and become a fine political hostess."

Lord Hedgeworth stared at her, his mouth slightly agape. Then he said earnestly, "Don't you do it, Freddie. You shan't like it in the least."

But Fredericka only shook her head, and turned away from him, still smiling, to lend an ear to one of the earl's illustrious guests.

Lord Hedgeworth was given food for thought by this short exchange, and he wondered what his sister was intending when she appeared to be entertaining thoughts of accepting the possible suit of the sort of gentlemen in attendance at the dinner party. They were all of the same sort, which he had no hesitation in stigmatizing as dull dogs.

However, his sister's concerns could not have been expected to exercise Lord Hedgeworth's thoughts for long. Through Lord Markam and a small number of invitations extended to him by way of introductions around town, Lord Hedgeworth soon found himself in the happy circumstance of being able to claim a growing number of acquaintances. Many of his new friends were just as youthful as himself, or at least were so in spirit, and it was not too many days before Lord Hedgeworth was being initiated into such things as a faro bank, laying odds at Tattersall's, attending bloody pugilist exhibitions, going off for an hour's shooting at Manton's, ogling bold-eyed opera dancers, and generally doing all the things that a dashing young blade might be expected to try.

Mr. Howard-Browne was the first to hear of Lord Hedgeworth's staggering losses in one night's play at a little house off Pall Mall. He relayed the gossip to Lord Satterwaite, shaking his head over it. "The boy is in deep, there is no mistake about it. I understand that he has lately been taken to Watier's by Markam. At least there he'll find honest play."

Lord Satterwaite frowned over the news. "I called on my uncle just last week and he chanced to mention that he had known

Hedgeworth's father. It seems that the late Lord Hedgeworth was a gamester of the worst sort."

Mr. Howard-Browne shook his head. "That's bad. It always runs in the blood. I suppose that we shall see the boy run off his legs. It's a pity that one can't give him a hint."

"Yes, isn't it? But only Miss Hedgeworth has that right," said Lord Satterwaite. "And I doubt that she is aware of all of her brother's doings."

"Quite right, too. Ladies never understand these things. It's best to keep them in the dark," said Mr. Howard-Browne.

While Lord Satterwaite did not entirely agree with his friend's sentiments, he nevertheless felt considerable constraint against telling Miss Hedgeworth what her brother was doing. He stood in no relationship to her, nor to Lord Hedgeworth. It would be the height of impertinence for him to interfere. Yet he liked Lord Hedgeworth, and he knew intimately the temptations and pitfalls of gaming at its worst. After all, he had been going much the same route.

However, there was a significant difference between himself and Lord Hedgeworth. He was possessed of a fortune. Lord Hedgeworth was not. Undoubtedly it was much like Mr. Howard-Browne had said, and Lord Hedgeworth would soon be punting on tick.

Lord Satterwaite was still wrestling with a moral dilemma when he was given the opportunity to observe Lord Hedgeworth's progress for himself. He strolled into the club late one evening with a couple of friends, Mr. Howard-Browne and Sir Peter, and instantly perceived Lord Hedgeworth sitting at a table across from a notorious gamester. Several gentlemen were standing about the table watching the play.

Lord Satterwaite gave only a single glance toward the table and then turned away with his own party. But he seated himself where he could observe what was happening. Another gentleman was hailed to make a fourth, and the viscount's game with his three companions began. His play was a little more careless than usual, but not enough for his friends to remark.

There was a concerted hush over Lord Hedgeworth's table, and when the hand was at last played out, general laughter broke out.

"The boy has done you to a turn, Bookering!" cried one gentleman.

"Aye, a cooler head I wish I may see!"

Lord Hedgeworth rose from the table the winner and he made a graceful disclaimer to his erstwhile partner. Lord Bookering had reddened of face at the good-natured ribaldry, but his countenance eased into a stiff smile with whatever Lord Hedgeworth had said to him. The gentlemen exchanged bows and Lord Hedgeworth went off arm in arm with his boon companion, Lord Markam.

Lord Satterwaite watched him go, an inscrutable expression in his eyes. Then he turned his attention fully onto his own game.

Shortly after this incident, Lord Satterwaite received a note from his mother that she desperately needed him as an escort to the opera, the earl feeling too unwell to accompany her. Lord Satterwaite groaned. He could definitely understand the earl's feelings, for the opera was not something that he himself enjoyed. However, he resigned himself and sent back a reply that he would hold himself ready to perform his duty.

The original party was to consist of Lady Chalmers and Miss Hedgeworth, the Howard-Brownes, Lady Markam, her ladyship's cousin, Mr. Pauling, and Miss Stoker. At the last moment, Lady Chalmers stunned her son by announcing that an elderly cousin was also joining them. Lady Chalmers met the viscount's reproachful gaze and said with a shade of defiance, "Cousin Maria particularly wished to attend this performance."

Because the decrepit old lady was nearly deaf, Lord Satterwaite could only shake his head and wonder at his mother's misguided notions of charity. When he chanced to meet his father as he was escorting his party toward the front door, he said feelingly, "You have made a fine escape at my expense, sir!"

Lord Chalmers allowed a smile to touch his face. He did not deny it, but simply wished everyone a good night. He complimented his wife and Miss Hedgeworth on their finery, but merely bowed over his cousin's gnarled hand. He was too used to her odd ways to be in the least put out of countenance when she loudly scolded him for burning too many candles in the drawing room. "Quite so, Cousin Maria. I shall have Moffet attend to it directly," he said without a blink. He retreated to the library and closed the door.

Without further ado, Lord Satterwaite and the ladies got into a carriage and rode to the opera house, where they were to meet the others of their party. Lady Markam was on the watch and soon sailed up to them, her companions in tow. Greetings were made and conversation quickly turned to the treat in store.

Mr. Howard-Browne said in a depressed voice, "I was caught off guard, Sebastion. My mother would have it that it was my duty to squire my sister just once this week and without even thinking it over, I agreed. So here I am, about to have my ears assailed with cat screechings."

"Cats? Cats? I cannot abide cats. I will not have it, Sarah. You must tell them that I will not have cats near me. It will bring on one of my spasms," said Cousin Maria querulously, having caught only a portion of the conversation.

Lady Chalmers soothed the elderly lady. "There will not be a single cat, I promise you, Cousin Maria. Now we must go to our box, for the opera is about to begin. You will like that, won't you?"

Mr. Howard-Browne rolled his eyes and followed in the wake of his excited sister, having offered his escort to Miss Stoker. Mr. Pauling gallantly squired Lady Markam and Lord Satterwaite offered his arm to Miss Hedgeworth.

He saw that she was biting her lip to keep from laughing and said reprovingly, "It is most unkind of you to laugh at the misfortunes of your fellow man, Miss Hedgeworth."

Fredericka did laugh then. She shook her head. "Oh, but poor Mr. Howard-Browne's expression! Especially when Lady Chalmers's cousin took up about cats!"

Lord Hedgeworth grinned. "Well, yes. However, I shall not enter further into lampooning my poor friend, for I share too closely in his sentiments."

"Do you not admire the opera, then, my lord?" asked Fredericka, her eyes lighting with comprehension.

"No, I do not," stated Lord Satterwaite unequivocally. As he ushered Miss Hedgeworth to the box, he resigned himself to one of the most uncomfortable evenings to which he had ever bee subjected.

The performance was as nerve-wracking as Lord Satterwait had anticipated. When the curtain dropped for the intermission h could scarcely believe that it was not over.

The ladies wished to visit between boxes and to take refresh ment, so it fell to the gentlemen to escort them out. Several ac quaintances were met up with and it was a relief to exchange pleasantries without the loud din from the stage making conversa tion an excruciating exercise. All too soon, the intermission was over and the operagoers returned to their seats. Lord Satterwaite thought that if he could survive the next half, he would know the worst that the evening could bring.

He was wrong.

When the performance was at last over and the ladies' wraps had been bestowed about their shoulders, the party left the opera house. The carriages had already been called for and there were others ahead of them at the bottom of the steps already preparing to depart.

It was seen that at least two of Miss Hedgeworth's admirers had attended the opera. Sir Lawrence and Mr. Thatcher both left their own companions for a brief moment to greet Miss Hedge-worth and her party. Everything was of an amiability, the gentle-men privately making asides to one another that it had been a ghastly business but they had managed to scrape through it well enough, while the ladies conversed with their swains and acquain-tances.

Suddenly a figure materialized out of the dark. It was a female, attired in what was obviously the costume of a servant maid. She caught hold of Mr. Thatcher's sleeve. He turned quickly, and his face drained of color. He tried to detach himself quickly, but the wench had a strong hold.

"Please! Please, ye must hear me! I've been turned out. Ye promised to wed me, so ye did!"

"My good girl, you must be mistaken! Must—must mistake me for another!" stammered Mr. Thatcher, acutely aware that all con-versation had been suspended and he was the center of all eyes. He tried to wrench the girl's hands off of his arm. "Let me go, I say!"

"No! No, ye cannot be so cruel! Ye promised me!" sobbed the girl. "They found out about the baby! I've been turned out, I tell ye!"

Lady Markam made hasty apologies to Lady Chalmers and began to herd her openmouthed daughter and her cousin toward their carriage. "Mr. Howard-Browne, you must see to your sister!" she commanded.

Mr. Howard-Browne came to himself with a start. "Quite right! Come, Amelia, we must be going!"

"But, Fitz, what of that poor unfortunate girl?" asked Miss Howard-Browne.

"Not our business," said Mr. Howard-Browne gruffly.

"Of course it is our business!" Fredericka stepped forward. "Mr. Thatcher, do you know this girl?"

Mr. Thatcher rolled his eyes, looking for help. He found none. Sir Lawrence had quietly removed himself from the vicinity and was polishing his quizzing glass. There was a particularly grim look about Lord Satterwaite's mouth, and as for the expression in the viscount's eyes, it was all too readable. Mr. Thatcher did not dare to encounter the gazes of the ladies. He was at last able to wrench himself free of the girl's grasp and he backed away. But he came up against an interested bystander and startled to one side. He was beginning to look like a hunted animal.

Lady Chalmers said hurriedly, "Fredericka, come with me at once! This is not for your ears, my dear."

"I am sorry, my lady. I cannot depart until I hear the truth of the matter," said Fredericka with quiet resolution. "Mr. Thatcher, this girl says that she has been cast out like a stray cat and that you promised to wed her. Is that true, sir?"

"Cat? Did she say there is a cat?" Cousin Maria peered about in alarm and then let out a startling screech. "There it is! Oh, oh, oh!"

Lady Chalmers caught her elderly cousin, who had gone alarmingly rigid and seemed in eminent danger of sliding to the flagway. Her expression harried, she snapped, "Fredericka! I implore you!"

Fredericka put her arm around the now weeping girl. "Pray do not cry. What is your name? Betsy? He shall make it right, I promise you!"

The Chalmers carriage had arrived. Lord Satterwaite took hold of one of his elderly relative's arms and helped his mother support the prostrate lady toward the carriage. "You must take her up at once, ma'am! I shall deal with Miss Hedgeworth."

"Yes! Thank you, Sebastion," said Lady Chalmers in relief.

After seeing the countess and her afflicted companion into the carriage, Lord Satterwaite turned again toward the scene on the flagway. Apparently some sort of admission had been dragged out of Mr. Thatcher that he did know the girl, and that he had been aware that she had been turned off, and why. Miss Hedgeworth's eyes flashed and before Lord Satterwaite quite realized what was happening, she made a thorough condemnation of her admirer's character.

Lord Satterwaite was appalled. Never in his life could he have imagined such a scene. The operagoers were still coming out of the opera house. Some had already heard enough to realize that something unusual and even newsworthy was happening. And here was Miss Hedgeworth dressing down in public a gentleman of the Honorable Oliver Thatcher's order. Granted, Mr. Thatcher was not the sort that he would himself admit to his own inner circle, but it was still the outside of enough that the man was being called to account in a public thoroughfare.

Mr. Thatcher was looking sick as a dog. His eyes darted here and there. There were enough observers who had stopped to listen that he was effectively hedged in, but at length his desire to escape was greater than his fear of giving offense and he shouldered and elbowed his way through the bystanders.

With Mr. Thatcher's hasty exit, most of the onlookers began to fade away. But there were such thoughtful and shocked and disapproving looks leveled on Miss Hedgeworth that Lord Satterwaite ground out a soft expletive.

Sir Lawrence's face was coldly expressionless. "Quite, Satterwaite." Without another word he turned on his heel and walked quickly away.

Lord Satterwaite took hold of Miss Hedgeworth's arm and drew her out of the lamplight. The girl stumbled along with them, still enfolded by Miss Hedgeworth's protective arm. "You have succeeded in setting the ton on their ears," he said tersely. "What do you mean to do now? Have you any notion what is to be done with this pitiful creature whom you have championed?"

"Why, yes, my lord," said Fredericka coolly. "I shall take her to Mrs. Savage, who runs a foundling home in the west end of London. If you will be so good as to hail a hackney for me, I shall do so at once."

Chapter Twenty-one

Lord Satterwaite was stunned. He looked from Miss Hedgeworth's resolute, steady gaze down at the tearful, cringing girl. He said explosively, "You cannot possibly go down in that neighborhood by yourself."

"I can and I shall. Betsy needs the sort of help that Mrs. Savage can provide to her." Fredericka regarded the viscount, her eyes sparkling with anger. "Come, my lord! You have already seen how disgracefully this poor female has been used. Shall I throw her into the gutter as well?"

Lord Satterwaite found that unanswerable. He had as much compassion as the next man, he thought, throwing another look at the fearful maid. From between clenched teeth, he said, "No, of course not. Nothing could be more monstrous. She shall go to Mrs. Savage. But I shall take her there."

This pronouncement threw Betsy into a fresh paroxysm of terror. She clung tighter to Fredericka, crying piteously, "No, miss! 'e'll abandon me for certain. I'm abegging you, miss, don't send me away wif 'im!"

"I shan't abandon you, girl. I give you my word," said Lord Satterwaite in a hard voice. He wanted only to be done with the matter. There were still passersby and they were getting no little curiosity.

But his assurance seemed to fuel Betsy's terror. "It were breach of promise. It were just what the other toff said, miss!" she cried. "Oh, don't send me off wif 'im!"

"I do not think that I could even if I wished to, such a hold you have of me," said Fredericka with a streak of humor.

The girl's screeching was beginning to attract fresh stares. "We must get out of here, Miss Hedgeworth. We'll have every nosy body in town upon us in another minute. Come, Miss Hedge-

worth! Here is a hackney. I shall escort both you and the girl to
Mrs. Savage's house." The words were bitten off with a good deal
of exasperation.

Fredericka thanked the viscount gratefully. If the truth was to
be known, she was not perfectly comfortable with the notion of
being driven down into the winding, narrow backstreets with only
the helpless Betsy as her companion. She caught up her skirts and
ascended into the hackney, urging the maid inside with her. As
Lord Satterwaite made to latch the door, she stopped him. "Are
you not getting inside, my lord?"

"I shall ride on top with the driver. I shall be better able to see
trouble coming if there should be any," said Lord Satterwaite.

"Thank you, my lord."

"Have I a choice, Miss Hedgeworth?" There was an edge of
temper in his voice, but nonetheless she detected a softening of
his expression. Fredericka smiled at him.

Lord Satterwaite abruptly slammed shut the carriage door with
unnecessary force.

During the jolting ride, Fredericka did her best to soothe and
reassure the maid, but with indifferent success. The girl seemed to
understand nothing beyond the fact that Miss Hedgeworth was the
one person in the world at that moment who was disposed to treat
her with kindness. The thought of leaving Miss Hedgeworth's
protection kept her sniffing morosely.

By the time that the hackney reached its destination, Fredericka
was exhausted by her efforts. She was never more glad of anything in her life when the carriage door was opened and she saw
Lord Satterwaite's silhouette. "We have arrived?" she asked
hopefully.

Lord Satterwaite handed her out, and Fredericka saw that she
was indeed in the dusty yard of the old coaching inn. "Thank
God," she breathed, turning then to help the maid out of the carriage, the girl having refused the viscount's hand.

Lord Satterwaite obligingly stepped back. "She is still watering
everything in sight, I see."

Fredericka threw him a look that was easily read, and he
cracked a laugh. In impatient accents, Fredericka asked the vis-

count to escort them to the entrance. He politely offered his elbow.

A lantern was burning beside the door. The door was already opened to them and the same dour individual who Fredericka had noticed before motioned for the trio to come inside.

They did so and Mrs. Savage met them in the hall. The lady cast one comprehensive glance over the trio and ushered them into the parlor. "Miss Hedgeworth, this is an unexpected surprise. Pray make known to me your companions."

Fredericka introduced Lord Satterwaite and then drew forward the maid. "And this is Betsy. She is in the family way. It was discovered today and as a result she has lost her post."

Mrs. Savage lifted a hand. "You have no need to say more, Miss Hedgeworth. It is not an uncommon story, unfortunately." She glanced at the viscount. Her voice turned markedly arctic. "Had you aught to do with this, my lord?"

Lord Satterwaite looked at the woman, his brows snapping together. Quite coldly, he said, "I am not certain what you mean, ma'am. If you are referring to the fact that I have provided escort to Miss Hedgeworth and this female to your door, then yes."

Fredericka realized suddenly what Mrs. Savage was inferring. She intervened hastily. "It was not Lord Satterwaite who gave her a slip on the shoulder, ma'am. Betsy was an undermaid in Lord Comberley's household. His lordship has a son—"

"It were breach of promise, mum," interjected Betsy tearfully.

Mrs. Savage glanced down at the maid and her countenance softened. "Yes, my dear child. I see just how it was."

Some minutes before Mrs. Savage had pulled a bell rope and now the door to the parlor opened to admit a portly dame. "Yes, Mrs. Savage?"

"Mrs. Stoeffer, this young woman is called Betsy. She is a former undermaid. Betsy would like some supper and a place to wash up," said Mrs. Savage.

"Of course she would. Come along, chick. I'll see that you have a nice cup of broth and some buttered bread," said Mrs. Stoeffer, coming forward to take the maid's hand and gently draw her away.

Betsy looked back uncertainly. Fredericka nodded reassurance.

'You may trust these good ladies, Betsy. They shall see that you are cared for properly."

"Thank you, miss," said Betsy, dropping an instinctive curtsy. Then, still sniffling, she went away with Mrs. Stoeffer.

When the door closed, Mrs. Savage shook her head. "That is a good girl. It is a pity that she was gotten into this predicament through blandishments and false promises," she said, sighing. Mrs. Savage turned once more to Fredericka and took her hands. "You have shown true compassion and kindness, Miss Hedgeworth. May the Lord bless you for it."

As though realizing that she had stepped out of her usual austere role, Mrs. Savage smoothed away her expression of sentimentality. "I shall not keep you, for I know that it grows late. You will not wish to linger in these streets."

Mrs. Savage did not encourage them to linger, but neither Fredericka nor Lord Satterwaite would have wanted to in any event. Fredericka got back into the hackney. Lord Satterwaite climbed up on the box again with the driver. He rode topside until the carriage had left the worst neighborhoods behind. Then he had the hackney stop and he climbed inside.

As Lord Satterwaite settled against the musty seat squab and the carriage set forth again, he commented, "There is scarcely a dull moment to be found when you are anywhere in the vicinity, Miss Hedgeworth."

Fredericka eyed the viscount askance. "I am not sure what you mean by that, my lord. It does not sound to be particularly complimentary."

"On the contrary. I never knew a Season to be so fraught with novel difficulties," said Lord Satterwaite. "I am becoming quite inured to it, I assure you."

Fredericka was becoming amused by his air of resignation. "Why, my lord, surely you are not implying that I am the cause of upset in your untrammeled existence?"

Lord Satterwaite uttered a short bark of laughter. "Implying, Miss Hedgeworth? I rather thought I was quite clear on the matter."

"What a horridly boring time of it you have had, then," said Fredericka. "You should be grateful to me, my lord, for enlivening your life."

"I foresee that I shall end by wringing your neck, Miss Hedge-worth," said Lord Satterwaite thoughtfully. "How dare you tell that woman that I was not the one who had given that wretched female a slip on the shoulder?"

"Well, you were not," said Fredericka calmly. "Oh, you are thinking that I should not have used such warm language."

"That thought did cross my mind," admitted Lord Satterwaite with considerable restraint. "You should not even know such a phrase, but undoubtedly you have a perfectly good explanation for it."

Fredericka let that last comment pass, feeling it unnecessary to explain that the daughter of one of the tenants at Luting had found herself in just the same predicament and that the girl's father had been too distraught to watch his language.

"Well, I shan't do so again. It is just that the circumstances seemed to warrant a rapid and unequivocal disclaimer." Freder-icka's glance was brimful of amusement, but she said meekly, "I was so concerned for your reputation, you see."

After a stunned instant, Lord Satterwaite said appreciatively, "You little wretch."

Fredericka laughed then. "I am sorry! But you must see the ex-quisite irony."

"I do. Believe me, I do!" There was a peculiar glint in Lord Satterwaite's eyes, compounded of humor, frustration, and some-thing else. Before Fredericka guessed what he had in mind, he had tilted up her chin with his long fingers and kissed her thor-oughly.

"Oh!" She drew back, blushing hotly.

In the passing lamplight, he observed this phenomenon with satisfaction.

The carriage was slowing. They were nearing their destination, it seemed. "Let that be a lesson to you, Miss Hedgeworth. Playing with fire has its inevitable consequences," he said.

Before Fredericka had recovered possession of herself suffi-ciently, his lordship had opened the door of the carriage and leaped down. Lord Satterwaite held up his hand to her to aid her descent. Very much on her dignity, Fredericka refused to look up into his face.

Astonishment was giving way to anger that he should have

treated her so freely, but she could not speak to him as she had in mind to do. There was such a confusing riot of emotions inside her that she recognized the sheer impossibility of addressing the viscount in any very coherent manner.

Lord Satterwaite escorted Fredericka up the front steps, but he declined to enter at the butler's invitation. Instead he took punctilious leave of Miss Hedgeworth. Taking her gloved hand and raising her fingers to his lips, he said, "I have rarely spent such an interesting evening at the opera, ma'am."

Her color considerably heightened, Fredericka swept into the town house.

The consequences of her compassionate action toward the servant girl were soon made apparent to Fredericka. Before she had gotten into bed, Lady Chalmers came into her bedroom and dismissed the maid. Then the countess read her a stern lecture.

"But could you have turned your back on that poor unfortunate soul, dear ma'am? I do not believe it," said Fredericka quietly.

Lady Chalmers faltered in the face of such confidence in her own character. "Well, my dear, I certainly did not have the opportunity to discover whether I would have or not," she said on the slightest laugh. "Cousin Maria had by that time tumbled into my arms and I could not have very well let her drop to the ground. Er—what did you decide to do with the girl?"

"Lord Satterwaite very graciously agreed to escort me to Mrs. Savage's, ma'am," said Fredericka with a smile. "We left her in that lady's very capable hands."

Lady Chalmers dropped onto the side of the bed as though she had no strength left in her legs. "Fredericka! You did not go there!"

"But of course I did. Betsy would not go with Lord Satterwaite without me," said Fredericka calmly, as though it was the most mundane thing in the world to have done.

"The neighborhood, my dear! Why, there is no saying what might have happened to you," said Lady Chalmers.

"However, nothing did and so you may rest easy tonight, my lady," said Fredericka.

Lady Chalmers rose to her feet. "I am very, very disturbed, my dear. And as for Sebastion's part in this— I shall have something to say to my son, I believe."

"I wish you will not blame the viscount, dear ma'am, for he truly had no choice in the matter, as he himself told me. He would not allow me to take a hackney there alone," said Fredericka.

"I should hope not! Folly to have allowed you to go alone!" Lady Chalmers realized that she had quite unconsciously absolved her son of all blame and she shook her head. "Very well. I shall not ring a peal of his head. And I suppose that I have done ringing one over yours, my dear." The countess approached her guest and bent to kiss her. "You are a brave but utterly foolish young woman. I quite see that your poor mother has had much to bear from your headstrong character."

Fredericka laughed. "Indeed she has, my lady. I do not deny it. However, we love one another dearly for all of that!"

Lady Chalmers's annoyance faded from her face completely. "Yes, I am certain that you do. Go to sleep, my dear. We shall hear all sorts of rumors tomorrow over this piece of work, of course. But we shall not let it affect us at all, shall we?"

Lady Chalmers's optimistic outlook suffered a setback on the following day, however. It seemed that everyone knew about what had happened on the steps of the opera house. Not content with making shocked observations on Mr. Thatcher's sad part in the drama, many of the ladies who called at Chalmers House wondered aloud how Miss Hedgeworth could possibly have taken up the defense of such a creature.

"For it is well known that one cannot trust the morals of that class," pronounced Lady Towrand.

"Perhaps one should also take stock of the morals of the higher class, as well," murmured Fredericka.

Lady Chalmers said hastily, "Perhaps you would care for more tea, my lady?"

"Quite right," said Lady Towrand, nodding. She was far too arrogant to expect any but corroboration of her own statements, and when it dawned on her precisely what had been said her long face turned cold. "Really, Miss Hedgeworth! The very idea! No, I think not, Lady Chalmers. I have had quite enough tea, I thank you!" She set down her cup and saucer with a decisive click and surged to her feet. "I shall take my leave of you, Lady Chalmers."

"Of course, Lady Towrand," said Lady Chalmers helplessly. She walked her guest to the door and after seeing her out, turned herself about. "My dear Fredericka, I was never more shocked in my life. How could you have said anything so—so graceless?"

"Lady Towrand does not believe in charity, my lady. She and Sir Lawrence once stigmatized your own efforts as worthless gestures," said Fredericka quietly. "I am sorry that I have upset you, ma'am. But I cannot abide such haughty self-importance."

Lady Chalmers stared at Fredericka, scarcely heeding the last part of her statement. A faint color was rising into her face. "Worthless gestures? When I have such admiration for what Letitia Savage is doing? How dare that overbred woman say such a thing! I never liked her above half." The countess drew a breath, visibly regaining control of herself. "I had thought better of Sir Lawrence. His manners have always been exquisite. Fredericka, I am sorry if I wound you, but I do hope that you have not chosen to encourage that gentleman. Such sentiments as Sir Lawrence expressed speak of a narrowness of character that I am persuaded you would not like in a husband."

"I do not believe that I need be anxious that Sir Lawrence will continue to press his suit, my lady. I suspect that he was given such a disgust by the whole spectacle that he has bowed himself out of the lists," said Fredericka.

"I see." Lady Chalmers reflected for a moment. "While it is unfortunate that the gentleman's defection should be due to such a contretemps, I nevertheless feel it is for the best. Sir Lawrence would not have suited you, my dear."

"No, my lady," said Fredericka with a sigh of relief. She had wondered whether Lady Chalmers had favored Sir Lawrence as an eligible *parti*. Little comments of approbation for the gentleman had casually dropped from the countess's lips and her ladyship had always bestowed warm approval on Sir Lawrence's visits to the town house. Lady Chalmers had also taken particular note of the numerous posies that were delivered which had borne Sir Lawrence's card.

"I suppose that we shall not be seeing Mr. Thatcher as often as previously," said Lady Chalmers mediatively.

"No, my lady," Fredericka admitted. "I do not think so."

Lady Chalmers looked at Miss Hedgeworth for a moment. A smile barely touched her lips. "Well, my dear. I once commented that I need not be anxious that you would be importuned by totally unsuitable offers, for you seemed well able to counter them. Let us hope that there are other gentlemen who shall not require such rough-and-ready treatment."

"No, indeed." Fredericka smiled, even though she knew that the countess was half in earnest. Almost as well as she knew her own thoughts could she read Lady Chalmers's obvious reflections. Her ladyship was a bit perturbed that she had virtually thrown over two of her most persistent suitors.

Though Fredericka had several admirers, there were only a handful who were generally considered to be serious in their pursuit. Mr. Everard was flatteringly attentive, but one never knew what lay behind that gentleman's faintly contemptuous smile. Mr. Thatcher and Sir Lawrence had exhibited definite signs of interest. Now obviously they would no longer make up part of Fredericka's inner court. Young Lord Alterwrop had certainly shown himself enamored, but no one had actually believed anything would come of his impassioned siege and so it had proved. The only others assumed to have thoughts of winning Miss Hedgeworth's hand were Mr. Howard-Browne, whom Fredericka had already decided would not do for her, Sir Thomas, and Lord Satterwaite.

Undoubtedly Lady Chalmers knew which gentlemen were still contenders, for it was reflected in her next question. Her gaze very steady, she said, "My dear, I should like you to be perfectly frank with me. I believe that both Sir Thomas and my son, Lord Satterwaite, harbor an interest in you. Could you possibly accept either of their suits?"

Chapter Twenty-two

Fredericka hesitated. It would not do to intimate to Lady Chalmers that she preferred either gentleman over the other when she did not really know herself. Yet it would be unfair to indicate that she did not care for the gentlemen at all. Slowly, she said, "I scarcely know how to reply, my lady. Sir Thomas is a very worthy gentleman. I have found him to be unfailingly considerate and the tone of his mind to be of a high order. Lord Satterwaite, too, is all that is amiable. In addition, we share many common interests. However, his lordship and I do not always agree as we should. Forgive me for saying so, my lady, but Lord Satterwaite can be rather autocratic and opinionated."

"No doubt my son was rather vexed over last night's affair and ended by behaving abominably to you," said Lady Chalmers dryly. "Oh, you have no need to blush. I am quite aware of Sebastion's abominable flashes of temper. Never mind, my dear! You have answered my question perfectly and indeed, I am encouraged. I have no doubt whatsoever that we shall eventually see you very credibly established."

The door opened and the butler stepped inside. "Sir Thomas, my lady." He stood aside to allow the gentleman to pass and then withdrew from the drawing room.

Lady Chalmers rose and offered her hand. "Sir Thomas! This is indeed a pleasant surprise. I am glad that you have called on Miss Hedgeworth and myself this afternoon."

Sir Thomas bowed correctly over her ladyship's hand and exchanged greetings with Miss Hedgeworth. "I trust that I am not intruding, my lady?"

"Of course not, dear sir! Pray come sit down with us. I am certain that nothing could be more delightful," said Lady Chalmers.

Sir Thomas was gratified at his reception. He sat down and proceeded to entertain the ladies with various amusing anecdotes that he had heard since he had last seen them. Then with a grave look, he said, "I am glad to have caught you alone, my lady, Miss Hedgeworth. I was never more shocked in my life to hear what happened yesterday evening at the opera. I had it from Lady Markam just this morning. My dear Miss Hedgeworth, I wish in particular you could have been spared such a distressing scene."

"It was indeed distressing, Sir Thomas, but more for that unfortunate young woman than for anyone else," said Fredericka quietly. "I am only glad that I was able to offer her some aid."

"What is this you say?" Sir Thomas glanced toward Lady Chalmers for enlightenment. "Have you indeed extended that poor girl sanctuary, my lady?"

"What Miss Hedgeworth means is that she knew of my interest in a foundling home and she conceived the happy notion to see that the girl was taken there," said Lady Chalmers, deliberately glossing over the details. She smiled at Fredericka. "I am really quite proud of her presence of mind at such a time."

"Quite!" Sir Thomas was much impressed. "Indeed, Miss Hedgeworth, there are not many whose compassion and strength of purpose would have dictated such an honorable course. In short, I am all admiration. It puts quite a satisfying conclusion to the terrible business. I congratulate you."

"It was little enough to be able to do, Sir Thomas," said Fredericka, somewhat dryly.

"It is like your modest nature to disclaim," said Sir Thomas, smiling. He turned to Lady Chalmers. "My lady, I know that it is highly improper—indeed, an impertinence! But may I request a few minutes alone with Miss Hedgeworth?"

Lady Chalmers glanced quickly at Fredericka. There was a dawning comprehension in the younger woman's eyes, and entreaty as well. Lady Chalmers decided to ignore Miss Hedgeworth's obvious dismay. "Of course, Sir Thomas. There are one or two things which I must say to my housekeeper."

Lady Chalmers rose to her feet, Sir Thomas rising at once with her. She gave the gentleman her hand. "I believe a quarter hour shall suffice for my little errand."

Sir Thomas bowed. When the countess had exited, he returned

to his seat. "Miss Hedgeworth, you must be wondering what has possessed me to request this unusual interview. Believe me, anything smacking of the unconventional is highly repugnant to me. I would not have gone this length if there had been anyone of your family who stood in some sort your guardian available to me."

"My brother is in town and he is accepted as the head of our family," said Fredericka, with a touch of mischief.

Sir Thomas looked nonplussed. His forehead creased. "I had not considered Lord Hedgeworth due to his lack of years, but naturally, if you think it more proper—"

"You have done just right, Sir Thomas. Jack is not my guardian. I am of age and my own mistress. You may speak your mind freely to me, sir," said Fredericka, taking pity on his obvious confusion, and resigning herself to the inevitable.

Sir Thomas was relieved. He smiled at her. "Thank you, Miss Hedgeworth. You are truly most kind. What I wished to say to you—that is, I hold you in such admiration and respect that I—" He had reddened with the effort of making himself clear. "In short, Miss Hedgeworth, I am offering for your hand." He looked at her hopefully.

Fredericka smiled, but gave the slightest shake of her head. "My dear Sir Thomas, I truly value your proposal. However, I must decline. I have found you to be a good friend. But I do not wish to wound you by pretending to those warmer emotions that I am persuaded you would wish the lady of your choice to feel toward you."

Sir Thomas's countenance had fallen. He sighed heavily. "I thank you for your frankness, Miss Hedgeworth. I am naturally disappointed. However, I shall not despair. Perhaps I have been too precipitate—my own ardency carrying me too fast. You may continue to count me one of your most devoted admirers, Miss Hedgeworth."

"You are too good, Sir Thomas," said Fredericka gently.

The door to the drawing room opened and Lady Chalmers entered. Sir Thomas got to his feet. He went to her ladyship, offering her a smile and a bow. "I shall wish you good day, my lady. No, no, pray do not put yourself out. I can easily find my own way out, I assure you."

When Sir Thomas had exited, Lady Chalmers instantly turned toward Miss Hedgeworth. "Pray tell me at once, my dear! Has Sir Thomas offered for you?"

"Yes, indeed he did, ma'am. However, I declined his flattering suit," said Fredericka. She watched as the countess's face underwent varied emotions.

"I do not perfectly understand, Fredericka. You spoke of Sir Thomas quite highly only an hour or so ago. He is in every respect imminently suitable. You have said so yourself. Why have you then refused him?" asked Lady Chalmers.

"I know that it is quite extraordinarily improvident of me, my lady, especially when you have gone to such pains to bring me to the notice of every eligible gentleman in London," said Fredericka apologetically.

"Well, never mind that," said Lady Chalmers, waving her hand. "That is scarcely the point, after all. I quite thought that you looked upon Sir Thomas with some favor."

"Indeed I have, my lady. I had almost decided that should he make an offer for me that it would suit me very well to accept him," said Fredericka. "However, when it came down to actually doing so, I found that I—I could not!"

"Oh, my dear. I suppose you know your own business best," said Lady Chalmers.

With a good deal of humor in her voice, Fredericka said, "You must not despair, my lady, for Sir Thomas does not. I am fairly certain that he will probably offer for me again."

Lady Chalmers stared very hard at her. "Indeed! Well, I hope it is not for some weeks, for perhaps by then you will better know your heart."

"So I hope, too, my lady," said Fredericka quietly. "If you will excuse me, Lady Chalmers, I should like to go upstairs for a while. As you may appreciate, I have a great many things to think about."

"Of course, Fredericka," said Lady Chalmers.

Fredericka went upstairs to her sitting room. She did indeed have much to reflect upon. She had done something that afternoon that she had never done before. She had actually declined an honorable offer from a most worthy *parti* and it bothered her to an unusual degree.

The problem was that she liked Sir Thomas very much. In nearly every respect he was faultless. He was kind and thoughtful and considerate. He was a man of considerable affluence. As his wife, she would want for nothing. Except, said a small voice inside her, a bit of excitement.

Her thoughts instantly gravitated to that thorough kissing she had received from Lord Satterwaite. Fredericka pressed her hands to suddenly warm cheeks. It was so horrid to compare Sir Thomas's punctilious attentions with Lord Satterwaite's rakish behavior. And that the viscount had had experience at that sort of thing, Fredericka was in no doubt. He had not been at all clumsy or, afterward, embarrassed. On the contrary, he had seemed rather pleased with himself.

If Lord Satterwaite was to offer for her, what would be her answer? The startling question had flashed across her mind and she discovered that her heart had automatically leaped in response. Fredericka got up to pace across the floor. Her brows were knit. It could not be possible that she was falling in love with the viscount.

She was still reflecting upon this most important concept when a knock fell on the door. She jumped, startled. "Come in!"

A footman opened the door. "Miss, Lord Satterwaite is belowstairs and requests to see you."

Fredericka's thoughts were still so thoroughly caught up that she panicked. "Oh, no! I could not possibly—" She met the astonished gaze of the footman and realized what a fool she was making of herself. Lifting her chin, she said, "Pray let his lordship know that I shall be down directly."

The footman bowed and went away to relay the message. Fredericka slipped into her bathroom to bathe her suddenly heated face. She glanced in the mirror and was startled to see how bright her eyes looked. "This will not do at all, my girl," she said aloud. She took a deep breath and practiced a calm expression until she was half-satisfied.

Fredericka finally started downstairs. She hesitated on the landing, a variety of thoughts tumbling through her mind. Uppermost was the memory of how she and the viscount had parted the night before. Her heart actually pounded at the thought of facing Lord Satterwaite now.

When she entered the drawing room, she saw that the viscount was dressed in buckskins and boots and that he held driving gloves and his whip. He had obviously tooled his carriage over to Chalmers House. She knew that he did not like to keep his high-strung horses standing and so she knew that it was to be a short visit. "Good afternoon, my lord."

As Fredericka approached him, her hand held out and with a polite smile fixed to her lips, Lord Satterwaite studied her narrowly. He thought that she looked too pale. He stepped forward to take her hand in his own. When she would have withdrawn it, he retained his grasp on her fingers and demanded, "Has my mother been ringing a peal over your head?"

Fredericka's expressive eyes rose quickly to his, then sank again. He could not know of her refusal of Sir Thomas, and so he could only be referring to the evening before. "Only a little, my lord. Her ladyship has been most forebearing, considering the depth of her distress." She managed to regain possession of her hand and she gestured at a wingback chair. "Won't you sit down, my lord?"

"I haven't come to sit, but to take you for a drive in the park," said Lord Satterwaite. He smiled slightly at her swift glance of surprise. "Did you think that I would cut your acquaintance, Miss Hedgeworth?"

Fredericka felt the flush that warmed her face. "I did not know what to think, my lord."

Lord Satterwaite flashed a grin. "Complimentary of you, my dear lady. However, I shall disregard it. It is almost five o'clock. You will want to be seen by all the high flyers and starched up personages, so go upstairs and change into something suitable. However becoming that gown is to you, it will not do for a drive in my phaeton."

Fredericka managed to retain her composure. He had obviously guessed or heard the talk that had gone forward over the episode at the opera house. She understood him well enough to know what he was about. However, she had begun to come to some conclusions regarding her feelings for him that made her rather shy at that moment of his company. "I thank you for your consideration, my lord. But I'd rather not go driving."

"Afraid, Miss Hedgeworth?" he challenged.

"Of course not!" exclaimed Fredericka, roused out of her restraint. "Merely, it is hot today and I would infinitely prefer to stay indoors this afternoon."

"Pudding-heart. Admit it, Miss Hedgeworth, you haven't got the fortitude for it," said Lord Satterwaite. "I suspect this is not the only fence that you have jibed at."

"I have never shied at a fence in my life," retorted Fredericka, a gleam of anger entering her eyes.

Lord Satterwaite held out his hand. "Then prove it to me. Come driving with me and stare down any and all who would attempt to put you out of countenance!"

Fredericka stared up at the viscount. She wavered, thoroughly detesting his tactics but anxious to show herself worthy in his eyes. She laid her palm in his. "Very well, my lord. I shall!" she said evenly.

Lord Satterwaite's eyes held a gleam of satisfaction. His fingers pressed hers, then let her go. "Good girl. I shall await you here."

"I will not be long, my lord. I know well that you do not like to keep your horses standing," said Fredericka. She did not wait for his reply before she turned on her heel and went swiftly out of the drawing room.

Within minutes, Fredericka had donned a carriage dress and returned downstairs. Lord Satterwaite walked out of the town house with her and handed her up into his phaeton. Climbing up beside her, he took up the reins and nodded to the groom who stood at the horses' heads to let them go.

Smoothly the viscount tooled the team into the traffic. He glanced down at the lady sitting beside him. "I hope that you do not feel that I have coerced you into driving out with me, Miss Hedgeworth."

"Of course you have," said Fredericka with asperity. "You knew very well that I could not allow those slights against me to go unchecked."

Lord Satterwaite laughed. "Well, yes," he admitted finally. "But I wished to lend whatever credit I might have to you. I know that the gossip is running high."

"We have indeed sustained several visits today from those who otherwise would have expired from their own curiosity," said Fredericka.

"You have a devilish sharp tongue," said Lord Satterwaite appreciatively. He nodded to an acquaintance in a carriage passing in the opposite direction. "The affair does not appear to have harmed you unduly, Miss Hedgeworth. You appear to be acknowledged as widely as ever."

Fredericka had caught sight of Sir Peter. He was promenading with a lady on his arm. She bowed to the gentleman and received in return only a cold nod. "There is at least one personage who shall not forgive me," she said cheerfully.

Lord Satterwaite had taken note of the passage. "You are rather more cheerful over Sir Peter's defection than I would have anticipated, Miss Hedgeworth. He was acclaimed as one of your prime suitors."

"Was he? How odd that he never attained to that position in my eyes," said Fredericka indifferently.

Lord Satterwaite glanced down at her profile, but he did not comment. Instead a slight smile touched his mouth. When he perceived that another carriage had stopped and the occupants were waving at him, he obligingly pulled up his team. "Well met, Miss Howard-Browne! Good day, Miss Stoker."

Fredericka leaned forward to greet the two young ladies as well. "I am so glad to see you. Do you go to the Suttons' ball on Saturday?"

Miss Howard-Browne and Miss Stoker both laughed. Her eyes sparkling, Miss Howard-Browne said, "I do not know! We have been invited to make up a party for the public masquerade. Fredericka, why do you not join us?"

"Why, I should like to very much. Lady Chalmers insisted at the beginning of the Season that I should have a domino and I have not yet had the opportunity to wear it," said Fredericka, smiling.

Lord Satterwaite interrupted. He was frowning a little. "A public masquerade? Surely that is an entertainment that is a bit fast."

Miss Howard-Browne made a face, laughing at the same time. "Pooh! Fitz has said the same thing! He is so disobliging, but I had quite thought that you would be more sportive, my lord!"

"I am certain that it will be very agreeable," said Miss Stoker. She glanced at her companion. "Only we do not yet have all of our party made up. It was Mr. Everard's notion and Lord Markam saw at once that it was just the thing to pull us all out of the doldrums that all of these assemblies and routs and balls have thrust upon us. He has promised to find us some respectable escorts, so there can be no objection."

"No objection in the world," said Lord Satterwaite, a faintly acid note in his voice. "My dear Miss Stoker, have you spoken to Lady Markam about this precious scheme?"

Miss Stoker looked a shade apprehensive. "No, of course not. We have only just finished discussing it with Mr. Everard and some others. Why, my lord? Surely you do not suspect that Mama will put the least rub in our way!"

"That is precisely what I do think, Miss Stoker," said Lord Satterwaite firmly. "Miss Howard-Browne, I suggest that in this instance you allow Fitz to guide you. I assure you that he will have the complete support of your mother."

Miss Howard-Browne wrinkled her pretty nose. "Oh, you are a spoilsport indeed, my lord! I wish that I had never waved for you to stop."

Lord Satterwaite laughed and flicked his reins. "No doubt. However, it was for the best, I assure you."

Chapter Twenty-three

As the carriages parted, Fredericka glanced up at her companion's face. "Is the notion really so very bad, my lord? After all, if Mr. Everard and Lord Markam see no objection—"

"Lord Markam is as foolish as he can hold together. As for my cousin, I would object to anything which he might suggest," said Lord Satterwaite shortly. He looked down at her. "I hope that you are not contemplating taking part in this ridiculous scheme."

"Why, as to that, my lord, I have not yet made up my mind," said Fredericka serenely. She did not meet his sharpened glance, but continued to direct her gaze ahead. "There is Mr. Everard now, my lord. Do, pray, pause for a moment."

Lord Satterwaite did so, with obvious reluctance. He nodded to his cousin. "Lucius."

From his seat on the back of a showy hack, Mr. Everard inclined his head. "Cousin, your very obedient." His suave smile widened when he directed his attention toward Fredericka. "Miss Hedgeworth! You appear in looks this afternoon. I am happy to see that the stirring events of yesterday evening did not bring a pall of shock to your lovely cheeks."

"I am made of sterner stuff, Mr. Everard," said Fredericka.

"I am certain that you are," he murmured.

Fredericka did not like the man, and neither did Lord Satterwaite. She could tell from the tension in his posture and his carefully schooled features. She had hesitated putting into action the impulse that had led her to urge the viscount to pull up for Mr. Everard, but Lord Satterwaite's intense dislike of his cousin reinforced the half-formed thought in her mind. "Mr. Everard, I understand from Miss Howard-Browne and Miss Stoker that there is to be a party gotten up for a masquerade this Saturday. I should like to know more, if you would be so kind."

"Alas, Miss Hedgeworth, I can tell you no more than you obviously already know. Such a scheme was certainly discussed, but whether a party shall actually be got up is an entirely different matter," said Mr. Everard, shaking his head.

"That is disappointing, indeed. However, it is probably all for the best. I have been told that these masquerades are really not at all the thing," said Fredericka.

Mr. Everard laughed gently. "Oh no, who could have said anything so prudish and old-fashioned?" His eyes had glanced toward the viscount's face as he spoke and then he looked again at Miss Hedgeworth. "If I hear anything more, Miss Hedgeworth, rest assured that I shall instantly apprise you of it."

"Thank you, Mr. Everard," said Fredericka.

Lord Satterwaite lifted the reins and gave his team the command to go. "We shall undoubtedly run into you again, Lucius."

Mr. Everard backed his mount a couple of paces so that the carriage could brush by him. He touched the brim of his hat in silent salute to Fredericka as the phaeton passed.

Fredericka slid a glance at the viscount. His jaw was held very tight and a muscle jumped in his cheek. "You are angry, my lord?" she inquired calmly.

Lord Satterwaite looked at her swiftly. "Of course not! It is nothing to me that you set yourself up to flirt with every man-milliner in town."

"Oh, I don't think that I flirt with all of them. Just Mr. Everard and a few others," she said.

Lord Satterwaite jerked his head around. His eyes narrowed. "You are deliberately offering me provocation, Miss Hedgeworth! You recall as well as I that I warned you against my cousin."

"Indeed you did," agreed Fredericka cordially. "However, I also recall that I made it quite clear that you do not have the least say in whom I befriend. Nor do you have the obligation to censor or approve of what I do."

"Do I not know it!" Lord Satterwaite gave a short bark of laughter. "Only witness that farce last night. I trust that you will not mind me telling you that you are headstrong and foolish to a disproportionate degree."

"Not at all, my lord, as long as I am able to observe that you are a bit too dictatorial and set in your opinions," said Fredericka promptly.

Lord Satterwaite was incensed. In a controlled voice, he said, "I suppose that you prefer my cousin's raffish style and manners, Miss Hedgeworth?"

Fredericka smoothed a crease from her skirt. "Why, I cannot say, my lord. How can I make any such rude comparison?" She stole a look upward at the viscount's set expression, and she was encouraged to continue. "Perhaps I should become better acquainted with Mr. Everard. I believe that he is counted as one of my most ardent admirers, after all."

"I believe that it will suit us both to cut our drive short today, Miss Hedgeworth," said Lord Satterwaite. "I shall set you down at Chalmers House directly."

Fredericka agreed to it with a serenity that the viscount found most irritating. He was not used to having himself looked upon as less than a most eligible *parti*. Every unmarried lady of his acquaintance would willingly cut out the heart of her closest confidante to sit up beside him in his phaeton so that the world could witness her triumph in attaching his interest. But not Miss Hedgeworth. Oh, no, that miss was singularly indifferent to the honor that he was paying to her. For some reason, the crowning insult was that she had preened herself upon attaching Lucius Everard's interest! If it was not so repulsive, he would shout with laughter, thought the viscount savagely.

Miss Hedgeworth, obviously supremely unaware that she had gravely offended him, capped her perfidy by casually commenting on every insipid sight that came within her vision.

The drive out of the park took an inordinate amount of time to accomplish. Miss Hedgeworth waved and bowed to every chance-met acquaintance, even requesting a number of times that the viscount pull up his horses so that she could exchange a few cordialities.

Lord Satterwaite was seething by the time he was able to draw up before Chalmers House. Yet nothing could have exceeded his polite manner in lifting Miss Hedgeworth down to the flagway, nor his beautiful address as he took leave of her.

Miss Hedgeworth walked up the front steps of the town house and entered it without a backward glance.

Lord Satterwaite slapped the reins and gave his startled team the office.

Fredericka was traversing the front hallway toward the stairs when she chanced to meet Lord Chalmers coming out of the library. "Good evening, my lord," she said sunnily. "I hope that you have spent an enjoyable afternoon."

"Good evening, Miss Hedgeworth. It has been quite pleasant, actually. It is kind of you to inquire. Allow me to bear you company upstairs, my dear. I have been informed that my valet is waiting for me. We are to dine at Carlton House tonight, you know," said Lord Chalmers.

"Oh, yes! I am looking forward to it no end," said Fredericka, beginning to unbutton the wrists of her kid gloves. "I have heard much regarding the prince's hospitality."

Lord Chalmers chuckled. "That I do not doubt! You have naturally been warned of the overheated rooms, but I shall also drop a word in your ear regarding the prince himself. His Royal Highness is partial to lovely women and he shall no doubt pay you quite lavish compliments when you are presented to him, so you are not to be too much put out of countenance when he does so."

Fredericka gave a throaty chuckle. Her eyes were alight as she slid a mischievous glance toward the earl. "I shall keep it in mind, my lord. Are we to be a party this evening?"

"I do not know. Lady Chalmers has not told me as yet. Her ladyship prefers to break these things to me quite at the last moment so that I do not have the opportunity to brood over my ill luck," said Lord Chalmers cheerfully.

Fredericka laughed again. The earl noticed that she appeared inordinately appreciative of his small foray into humor. No doubt there was a deeper explanation and he was made curious. In the normal course of things he would have thought it beneath him to satisfy his inquisitiveness, but he had had his own thoughts about certain matters and he made delicate inquiry.

"You appear quite delightfully radiant this evening, Miss Hedgeworth. But I perceive that you have been out driving. No doubt that accounts for it," said Lord Chalmers. "It is a beautiful day for it."

"Is it? Oh, of course it is," said Fredericka, beginning to pull off her kid gloves. She flashed a bright smile. "I do not think it would have mattered if it had been pouring rain, my lord. I have been out with Lord Satterwaite. You will scarcely credit it, I daresay, but we have just enjoyed the most splendid row."

"Have you indeed, my dear," said Lord Chalmers, eyeing her in considerable astonishment.

Fredericka was concentrating on a particularly obstinate thumb. "Yes! I discovered that he quite despises Mr. Everard and that was what began it. So you see!"

"Quite. It is marvelous indeed. You are to be congratulated," said Lord Chalmers dryly.

Fredericka looked around at the earl. Realizing what her inattention and impulsive tongue had led her to confide, she colored hotly. "I am sorry, my lord! I have been going on in the most non-sensical way."

"No, no, I shall not allow you to say so, Miss Hedgeworth. Indeed, I am profoundly interested in everything that you may find to say to me," said Lord Chalmers reassuringly. "Forgive me for my lamentable lack of imagination, but why is it wonderful to have quarreled with my son?"

Fredericka flushed even brighter. "My wretched tongue! Do, pray, forget that I have ever said anything at all, my lord!"

"That is highly unfair, Miss Hedgeworth. You have roused a perfect passion in me to discover the truth. You cannot deny me now!" said Lord Chalmers.

"Oh dear!" Fredericka gave a rueful laugh. "I suppose that I am finely caught, am I not? Very well, my lord! But I warn you that it scarcely rebounds to my credit!"

"All the better, my dear Miss Hedgeworth!" assured the earl, a twinkle in his eyes.

"It is terrible of me, I know, but I am afraid that I tried to incite Lord Satterwaite to—to jealousy," confessed Fredericka.

"And were you successful?" asked Lord Chalmers, regarding her with fascination. Fredericka laughed and shook her head. "It is a great deal too bad to admit to it, but yes, I believe that I was!"

"Excellent, Miss Hedgeworth! I am delighted. My son has had is own way for too long," said Lord Chalmers, chuckling.

"I have never before done such a thing in my life, my lord," aid Fredericka ruefully. "I am a little ashamed now."

"No, why? It will not do my son the least harm in the world. On the contrary! I am glad to hear that at least one young lady is managing to stir him up," said Lord Chalmers. He paused, throwing a level glance toward her. "I heard about the affair of yesterday evening, of course."

"Have you, my lord?" murmured Fredericka, with a sinking feeling. The countess had been greatly disturbed by the role that her houseguest had played in the unfolding drama and undoubtedly had related her upset to the earl. No doubt Lord Chalmers wished to call her to account and Fredericka set herself to accept it gracefully.

"A regrettable incident, of course. I trust that Lord Satterwaite rose nobly to the occasion?" asked Lord Chalmers.

Fredericka looked at the earl in swift surprise. A smile trembled on her lips. "The viscount was considerably put out, my lord."

Lord Chalmers gave a bark of laughter. His eyes gleamed. "Was he, indeed! No doubt he had reason, too. Miss Hedgeworth, I must tell you that I am delighted at the way you are injecting a bit of turbulence into Lord Satterwaite's life. Pray do not allow your maidenly scruples to hinder you in continuing to do so."

They had by this time reached the head of the stairs. Lord Chalmers nodded to her and turned off with his limping step toward his own quarters. Fredericka walked to her own bedroom and entered it, rather bemused.

When she had refreshed herself and changed into her evening gown, Fredericka returned downstairs to meet the Chalmerses in the drawing room. As she was crossing the entry hall, she was stopped by a footman and handed a note.

"This came for you a short while ago, miss. There was no reply requested," said the servant man.

Fredericka thanked the footman and unsealed the sheet. Her eyes at once dropped to the signature. With astonishment, she saw that it was from Mr. Everard. Fredericka read with startled dis-

may that Mr. Everard had obeyed her behest and had concocte‹
what he hoped would be a congenial party to attend the publi‹
masquerade to be held on Saturday. He hoped that Miss Hedge‹
worth would be pleased to add her presence to the gathering.

Fredericka frowned. She folded the note and slipped it into he‹
reticule. She felt herself to have been placed in an awkward posi‹
tion. It was quite her own fault, of course. She had made the ini‹
tial overture to Mr. Everard and that would make it very difficul‹
to draw back from an engagement that she knew would not be ap‹
proved by Lady Chalmers.

Yet, Fredericka felt that she was almost constrained to accept‹
Mr. Everard's invitation, for offhand she could not think of any‹
way to gracefully decline. However, if it was to be such a party as‹
Mr. Everard had said, perhaps it would not be so very bad after‹
all. She needed the countess's wise guidance. Her ladyship was‹
vastly experienced in such social matters and could no doubt‹
guide her to the best conclusion.

Now was not the time to think about her dilemma, nor to seek
Lady Chalmers's advice, however, and so as she walked into the
drawing room Fredericka put the problem out of her mind.

That evening at Carlton House, Lord and Lady Chalmers, with
Fredericka, joined the crowds. The ornate rooms were just as hot
as Lord Chalmers had predicted and Fredericka applied her fan
continuously. She had no desire to dance, but instead thought
longingly about stepping outside.

Lord Satterwaite appeared at her elbow. He smiled at her with
a lazy gleam in his eyes. "Would you care for an ice, Miss Hedgeworth?"

"Oh, yes! That would be wonderful," said Fredericka gratefully.
She glanced at Lady Chalmers for permission and the countess
nodded, smiling. Fredericka placed her fingers on the viscount's
elbow and allowed him to steer her slowly through the milling
crowd toward the refreshments room. An orchestra was playing,
but the music merely underlaid the din of conversation that rose on
all sides. "Is it always like this, my lord?"

"Invariably," said Lord Satterwaite. "His Royal Highness does
not like the night air and consequently has the windows shut tight
at all times."

"I was speaking of the crowd, my lord. I have never seen such a magnificent gathering," said Fredericka.

Lord Satterwaite laughed. His eyes had narrowed with amusement. "The prince likes to entertain and there are few who are foolhardy enough to reject his highness's invitations. You will see all the ton who are presently residing in London here tonight."

"That I can well believe, my lord," said Fredericka dryly as she was bumped by a large woman who had surged past them.

At almost the same instant, Mr. Everard sauntered up to the couple. He saluted the viscount lazily, his eyes hard. "Cousin. I trust that I see you well. But how can it be otherwise when you have the lovely Miss Hedgeworth on your arm?"

"As you say, Lucius," said Lord Satterwaite, not pleased by his cousin's appearance. However, there was nothing that could be gained by being uncivil. He had already learned some months previously, when he had allowed his temper to run away with him, that regrettable circumstances could arise out of his own lack of control. No matter how his hackles rose in his cousin's presence, he was determined not to allow himself to be drawn into conflict. He therefore smiled with every appearance of affability. "I have the distinction of squiring Miss Hedgeworth in for refreshments."

"Heady stuff indeed," said Mr. Everard with the faintest thread of mockery. "However, I believe that I shall shortly have the honor of adding Miss Hedgeworth to my own pleasure party. I trust that you received my note this evening, Miss Hedgeworth?"

"Yes, of course," said Fredericka, very aware that the viscount had stiffened beside her. "I do not yet have an answer for you, Mr. Everard. I do not know precisely what my engagements may be and—"

"Come, come, Miss Hedgeworth! I know well that the fascination of a masquerade must make all other engagements pale in comparison," said Mr. Everard tolerantly, his smile wide. "Indeed, the notion has already generated some excitement in certain quarters. Miss Hedgeworth! You cannot be so cruel as to deny me the pleasure of your company when you had indicated that you would attend!"

"That is precisely what she is saying, Lucius," snapped Lord Satterwaite. "Miss Hedgeworth shall not be available to your party."

Mr. Everard raised his brows in astonished surprise. "Forgive me, my lord. I did not realize that you were Miss Hedgeworth's mouthpiece or her censor."

Fredericka flushed, both angered and dismayed by the manner that this scene had been forced upon her. "Lord Satterwaite is neither, Mr. Everard. But—"

"Good. Then I may count upon you after all, Miss Hedgeworth," said Mr. Everard. He bowed and slipped away in the press around them before another word could be exchanged.

Lord Satterwaite turned, letting Miss Hedgeworth's fingers slip from his elbow. His green eyes blazed. "I did not think it possible that you could be such a little fool. I had thought you had more sense than to encourage that fellow when both my mother and I have warned you against him. And now you intend to sit in his pocket, at a masquerade, no less!"

Fredericka was stung. "Lord Satterwaite, I am not encouraging Mr. Everard. He has made an assumption, helped along, I might add, by your completely unsolicited interference."

"Yes! What else could he think when you so brazenly inferred to him that you wished to be in his company!" exclaimed Lord Satterwaite.

There were a number of things that Fredericka wished to say. Among them a denial that she had said any such thing or had even desired it; that she had only spoken to Mr. Everard about the masquerade at all to pique Lord Satterwaite's jealousy; that she earnestly desired nothing more than to decline Mr. Everard's invitation; that she disliked Mr. Everard intensely, but cared more for Lord Satterwaite than was comfortable. But she said none of those things. Instead, very coldly, she said, "I find that I do not wish to have an ice after all. Pray return me to Lady Chalmers, my lord!"

Without a word, but his expression grim, Lord Satterwaite did exactly as she had asked. Then he turned on his heel and walked off.

Fredericka, watching the viscount go, felt strongly inclined to burst into tears.

Chapter Twenty-four

In the end, Fredericka did accept Mr. Everard's invitation to attend the masquerade. She did not seek Lady Chalmers's advice for her bleak decision, nor did she inform that lady of her intentions. Fredericka felt much as though a schoolgirl must who was sneaking away from her governess. She consoled herself with the reflection that it would not be for long and that there would be a large party, so that it would all seem quite respectable.

However, her assumption suffered a severe setback when she met Mr. Everard and saw that he was alone. As she stepped out of the carriage, her domino and mask in place, she asked, "Where is everyone else, Mr. Everard?"

Mr. Everard tucked her hand into his arm. He was wearing a mask, but he was easily recognizable from his wide smile and his height. He pressed her hand. "Alas, Miss Hedgeworth! It is most unfortunate. Lady Markam was taken by a temporary spell of dizziness and Miss Stoker naturally went with her ladyship to see that she completely recovered. The others have all drifted away from the booth in order to see the sights. I assured them that I would meet you and see that you were safely ensconced in the booth until their return."

Fredericka stood for a moment in indecision, but she could not perceive in Mr. Everard's respectful tone anything other than a concern and a ruefulness natural to a gentleman whose party had undergone such an unexpected crisis. She nodded, therefore, if somewhat reluctantly. "Very well, Mr. Everard. Pray escort me to the booth. I hope that Lady Markam will not prove to be so indisposed that she will not be able to join us."

"Oh, have no fear of that, Miss Hedgeworth. Lady Markam is a remarkably resilient woman," said Mr. Everard. He drew her into the gardens and kept up a steady stream of gentle conversation as they walked. When they emerged into the cleared area where the booths were located, he politely ushered her into one.

When Fredericka saw that the table was set for several places, she was reassured. Surely the remainder of the party would return in only a few moments. In the meantime, she would do her best to be an amiable guest, even though she really did not care to be alone with Mr. Everard. It was simply not done to be totally without chaperonage, and Fredericka hoped that her own mask and domino disguised her identity from the many masked personages promenading past the booth.

Mr. Everard set Fredericka into her chair with a solicitous flourish. His eyes glittered behind his mask and his mouth smiled. "I shall have a supper plate for you momentarily. In the meantime, allow me to pour you a glass of champagne."

Fredericka smiled and agreed. She watched the frothy wine cascading into her glass. Her brows knit slightly at the amount that Mr. Everard had poured. "I shall not be able to drink the half of it, sir," she said, glancing up at him.

Mr. Everard lay back against the cushion of his seat. He smiled, swirling his own glass. "Oh, I fancy that you will find that you have quite a taste for it, Miss Hedgeworth. To your good health, my dear lady." He raised his wineglass in a toast and waited, while Fredericka reluctantly raised her own. He gave a low laugh and tossed off his wine.

Fredericka sipped at the champagne and looked around her. Several couples were dancing to the orchestra's offering, but in a free manner that quite shocked her. Laughter and scraps of conversation came to her ears. Everyone she saw was masked and wore a domino and she thought it was a good thing. Surely that silly little female sidling up so boldly to her escort would not have wished anyone to know who she was, she thought, watching with dismay conduct that could only have been stigmatized as disgraceful.

Fredericka was feeling more and more ill at ease. Attending a public masquerade had seemed to be an outrageous, but yet a rather harmless, thing to do.

Now she bitterly regretted the sequence of events that had led her to accept Mr. Everard's invitation. His glance was bold, his hands had lingered on her shoulders as he seated her. She disliked his knowing laugh and his thinly veiled amorous remarks as time plodded on. In short, he was not in the least respectful toward her as he had been when she had arrived.

It was as though he had spun some sort of web and now considered that she had been finely caught. Fredericka did not care for that analogy. It made her shiver.

However, she reassured herself by recalling that Mr. Everard had promised that he would return her to Chalmers House before the midnight unmasking. Above all, Fredericka knew that she could not allow herself to be unmasked and perhaps recognized.

This function was altogether different from what she had envisioned. The vulgar strolled about with the quality. Raucous laughter and delighted squeals and loud flirtations were now heard on every side. The orchestra was very nearly drowned out, but the whirling couples on the dance floor were oblivious.

Fredericka reluctantly admitted to herself that the viscount had known what he was talking about. He had been right when he had warned her that this was not the sort of thing she would enjoy. But she was here now and with no prospect of leaving for at least a little while.

Fredericka had already realized that the party that Mr. Everard had so suavely spoken about had no other existence than in his own airy statements. Mr. Everard had more than once alluded to Lady Markam and others, voicing concern that they had not yet returned, but with such an indifferent tone that Fredericka was convinced that they had never been to the masquerade at all. She therefore had no one to whom she could appeal in making an early withdrawal. Mr. Everard had ordered supper and she did not anticipate that he would willingly take her home until they had finished eating.

Fredericka took another small sip of champagne. She grimaced slightly. It was a cheap champagne, but she would not complain. Perhaps that was all that was to be had at this sort of function, or perhaps it was the best that Mr. Everard could afford.

Supper was served to them in their box. Fredericka made an effort to do justice to the mediocre repast. Mr. Everard noticed that she was not eating much. "Is dinner not to your liking, Miss Hedgeworth?" he asked.

"In truth, I am not very hungry," admitted Fredericka.

"It is paltry fare, I fear," said Mr. Everard, pushing aside his own unfinished plate. He lifted the wine bottle and tipped it over her glass. "Allow me to replenish your glass, Miss Hedgeworth. It is the least I can do when the supper has become a disappointment."

Fredericka thanked him politely, but with a sinking heart. If she drank the half of what he pressed upon her, she would undoubtedly become tipsy. She felt a strange need to keep her wits about her this night.

"You do not drink, Miss Hedgeworth!"

Fredericka smiled at him from under her mask. "I have had my fill for the moment, Mr. Everard. Actually, I would like to leave the box and—"

"A capital idea!" exclaimed Mr. Everard, at once rising and holding out his hand to her. "I will be happy to escort you onto the floor, ma'am."

Fredericka was dismayed. She rose, but said, "I do not wish to dance, Mr. Everard. I am sorry. What I should really like to do is to—"

"It is hot here under the pavilion, is it not? You are uncomfortable," said Mr. Everard.

Fredericka felt a measure of relief. "Yes, that is it exactly! I should like to be taken home."

Mr. Everard did not appear to have heard her. He had taken her hand around his elbow and was holding her fingers captive against his sleeve. The noise and the chatter seemed to have deafened him as he escorted Fredericka out of the box. He was saying something to her, which she could not quite make out.

"What did you say, Mr. Everard?" she asked.

He laughed and shook his head. Very loudly, he said, "It is far too noisy in here to make oneself properly heard. Let us go elsewhere."

Mr. Everard drew Fredericka across the crowded floor. Men and women attired in masks and dominoes dashed past them. Fredericka was rudely shoved aside by one buck intent on his pursuit of a shrilly laughing nymph and she stumbled. Mr. Everard steadied her. She thanked him, but then realized that his protective arm about her shoulders had not been removed. Fredericka edged a little sideways. "Sir, I must protest."

Mr. Everard glanced down swiftly. He flashed an amused smile. "I apologize, Miss Hedgeworth. I am thoughtless in this press." He took her hand again and continued to guide her toward the fringes of the crowd.

Fredericka saw their direction and she was relieved. Once out of the pavilion it would be a simple matter to go to find their carriage. But when they emerged out of the pavilion, they were standing in a far different area than that through which they had entered. Fredericka glanced around in bewilderment. "But where are we?"

"These are the pleasure gardens. Come, we shall stroll the walks for a few minutes and cool ourselves," said Mr. Everard. He felt her sudden resistance and smiled down at her. "Miss Hedgeworth, your maidenly reservations do you nothing but credit, believe me. But it is rather warm in the pavilion and we are standing in a very exposed spot. It would be easy to be recognized under this blaze of lights."

Fredericka glanced about quickly. It was as he had said. They were standing directly in the light of several lamps that were set about. She started forward toward some shadow. "Are we near the carriages, sir? As I told you inside, I wish to return home."

"So soon! I am devastated. I fear that I cannot have been good company this evening," said Mr. Everard mournfully.

"I have not said so," said Fredericka, smiling slightly. Little as she had liked his increasing familiarities, she still had no wish to insult him or to wound him. "It is the masquerade. And the lack of a proper party. It—it is not at all as I had thought—hoped—it would be."

Mr. Everard nodded as though he perfectly understood. "Come, we shall do better to go this way. It is the quickest."

Fredericka allowed herself to be guided down a broad lighted walkway. She felt a momentary qualm at leaving the safety of numbers that the crowd represented, but then she reassured herself. Mr. Everard was a gentleman. He had understood her dismay and he had acquiesced in her desire to be taken home. Soon now they would come upon the carriages and she would be safely away from the masquerade.

Mr. Everard turned a corner into a smaller path. It was less well-lighted and Fredericka paused. "Surely this is not the way?" she asked.

Mr. Everard smiled. He said confidently, "Of course it is. I am never at a loss on these paths. I know precisely where we are."

Fredericka was only partially reassured, but rather than make a scene, she allowed herself to be drawn on by Mr. Everard's insistence. But her own sense of direction was good and she began to feel uneasy, for it seemed to her that with a couple of turnings they were walking in the opposite direction from where they had started. And too, the lamps had become fewer and farther between, so that she and her companion were more in the dark than they were in the light.

Much of the noise had faded behind them, but there were still sounds. There must be other promenaders out roaming the gardens, thought Fredericka, trying to reassure herself. But it was impossible to deny that she was now in an extremely uncomfortable position. She had allowed herself to be taken off alone by a gentleman. If she were to be discovered in such compromising circumstances, she would be mortified and instantly become the subject of gossip.

With all of her heart, Fredericka wished that she was back at the pavilion. At least there, in that crowd, she would have felt less vulnerable.

Fredericka stopped. She slipped her hand free of Mr. Everard's grasp. In a controlled voice, she said, "Mr. Everard, this has gone on long enough. It is your notion of a joke, I suppose, but I do not find it amusing. Pray return me to the pavilion now. I should like to go home."

"All in good time, my dear. All in good time." Mr. Everard glanced about them. They stood alone on a lonely overgrown path. A single lamp was lit behind them, now half-obscured by leaves. It was dark ahead of them. "This will do admirably, in any event."

"What do you mean?" asked Fredericka sharply, taking a step backward. She did not like his tone, nor his low laugh.

Mr. Everard grasped her wrist and pulled her to him. He bent

—er arm behind her back. With the other hand he grasped her chin. "This, my dear Miss Hedgeworth." He lowered his head and kissed her.

Fredericka twisted her head free. Panting, she stared up at the gentleman. He was faintly smiling. "Let me go at once!"

"Oh, I shall let you go. But not just at once," he murmured, preparing to gather her closer.

Fredericka had grown up around two brothers and their male friends. She lifted her knee sharply and at the same time twisted her body. Mr. Everard jerked. His hold on her slackened and Fredericka spun free. Instantly she darted back down the path.

"Jade!" Mr. Everard shouted after her. As quickly as his condition would permit, he started after her. "I shall catch you, never fear. And when I do—" He laughed again, unpleasantly.

Fredericka fled on winged feet. She was not quite certain of the paths, but she knew roughly where the pavilion was situated and she took those walks that seemed to lead in that direction.

Her breath coming fast, Fredericka rounded an abrupt corner and collided with someone. She drew back, giving a sharp gasp. Her arms were held in a nonpersonal way that swiftly changed.

" 'ere now! Look at wot Oi've caught!"

"Unhand me at once!" exclaimed Fredericka. She tore herself free, only to be confronted by two other roughly dressed men. They were both beginning to smile and she backed up a step.

"Aye, 'tis a rare piece. Let's 'ave a look at 'er face!" One reached out with a dirty hand.

Fredericka ducked, her own hands going out to stave him off. Nonetheless, his fingers tore at her mask and ripped it free. She glared at them all.

"My, my, it is a rare spitfire," said the first man. His voice took on a cajoling note. " 'ere now, missy, we mean ye no 'arm." His companions laughed as though at a good joke.

Fredericka was desperate. She had wandered into a nightmare. One of the men held a stave. She darted forward and snatched it from his slackened grip. Brandishing the wooden stave, she warned, "Let me pass or it will go roughly with you."

The three men laughed uproariously. They stepped toward her. Fredericka swung the heavy stick as she had been taught in her childhood by one of her father's tenants. The end caught one of the men a hard blow in the abdomen. He crumpled instantly with a cry of pain. One of the other men had come into range and Fredericka whirled the other end of her makeshift weapon. The end cracked up against the man's chin. Down he crashed.

The last of the trio leaped toward her and his hand dragged at her shoulder. But then he was suddenly gone. Fredericka looked up. She saw an unknown gentleman in a swirl of satin domino level her third assailant with a quick fist.

The gentleman did not even wait to watch his opponent sprawl to the ground. He held out his hand. Breathing quickly, he said in a low voice, "Come! We must get away from here at once. The pavilion is this way."

Without giving a second thought to what she might be doing in trusting this stranger, Fredericka placed her hand in his. He strode off quickly with her keeping pace beside him.

The noise of the revelers became louder. Fredericka was never more glad in her life to see the pavilion and the crowd. She started to run forward, but her companion held her back.

"Your mask!" he said. "It's gone."

Fredericka put up her hand to her face. Dismayed, she said, "I remember now. Those men—"

The gentleman reached up to the strings of his own mask. "Here, wear mine. You can't be recognized here."

He pulled off the mask and handed it to her, at the same time meeting her startled glance. With a sardonic curl of his lips, he asked, "Surprised, Miss Hedgeworth?"

Fredericka took the mask from his fingers and quickly tied it in place. Her cheeks were burning. More than the fear of being discovered by someone she knew, she wanted to hide her embarrassment. It was the worst possible thing to have happened. Viscount Satterwaite had witnessed and even rescued her from her folly. "I cannot deny it, my lord," she said tightly.

"I thought not. However, this is not the time nor the place to explore it," said Lord Satterwaite. He was looking around, his lean face grim in expression and his green eyes glittering. "It is unfortunate that I shall be recognized, but my reputation will absorb it, I think." His hand tightened around her elbow. "Come!

Let us leave this place as quickly as possible. You cannot be seen here."

A dominoed gentleman came rushing up behind them. He seized Fredericka's shoulder. "There you are, my dear! I told you hat I would catch you."

Fredericka sucked in her breath in fear and dismay. All too aware of the viscount's stiffening presence, she felt ready to sink. 'Leave me alone, sir. I am going home."

Mr. Everard laughed. "You have found a new protector, have you?" He looked at last at her companion. His mocking smile was wiped away. "Satterwaite!"

"Lucius." Lord Satterwaite's voice was utterly cold. "Somehow I am not surprised to find you here."

Mr. Everard stood fiddling with the strings of his domino. He smiled. "No, I don't think you should be surprised. However, I am a great deal astonished by your awkward presence, my dear cousin. But perhaps it can be explained easily enough. The lady is an attractive minx."

Lord Satterwaite's fist shot out and connected with Mr. Everard's jaw. His cousin went down like a sack of meal. The viscount reached down and fumbled for a moment. When he straightened, Mr. Everard's mask dangled from his fingers. Glancing at Fredericka, he said, "A fortunate meeting indeed. Now I need not brazenly advertise my presence here this night." He put on the mask. Then he took hold of her elbow again. "Now, my dear lady, we shall leave with all speed."

Fredericka was perfectly willing. Mr. Everard was beginning to stir and he uttered a low groan. She wanted to be far away before that gentleman came to his senses. She was trembling over the nasty scene. The whole evening had been one terrifying experience. It was unpleasant, certainly, that the viscount had appeared in all of his grim and righteous anger, but still she was so very relieved that he had come. She felt safe in his company, at least.

Lord Satterwaite and Fredericka made their way as swiftly as possible out of the pavilion. Fredericka tried to express her gratitude, but the words would scarcely leave her throat. She could feel the anger vibrating from the viscount. He was furious with her. It made her at once desperately unhappy and angry as well.

The viscount motioned for his carriage. When it drove up beside them at the curb, he handed Fredericka inside and climbed in after her. He shut the door and gave the signal to his driver. The carriage started off as he settled back against the seat.

Lord Satterwaite looked across at his companion. In the flickering lights of the streetlamps, he could see that she had turned away so that her profile was to him. The mask obscured her face, lending a hint of mystery. She appeared undeniably intriguing. He wanted to drag her into his arms and snatch off the mask and kiss her. But he held himself still. Fury at himself and at her for what had happened coursed through him.

Neither uttered a word during the interminable drive to Chalmers House. When they arrived, Lord Satterwaite descended first from the carriage and then turned to offer his hand. She stepped down to the walkway and when she would have withdrawn her hand, he tightened his hold. "I shall escort you inside," he said.

Fredericka looked up at him. "Of course, my lord," she said expressionlessly.

They were admitted into the house by a sleepy porter, who at sight of the masks became more alert. Lord Satterwaite took off his mask and held out his hand for hers. When Fredericka gave it to him, he stuffed both into his pocket.

"We shall be private in the drawing room, I think," he said. He told the porter to light a few candles, which the manservant swiftly did.

Chapter Twenty-five

Fredericka preceded the viscount into the drawing room. She wandered aimlessly from the occasional table to the hearth while the porter lit the candles. She was aware that the viscount was watching her from near the door. When the porter was at last done with his task and had exited, Fredericka turned toward the viscount. He had shut the door and advanced into the middle of the room.

"I am constrained to admit to you that you were right, my lord," she said tightly. "It was not at all the sort of affair that one might enjoy."

Fredericka knew well that she was grossly at fault. She could not now rationalize away her actions. She had been affronted and angry when he had interjected himself into her affairs at Carlton House. She should not have allowed matters with Mr. Everard to come to a head, but she had also wanted to show Lord Satterwaite that she had no need of the self-appointed guard that he had set over her. Instead she had made a fool of herself, in his eyes and her own. It was insufferable. His reaction to her apology was not balm to her spirit.

"You are a hoyden!" said Lord Satterwaite coldly. "I do not understand why my mother does not send you packing."

"Your opinion is of little consequence to me, my lord!" said Fredericka, her eyes blazing. "Indeed, it is laughable that *you* should censor *me*!"

Lord Satterwaite seized her wrist when she would have whirled away from him. "What do you mean by that?" he demanded.

Fredericka tossed her head. "Only that I have learned a great deal since I have been in London. You are a byword in some quarters, my lord. And it is rumored quite openly that Lord Chalmers is so overtaxed with your scrapes and escapades that he has threatened to disown you. If only half of what I have heard is true, it is truly a wonder that the earl has not long since done so. So do not dare to call me on the carpet, my lord! You have not the credits for such a role!"

Lord Satterwaite was white about the mouth. "You dare! Your impertinence is insufferable! If I were your brother, I would soon teach you better manners!"

"How fortunate for me that you are not!" snapped Fredericka. She jerked free her wrist. "As for my impertinence, what of yours, my lord! You have seen fit to rake me over the coals. You have not the right nor the respect that task requires. You would do well to remember that I am not your sister, nor any sort of relation whatsoever!"

"Thank God!" he interjected from between set teeth.

"Yes!" flashed Fredericka. "How I should hate to be under any obligation to you. You are autocratic and arrogant and a hypocrite to boot! I have learned to detest everything about you. You deal fast and loose with Lord and Lady Chalmers. You protest friendship, but you turn your face at the least adversity. You pretend compassion when you have a heart of stone. In short, I suspect that I hate you!" She was trembling with the force of her emotion.

"Are you quite finished?" he asked. His brows were contracted and his eyes were narrowed to slits. His mouth was held very tight. His voice vibrated with his anger.

"No, I am not! But I find that it would be a waste of my time and breath, for you do not care in the least! Good-bye, my lord! I hope that we shall never meet again!"

Fredericka spun and hurried away from him. She wrenched open the door and fled from the drawing room. She was half-afraid that he would follow her, for he had looked like a thundercloud. His fists had been bunched, too. It was obvious that it had taken the greatest self-control for him not to reach out and do her violence. At that frightening thought, Fredericka increased her pace. She picked up her skirt and ran up the stairs.

Reaching her bedroom, Fredericka went in and shut the door, turning the key in the lock. That done, she loosened the strings of the domino and let it slip to the floor. Then she threw herself across the bed and burst into tears.

There was a knock at the door. "Miss! Miss, are you all right?"

"Oh, go away! Just go away!" Fredericka cried, and then buried her face in the pillow to muffle her sobbing. After a while, she sensed that the maid had indeed crept away. She gave way to the full weight of her humiliation and sorrow, until she was at last emptied of tears.

Fredericka was exhausted and drained. Something hideous had happened tonight. She knew that she would never be the same again. For several minutes she stared up at the darkened ceiling. It was a long time before she slept.

Lord Satterwaite left Chalmers House burning with outrage and resentment. Miss Hedgeworth had used him abominably. She had not shown the proper gratitude for his timely rescue, nor repentance for her foolhardiness. It seemed to him that Miss Hedgeworth was utterly graceless and lacking in common sense.

"She needs a keeper. No! A bear-leader," he said to himself, pausing on the walkway. He stood frowning a moment. It was not outside the realm of possibility that Miss Hedgeworth would continue in her headstrong, heedless ways. She obviously had no intention of attending to any advice of his, he thought bitterly.

Lord Satterwaite knew that the best thing, the easiest thing, for him to do would be to wash his hands of the entire matter. He should step back and allow Miss Hedgeworth to continue in her path of destruction.

Quickly enough, she would learn the folly of her ways. Already the starchiest of society were looking askance at Miss Hedgeworth. The tale about what had happened at the opera house had gained in the telling, bringing with it the inevitable censor.

The ton had closed its ranks. Mr. Thatcher was one of them, and though the evil attending his actions was recognized, it was yet felt that a young lady such as Miss Hedgeworth should not have been involved at all in such a sordid scene. That she had been hinted at a faint lack of breeding.

Miss Hedgeworth was slowly attaining a reputation for being a little fast. It would not be many more weeks, or take many more floutings of social conventions, before Miss Hedgeworth found herself on the outs with the ton. She had risen quickly to popular-

ity. Her descent to oblivion could be just as swift, thought Lord
Satterwaite grimly.

If Miss Hedgeworth persisted in pursuing friendships with such
individuals as Lucius Everard, certainly social ostracism would be
only her just desserts.

Even as the thought arose, Lord Satterwaite denied its truth.
Miss Hedgeworth might be unpredictable and lively and perhaps
a shade too ready at hand for any mad dash, but she was also one
of the most unspoiled, capable, and fascinating ladies of his experience.

Lord Satterwaite made his decision. He would not simply stand
by and watch Miss Hedgeworth make a complete disaster of her
first Season in London. There must be someone whose advice she
would give an ear to, if not his own or Lady Chalmers's.

Lord Satterwaite thought then of Miss Hedgeworth's brother.

The baron was young but he bore himself well. Lord Hedgeworth had made a few mistakes since coming to London, but he
had swiftly proven that he was not to be drawn into complete disaster. His gaming debts were reputed to have been honorably settled and he had not returned to the halls after that singularly
unprofitable foray.

Lord Hedgeworth had committed the natural errors of a fledg-
ling unused to town ways. However, he had also come about in an
amazingly short time. He appeared to have a head on his shoulders and to be of a shrewd, even sharp, understanding.

Lord Satterwaite set out for Lord Hedgeworth's lodgings. The
viscount wanted to get the unpleasant business over and settled
before another hour had elapsed. There was no knowing what
Miss Hedgeworth would take into her head to do when she rose
from her bed in the morning.

At Lord Hedgeworth's lodgings, the viscount learned that the
young gentleman had gone out for dinner and had not been back
since. Upon Lord Satterwaite's inquiry where Lord Hedgeworth
might have gone after his dinner engagement, the young gentleman's man could only speculate.

Lord Satterwaite swallowed his impatience and proceeded
upon a search for Lord Hedgeworth. He thought he had a fairly
shrewd notion of what sort of entertainment Lord Hedgeworth
might seek in the company of other young bucks like himself, and

Lord Satterwaite set out on a tour of all the more popular gaming houses.

Lord Satterwaite ran his quarry to earth in an amazingly short time. He stood watching the play for a few moments. He noted that Lord Hedgeworth played recklessly but with a good deal of shrewdness, nevertheless. He strolled away for refreshment and a quiet hand or two with acquaintances, but always kept one part of his attention on Fredericka's brother.

When Lord Hedgeworth rose from the table at last, it was nearly three in the morning. Lord Satterwaite threw in his hand and made his excuses to his friends. He casually followed Lord Hedgeworth out of the room and hailed him at the doorway. "Hedgeworth! You are going in my direction, I suppose?"

Lord Hedgeworth looked around in surprise. His eyes were heavy-lidded and reddened from the smoke and the brandy and the hour, but were surprisingly alert for all of that. "My lord Satterwaite. Yes, I am walking to my lodgings."

"I shall bear you company part of the way," said Lord Satterwaite.

Lord Hedgeworth's face registered surprise and a hint of wariness. But he waited courteously enough for the viscount to claim his own hat and gloves. The gentlemen left the portals of the club with the porter's good night echoing in their ears. They walked companionably down the walk, neither saying anything for a few minutes.

Finally, Lord Hedgeworth's curiosity got the better of him. "What did you wish to discuss with me, my lord?" he asked abruptly.

Lord Satterwaite threw the younger man an amused glance. "Must I have something to talk over with you?" he asked.

Lord Hedgeworth made a gesture. "I am not an intimate of your circle, my lord. The only connection between us is my sister. I cannot think of any other reason for you to seek out my company."

"You are not a stupid young fellow, in any event," remarked Lord Satterwaite. "You have guessed correctly. I wished to talk to you about your sister. Miss Hedgeworth has gotten herself embroiled in a rather awkward matter. I have hopes that you might be able to help her come about."

Lord Hedgeworth stopped on the flagged walkway. He stared up at the taller man with a pugnacious expression that was fully discernible in the light of a streetlamp. "I will not tolerate any scandalmongering, my lord. I warn you to take care in what you say to me about my sister."

"Smooth your feathers, bantam. I do not seek to insult Miss Hedgeworth," said Lord Satterwaite, his lip curling a little. "On the contrary, I hope to protect her from her own folly."

Lord Hedgeworth's brows were drawn together in a heavy frown. "You speak in riddles, my lord. Confound it, my head is pounding so loud that I can scarce make sense of what you are saying. Come with me to my lodgings. I must have some coffee."

Lord Satterwaite indicated his willingness to fall in with this plan and the gentlemen continued on their way. Lord Hedgeworth's hotel was soon reached and the two men entered and went upstairs.

Lord Hedgeworth showed his companion politely into his rooms. Shutting the door, he crossed to the bellpull. Tugging on it vigorously, he then waited with impatience for his man to appear. When the valet opened the door, Lord Hedgeworth requested that a pot of coffee be brought up. He inquired whether his guest wished anything and upon Lord Satterwaite's negative, he sent the man away.

Lord Hedgeworth threw himself carelessly into a wingback chair. He gestured at a companion chair. "Sit down, my lord. I shall be in a fair way to treating you with due consideration in a few minutes." He closed his eyes, giving the impression of falling asleep. Only the tenseness of his hands on the chair arms gave true indication of his continued consciousness.

Lord Satterwaite privately doubted it, but he sat down as he had been invited. Crossing his legs, he gently swung one booted toe. He began to wonder whether he had made a mistake in seeking out the young cub at the club. The boy was obviously three quarters to the wind. It would probably have been best to have sought out Lord Hedgeworth in the morning after he had had some sleep.

Shortly, the door opened and the valet entered. He had obviously anticipated his young master's order and had brought sandwiches as well as a pot of coffee. Lord Hedgeworth sat up. With a silent gesture, he invited Lord Satterwaite to join him.

Lord Satterwaite smiled, but politely declined.

Lord Hedgeworth wolfed down a couple of the sandwiches, washing them down with several cups of coffee. In an astonishingly short time, he was finished. He looked over at the viscount, who had been watching him with amused astonishment, and grinned. "I am always hungry after going to the club," he said.

"So I see," said Lord Satterwaite. "Are you sufficiently fortified now?"

"Oh, yes," said Lord Hedgeworth casually. "I am never completely awash. I eat a large supper before I go and I do not drink overmuch. I find that some coffee and a light meal put me to rights at once."

Lord Satterwaite looked into his host's eyes and he saw that Lord Hedgeworth had spoken only the truth. The boy had a more level head on his shoulders than he had thought. And that was all to the good. "I am glad to hear it, for I have something of consequence that I wish to discuss with you."

"Yes, about my sister," said Lord Hedgeworth, his smile fading. He picked up a butter knife and played with it. "What is it that you wished to convey to me, my lord?"

"Miss Hedgeworth has managed to set the ton on its ear almost from the first day that she arrived in London, as I believe you know," said Lord Satterwaite.

"Of course. What is there in that?" said Lord Hedgeworth.

"What you do not know is that tonight Miss Hedgeworth attended a public masquerade. She had as her escort my cousin, Mr. Lucius Everard. Perhaps you have heard of the gentleman?" said Lord Satterwaite.

Lord Hedgeworth stared at the viscount, his expression becoming set. "Yes, I have heard of him. Without wishing to give offense, my lord, your cousin is something of a loose screw."

Lord Satterwaite nodded. "You will understand, then, my concern when I discovered what Miss Hedgeworth had done. I followed her at once to the masquerade. I wish I had been a few moments earlier, but unfortunately I was not. Before I arrived on the scene, Miss Hedgeworth had been mauled by my cousin. Escaping from his unwelcome attentions, she ran into even worse company. When I found her, she was attempting to preserve her virtue from a trio of blackguards from the gutters." He suddenly grinned in recollection. "I will say this much, Miss Hedgeworth is a formidable opponent with a stick."

Lord Hedgeworth was white about the mouth. His eyes burned black in his face. "Was my sister harmed, my lord?"

"Not in the fashion that you mean. I believe that she was more shaken and shocked than anything else," said Lord Satterwaite, quick to reassure.

"Thank God," said Lord Hedgeworth. His lips tightened. "I think that I shall have something to say to your cousin in the morning, my lord."

Lord Satterwaite shrugged. "That is a matter of indifference to me. I did not search you out to encourage a duel, but rather, to enlist your help on your sister's behalf. You see, my lord, at some point during her struggles, Miss Hedgeworth's mask was ripped off. There were a great number of people in attendance and I am fairly certain that at least a few must have been from our circle of acquaintances. These public masquerades are not the thing, but they do entice certain adventuresome sorts out who delight in rubbing shoulders with the hoi polli."

Lord Hedgeworth looked narrowly at the viscount. "You are saying that Freddie might have been recognized?"

"I would wager on it," said Lord Satterwaite harshly.

"And you fear a scandal," said Lord Hedgeworth tersely.

"You have it in a nutshell. Miss Hedgeworth has played with the ton all Season. She has been remarked upon as an original, a free spirit, a delightful scamp." Lord Satterwaite almost snorted. "What Miss Hedgeworth has not realized in her progress to make herself the toast of the town is that she has gradually offended the sensibilities of many who are of consequence. This wild indiscretion would undoubtedly spell her social demise if it becomes generally known."

"I understand you perfectly," said Lord Hedgeworth. "What do you wish me to do?"

Lord Satterwaite leaned forward. "My lord, if you have any influence upon your sister at all, persuade her that she must curb her wild starts. She is well on the road to ruin now. If she is not to be utterly cast out of polite society, she must reform her ways!"

"I did not realize that Freddie had gone so far," said Lord Hedgeworth. He wondered what could possibly have been going through his sister's head to put herself on the line in such a fashion. "I will speak to her, of course. But what is to be done about the masquerade?"

"I shall do my part in burying any rumors that might surface. My mother will naturally pledge herself to do the same. It shall become universally known that Miss Hedgeworth was with friends on the night of the masquerade. Anyone who jumps up to claim otherwise, that she was seen at the masquerade, will likely be a hanger-on of society and might very well not be believed," said Lord Satterwaite.

"I hope that you are right, my lord," said Lord Hedgeworth.

"So do I," said Lord Satterwaite grimly. "As for Lucius Everard, you must deal with him as you see fit. However, I will point out that to force a duel on him may give rise to the very sort of talk that we want least."

"Yes, I can see that, of course. But the fellow must be called to book somehow," said Lord Hedgeworth. "I will not allow my sister to be insulted in such a fashion with impunity."

"I did not think that you would," said Lord Satterwaite. "If you will permit me to make a suggestion?"

He waited for Lord Hedgeworth's wary nod before he continued. "Lucius is known as a bad man, but his reputation notwithstanding, he does have his vulnerabilites. He skates on the thin edge of respectability now. Allow him to fall of his own accord, my lord, and keep your own hands clean. You will see my cousin humbled, never fear."

"I wish that I could believe that," said Lord Hedgeworth.

Lord Satterwaite shrugged. "Lucius is second in succession to my father's shoes. I do not intend to give up my place to him. He has already squandered his own inheritance. It will not be long, according to the whispers that I have heard, before Lucius is clapped in debtor's prison."

Lord Hedgeworth stared narrowly at the viscount. "You speak coldly enough about it, my lord."

"There is little love lost between me and my cousin. He has always been envious of me, which has often led him to utter malicious and slanderous insinuations against me. One learns to mistrust and avoid such a person. We have never run in the same circles. It is a pity, for at one time I believe that Lucius could have made something of himself," said Lord Satterwaite. "But we run the path of our own choosing, do we not? I am fortunate. I have already been made to see the destruction that laid in wait for me."

Lord Hedgeworth was not sure that he understood the viscount's last murmured statement. But it was of little consequence, for his lordship apparently did not require a reply.

Lord Satterwaite rose from his chair. Lord Hedgeworth stood up, also, and he was gratified when the viscount held out his hand to him.

"I wish you good fortune in your audience with your sister." Lord Satterwaite hesitated a moment. "I must tell you that I attempted to reason with her last night. She did not attend to me."

"Though I am fully cognizant of our obligation to you, my lord, you had no right to censor my sister," said Lord Hedgeworth quietly, at once understanding more than the viscount had said. Fredericka had for long made her own decisions and shouldered responsibilities. It would naturally put her in a flame to have someone attempt to override her.

Lord Satterwaite smiled briefly. "So I was informed, in no uncertain terms. However, pray excuse my extraordinary lapse in good manners. My natural anxiety for Miss Hedgeworth and concern for my mother's peace of mind led me into passing the line," he said. "My mother will be quite shattered to be told what had happened. After all, Miss Hedgeworth is under her aegis."

Lord Hedgeworth nodded unhappily. "I am grateful, my lord, both to you and to her ladyship. Never think that I am not. I shall of course do just as you have asked. I will speak to Fredericka."

"Thank you, Lord Hedgeworth," said Lord Satterwaite. The gentlemen shook hands again.

Lord Hedgeworth looked at the viscount, a measure of questioning shrewdness in his eyes. "Why have you put yourself to such trouble on Freddie's behalf, my lord?"

"As I have told you, my mother will be much affected by this affair," said Lord Satterwaite coolly.

"And perhaps you care a little for Freddie herself?" suggested Lord Hedgeworth.

Lord Satterwaite was startled. The question acted as a blinding light, shone suddenly upon his strangely tangled emotions that night. He was staggered by the implication.

But it was not in him to confide in a casual acquaintance like Lord Hedgeworth or, indeed, in anyone. His expression became closed. "I shall take my leave of you, Lord Hedgeworth. It grows abominably close to dawn."

"Yes, of course." Lord Hedgeworth saw the viscount out. When he had returned to his room, he stood frowning for a long moment. Then he shook his head. "Any sensible man would simply go to bed," he said aloud. Banishing any further thoughts and questions, he tumbled into bed. He was snoring within minutes.

Chapter Twenty-six

When Fredericka wakened, it was morning. Pale sunlight glimmered around the edges of the heavy drapes drawn over the windows. She lay still for a long time before she sat up. The bedclothes were tumbled and the gown that she still wore from the night before was rumpled and creased beyond recognition. Her head pounded. Her eyelids felt puffed and heavy and she ached in every limb. Fredericka dragged herself out of bed and unlocked the door. Then she returned to the side of the bed and pulled the hanging bellpull.

A few minutes later, her maid entered the room. When the girl saw Fredericka, her face registered consternation! "Miss! Ye didn't sleep in your dress?!"

Fredericka looked down at herself. She could not even smile. "I do look a fright, do I not? Pray help me get out of it."

"Of course, miss!" The maid expertly undid the many hooks and slid the gown off. She shot a quick glance at her mistress's tired face. "I shall throw a sleeping gown over your head, miss. It is early yet. Ye'll want to sleep a bit more."

Fredericka listlessly agreed to it and she allowed herself to be properly made up for bed. Then she obediently got between the sheets after the maid had smoothed them. She turned her head on the pillow and closed her eyes. Almost at once she was asleep.

The maid was shaking her head and murmuring to herself as she picked up the discarded gown to inspect it. She found at once a rip in the hem and torn lace at the bodice. "What is this, now?"

She glanced again at her sleeping mistress, this time speculatively. Then she nodded. "Aye, miss, ye've had a rare night of it, I'm thinking. I will tell her ladyship that ye are feeling under the weather a bit and that ye desired to sleep late. It is but the truth, after all." She trod across the bedroom to the door, carrying the

shandled gown draped over her arm, and exited the bedroom,
ftly closing the door behind her.

Lady Chalmers was not at all surprised to be informed that
iss Hedgeworth had elected to remain abed late that morning.
er son had come to pay her a visit only a half hour before and in
at time she had sustained a horrid shock. Lord Satterwaite's
rse round tale was scarcely believable, but she was forced to
cognize its truth.

"The girl is utterly unprincipled!" she exclaimed in distress.
And she is a coward to boot! She is simply too frightened and
hamed to show her face!"

Lord Satterwaite apparently thought the same, for he remarked,
Yes, doing it too brown!" He rose from his chair. From his com-
anding height, he said, "I shall leave you now, Mama. You will
ant to deal with this in your own fashion."

"Yes, and I shall do so." Lady Chalmers also rose to her feet.
he gave her hand to her son. "I trust that I may rely upon you to
eep silence, Sebastion?"

Lord Satterwaite frowned down at her. "Of course I shall. What
o you take me for, Mama? I know what a trial this Season has
een to you. I would never add to your burden by letting my
ngue run away with me."

"Thank you, Sebastion. I do not know why I even asked it of
ou, for I do know better," said Lady Chalmers. She drew a deep
nhappy breath. "I suppose that I am still so shaken at what you
ave told me that my wits are completely addled."

He squeezed her fingers, and then let them go. "I took no of-
ense, Mama. I know how affected you must be. She is the daugh-
er of one of your oldest friends, after all. It will come as a shock
o Lady Hedgeworth, as well, I imagine."

"Victoria!" Lady Chalmers spoke in bitter accents. "She should
ave warned me, given me some hint that Fredericka was so wild
and ungovernable. But I was told nothing, nothing!"

"Perhaps Lady Hedgeworth did not know, ma'am. You yourself said that Miss Hedgeworth had never been exposed to society. Perhaps it was finding herself in such heady circumstances
that has led Miss Hedgeworth into this heedless indiscretion,"
said Lord Satterwaite.

He was uncomfortable in the role of castigating Miss Hedge
worth's conduct and character. As his mother had condemne
Miss Hedgeworth, he discovered excuses for the young lady, an
for himself, as well, for he knew far better than anyone how od
had been his reaction to her all along.

Lady Chalmers shook her head, quickly. "Ah, no! You are to
tolerant, Sebastion. The girl is wild to a fault. I am positive tha
there must have been some sign of it before and that played
strong factor in Victoria's positively leaping at accepting my invi
tation to sponsor her daughter. She obviously hoped that sh
would be rid of Fredericka and all the possibility of scandal by
seeing the girl married off."

The countess smiled at her son and laid her hand on his arm
"How glad I am that you did not succumb to her, Sebastion! I de
not think that I could have borne that. You would have regretted i
all of your life."

Lord Satterwaite covered his mother's hand with his own, bu
after a moment removed her fingers from his sleeve. "No doub
you are right, Mama. However, that is neither here nor there. The
question is, what shall you do with her now?"

"I scarcely know. Fredericka could very well have destroyed
her good name with this outrageous start. Coming on top of that
debacle with Oliver Thatcher, it could put her totally beyond the
pale. If anyone at all recognized her last night—" Lady Chalmers
shuddered. "It is not to be thought of, Sebastion. My own credit
will be badly dipped, for it was I who introduced her into society."

"You must send her home," said Lord Satterwaite, frowning.

Lady Chalmers threw up her hands. "How can I? I promised
Lady Hedgeworth to keep her to the end of the Season. Yes, and
to launch her successfully! With the exception of Sir Thomas's
rejected suit, I have yet to receive a decent offer for her hand.
There have been one or two that were marginal, but Fredericka
has refused them."

"That was her choice, ma'am. You can scarcely be held ac-
countable for that!" said Lord Satterwaite. He was glad that Fredericka had turned down those offers. It was only because he could
not presently think of anyone whom he thought could manage
Miss Hedgeworth, he assured himself. She ought to be sent back

where she came from. Her brother would see that she was
red for and she could remain under his protective eyes until
ne had erased the sting of her scandalous behavior.

Lord Satterwaite was unsure what he foresaw after that, for cer-
inly he did not wish his mother to bring Miss Hedgeworth back
London for another Season. The countess had endured enough.
o, something else must be done with Miss Hedgeworth.

The thought crossed his mind that once Miss Hedgeworth was
ack with her brother, he could at last wash his hands of her. But
e rejected that notion without even wondering why he did so. As
ong as Miss Hedgeworth was unattached, she was a menace to
veryone's peace. She must be gotten a stern husband. Perhaps
ie royal hangman might do for her, he thought with black humor.

"No, I know that, Sebastion! It is just that I detest to admit fail-
re. But in this instance—" Lady Chalmers cut off what she was
bout to say. Instead, she made herself smile. "Well, it is not your
vorry, after all. Never mind, my dear. I shall come about. I shall
o my best to scotch any ugly rumors that may arise from this
pisode and I implore you to do the same."

"I shall do my best, of course," said Lord Satterwaite. He lifted
iis mother's hands to his lips and brushed a salute across her
:nuckles. "Do not put yourself into a fret on Miss Hedgeworth's
oehalf, Mama. I have contacted her brother and enlisted his help
n this regard. He has agreed to speak to his sister. He, at least,
seems to know what is due to his name!"

"Very good!" approved Lady Chalmers. "Lord Hedgeworth
seemed eminently levelheaded. Perhaps he might exert some influence over his sister."

"I doubt that anyone has that much influence, dear ma'am,"
said Lord Satterwaite dryly. "But I do have hopes that Lord
Hedgeworth might advise you how best to handle her when she
has taken the bit between her teeth."

"Yes, and so do I!" declared Lady Chalmers.

Lord Satterwaite smiled. "It is a pity that I do not stand in some
authority to her. I could school her. I have broken some spirited
fillies in my time."

"Unfortunately, Fredericka is not a horse," said Lady Chalmers
tartly. "Now pray go away, Sebastion. I do not want you in the

house when she comes downstairs, for lately you and she do nothing but spit and snarl at one another when you meet. She will fl
up into the boughs if she meets you. And I have the headache."

The viscount bowed, his smile widening. He took leave of hi
mother and exited.

Fredericka did not come downstairs when Lady Chalmers had
anticipated that she might. Her ladyship grimly considered tha
young woman's rebelliousness and decided to attend to her own
obligations. There would be time enough to speak her mind to
Miss Hedgeworth.

For a fleeting moment Lady Chalmers was tempted to stay at
home, denying herself to visitors, and pour her woes into Lord
Chalmers's ears. But she rejected that inclination at once. The
earl would be appalled by the tale. It was far better to say nothing
to his lordship until she had done something to help mend the unfortunate situation.

In any event, Lord Chalmers would hear speculation bruited
about by his acquaintances. Though it would catch Lord
Chalmers off guard, he would automatically downplay the rumors
and that was just what was needed from him.

In fact, downplaying the tale was of paramount importance,
and Lady Chalmers knew that every moment she put off the task
would make it that much more difficult to accomplish.

The first matter to be taken care of was to enlist the help of her
oldest and dearest of friends, Madame Potterley. Margaret Potterley lived quietly due to ill health, but she often entertained with
small select parties. Once Margaret Potterley had agreed to put it
about that Miss Hedgeworth had been at her home the evening of
the public masquerade, Miss Hedgeworth would be provided with
an unexceptional alibi.

Lady Chalmers remembered the other morning calls that she
would be making and her thoughts became a bit grim. She was
not looking forward to going about that morning, no matter how
prettily the sun was shining. Steeling herself, she got up and made
ready to go out on her morning calls.

Chapter Twenty-seven

Fredericka awakened heavy-eyed and with the headache. She could see by how light the bedroom was that it must be late morning. She had to get up. She sighed and raised herself onto her elbow. She reached for the bellpull and gave it a tug to call her maid.

Shortly thereafter her maid was at the bedside. "Ye've awakened at last, miss," said the maid cheerfully. She set a tray on the table beside the bed. "I've brought for you some tea and crackers. That will make you feel more the thing."

"Thank you," said Fredericka. She frowned. "What o'clock is it?"

"Oh, 'tis after luncheon," said the maid. She had bustled over to the drapes and now pulled them back. Bright sunlight streamed into the bedroom, dispelling its former deceptive gloom.

"After luncheon!" Fredericka exclaimed. She threw back the bedcovers. "I must get up. What must her ladyship be thinking?"

"Never fret, miss. I told her ladyship this morning that ye were staying abed late, for I could see plain that ye were burnt to the socket. And so I told her ladyship," said the maid reassuringly.

Fredericka subsided. She was grateful to the maid and said so. "I appreciate what you've done for me. It was kind."

The maid flushed. "Ye've been a kind mistress, miss." She started bustling again toward the wardrobe. "Now let us look at what ye might wish to wear, miss."

A quarter hour later, neatly dressed and coiffed, Fredericka entered the dining room where luncheon was being served. Lord Chalmers greeted her pleasantly, even affectionately. But Lady Chalmers bestowed a frosty smile upon her.

Fredericka's heart sank. She could only conclude that the earl had heard nothing of her contremps, but that the tale had already

reached the countess's ears. Her ladyship was obviously e
tremely displeased with her. Her supposition was enforced whe
that lady did not vouchsafe more than two sentences to her, Lad
Chalmers confining most of her remarks to the earl.

When Lady Chalmers rose from the table, expressing her inter
tion to make a few calls that afternoon, Fredericka hastened to sa
that she would be glad to join her ladyship.

Lady Chalmers regarded her thoughtfully. "I think not, Frede
icka. Your maid told me this morning that you did not feel en
tirely well. You would do better to conserve your energy and res
the remainder of the day." She smiled coolly. "We shall talk late
I promise you."

"As you wish, my lady," said Fredericka quietly.

Lord Chalmers looked at their young houseguest. Now that h
scrutinized her face, he realized that she did indeed appear fa
tigued and paler than usual. Annoyed that he had not noticed a
once, he said shortly, "Lady Chalmers is in the right of it, Mis
Hedgeworth. You would do well to recruit your strength. It come:
from burning the candle at both ends, of course. But no doub
there is not a single young lady or youth, if it comes to that, whe
will listen to wiser counsel."

"That is undoubtedly true," said Lady Chalmers.

"Yes, my lord. I shall endeavor to do just as you suggest," saic
Fredericka.

Lady Chalmers smiled again. It was that same chilly smile that
did not engage her eyes. She sailed out of the dining room.

Fredericka remained just a few minutes longer in company
with the earl before she excused herself by pleading the headache.
It was no fabrication, for the dull ache she had awakened with had
become more pronounced. The earl elicited her promise that she
would immediately go upstairs to rest and Fredericka was glad to
give it.

Shortly over an hour later, Fredericka went back downstairs.
She clung to the banister and moved without her customary
spring. Her head still pounded with a dull ache and she felt as
though she had not rested at all. But she brushed the symptoms
aside. The megrims would be shaken quickly enough. She just
needed to be up and about.

She had been informed a few minutes before that her brother

d come to call on her. He was waiting in the drawing room.
edericka did not wish to talk to anyone just then, but she knew
at if she did not visit with Jack, then he would instantly wonder
hat was wrong. Fredericka did not want to make any explana-
ons that might lead to her experiences of the evening before, and
she decided simply to see him.

When Fredericka entered the drawing room, she smiled at her
rother and went to him with outstretched hands. "Jack, how
ood of you to call on me."

He took her hands, but he bent a stern stare on her face. "You
ay think so, Freddie. You look ghastly today. Didn't you sleep
all?"

Fredericka withdrew her hands from his light clasp. She indi-
ated the settee to him and seated herself. "No, I did not sleep
ell last night, as a matter of fact. But I hope that I do not look
hat haggard, Jack. I have been called the toast of the town. I have
reputation to maintain."

"That is just what I wanted to talk to you about," said Jack,
lancing at the drawing room door. Satisfied that it was shut, he
aid, "Lord Satterwaite paid me a visit last night."

Fredericka's smile was wiped from her face. She stiffened. "Is
is lordship's effrontery never satisfied?"

"I told him that he had overstepped his bounds in reading you a
ecture, Freddie, but damned if I don't blame him," said Lord
Hedgeworth frankly. "What maggot got into your brain that led
you to attend such an affair and especially in Lucius Everard's
company?"

Fredericka put her hand to her head. The headache seemed to
be getting worse. "Pray do not ring a peal over me, Jack. I feel so
badly about it as it is."

"So you should! Freddie, I don't mind telling you that I was
deuced glad that Satterwaite was where he was. I don't know how
he chanced to be there, but—"

"He followed me," said Fredericka bitterly. "He followed me
because his arrogance is such that he could not abide the thought
that I had gone against his advice."

Lord Hedgeworth stared at his sister, absorbing the implications of everything she had said. "Followed you? But hold on a

moment, are you saying that Satterwaite advised you again
going to this public masquerade?"

Fredericka realized that she had neatly pricked herself. Sh
sighed, for it was too late now to stave off the conclusions th.
were certain to follow. "Yes, he did. He had overheard me inqui.
ing about it after an acquaintance had mentioned it. Lord Satte-
waite took it upon himself to rebuke me. As though he was m
guardian! And then he ordered me to put it out of my head. Oh,
know that it was no excuse to have done what I did. But the situa
tion was such that my judgment became clouded." Frederick
made a gesture with her hand.

Lord Hedgeworth stared at her, frowning. Finally, he said, "
sounds to me as though you and the viscount have been playin;
some deep game of your own. Freddie, I am going to ask yo
straight from the cuff. Do you care for Lord Satterwaite?"

Fredericka shook her head, almost too quickly. "He is insuffer
able, Jack. How could I? He puts me into such a passion."

"I see." Lord Hedgeworth's frown deepened. There was some
thing here that he did not understand. He had a strong suspicio
that Fredericka was hiding something from him. But she probably
wouldn't tell him what it was. "Freddie, I assured Satterwaite tha
I would speak to you about the course that you have been pursuing."

"Did you indeed!" Fredericka's eyes blazed. "And did his lordship inform you that I am in a fair way to disgracing myself?"

"Believe me, I was never more shocked than when he told me
how fast and loose you have been playing with the proprieties,"
said Jack, perhaps unwisely, tactlessly.

Color surged into Fredericka's face. "How dare he make such
judgments, and yes, carry them to you, too!"

Lord Hedgeworth regarded her obvious temper with misgiv-
ings. "I know that you are older than I am, but a fellow sees and
hears things. Freddie, I don't want my sister's name bruited about
by the vulgar. I don't mean to offend you, but you must see that
you must behave more circumspectly."

Suddenly Fredericka's face crumpled. "Oh, Jack! It is all such
a muddle. I haven't meant to disgrace myself. But Lord Satterwaite assured me that I have and Lady Chalmers is so chillingly
polite. And this is only the worst of it. There was that affair over

Oliver Thatcher's mistress, too, and I offended Lady Towrand. Then I used Lord Satterwaite's dislike for Mr. Everard so that I could play them off against each other. Oh, I have been despicably foolish, Jack!"

"Whatever made you do it, Freddie?" asked Lord Hedgeworth, out of natural bewilderment. He had never known his sister to behave with anything other than good sense, and these fits and starts that he was beginning to learn about had greatly confused him.

Fredericka made a gesture. She sniffed a little. "Oh, it started as a bit of a game."

"A game!" Lord Hedgeworth stared at her. "Freddie, were you mad?"

"I think that I may have been," said Fredericka with a dry little laugh. "I disliked most of the set I was introduced to, you see. The gentlemen considered to be eligible for me were mostly either arrogant bores or lisping dandies. There was not one that I liked. At least— But that is neither here nor there! In any event, I couldn't envision forming an attachment to any of them. Lady Chalmers was so good in making certain that I was well-noticed and I knew that Mama was depending upon me to make the most of my opportunities. Jack, I felt so guilty. I did not want to entertain a suit from any of them! And yet, if one of them did offer for me, how could I tell Mama that I had turned down a perfectly good offer? But that is just what I did do, and now that I have disgraced myself, Sir Thomas will not wish to offer for me ever again."

"You nitwit," said Lord Hedgeworth levelly. "Did you really believe that Mama would reproach you for turning away someone whom you held in repugnance or indifference? What a fool you have been, Freddie!"

"Yes, I have," said Fredericka unhappily. "One thing led to another, until I found myself going to that horrible masquerade with Mr. Everard. Believe me, I do regret that! It was all exceedingly uncomfortable and if I was recognized, which Lord Satterwaite thinks I probably was, the end will probably be social ostracism."

Lord Hedgeworth got up from the settee and took a turn about the drawing room. He faced her again. Rather sternly, he said, "You've made a rare mull of it, Freddie. I can't deny that you have. However, Satterwaite assures me that he and the countess will do all in their power to head off any unpleasant rumors. You were at a private party with friends last night, by the way. You will have to inquire of Satterwaite whose party it was, for I am sure I don't know!"

"No, nor I," said Fredericka. She was silent for a moment. "Jack, do you think that I ought to retreat to Luting?"

"Retreat!" He looked at her. "Of course you will do no such thing. You have to ride this one out, Freddie. Otherwise everyone will be bound to think that there was some truth in the rumors of the masquerade."

"I'd much rather not," said Fredericka, looking down at her hands.

"It's the highest fence you've ever been faced with," said Lord Hedgeworth, quite readily understanding the basis of her reluctance. "But you mustn't shy off now. You must finish the course, Freddie."

Fredericka laughed quietly at herself. "I thought that I would be happy when I had gone my length and I could return to Luting. But I'm not, Jack. I am not at all happy."

Lord Hedgeworth went over to her and put his hand on her shoulder, pressing it. "No, I don't suppose that you are. And whatever else you have on your mind does not help matters, I'll warrant."

Her startled eyes rose swiftly. "How did you know?" she whispered.

"Dash it, Freddie! You're my sister. We've been too close for me to suddenly grow blind," growled Lord Hedgeworth. "Now cut line, girl. What had really cut up your peace so badly? Is it Satterwaite?"

Fredericka dipped her head. She wound her fingers together. "It is so terribly inconvenient, Jack, for he doesn't like me. Not even a little bit."

Lord Hedgeworth stared down at her bowed head, astonishment on his face. "Freddie, you've not gone and fallen in love with Lord Satterwaite?"

She looked up, her lips trembling. She smiled waveringly. "That is precisely what I have done, Jack. Isn't that stupid?"

Lord Hedgeworth thought it would be best if he kept his

thoughts to himself on that end of it. "I would never have guessed it. You and Lord Satterwaite! Still and all, it would not be a bad match."

"But I have just told you, Jack! He doesn't care about me. There is not the least chance of Lord Satterwaite offering for me," said Fredericka.

Lord Hedgeworth regarded her for a long moment. He was thinking about what lengths the viscount had gone to on Fredericka's behalf. Surely a gentleman's concern for his mother's peace of mind could carry him only just so far. Lord Hedgeworth smiled and shook his head. "I tell you what, Fredericka. You have as little sense as any peagoose on occasion."

"What do you mean?" asked Fredericka, mystified.

Lord Hedgeworth shook his head. "Never you mind. It isn't for me to say." He took her hand. "I shall leave you to it, Freddie. You will keep your head up, I know. And I hope that you have learned your lesson. You will refrain from creating any more scandals, will you not?"

"Of course," said Fredericka. She was reluctant to let him go. There was something in his expression that bothered her. He looked as though something had amused him. "Will you come to dinner on Friday? We dine here at Chalmers House that evening."

Lord Hedgeworth shook his head. "No, I had already decided before this matter came up that I was ready to go home. I shall be leaving tomorrow, I expect."

Fredericka felt a lowering of her spirits. "Oh, I see. I did not realize that you were leaving London. But of course you must be anxious to get back to Luting. There will be things that Bartram will wish to discuss with you. And Mama and the others will be glad to see you, too."

Lord Hedgeworth grinned at her. "True, true. I am a favorite wherever I go. I shall give Mama your love."

"Yes, and give my love to Thomas and Sarah, too. Tell them all that I miss then most prodigiously," said Fredericka, rising from the settee and walking with him to the door.

"I will do so," promised Lord Hedgeworth. He turned at the door and pointed a finger at her. "Now mind, you are to behave yourself!"

Fredericka laughed and tossed her head, pretending a lightness that she did not feel. "Of course I shall, Mr. Saucebox!" She saw her brother out with a pretense of renewed spirits, but after he had left, her cheerful expression vanished. She sighed and directed her steps back upstairs.

Chapter Twenty-eight

That afternoon, to all inquiries concerning Miss Hedgeworth's absence, Lady Chalmers replied with a smile and a gracious word. "The poor girl feels quite pulled today. She has been burning the candle too fast, I fear. Her maid told me this morning that she was exhausted and so I allowed her to remain quietly at home today."

Her excuses were met with polite smiles and unbelieving glances. However, few had the effrontery to actually voice their disbelief and merely requested that they be remembered to Miss Hedgeworth. By the time that Lady Chalmers had returned home, she was in a thoroughly bad temper. It was bad enough that Fredericka had behaved so disgracefully. It was worse that she—she!—must make the wretched girl's excuses and pretend that all was well, when it wasn't. She had constantly been on tenterhooks that something would be said at any moment about that stupid masquerade.

There had been a few bad moments, but she had scraped through them fairly well. As Lady Chalmers had hoped, her friend Margaret Potterley had agreed to support her story. Once word had gotten around that Miss Hedgeworth had been at Madame Potterley's, and Lady Chalmers had deliberately let drop that tidbit, the matter could be depended upon in a fair way to being hushed up.

However, there was another matter to resolve. Lady Chalmers sent up a request for Miss Hedgeworth to join her in her sitting room.

Fredericka went to Lady Chalmers almost immediately. "You wished to see me, ma'am?" Her countenance was pale, but she met the countess's gaze steadily.

Lady Chalmers had put off her outer garments and now she signaled for her maid to leave them. She waited until the woman had exited and they were alone before she turned to the young woman. "Fredericka, I have asked you to come because there is a matter of some gravity that I wished to discuss with you. Lord Satterwaite came to see me this morning. You may guess what he related to me."

"Yes, ma'am, I can," said Fredericka quietly. "I am sorry to have acted so foolishly, my lady. It will not happen again."

"I should hope not, indeed!" exclaimed Lady Chalmers. "Fredericka, how could you have done such a thing? If Sebastion had not come up to you when he did, I shudder to think what might have happened to you. Though naturally I am thankful that you are safe, there have been other repercussions of your unthinking folly. I am greatly disappointed in you, my dear, greatly disappointed!"

Fredericka winced. "I am sorry, ma'am. I cannot find words adequate enough that will express my feelings. I know how wrongly I have acted. Indeed, I have not paused once since this has happened in castigating myself. I am truly, truly very sorry."

Lady Chalmers was silent for a moment as she regarded the younger woman. Finally, she said, "I believe you, my dear. However, I am forced to tell you that sponsoring you this Season has not been at all what I had envisioned it would be. I have felt on several occasions that you have showed a complete lack of regard for my feelings, as well as a carelessness toward your own reputation that is distressing. It has made it difficult for me to regard my promise to your mother in the glad light that I once did."

"I know it, dear ma'am," said Fredericka in a low voice. "I can offer you no explanation that would not sound selfish, as, indeed, I have been. I can only assure you that I shall not do anything else to distress you."

Lady Chalmers sighed. "Oh, my dear. If it were only so simple. Though you may be a pattern card for the remainder of the Season, yet your credit, and mine, have already been affected. I can but pray and hope that this latest, and worst, spot of mischief does not disgrace you altogether."

Fredericka looked at the countess. Her face was exceedingly pale. For once, her hazel eyes held no hint of the laughter that was characteristic of her; instead they were somber. "Is it so bad, ma'am?"

"I am sorry, Fredericka." Lady Chalmers spoke quietly, with finality. "I will not disguise from you my deep forebodings. Already this morning while I was out I have had to field several delicately phrased questions. If it were not for Margaret Potterley agreeing to provide you with an alibi, we would have had nothing with which to counter the whispers of the curious. As it is, we must hope for the best. Now I must send you away. I have an appointment with my jeweler."

Fredericka knew herself to be dismissed. Without another word, she left Lady Chalmers's sitting room. She was devastated by the countess's recriminations and the cooling of that affection which Lady Chalmers had always shown her.

There was no one to whom Fredericka could confide her unhappiness, except to her brother Jack. But he was shortly due to leave town and she did not want to burden him with her depression of spirits when he was already anticipating his return to Luting.

How very much she wished that she was returning to Luting with him!

Fredericka's heart yearned suddenly for her home, where she would be safely immured from the gossip and the upset of her equilibrium.

It would have been wonderful indeed if she could have talked with Lord Satterwaite. He had once been her friend, but he had made it quite clear that he was no longer. She had managed to give the viscount such a disgust of her that to Fredericka's agitated mind it would be surprising if he deigned to make a civil bow in her direction.

Fredericka felt positively unwell over the mess she had made of things. After relaying a message downstairs that she wished to be denied to any callers, she shut herself into her sitting room.

It was a completely uncharacteristic thing for her to do, but the household at Chalmers House did not know her well enough to recognize that fact.

After meeting with her jeweler, Lady Chalmers decided that she would do a little shopping. The outing might mitigate some of the frustration and anger and despondency that threatened to overwhelm her. She asked after Miss Hedgeworth as she was pulling on her gloves. "Has Miss Hedgeworth gone out, Moffet?"

"No, my lady," said the impassive butler. "Miss has, however, requested that she be denied to callers."

Lady Chalmers's eyes rose to meet the butler's gaze. She frowned, then shook her head. "I am going shopping, Moffet. Pray inform Lord Chalmers when he returns from his club that I shall be out for a few hours."

The butler bowed. "Very good, my lady."

Lady Chalmers was not informed until she returned late that evening that Miss Hedgeworth had remained in her bedroom all day. It was Lord Chalmers who told her. "I am informed that Miss Hedgeworth has felt ill today," he said.

Lady Chalmers snorted. "I do not doubt it in the least. The girl is undoubtedly suffering from a guilty conscience. I am certain that you must have heard the rumors at your club this afternoon."

"I did, and I am not pleased that I was kept in the dark, my lady," said Lord Chalmers with a deep frown.

"I am sorry, Edward. I felt impelled to do something at once on Miss Hedgeworth's behalf, for I know how much you dislike wagging tongues. I have enlisted Margaret Potterley as an ally. She promised faithfully to furnish Fredericka with an alibi and I have already set it about to everyone during my calls today," said Lady Chalmers.

Lord Chalmers was mollified, both by the apology and the knowledge that an effort to scotch the rumors had already been set in motion. "I am glad to hear it. But how much truth is in this tale that Miss Hedgeworth attended a public masquerade and made a wanton spectacle of herself?"

Lady Chalmers sighed. "Well, much of it was true. I do not say that Fredericka displayed herself in a *wanton* manner, but she has behaved abominably! If it had not been for Sebastion, who found and escorted her home, there is no saying what the consequences might have been. I simply do not understand what got into her that she could ever do such a thing."

Lord Chalmers was uneasily recalling how he had applauded and encouraged Miss Hedgeworth's mischief making. Feeling that it was required of him, he unexpectedly defended her. "For my part, I like the girl's spirit. And she has certainly managed to ring herself to everyone's notice. That is quite a feat for a young lady who is past the debutante age."

"She has brought disgrace and scandal down upon her head, Edward! You have no notion what contortions I have had to perform to keep her name from being irretrievably tarnished. I am so utterly fatigued that I positively long for the Season's end!" exclaimed Lady Chalmers.

"Then I am doubly in Miss Hedgeworth's debt, for I should like nothing better than to return to Chalmers," said Lord Chalmers.

"Edward! I did not realize that you were bored. You should have said something, my dear," said Lady Chalmers, at once concerned and contrite. She had been so wrapped up in her own troubles that she had not noticed that the earl was restless.

"Bored? Nonsense! How could I be bored when I have had Sebastion's antics to entertain me," said Lord Chalmers, chuckling. "I meant merely that I miss our quiet evenings together, Sarah. We have had scarcely a moment to ourselves since we came up to London."

"I feel it, too," said Lady Chalmers, but her smile was preoccupied. She had been surprised by his good humor and at what he had said. "What did you mean by 'Sebastion's antics'?"

"Why, his flights of knight errantry, of course. I have never been more amused by anything. Miss Hedgeworth has kept my son completely unbalanced for all of these weeks. It has done me good to see it," said Lord Chalmers. "And certainly it has done him untold good!"

Lady Chalmers stared at her spouse. "Whatever are you talking about, Edward? Surely you do not suspect that Sebastion has a—a *tendre* for Fredericka?"

"Suspect? My dear Sarah, I do not quibble over a word. No, Sebastion is head over heels in love with Miss Hedgeworth. I think it a wonderful development," said Lord Chalmers.

"Well, I do not!" said Lady Chalmers roundly. "Why, if I thought that there was the least possibility that you were right, I would send that girl back to the country on the instant!"

"Why would you do such a nonsensical thing as that?" asked Lord Chalmers, frowning at his lady.

"The girl is hopeless! Every time I turn around, she is doing something yet more outrageous than what she did the week before! My dear sir, Sebastion cannot possibly contract a match with Fredericka. I will not countenance it," said Lady Chalmers earnestly.

"It is scarcely for you to countenance it or not, Sarah," said Lord Chalmers calmly. "Sebastion is of age. He will do what he deems to be best."

"But Fredericka! You cannot possibly entertain the thought of her as our daughter-in-law. Oh, yes, yes! I once had aspirations of making a match between her and our son. I admit it! But that was before I came to know her. She is wild to a fault!" exclaimed Lady Chalmers.

"What is there in that? Sebastion has his wild streak, as you must own, and I am in no doubt that that is what began the attraction between them. I say let Sebastion work out his own destiny, my dear. He will come about, never fear. And the succession shall be secured," said Lord Chalmers comfortably.

Lady Chalmers subsided. Her astonishment and distress were such that it was a struggle for her to do so, but she recognized that there would be little point in trying to bring the earl to see reason. He was obviously besotted and thus unaccountably blinded to the evils of Miss Hedgeworth's character.

The only consolation that Lady Chalmers had was that the viscount had expressed himself in such strong terms against Miss Hedgeworth. He had not sounded like a man in love, thought Lady Chalmers. Quite the contrary, in fact. She began to regain her composure, becoming more and more certain of her conclusion. No, Sebastion would not make an offer for Miss Hedgeworth. More than anyone else, he would applaud either her betrothal to someone else or her return to her home.

Lady Chalmers sighed. She did so look forward to the end of the Season. Miss Hedgeworth would then become someone else's concern and she could at last wash her hands of her.

It would be a pity if the girl did not receive any further offers during what remained of the Season, but the countess resigned herself to the distinct possibility. After all, Fredericka had managed to outrage much of society over the Thatcher affair. Now there were these fresh and incredibly damaging rumors. Sir

Thomas had declared himself to be as much Fredericka's admirer as ever, but such a stumbling block as this fresh assault against all that the ton deemed proper must make even such a stalwart as the worthy Sir Thomas blanch. It would be wonderful indeed if there was now any gentleman willing to risk himself with such a bumptious female.

Lady Chalmers could easily envision Lady Hedgeworth's natural dismay to have her untractable daughter once more at home. She was only glad that she was going to be able to send Miss Hedgeworth back without there having been formed an attachment with her son.

Miss Hedgeworth's maid sought out the Countess of Chalmers. The servant woman dipped a curtsy. "My lady, it is my duty to inform you that Miss Hedgeworth is ill. Her fever has climbed and she has been ever so sick. She has not eaten a bite since this morning," said the maid.

Lady Chalmers frowned. Though she was thoroughly put out with Fredericka, her heart was not made of stone. Setting aside her embroidery, she said, "I shall come at once."

Lady Chalmers went upstairs and into Fredericka's bedroom. Lady Chalmers advanced on the bed and saw at once that the maid had not exaggerated. Fredericka's face was deeply flushed and perspiration beaded her brow. She muttered and tossed her head, obviously uncomfortable. Lady Chalmers took the girl's limp wrist between her fingers and at once felt her tumultuous pulse.

"I shall send for a physician to come see her as soon as possible," said Lady Chalmers, her natural compassion aroused. She gently laid down the girl's hand on the coverlet. "Pray see to it that Miss Hedgeworth is given some barley water to drink and that she is made comfortable. She needs a fresh gown and sheets. I will send one of the other girls to assist you."

"Yes, my lady," said the maid. She was glad to have been relieved of making any decisions.

Lady Chalmers sent at once for the physician and herself escorted him up to Miss Hedgeworth's bedroom. Then she retreated to her sitting room, where she waited for half an hour to receive the man's verdict. "Well?"

"It is a bad attack of influenza, my lady," said the physician matter-of-factly. "Miss Hedgeworth's fever is extremely high. I have had to bleed her so that she will not be so restless. I have given her a powder for the fever and will leave a few more packets to give her as they are required. She should be given as many fluids as possible. Over the next several days, she must be kept quiet and encouraged to rest. I would suggest, too, quarantining these maidservants with Miss Hedgeworth so that there will be less likelihood of the infection being carried throughout the rest of the household."

"I shall order all as you have said," said Lady Chalmers. She extended her hand. "Thank you for coming, sir. We are indebted to you."

The physician bowed to her and then made his exit.

Fredericka did not bounce back from her illness, as might have been supposed of such a vigorous young lady. She took a longer time than anyone had anticipated to leave her bed.

When the physician returned to check on his patient two weeks later, he frowned. "I shall not disguise from you, my lady, that I am concerned by Miss Hedgeworth's slow recuperation. Was the young lady perhaps doing too much before she was taken ill?"

"I had not thought so, for Miss Hedgeworth always seemed so indefatigable," said Lady Chalmers, her brows contracted. "However, it is true that we have scarcely been home one evening this Season."

The physician nodded, satisfied. "Depend upon it, my lady, that is the cause of her continued languishing in bed. I am certain that given a few more weeks of rest, Miss Hedgeworth's naturally strong constitution will reassert itself and she will make a complete recovery."

When Lady Chalmers repeated this assurance to the earl, Lord Chalmers snorted. His heavy brows drawing down over his fierce gaze, he said, "Quack! Of course Miss Hedgeworth will recover. She is a fine girl, not one of these doddering females who think everything in the world is wrong with them."

Fredericka did leave her bed a day or two later, but the influenza had left her physically weak and her spirits were noticely low. Lady Chalmers said that there could be no question of suming the social round when Fredericka could scarcely bear up der an afternoon of greeting callers.

And there were those who called, even during the worst of redericka's ilness. Sir Thomas was one and he was greatly disessed to hear of Miss Hedgeworth's malady. Each day he had elivered a fresh posy with his card. Cards and flowers came in om other admirers and acquaintances as well. The Howardrownes called, as did Lady Markam and her daughter, Miss toker. All professed themselves regretful that Miss Hedgeworth as ill and promised to come again when she was better.

Another who made it a point to call was Lord Satterwaite. He lways spent a few minutes visiting with his mother, before inuiring politely after Miss Hedgeworth. His expression never reealed more than civil interest and so Lady Chalmers never uessed at the anxiety and turmoil in his mind.

The truth was that Lord Satterwaite was plagued by uncerainty, and even fear. He had realized with Lord Hedgeworth's question that he had fallen in love with Miss Hedgeworth. More han anything else he desired to declare himself to her, and cerainly he would have done so if she had not been taken ill.

But as time went on, he recalled with more and more intensity he scorn and contempt in her expression when they had last been ogether. Nor could he brush aside the memory of how she had utered her hatred of him.

For the first time in his life, Lord Satterwaite was afraid. If he did not act upon what he felt for Miss Hedgeworth, he would lose her. Yet he feared a fresh avowal of her scorn and contempt. So he wrestled privately with tormenting indecision.

The mild rumors that Lady Chalmers had quietly removed Miss Hedgeworth from society until the young lady's adventures could be said to be forgotten died when later visitors had the opportunity to see Miss Hedgeworth. She had lost weight and her pale face and subdued manners alike were all shocking to those who had been used to her sparkling good humor and energy.

Lord Satterwaite visited once during Miss Hedgeworth's later convalescence. Her white countenance; the way that her eyes flew to his face, then dropped; the reserved way that she received

him, were as hot irons to his uncertainty. He wanted to gather her
up in his arms and whisper reassuring endearments in her ears,
but of course that was impossible. She was obviously made uncomfortable in his presence. He stayed only a very few minutes
before shortly taking his leave. Fredericka watched him go, but
she could say nothing in front of the other visitors making claim
on her attention.

There was no question that Miss Hedgeworth had indeed been
gravely ill. All expressed their sincere sympathy to Fredericka,
assuring her that it was quite normal to feel a lowness of spirit
after such a bout of illness.

Fredericka expressed her gratitude for these solicitous reassur-
ances, but privately she knew that she could not blame her
malaise completely upon her recent illness. Rather, the depression
of spirits that afflicted her was due in large part to the tumbling
thoughts that kept going round and round through her mind. She
had said such terrible things to Lord Satterwaite. She could tell
from his short visit that he was thoroughly disgusted with her.
Her case was hopeless. He would never come to love her. She
would be better off away from London so that she could try to
forget that he felt only indifferent contempt for her.

Luting. How nice it would be to go home to Luting.

Fredericka began to beg Lady Chalmers to allow her to return
home. "I am a burden to you, ma'am. Pray, pray, let me go
home," she said.

Lady Chalmers considered it. She turned it all over carefully in
her mind. She had promised to sponsor the girl to the end of the
Season. But the Season was nearly over. Fredericka had spent the
last two and a half weeks in her bed and she was still not up to attending a number of parties or other functions. She tired too easily. Actually, it was rather alarming at how slowly Fredericka was
recovering from her recent illness. Surely Lady Hedgeworth
would not blame her for acceding to Fredericka's own wishes in
the matter. Surely Lady Hedgeworth would be grateful that she
had shown enough concern over Fredericka's health that she
would not insist upon the girl continuing in London to the end of
the Season.

At last making up her mind, Lady Chalmers granted Fredericka
permission to return home. "I am sorry to see you go when you

el so poorly, my dear. I am reluctant to risk your health by such
journey, but I quite see how it might prove to be the best thing
or you. One can rest so much easier in one's own bed," said
ady Chalmers, covering her own relief that her responsibility
as ending so much sooner than she had anticipated. "And your
lother will know just what to do for you, besides."

"You have been kind to me, my lady. I am sorry that I have
een such a charge to you," said Fredericka quietly. There were
ears standing on her lashes. She brushed them away.

Lady Chalmers was embarrassed, fearing that her inner relief
lust have shown through. "Think nothing of it, my dear. As I
old you in the beginning, I enjoy nothing better than entertaining.
had hoped to see you credibly established, of course."

She saw the expression in Fredericka's eyes, and said hastily,
But that is neither here nor there. We shall not speak of that."
She patted Fredericka's hand. "I shall give the orders for your
hings to be packed away. You shall naturally be driven home in
ny own carriage."

"Thank you, my lady," said Fredericka, relieved. She knew that
she would rest easier at Luting. She let her eyes close. It did not
matter what Lady Chalmers thought of her rudeness. She was so
tired. Already half-asleep, Fredericka heard the countess steal
away.

Two days later, Fredericka looked anxiously out of the carriage
window for her first sight of Luting Manor. When it came into
view, she smiled tremulously. Soon, soon, she would be home.

The carriage rolled up to the front steps where there was already a welcoming party gathered. The door was opened, the step
was let down. Then one of the footmen helped Miss Hedgeworth
to alight. She gratefully leaned on the man's arm while she
greeted her mother.

Lady Hedgeworth was shocked by her daughter's appearance.
Fredericka was pale and gaunt and she appeared grateful to be
able to lean upon someone's arm. This was not the vigorous
daughter that Lady Hedgeworth was used to seeing.

"My dear Fredericka," she said quietly. She embraced her
daughter and felt how thin she had become. Her heart smote her
and her emotions nearly overcame her. Rallying herself, she said

brightly, "You must go upstairs at once and put off your traveling things. I shall let you rest before dinner, for I know that the journey was tiring for you."

"Thank you, Mama. I own, I am feeling rather pulled," said Fredericka with an attempt at her old sparkle.

Lady Hedgeworth smiled with her daughter, but inside she was bleeding for her. "I expect that Lady Chalmers sent a message by you?"

"Oh, yes. I had almost forgotten. Here, in my reticule," said Fredericka. She hunted through her bag for a moment, then drew out the letter. "Her ladyship was most kind, Mama. I fear that led her a sorry dance toward the last and this illness was merely the coup de grace."

"Never mind, my dear. You must go upstairs now and rest," said Lady Hedgeworth. She waited until she had seen Fredericka supported up the stairs by a solicitous footman before she turned and made her way blindly into the drawing room, the Countess of Chalmers's letter clutched in her hand.

Lady Hedgeworth lost no time in breaking the wax seal. She unfolded the sheet, hoping to find some explanation for her daughter's condition.

> *"My dear Victoria,*
>
> *"It is with reluctance that I write to you, for I know that you will be saddened and shocked by Fredericka's condition. You will undoubtedly wonder that I did not take better care of her. I almost castigate myself. However, I console myself with the reflection that contracting the influenza is not something that one can readily control.*
>
> *"I was dismayed, however, at Fredericka's extremely slow recovery. She is such a vigorous girl that one would never have suspected that an illness could strike her down so thoroughly, but thus it has been. She has begged me to be allowed to return to you and I have agreed, for I think that being under your care at this time will be most beneficial to her. I do not believe that you will blame me for yielding to her entreaties.*
>
> *"Fredericka enjoyed all the success that one could have hoped for her during this Season. She received a small num-*

ber of offers, none of which she either cared for or were completely eligible. There are a number of reasons for this, but I shall not weight you with them all.

"I shall mention, however, that Fredericka was at times quite a handful. Often her escapades skated narrowly close to social disaster. Just before she became ill, she attended a public masquerade in the company of one who is quite beyond the pale. It was bidding fair to become a pretty scandal, but fortunately Sebastion was able to spirit her away before too much damage was done. I was able to make light of the worst of the rumors and talk.

"I do not tell you this to give you pain, but simply to explain Fredericka's ultimate failure in securing for herself an eligible parti. *It is unfortunate in the extreme. I know how you must have pinned your hopes on this Season, and now it is ended early due to Fredericka's illness. I am very sorry to have to relay such gloomy tidings to you.*

"My lord and I return to Chalmers shortly.

"I remain, your friend,

"Sarah"

Lady Hedgeworth allowed the single sheet to fall to her lap. She stared into space for a few seconds. Varying emotions warred in her breast. Anger at Fredericka for throwing away her chances. Anger at the Countess of Chalmers for not taking a firmer hold on Fredericka. But most of all, anger at the countess for the restrained style in which she had written.

It was patently obvious that the Countess of Chalmers would not again offer to sponsor Fredericka. Fredericka had apparently so disgraced herself in the countess's eyes that her ladyship had withdrawn her favor. And it was utterly, positively, obvious that there would be no match between Viscount Satterwaite and Fredericka.

All in all, Lady Hedgeworth was thoroughly incensed and depressed. Nothing had gone the way she had anticipated. She had had such high hopes. She knew Fredericka's worth. She had thought that others would recognize it as well.

The door opened and Lord Hedgeworth entered. He was attired in riding clothes and he still wore his gloves and carried his whip.

"Mama! I have just come in. I am told that Freddie is back home. Where is she?"

"She is upstairs resting, my dear," said Lady Hedgeworth, slowly folding the letter.

Lord Hedgeworth stared at his mother. "Upstairs resting? That doesn't sound like Freddie. Why, it is only two days' journey from London. She would not regard that!"

Lady Hedgeworth shook her head. She rose out of her chair. "You will find Fredericka greatly altered, Jack. She has been very ill with the influenza. Lady Chalmers sent her back because she was recovering so slowly."

Lord Hedgeworth wore an expression of alarm. "But Freddie is never ill!"

"Perhaps that is why the influenza struck her down so hard. I have observed before that those who are rarely sick often seem to suffer more than others when they do become ill," said Lady Hedgeworth. "I am on my way up to her room now, Jack. Is there anything that you wish me to tell her?"

Lord Hedgeworth shook his head. "No, it was nothing important. I just wished to ask her about London and—" He looked at his mother. "Dash it, Mama, I don't mind telling you that hearing about Freddie has knocked me all awry. She has always been a tower of strength for the rest of us. Do you recall that outbreak of pox and how she helped to nurse the girls and Thomas? Yes, and half the neighborhood as well! She was never touched by it."

"Yes, I do recall it. That is why I, too, have been unsettled by Fredericka's present condition. However, I shall myself nurse her and I am certain that we shall have her back on her feet in a trice," said Lady Hedgeworth, moving toward the door. "Fredericka was never one to languish in her bed for any reason."

"No, that is true." Lord Hedgeworth's face cleared. "I expect that she will be her old self in a day or two."

Lady Hedgeworth smiled but she did not reply. She rather suspected that it would be a bit longer before the old Fredericka was back with them. The daughter she had greeted just a half hour previously was only a pale reflection of the real Fredericka, she thought.

Chapter Twenty-nine

Fredericka had walked into the village to the parsonage, preferring the exercise over driving herself in the gig. She had taken a shortcut along the stream and so it was not that long of a walk. She was still not in such vigorous health as she had been formerly, but her strength was noticeably increasing. A few weeks earlier she would have been completely winded by such paltry exercise.

She had had a pleasant visit with Mrs. Reading, having taken a basket of jams and jellies to her that were to be distributed to the children in the parish. The good woman was plain in her manners and gentle in her speech, and Fredericka and the older lady had quickly established a rapport with one another.

It had come as a bit of a shock to Fredericka to discover upon her return to Luting that Reverend Reading had found himself a wife. There had been other changes in the county, too. Sir Julian was betrothed to Miss Eleanor Delacorte, her friend Dorcus's younger sister. And Mr. Hollingworth, he of the disconcerting sharp stare, had left the county, having obtained an army commission. There were other former admirers who were still unattached, of course, but these three had formerly formed the core of Fredericka's local court. However, when she had gone away to London, it seemed to her that each of the gentlemen had not seemed to repine much and had quickly turned their eyes and affections elsewhere.

Fredericka allowed her reflections free rein. So much had happened. So much had changed. How odd to recall that it had been a matter of just nine months since the Countess of Chalmers had first extended her invitation for the Season.

Fredericka had gone up to London with mild feelings of resentment and rebelliousness. She had returned practically disgraced, recovering from physical illness, and heartsore. It was enough to lower the spirits of any young woman.

Fredericka allowed her gaze to wander over the green fields through an opening in the hedgerows. Her thoughts turned naturally to Luting. The fields were green and gold, ripening in the late season sun. The herds were prospering. The irrigation projects were a resounding success.

Her brother Jack had turned out to be quite capable in administering the estate and the decisions that the position had required. He had grown in confidence and stature. There was now an informal agreement between himself and Miss Dorcus Delacorte. The two would wed as soon as Jack attained his majority.

Lord Hedgeworth's short stint in London had apparently satisfied all of his longings and imaginings. He was quite ready to settle down to a staid country gentleman's lot. In a year or two, there would be a wedding and shortly afterward a nursery would probably be established. There would be a new generation of Hedgeworths at Luting.

Fredericka was happy that it would be so. Yet she felt a disquiet. Many of her old responsibilities were gone from her forever, but she did not refine too much upon that anymore. She had found since returning to Luting that her feelings had changed about her home. She was no longer as content as she had once been simply to ride across the fields or to visit in the county. The activities of the village seemed sleepy to her now. She had become accustomed to London and the faster life there.

"Oh, be honest with yourself, you idiot!" she scolded herself. "It is Lord Satterwaite that you became accustomed to!" That was the most lowering reflection of all. Everything and everyone had continued to progress into a blithe future, except herself.

She could have changed her future, if she had wished it. But she had arrogantly thrown away the opportunities she had been given. She had viewed London from a selfish perspective and had been too blinded by her own conceit to see what was before her eyes.

Lord Satterwaite had been the one gentleman whom she would gladly have shared her life with, but she had created in him such a disgust that during those last weeks before she had left London he had deliberately avoided her company. He had called to inquire after her during her illness, of course, and he had sent her flowers with his card. But it had been no more than the gesture of a gentleman, whatever her swiftly pounding heart had hoped for otherwise.

What an utter little fool she had been, thought Fredericka. Now she had a few bittersweet memories that perhaps in time might fade to a dull ache.

Fredericka caught herself up out of her melancholy thoughts. She squared her shoulders and lifted her chin. Never would anyone be able to say that she was lachrymose. She would hold her head high and laugh. She would be a cheerful sister-in-law and a fond aunt. Eventually she might be able to set up house with her mother and live as her companion, sharing in the joys of their extending family from a distance. It would not be a bad life, though somewhat staid, thought Fredericka.

On a tiny smile, she recalled Sir Thomas's last visit to her. He had come to pay his respects and reiterate his admiration. But he had not offered for her hand again. At the time, Fredericka had been relieved. Now she had rather mixed emotions. A half loaf was better than none, was it not? But she had promised herself to have no regrets, and she would not.

A private chaise came barreling down the road. Fredericka moved off to the side near the hedgerow, expecting the chaise to pass her in a swirl of dust. Instead, to her surprise the chaise pulled up and then was backed toward her.

Fredericka looked up inquiringly at the driver, expecting to be asked directions. The door to the chaise opened and a gentleman leaped out. Before Fredericka quite knew what was happening, the gentleman had seized her and lifted her into the chaise.

She let out a cry of mingled outrage and fear. Then she had a fleeting glimpse of a familiar face under the beaver and her heart started pounding.

The gentleman leaped inside after Fredericka and slammed shut the door. The chaise started off again at a spanking pace.

Lord Satterwaite turned his head. His lean face was grim, his mouth held firm. There was an odd expression in his green eyes that made Fredericka feel oddly breathless.

"What have you done, my lord?" she asked.

"I have abducted you," he said in a clipped voice. "I would have worn a mask, but I seem to recall that I left it with you."

Fredericka was shocked. Disregarding the flippancy of his last statement, she stared at him in consternation. Suddenly a tide of anger made her eyes flash. "You cannot! You must put me down instantly."

"I shall do so, of course, if you satisfy me that is your true desire," said Lord Satterwaite coolly.

"Of course it is! How could you possibly think otherwise?" said Fredericka furiously.

The viscount lifted his hand, warding off her swift reply. "Before you decide, you should know that I have the permission of your mother to importune you. I have just come from Luting. When I described my feelings for you and my hope that I might pay my addresses, Lady Hedgeworth granted me her blessing. Your esteemable brother went so far as to wring my hand and declare that I was a trump of a fellow."

"This is outrageous. How dare you? I have never been more angry in my life," said Fredericka, but there was a trembling about her lips. She scarcely dared to hope. What had his lordship told her mother and Jack? Surely Lady Hedgeworth had not given her blessing to an abduction! As for her brother, he would have come riding neck-or-nothing at even the hint of such a thing befalling her. "My mother and brother never understood that you meant to abduct me!"

"No," conceded Lord Satterwaite. "I admit that was my own notion. I thought that it would appeal to your sense of adventure to be abducted in broad daylight."

Fredericka sniffed, but she did not dare to dispute him. She could not very well do so when she had set people on their ears all Season. Instead, she demanded, "Where are you taking me?"

"I am returning to Luting. I hope to have my answer from you before we arrive," said Lord Satterwaite, looking at her narrowly.

"What answer? What do you mean?" asked Fredericka, again suddenly breathless. She had seen that expression in the viscount's eyes before. He had kissed her then. She wondered rather giddily if he was going to kiss her again, and the thought was a pleasant one.

But the viscount merely possessed himself of her gloved hands.

"My dear Miss Hedgeworth, I have come to humble myself before you," he said. His expression became exceedingly grim. "You spoke such words to me that I have never forgotten them and they have placed me in torment from that day to this. Miss Hedgeworth, do you truly hate me?"

Fredericka felt as though she could not breathe at all. Her color rose hot in her face. "My lord! I do not hate you. I spoke out of anger and pride and—" Her voice became suspended for a moment as she fought back a foolish impulse to burst into tears. "No, I do not hate you, my lord."

Lord Satterwaite's fingers tightened on her hands. He was staring at her intently. "Miss Hedgeworth—Fredericka! I—" Suddenly he pulled her toward him and into his arms. He held her close. "Dear God, how I have feared your scorn, your contempt! My spirit has been writhing inside me. I love you, Fredericka! My heart beats in horrible apprehension that you do not return my love for you."

Fredericka pulled away from him. She looked up at him in astonishment. "You love me?"

Lord Satterwaite gave a shaking laugh. "Love you? No! I adore you. I can't think why I did not know it months ago."

"I made you very angry," said Fredericka in a small voice.

"Yes, but not without provocation, my dear torment. Fredericka, I am trying in my clumsy way to ask you to become my wife," said Lord Satterwaite. He was tense and his eyes held a strained expression, at once hopeful and fearful. "But I shall not press you if you have an—an aversion to me or cannot return my affection."

For reply, Fredericka flung herself back into his arms. She took hold of his face in both hands and kissed him. His lordship uttered an inarticulate groan and swept his arms tight about her. For some moments they clung to one another.

When they broke apart, Fredericka started laughing. "My very dear Sebastion, what an odd courtship we have had!"

"Do you love me, then?" he demanded, a smile on his lips and in his eyes.

"Oh, yes! I can't think why, but I do," said Fredericka. She tilted her head. "But why ever did you set about to abduct me? Even for you, it is outrageous conduct."

"I thought such a scandalous maneuver would add luster to my offer for your hand," said Lord Satterwaite, grinning crookedly.

"You are an awful man," said Fredericka, frowning at him. But her eyes twinkled. She snuggled comfortably back into the circle of his arms. "I do hope that you have a special license in your pocket, for I do not wish to wait for banns and have a tame sort of wedding."

"I have it here," said Lord Satterwaite, tapping his coat pocket. "I mean to wed you completely out of hand, Miss Hedgeworth. We shall have the local parson to officiate and all of the household at Luting Manor for witnesses."

"Oh, how wonderful. I shall like that very much," said Fredericka. "Will you mind that I do not have a proper gown?"

"Not a bit," said Lord Satterwaite instantly. "I expect you to be the envy of all eyes whatever you wear. Besides, my mother has sent down with me a dress of her own choosing for you. She assured me that it is offered with her blessing."

Tears stung Fredericka's eyes. "Lady Chalmers has forgiven me, then?"

Lord Satterwaite settled her closer against his side. Humor laced his voice. "My dear girl, how could it be otherwise when you have succeeded in snatching me from the brink of disaster? I adamantly refused to wed anyone but you. Upon my declaration, I was reinstated as my father's heir. He sends his regards and blessings, by the way. He thoroughly approves of you."

"Dear Lord Chalmers," said Fredericka with fondness. She turned her head to look up into her betrothed's smiling face. With a teasing light in her eyes, she asked, "Shall we live with them, my lord?"

The viscount frowned down at her. With restraint, he said, "I think not. I wish to have you to myself."

But there was nothing restrained about his kiss, and Fredericka was glad.